The Lady Chapel

Brother Michaelo pushed the young messenger behind him, but not before Owen had seen the boy's foot raised to kick some more.

'What do you want?' Owen growled, turning to Michaelo.

Brother Michaelo gave Owen a dazzling smile and bowed. 'Forgive me for the early hour, Captain Archer. But His Grace the Archbishop sent me. It is most urgent that you come to his chambers as soon as you are dressed.'

'Is the Archbishop lying on his deathbed?'

'No, praise God,' Brother Michaelo said, crossing himself. 'But there has been a murder. In the minster close.'

Candace Robb has read and researched medieval history and literature for many years, having studied for a PhD in Medieval and Anglo-Saxon Literature. On visiting York she was struck by its potential as a setting for a medieval novel and started work on *The Apothecary Rose*, which is also available in Mandarin. *The Lady Chapel* is her second novel.

Also by Candace Robb

The Apothecary Rose
Nun's Tale
King's Bishop
Riddle of St Leonard's

The Lady Chapel

AN OWEN ARCHER MYSTERY

Candace Robb

ARROW

Reprinted in Arrow Books 1997

13 15 17 19 20 18 16 14

First published in the United Kingdom in 1994 by William Heinemann
This edition first published in 1996 by Mandarin Paperbacks,
reprinted eleven times

Arrow Books Limited
Random House UK Limited
20 Vauxhall Bridge Road, London SW1V 2SA

Random House Australia (Pty) Limited
20 Alfred Street, Milsons Point, Sydney,
New South Wales 2061, Australia

Random House New Zealand Limited
18 Poland Road, Glenfield
Auckland 10, New Zealand

Random House South Africa (Pty) Limited
Endulini, 5a Jubilee Road, Parktown 2193, South Africa

Random House UK Limited Reg. No. 954009

A CIP catalogue record for this book
is available from the British Library

Papers used by Random House UK Limited
are natural, recyclable products made from wood grown in
sustainable forests. The manufacturing processes conform to
the environmental regulations of the country of origin

Printed and bound in the United Kingdom by
Cox & Wyman Ltd, Reading, Berkshire

ISBN 0 7493 1884 8

Table of Contents

ACKNOWLEDGEMENTS vii

GLOSSARY x

1   The Last Judgement 1
2   The Offending Hand 11
3   Ridley's Pride 29
4   An Impertinent Lady, a Humbled Man 50
5   The Ridley Women 61
6   Goldbetter & Co 80
7   A Bloody Treasure 92
8   Down by the River 111
9   Tonics and Waits 122
10   Forebodings 129
11   The Wool War 152
12   A Gleeful Conspirator 164
13   Liaisons 176
14   The King's Mistress 183
15   Nightmares 195
16   Uncomfortable Encounters 209
17   Jasper's Quest 220
18   Tildy's Secret 234
19   Grief 245
20   Desperate Measures 257
21   Martin Wirthir 271
22   Complications 283
23   St John's Day 301
24   Connections 309
25   Wirthir's Doom 320
26   Revenge 337
27   The Quick and the Dead 354
28   Blood Enemies 364

Author's Note 373

Extract from *The Apothecary Rose* 378

For Taddeus Wojtaszek

Acknowledgements

I thank Michael Denneny for enthusiastic feedback; Lynne Drew for a critical reading that helped clarify things; Victoria Hipps for a keen-eyed edit; Paul Zibton for the map; Walden Barcus and Karen Wuthrich for thoughtful readings; Evan Marshall for being everything an agent should be; Keith Kahla and John Clark for all their good humoured help behind the lines; and Charlie Robb for publicity.

Research for this book was conducted on location in Yorkshire and in the libraries of the University of York, the University of Washington, King County, Washington, and the city of Seattle.

And many thanks to my support group that includes The Book Club, Paula Moreschi's Physical Culture regulars, my family from coast to coast, and most of all the person who never lets me down, Charlie Robb.

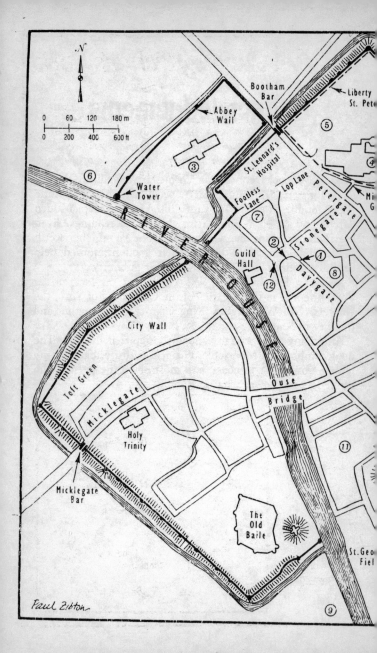

N

0 60 120 180 m
0 200 400 600 ft

Bootham Bar

Liberty
St. Pet

⑤

Abbey
Wall

③

④

St. Leonard's
Hospital

⑥

Lop Lane

Petergate

Mi
G

Water
Tower

Footless
Lane

⑦

②

Stonegate

①

Guild
Hall

⑫

⑧

Davygate

R I V E R   O U S E

City Wall

Ouse

Toft Green

Micklegate

Bridge

Holy
Trinity

⑪

Micklegate
Bar

The
Old
Baile

St. Geo
Fiel

Paul Zibton

⑨

Owen Archer's York

1. Wilton's Apothecary
2. The York Tavern
3. St. Mary's Abbey
4. York Minster
5. Archbishop's Palace
6. Magda's House
7. Ambrose Coats' House
8. Fletchers' House
9. St. Clement's Nunnery
10. St. George's Chapel
11. Franciscan Friary
12. St. Helen's Square

Monk Bar

ing's Square

Mercers' uild Hall

Foss Bridge

River Foss

KING'S FISH POND

Ripon
Boroughbridge
Aldborough
Alne
York
Beverley

England

Kenilworth

London
Windsor

Glossary

archdeacon   each diocese was divided into two or more archdeaconries; the archdeacons were appointed by the archbishop or bishop and carried out most of his duties

bedstraw   a plant of the genus *Galium*

butt   a mark or mound for archery practice

crowd   an old Welsh stringed instrument, four of its six strings played with a bow, two plucked by the thumb; a fiddle

jongleur   a minstrel who sang, juggled, tumbled; French term, but widely used in an England where Norman French was just fading from prevalence

Lady Chapel   a chapel dedicated to the Blessed Virgin Mary, usually situated at the east end of the church

leman   mistress; another French term widely used in medieval England.

liberty   an area of the city not subject to royal administration; for example the liberty of St Peter is the area surrounding the minster which comes under the Archbishop's jurisdiction

mercer   dealer in textiles, especially the more costly; a dealer in small textile wares

minster	a cathedral originally founded as a monastery; to this day, York's cathedral of St Peter is called York Minster
pandemain	the finest quality white bread, made from flour sifted two or three times
pillory	a wooden frame, supported by an upright pillar or post, with holes through which the head and hands were put as a punishment
rebec	a medieval instrument of the viol class shaped like a mandolin, usually with three strings
reredorter	privy behind a monastic dormitory
trencher	a thick slice of brown bread a few days old with a slight hollow in the centre, used as a platter
summoner	an assistant to an archdeacon who cited people to the archbishop's or bishop's consistory court, which was held once a month. The court was staffed by the bishop's officials and lawyers and had jurisdiction over the diocesan clergy and the morals, wills and marriages of the laity. The salary of a summoner was commission on fines levied by consistory courts – petty graft formed a large part of his income. More commonly called an 'apparitor,' but I use the term Chaucer used to call to mind the Canterbury pilgrim he so vividly described.
waits	musicians employed by a town to play on ceremonial occasions
wastrel	good quality white bread made from well-sifted flour; not as fine as pandemain

One

The Last
Judgement

Corpus Christi day dawned mild and sunny,
answering the prayers of the guildsmen of York,
and of all who looked forward to the Corpus
Christi pageants. Many saw the dawn, for the plays
began with the blessing of the players on the porch
of Holy Trinity Church, Micklegate, before dawn,
followed immediately by the first performance of the
day as the sun rose. Twelve stations had been marked
the evening before by banners displaying the arms
of the city. Here the audiences would gather. The
pageant wagons, over forty of them, would wind their
way through the streets, stopping at each station to
perform to the waiting people. It would be a long day
for the guild members and other players, ending after
midnight – a glorious day in which the history of
mankind's salvation by Christ's sacrifice was brought
to life, from the fall of the angels to the Last Judgement.

The Mercers' pageant wagon had just left the
station beyond Ouse Bridge, heading for the stands
in St Helen's Square. It was the last wagon; on it
was played out *The Last Judgement*. Young Jasper de

Melton trotted along beside the pageant wagon with his greasehorn, trying to take in all the sights and sounds of the day while listening for the creaking of the wagon wheels, his signal to slather on grease. It was an important job for a boy of eight. The large wooden wheels would soon come to a halt on the narrow, uneven streets without constant attention. Jasper was proud of his responsibility. And for the play of the Mercers' Guild no less, the richest guild in York. This was a step towards his acceptance as an apprentice in the guild, an honour that thrilled him and filled his mother with pride and hope for a better life for her son than she had been able to provide as a widow. Kristine de Melton had made Jasper a new leather jerkin for this important day.

Jasper should see his mother soon. She had promised to wait at the station in St Helen's Square, in front of the York Tavern.

As the wagon trundled towards the square, Jasper saw a red-faced man step close, calling out to Master Crounce. The flaps of the performers' tent opened and tall, lanky Will Crounce jumped down off the wagon, almost knocking Jasper over, and joined the heavyset man, slapping him on the back.

'Why are you not in the pageant at Beverley, my friend?' Crounce asked.

'Me?' The heavyset man laughed. 'I have no gift for yelling myself red in the face a dozen times in one day.'

The two turned and walked away, heads close together. Jasper was surprised. What if Master Crounce lost track of time and missed his turn in the play? He played Jesus. His absence would be noticed. It made Jasper nervous just to think of it, for Master Crounce was the man who had sponsored him for his job today and was sponsoring him as an apprentice in a few weeks. Dishonour to him meant dishonour to Jasper.

'Boy!' an elderly actor called out. 'Wheel be squealing like stuck pig.'

Jasper flushed and hurried to do his job. He must keep his mind on the wheels. He would only get in trouble worrying about other folk.

As Jasper rounded the front of the wagon, hurrying out of its way, he saw that the Mercers were next to perform. Squinting against the sun, Jasper searched the crowd outside the York Tavern. At first he did not see his mother. And then there she was, waving and calling his name. He waved back, grateful that he'd been hard at work when she'd spotted him. He would hate to disappoint her.

With a grinding shudder, the long, heavy wagon came to a halt. A small band of town waits played a flourish, and the actors came out from the tent. All but Master Crounce. Jasper bit his nails. Master Crounce must have heard the flourish. But where was he? The actors moved to their places. At last, just as his fellows had begun to murmur about his absence, Master Crounce jumped onto the wagon from behind and climbed to his perch, a rickety platform that would lower him from Heaven to Earth after his first speech.

The crowd hushed as God the Father began. Always they chose an actor with a bass voice for the part.

> 'First when I this world had wrought –
> Wood and wind and waters wan,
> And all-kin thing that now is aught –
> Full well, methought, that I did then. . .'

The player's voice rumbled like distant thunder. God would sound like this, Jasper thought.

'Angels, blow your bemes forthwith,
Ilka creature for to call!'

The angels blew their trumpets.

It gave Jasper chills to think that on this day they were given a glimpse of the Last Judgement. He vowed to live a good life so that he might not fear as did the Bad Souls on this day of reckoning –

'We mun be placed for our sins' sake
Forever from our salvation,
In Hell to dwell with fiends black,
Where never shall be redemption.'

As the third Angel spoke, Jasper looked up at Jesus, who finally came into the play.

From Heaven, Jesus spoke, 'This woeful world is brought to end . . .'

Someone in the crowd giggled. Jasper looked around and saw a pretty woman standing with two men, the heavyset man who had hailed Master Crounce and another. It was the woman who had giggled. The heavyset man glared at her; the other man frowned and bent towards her to say something.

Jasper wondered at the woman's blasphemy. For even though it was Master Crounce who played the role, a mere mortal touched with sin as all men were, yet he was Jesus this day.

But Jasper soon forgot the incident as Jesus spoke the words, 'All mankind there shall it see,' and the platform began its creaky descent through smoke. It was Jasper's favourite part. When the smoke cleared, Master Crounce as Jesus was standing on the main platform, his cowl thrown back. And then Jasper could see his eyes, shining with the sanctity of his role.

Master Crounce was transformed by the part. 'My apostles and my darlings dear . . .'

Jasper thought his master wonderful. He loved listening to him. Unfortunately, as Jesus's last words were spoken, Jasper had to begin the circuit of the wheels, greasing them for departure. He strained to hear the last lines:

> 'They that would sin and ceased nought,
> Of sorrows sere now shall they sing;
> And they that mended them while they might,
> Shall remain and dwell in my blessing.'

As Jasper reached the last wheel, he looked up where his mother had sat. She was gone. Jasper was puzzled. How could she leave while Master Crounce still spoke? And then he saw her being led away, supported by two neighbours. Her feet shuffled and her head lolled to one side. Holy Mary, Mother of God. What had happened? The sight haunted Jasper for the rest of the day. Even the sight of Master Crounce's shining eyes could not ease his fear.

Jasper did not return home until just before dawn the next morning. His mother was asleep; Mistress Fletcher, a neighbour, watched over her. The small, windowless room reeked of blood and sweat; the smell frightened Jasper.

'What happened?' he asked.

Mistress Fletcher's large eyes were sad as they gazed on Jasper. 'Women's trouble. Came on her in the crowd. A woman in her condition had no business in such a crowd.'

Will she live? the boy wondered, but he could not bring himself to utter the question.

Mistress Fletcher sighed and stood. 'I'll be off for a bit of sleep. Be a good boy and lie beside her so you wake if she wakes, eh?' She patted him on the head. 'I'll check in after I've fed my own lot in the morning.'

Jasper took off his new jerkin; he would need it clean for his interview with the guildmaster of the Mercers. He tucked the jerkin into a small chest that held his mother's treasures, a carved wooden cup and an elaborately painted longbow that had belonged to Jasper's father. Weary to the bone, the boy climbed onto the straw-stuffed pallet next to his feverish mother and fell asleep.

Though the room had no windows, the sounds of the city wakened Jasper. The walls were thin, letting out the heat in winter, letting in the heat in summer. Bells rang, shutters banged, carts clattered by, folk yelled their greetings to one another, a dog barked as if it were being beaten. Jasper's mother slept on, the blankets pulled up to her chin. Jasper relieved himself in the bucket in the corner, then took the bucket down the outside stairs and emptied the night waste into the gutter that ran down the middle of the street. He would be fined if caught, but it was more important to return to his mother as soon as possible. He would wait to fetch water until Mistress Fletcher returned.

Shortly before midday, Mistress de Melton opened her eyes. 'I saw you in your jerkin,' she said, her mouth working so little that the words were more guessed than heard. She managed a sad smile. 'Proud of my boy.'

Jasper bit his lip, a lump in his throat. His mother was dying. He had seen enough death in his eight years that he recognised it. 'I was waiting for Mistress Fletcher to come before I went for water,' he said. 'Are you thirsty now? Will you be all right if I go for it and leave you alone?'

'I will stay put.' Again the weak smile.

Jasper picked up the water jug and went out, scrubbing his face with his sleeve to remove any sign of tears. He was relieved to meet Mistress Fletcher on the stairs.

'Ma's awake. I'm fetching water,' he said.

'Good boy. I'll just go up and see if she needs anything.'

In the evening, Mistress de Melton began to toss and sigh. Her fever rose.

'Jasper,' she whispered to her son, 'go to the York Tavern. Find Will. He has a friend there, he will be with him.'

Jasper looked at Mistress Fletcher, who nodded. 'I'll watch beside your mother. Go get Will Crounce. He should be here.'

The York Tavern was not far. Jasper peeked inside and saw Master Crounce sitting with the fat man who had hailed him from the crowd yesterday. They were arguing. Jasper, thinking it a bad time to interrupt, backed out the door. He would wait a bit, then check again to see if things were peaceful. He brushed against a hooded person standing just outside the door beneath the lantern. From the scent, Jasper guessed it to be a woman. He moved across the way and sat in the darkness of the overhang.

It was not long before Master Crounce appeared in the doorway, swaying slightly, his face screwed up in anger. Jasper had never seen Master Crounce with such a face. The tall man lurched out the door. Jasper hesitated, frightened, and lost his opportunity. The hooded woman reached out for Master Crounce with a white, delicate hand. Crounce turned, gave a little cry of pleasure, and headed away with her.

Jasper did not entirely understand his mother's relationship with Master Crounce, but he suspected. And if he was right, then this mysterious woman had taken his mother's place. So should he follow anyway? What would Master Crounce say? What could Jasper say in front of his master's new leman?

He decided to follow them. Perhaps they would part company soon and Jasper could then speak with Master Crounce without embarrassing the man.

The couple went through the minster gate. The woman must live inside the liberty. Perhaps she worked for the Archbishop or one of the archdeacons. It was no problem for Jasper to go through. He often did day work for the masons and carpenters. His father had been in the carpenters' guild. They paid for the room Jasper and his mother lived in, and gave him work from time to time. The guards all knew Jasper. The one on duty tonight knew him well.

'Young Jasper. Out late, are you?'

'My ma's took ill,' Jasper explained. 'I'm after help.'

'Ah. I did hear. During the pageants, was it?'

Jasper nodded.

The guard waved him past.

Jasper stood still in the shadow of the great minster, listening for the couple's footsteps. They had turned left, towards the west entrance. Odd direction. That was the minster yard, the jail, the Archbishop's palace and chapel. Perhaps she was a maid in the palace. Jasper hurried to catch up. He did not know his way so well in this direction. He did not like this place in the dark. The minster loomed high above him to his right, a towering darkness that echoed with breezes and the skittering of night creatures. The two he followed rounded the great west front. Jasper hurried past the towers, stumbling in his fear of being alone in this place best left to God and the saints at nightfall.

As the couple stepped around the northwest corner into the minster yard, a laugh rang out, echoing weirdly. Jasper stopped and crossed himself. It did not come from Master Crounce or the lady, and it was not a friendly sound. Master Crounce stumbled. To Jasper's puzzlement, the woman broke from Master Crounce and ran back towards Jasper, who ducked into the shadow of the great minster so that she would not find him spying.

The laughter rang out again.

'Who's there?' Crounce demanded, though his words were so slurred with drink they hardly sounded challenging.

Two men dashed at Crounce from the darkness, knocking him to the ground. One bent down to the fallen man, and Crounce's scream dissolved into a gurgle and a sigh. The other attacker reared up, a sword raised above him, and brought it down with frightening force. He stooped, picked something up, and then the attackers ran.

Jasper hurried to his mother's friend. 'Master Crounce?' The man did not respond. Jasper knelt and felt Will Crounce's face. The eyes were open. The smell of blood was strong. 'Master Crounce?' The boy reached to tug on the man's hand. But there was no hand, only a hot, sickening wetness. Speechless with shock, Jasper ran for the guard.

'What is it, boy? Seen an angel, have ye?'

Jasper gasped and then bent double, retching.

Now the guard was alarmed. 'What is it?'

Jasper wiped his mouth with a handful of grass and then took a few deep breaths. 'Master Crounce. They've killed him. They've cut off his hand!'

As daylight reached his bed in the York Tavern, Gilbert

Ridley cursed and turned over. His head hammered. Too much ale, and oh how he regretted last night's bitter words with Will Crounce. If he lived through the morning he would go to the minster and do penance for his sinful pride and anger. Ridley turned over and held his breath as the hammers sent sparks shooting across his vision. Carts rattled by, bells rang. Blast the city. Blast Tom Merchet's excellent ale.

A smell turned Ridley's attention to the centre of the room. Something lay there, right there in the middle of the room, ready to trip him. He could not remember what he had dropped there. Meat? He must have left the door ajar. How drunk had he been to pass out before shutting out the sounds from below? Ridley closed his eyes, felt sick to his stomach. It was his bladderful of ale, that's what hurt. He sat up, clutching his head and his stomach, and waited until the room settled around him. That thing on the floor. It looked for all the world like— Oh dear God, it was a hand. A severed hand. Ridley rushed to the chamber pot and retched.

Two

The Offending Hand

F ather Gideon had given Mistress de Melton the last rites. Now Jasper knelt beside his mother, praying that he might be taken in her place.

Jasper was frightened. On Thursday morning he had been so happy he thought his heart would burst with joy. Now it was Saturday morning and his joy was a memory. His mother was near death and his sponsor for the guild had been murdered. When his mother woke, Jasper would have to tell her the awful news about her beloved Will.

What had Jasper done to be so punished by the Lord God Almighty?

'Jasper?' The hand that reached for his was icy. How could she burn with fever yet have such cold hands?

'Ma, let me get you some water.'

Kristine de Melton's lips were cracked from the heat of her fever. 'Will? Is he here?'

Jasper could not say it. He could not send his mother to Heaven worried for him. 'Master Crounce cannot come right away, Ma. But he sent his love.'

'He is a good man, Jasper. Let him care for you.'

Jasper nodded. He could not speak with the lump in his throat.

Mistress de Melton smiled, touched her son's cheek and closed her eyes. 'So sleepy.'

Jasper prayed that God would forgive his little lie.

Bess was at the bakery when she heard about the body. A wool merchant from Boroughbridge.

'What was his name?' she asked Agnes Tanner.

Agnes frowned down at the child who clung to her skirts. 'Will. Like my little 'un.'

Bess considered the information. Will, a merchant from Boroughbridge. 'Crounce? Did he go by that name?'

'Could be. Sommat like. You knew him?'

'Customer is all,' Bess said. 'Seemed a gentle sort.'

'A boy found him. Poor chit.'

'Terrible thing. Was it robbery?'

'Most like. Why else cut off his hand?' Agnes scooped up the child and barked at her eldest to hold the basket of bread straight. 'Must be off, then. Greetings to Tom.'

The pounding at the shop door woke Lucie, but Owen had her pinned to the mattress with an arm and a leg. Lucie closed her eyes and hoped whoever it was would go away. She hated to disturb Owen, and she certainly did not want to go downstairs herself.

But the pounding continued. Lucie felt Owen's

muscles flex, and he sat up with a jolt. 'Who is it?' he yelled, though of course the person at the door could not hear him.

'Why don't you go down and see?' Lucie suggested.

'They'll want you. If it's an emergency, they'll want the master apothecary, not her apprentice.' He lay back down with a contented sigh.

'But it's the apprentice's duty to find out who it is and what they want.'

'I'm naked.'

'So am I.'

'So you are.' Owen grinned and reached out to grab his wife, but the pounding began again, faster now, louder, as if a boot had replaced the hand. 'Blast them.' Owen threw on his shirt, slipped the patch over his scarred left eye and marched down the stairs.

Brother Michaelo pushed the young messenger behind him, but not before Owen had seen the boy's foot raised to kick some more.

'What do you want?' Owen growled, turning to Michaelo.

Brother Michaelo gave Owen a dazzling smile and bowed. 'Forgive me for the early hour, Captain Archer. But His Grace the Archbishop sent me. It is most urgent that you come to his chambers as soon as you are dressed.'

'Is the Archbishop lying on his deathbed?'

'No, praise God,' Brother Michaelo said, crossing himself. 'But there has been a murder. In the minster close.'

'Well I didn't do it.' Owen began to close the door.

Michaelo put out his arm. 'Please, Captain Archer, His Grace does not wish to accuse you, but rather to confer with you on the matter.'

That old debt again. Damn the man. 'And he cannot wait till decent folk are up and about?'

'He is most distressed by the situation.'

'Is the corpse anyone I know?'

Brother Michaelo's nostrils flared in surprise. 'I doubt it. Will Crounce, a wool merchant from Boroughbridge.'

Well, thank the Lord it was no acquaintance of Owen's. 'I'll be there shortly.' He slammed the door. Brother Michaelo was no friend to the household, and Owen did not consider him worth courtesy.

Lucie touched Owen's hand. He had not heard her come down behind him. 'You must go, you know,' she said quietly. Owen heard regret in her voice.

He squeezed her hand. 'Aye.'

Bess Merchet hurried back to the York Tavern and straight up to Gilbert Ridley's room. She stopped at the door with a start. Lying on the floor like a discarded toy was a human hand, fingers curled inward. She would have thought it a doll's hand made with devilish cunning, except for the horror of the wrist, where hand and arm had been messily severed. 'Blessed Mary and all the saints, what has Gilbert Ridley gone and done?' She noted with irritation that Ridley's belongings were gone. Just like a man to run and leave a mess. She scooped the disgusting thing onto a mat, folded it over so Kit, the serving girl, wouldn't see it, and took it with her, taking care to close the door behind her. Damn the man. Bess stomped down to question her husband, Tom.

He looked up from the wood peg he was whittling to repair a stool. 'Master Ridley paid and left in no particular hurry,' Tom said to her question.

'Why, Bess? What's amiss?'

'That Will Crounce he argued with last night was lying in his own blood this morning, that's what's amiss. Throat slit open and his right hand cut off.'

'Right hand? After a ring, were they?'

'What do you think?' Bess tossed the mat on the table, letting the hand roll out.

Tom dropped his whittling and crossed himself. 'Jesus have mercy, where did you find that, Bess? Is that—'

'I hardly think there's more than one hand gone missing in town this morning, do you?'

'Well, no—'

'I found it in Gilbert Ridley's room.'

'Ridley's?' Tom frowned and scratched his chin.

'So where is he?' Bess demanded.

'You think he put it there?'

'Whether he put it there or no is not for me to judge, Tom Merchet. What I know is they argue and the man is murdered, Ridley runs off, and I find the murdered man's hand in Ridley's room. If I were to judge, it wouldn't look good for him.'

Tom shook his head. 'If he meant to run, would he stop to pay his bill? Or be fool enough to leave evidence? Why move it at all? Let it lie there beside body. That'd be fearsome enough, to my mind.'

All true, but it did not clear Ridley in Bess's mind. 'He's got some explaining to do, that's all I know.' Bess wrapped up the hand. 'You watch this while I tidy up.'

'Tidy up? Where do you mean to go, wife?'

She could not believe the simplicity of the man. 'To the minster, Tom. I must take the evidence to Archbishop Thoresby.'

'Why him?'

'It happened in the minster liberty. Agnes Tanner said. So it will be the Archbishop's headache.'

'Why not just take it next door to Owen? He's Thoresby's man.'

'Owen is not Thoresby's man any more. He's Lucie's apprentice.'

Tom snorted. 'You're wrong there. You'll see.'

He smiled smugly as he bent back to his whittling. What Tom knew from chats with Owen over tankards late at night was Owen's debt to the Archbishop.

Last September, a messenger had arrived from John of Gaunt, Duke of Lancaster, ordering Owen to return to his service. An impertinence, for Owen had not been Gaunt's Captain of Archers, but Gaunt's father-in-law's, the old Duke of Lancaster, Henry of Grosmont. Owen had lost the sight in his left eye in the old Duke's service. When Owen told the old Duke that he wished to resign his post, that he no longer trusted himself in the field, the old Duke had put him to a new task. Owen had learned to read, write, and carry himself as a minor lord, and had thus become the old Duke's spy. But shortly the old Duke had died, without sons, so that his duchy went to his daughter Blanche's husband, John of Gaunt, third son of King Edward. Owen had hardly thought Gaunt would desire the services of a one-eyed archer or spy, so he had prepared to seek his fortune as a mercenary in Italy; but John Thoresby, Lord Chancellor of England and Archbishop of York, had chosen to honour the old Duke's request to watch over Owen's future. He had given Owen a choice – serve him or the new Duke of Lancaster. Not liking what he'd heard of John of Gaunt, Owen had chosen Thoresby.

Gaunt's sudden interest had had to do with Owen's skill as an archer and a trainer of archers. The return of the plague in 1361 had taken its toll in archers as in all other walks of life. King Edward, obsessed with his ongoing war with France, knew his longbowmen were his most important assets. He had gone so far as to outlaw all sports but archery. And then he had made it compulsory for all able-bodied men to practise at the butts on Sundays and holy days.

No doubt Bertold, Owen's friend who had succeeded him as Lancaster's Captain of Archers, had talked him up to his new lord, thinking it certain that Owen could not be content in his new life. And it was true that nothing since had felt as comfortable to Owen as the evenings spent drinking with his men after a day of training. He enjoyed learning the art of the apothecary, and he found peace working in the medicinal garden, but his body yearned for more activity.

However, he yearned for nothing so much as Lucie, and the summons from John of Gaunt had come less than two months before they were to be wed. Owen had gone to Thoresby with his problem, feeling the Archbishop owed him something.

Archbishop Thoresby had been happy to help. It happened that he had just returned to York from Windsor Castle and his duties as Lord Chancellor to settle a dispute about a relic between one of his archdeacons and a powerful abbot. Archer had been sent north to see to the problem. Meanwhile, Thoresby had returned to court and argued that Archer's talents would be better spent training bowmen on St George's Field on Sundays and holy days. York could in this way provide a skilled troop of bowmen at need. King Edward fortunately had told his son to desist.

Owen was thus beholden to Thoresby, and the Archbishop's summons could scarcely be ignored, no matter what Bess thought. Tom nodded at the smooth peg and put his knife away.

An unsmiling Michaelo showed Owen in to the hall of the Archbishop's palace. Thoresby sat in the light of a casement window, examining a parchment. He looked up as Owen entered and gestured for him to join him at the table.

'Word of the murder has probably travelled through the city already, Archer.'

'No doubt.'

'We must get to the bottom of this before I leave for Windsor.'

'I am to investigate?'

'I have no choice. I am surrounded by incompetence. I asked the guard how it happened that he did not hear the attack. He made a speech about how the murder happened on the far side of the minster, and that I would have been more likely to hear it. It is a wonder my plate is not stolen while I am away.'

'Murder within the minster liberty is rare, Your Grace. The guard would not be alert to the sounds.'

'Hmpf.' Thoresby looked back down at the parchment. Owen noted it was a map.

'You are leaving soon?' Owen said.

'The wedding of Princess Isabella is in three weeks. As Lord Chancellor I am needed to work out the details of the marriage agreement.'

'Surely the negotiations were completed long ago?'

'The bridegroom presents unique problems.'

'Enguerrand de Coucy? But he's been the King's prisoner of war for some time. There at court, right there where you can watch him. What problems does he have power to make?'

'He owes the King ransom money. He insists he be released of this as part of the dowry the King settles on Princess Isabella. De Coucy claims the ransom will impoverish him. We must be certain de Coucy is telling us the truth about his holdings. I have spies all over France and Brittany. And spies spying on the spies. Nothing will be certain until the day of the ceremony.'

'With such affairs of state to attend to, why concern yourself with the murder of a wool merchant? Give the headache to Jehannes. He's Archdeacon of York.'

'Will Crounce was a member of the Mercers' Guild. The guild is too important to me. I count on them for much of the minster fund.'

'The minster fund. I understand that's also why you took Brother Michaelo as your secretary – his family offered you a large sum.'

Thoresby let the map curl up and tossed it aside. He glared at Owen. 'I do not owe you an explanation, Archer.'

'No. Of course not.' Owen sat down.

'I want you to find out whatever you can about the murdered man.'

Owen settled back, stretching out his long legs. 'It would help to hear the details.'

Thoresby glanced down at Owen's outstretched legs as if about to reprimand him, then met Owen's eye and shook his head. 'The story is not so long as that. Two or three men attacked Crounce as he walked past the minster last night with a lady friend. The men slit Crounce's throat and cut off his right hand.'

Owen nodded. 'And the lady?'

'She fled.'

'Can she identify the men?'

'We do not know who she was.'

Owen frowned. 'Then how do you know—'

'A boy was following them.'

'Why?'

'The boy's mother is ill. She asked for Crounce.'

'And the boy does not know the woman Crounce was with?'

'He says she wore a hooded cloak.'

'In June?'

Thoresby shrugged. 'The hand is missing, by the way.'

Bess Merchet rushed past Brother Michaelo and barged into the Archbishop's chamber.

Thoresby rose with an exclamation of irritation. 'Where's Michaelo?'

'He's about to come through that door and complain that I ran over him,' Bess said. She placed her bundle on the polished wood table and nodded towards it, her cap ribbons aflutter. 'Do you look at that, Your Grace. Found it in one of my guest rooms.' She looked at Owen, surprised. 'So Tom's right. You are still the Archbishop's man.'

Brother Michaelo appeared in the doorway, nostrils flaring and slender body quivering with righteous indignation.

Thoresby glanced at Bess Merchet and back at his secretary. 'Are you coming in to announce Mistress Merchet?'

'She burst into the ante-room, Your Grace. I could not stop her.'

'I am sure that has been the complaint of better men than you, Michaelo. Would you bring us some brandywine?'

Michaelo sniffed, but hurried away to obey.

Thoresby smiled at Bess. 'You have not made

a friend.'

'I am not here in the busiest time of my day to make friends, Your Grace. Examine the bundle if you will.' Bess sat down without invitation and leaned forward expectantly.

Thoresby had a good idea what the bundle contained and wished to delay the unveiling until the brandy-wine arrived. Such unpleasant experiences were better softened with a drink.

But Bess was impatient. 'Please examine it, Your Grace. As I've said, I'm a busy woman.'

'I presume it's the hand of the man found murdered in the minster close?'

Bess sat up straight. 'Indeed it is. How did you guess?'

'It is the way of such a disturbing event that any-thing unusual happening on the same day is connected to it in some fashion. The bundle is the right size for the missing hand.'

'I found it in the room Gilbert Ridley vacated this morning. They'd argued last night, you know.'

It was Thoresby's turn to lean forward. He knew Gilbert Ridley. A representative of Goldbetter and Company in London and Calais, important merchants in the King's financial dealings. Ridley was also a member of the Mercers' Guild. 'Who argued?'

'Gilbert Ridley and the dead man, Will Crounce.'

'How do you know the name of the dead man?'

Bess shrugged. 'Heard it at the bakery this morn-ing. Did you mean to keep it a secret?'

'Not at all.'

Michaelo came in with the wine. He filled three cups and departed silently.

Thoresby took a drink. 'Tell me about this argu-ment.'

'Little enough to tell,' Bess said. 'They were at the inn last night. Raised voices and red faces. I marched over to tell them to behave. Will Crounce left in a huff. Gilbert Ridley apologised and went to his room.'

'You overheard nothing?' Owen asked, breaking his silence.

Bess glanced at Owen and then dropped her eyes to her cup. She hated to admit to a customer that she eavesdropped.

'I know that it is not your way to gossip,' Owen said, 'but it would be most helpful if we had an idea what they argued about.'

'Well, they *were* loud, as I've said. From what I could hear, Crounce accused Ridley of ruining the lives of two good women.'

'Gilbert Ridley a womaniser?' Thoresby said. 'That fat, gaudy man with the piggish face? I never would have guessed. He must buy favours.'

Bess snorted. 'Nay, Crounce spoke of Ridley's wife and daughter. Mistress Ridley never saw her husband, the daughter is married to a man whom Crounce called a brute and Ridley called ambitious, determined to be knighted.'

'Where is Gilbert Ridley now?'

Bess shrugged. 'Paid his bill and left while I was at the ovens. My husband let him go without questioning him. Tom had not heard about the trouble.'

'And you found the hand in Ridley's room?'

'Right there in the middle of the floor. If Kit had seen it when she came up to clean the room we would have had a fine scene, I can tell you. We'd have had no work out of that girl for a fortnight at least.'

'This argument,' Owen said, 'would you say it was serious enough to end in murder?'

Bess smiled at her best friend's handsome husband and gave a decided shake to her ribbons. 'Nay. 'Twas friends getting too honest in their cups, just as Master Ridley said.'

'Ridley went up to his room after Crounce left and stayed there?' Owen asked.

'It's a private room. What he did after we were all abed, I cannot say. The hand could not have walked up there itself.' Bess looked them both in the eye. 'And there's something else.' Before Thoresby could stop Bess, she had leaned over and unwrapped the unsavoury bundle. 'Crounce wore a signet ring on his right hand, the hand that lifted his tankard. Gone now. Find the ring, find the murderer I would say.'

Thoresby used a quill to flip the cover back over the hand. 'I trust I can count on you not to speak of your discovery to anyone else, Mistress Merchet? We do not want to ruin Gilbert Ridley's good name.' Ridley had once hinted that he would pledge a large sum to the minster fund.

Bess sniffed. 'We'll see about that good name, won't we? But never fear, I can be trusted, Your Grace. And I hope I can trust you not to reveal to the world at large that such a thing was found in my inn.'

'Captain Archer and I will use the information only as necessary.'

Bess nodded with satisfaction and sipped her wine. 'I hear it was a boy found the body.'

Thoresby did not like the way Bess Merchet was settling in for a long talk. He rose. 'I will keep you no longer, Mistress Merchet. As you say, you are a busy woman.'

Bess drained her cup and stood, smoothing out her skirts. 'Your Grace,' she said with a little curtsy.

'Thank you for your assistance, Mistress Merchet.'

'I could do no less, Your Grace.' She swept out of the room with haughty dignity.

Owen waited until he heard the outside door latch shut before he spoke. 'So. Are you thinking that Ridley murdered Crounce after the argument last night?'

Thoresby shook his head. 'Too obvious. My guards are idiots enough to leave damning evidence behind them – but Ridley has been a key negotiator in Goldbetter and Company's business in Calais and London for years. To last that long in such a position takes a clever man. A man good at covering his trail.'

'Crounce was a business associate?'

'According to Jehannes, yes. Crounce was Ridley's man here in York and Hull.'

'Someone cut off Crounce's right hand to accuse him of theft? And left that accusation with his business associate?'

Thoresby shrugged. 'That is what we must discover.' He walked over to the fire and stood quietly contemplating its depths, his hands clasped behind him. Suddenly he turned. 'I want you to go after Ridley. He will not be far from the city yet. I presume he is headed home. To Riddlethorpe. His manor near Beverley.'

'You want me to leave at once?'

'Yes. Catch him while he's in shock. See what he knows. Offer to escort him home. You might search his bags. She could be right about the signet ring, but perhaps Ridley took it for safekeeping. As I said, I want this cleared up quickly. I do not want this worry on my mind at Windsor.'

'I would hate to dampen your enjoyment,' Owen said, making no effort to hide his irritation with Thoresby's priorities.

'It will hardly be a pleasurable sojourn for me, Archer. I will be busy with official duties throughout the celebration.'

Owen shrugged. 'What of the boy who witnessed the murder?'

'Jasper de Melton?' Thoresby shook his head. 'His mother is dying. Jasper told us what he saw. Leave the boy alone for now.'

'He may know something more.'

'Not now.'

'He may be in danger.'

'It was dark. He could not make out the faces, so neither could they make out his.'

'You know full well the whole city will soon hear this Jasper witnessed the murder.'

Thoresby dismissed the subject with a shake of his head. 'Ridley is more important to us. Michaelo will deliver a letter with my seal introducing you to Gilbert Ridley.'

'Your Grace does not afford me the courtesy of asking for my co-operation?'

Thoresby raised an eyebrow. 'I never ask.'

Owen strode out of the Archbishop's presence bristling; beneath the patch, needles of pain shot across his useless eye. What bothered Owen, besides Thoresby's power over him, was the Archbishop's cold unconcern for the boy. Jasper de Melton was of no significance because he was neither a prominent guild member nor was he rich. Owen hated Thoresby for that shake of the head.

But Owen could not deny the thrill he felt at a chance for a trip outside the city.

Lucie slowly mixed calendula oil into a spoonful of cream with a small wooden spatula. 'Beverley?'

she repeated without looking up from her work, 'they say the minster there is grand.' She was mixing a supply of the salve that kept Owen's scar from drawing and burning. More than four years and it still gave him pain.

'My purpose is not a pilgrimage,' Owen said.

Lucie handed Owen the jar. 'Keep it safe. And use it. I don't want a rough cheek scratching me at night.' She kissed his scar. 'I will miss you, but you have yearned to get out of the city. Too many years of soldiering. You find it hard to sit still.'

Owen shook his head, amazed. He thought he'd kept the excitement out of his voice. 'How is it that you divine my thoughts and I still find you an enigma?' He also found it disappointing that she had not protested against his going away. 'Will you miss me?'

Her blue eyes widened. 'Of course I will miss you. I said I would.'

Owen grinned.

'It is hard to run the shop without an apprentice.'

The smile froze on Owen's face.

Lucie laughed at his consternation. 'Silly oaf. I'll lie awake missing you.'

As Owen gathered what he would need for his journey, Lucie paced their bedchamber. 'I wonder if Gilbert Ridley has any idea whose hand he found in his room?'

'How could he?'

'How will you give him the bad news? Ridley told Bess that Crounce was his dearest friend.'

'Better that than breaking the news to Crounce's wife. I wonder who will handle that?'

'No need to worry. Joan Crounce died of plague

four years ago.'

'Now how did you discover that piece of information?'

'The stranger I brought to York. He said he was coming to watch the Mercers' play in particular, and mentioned that Will Crounce had lost himself in his play-acting since his wife's death of the plague.'

Owen looked at Lucie. Her startling blue eyes were fixed on him, waiting for an answer. They had argued about the stranger, spent several cool evenings after Lucie had returned from nursing her Aunt Phillippa. Owen had warned Lucie not to pick up strangers on the road. She was so lovely. Dear God, he knew what the stranger had been after. 'Have you seen him again?'

Lucie sighed. 'That is not the topic of discussion.'

'Have you?'

'No I have not, Owen Archer. And if I had, what would be the harm in it? I can service only one man at a time, and at the moment I have all I can do to keep you satisfied.' Lucie grabbed Owen's arm and put it around her slender waist, then pulled his head down for a kiss.

He resolved to forget the stranger. 'You can do something for me.'

'I have enough to do with the shop.'

'Just ask any customers about the boy, Jasper de Melton. Find out how his mother is, what will happen to Jasper if his mother dies. I take it he has no father.'

'You think Will Crounce was her lover?'

'It seems likely. Will you ask about him for me?'

Lucie gave Owen another kiss. 'Of course.'

'Just ask customers to the shop. I don't want you hunting the streets for him.'

'I won't have time to get into trouble, Owen.'

'Thank God for that.'

Three

Ridley's Pride

Ridley shifted on the low rock wall on which he had seated himself once he was convinced that Owen had come from the Archbishop. The merchant's face was reddening with the sun. He shielded his eyes with his right hand to look up at Owen. The gems on his fingers twinkled in the sunlight. 'I know why you've come. Bess Merchet found the—' Ridley swallowed. 'Why should someone put that hand in my room?'

Owen noted the rings. Travellers were attacked on the road for far less. Ridley risked his own life and the lives of the two servants who accompanied him. No doubt he considered his servants little better than pack-horses. What an arrogant half-wit to flaunt his wealth so recklessly.

Owen opened his mouth, closed it. Some of his irritation stemmed from having to blink his good eye against the reflections. He detested being so blinded. But he must curb his tongue and get to the point. 'One of your business associates was murdered last night. Near the minster.'

29

'One of my—' Ridley shaded his eyes with both hands and peered at Owen. 'Not Will Crounce?'

Owen, blinded again, suggested they move into the shade. 'Your face is reddening at an alarming rate.'

Ridley obliged, then repeated his question. 'Was it Will Crounce?'

'Yes. Did you realise that was his hand?'

'Will's?' Ridley choked. 'I— Dear Lord, no. I did not look closely. But even if I had, how would one recognise—? I do not think I would know my own hand lying severed.' Ridley shivered.

'Why did you leave without a word to anyone about it? At least a warning to the Merchets?'

Ridley bobbed his head and averted his eyes, embarrassed. 'It was cowardly and thoughtless, and they have been good to me. But I could not think what to do. All I wanted was to get far away.'

'What did you think it meant?'

'I wondered who would play such a hideous trick on me.' Ridley made the sign of the cross with a trembling hand.

Owen stared out across the summer meadows. This road paralleled the Ouse, though they were far enough north that the river was not visible. Still, it was the rich soil of a flood plain, quite different from the moors and dales to the north and west. A gentle landscape. Besides Owen, Ridley, and Ridley's two servants, there was no one in sight, though Owen could see cultivated fields. It must be midday, and all the labourers off in some shady spot, eating. A breeze stirred the wild flowers. It was so quiet Owen could hear the bees humming. Occasionally one of the horses whinnied or a bird sang out. Such an inappropriate setting for talk of murder.

'You thought of nothing more sinister than that someone was playing a trick on you?' Owen asked.

'That was as horrible as I cared to imagine. And my mind was muddled. I had much too much ale last night. Will and I—' Ridley shook his head. 'This must mean he was murdered?'

'It would seem so.'

Ridley took a deep, shuddering breath. 'No doubt you have heard from Bess Merchet that I spent the evening with Will at the York Tavern and he left in a temper.' Ridley rose and went to his horse, got a leather bottle out of his pack. 'Sweet Mary and all the saints,' he breathed and took a drink. 'I meant to make it up to him today. I did not like his going away angry.' He took another swig and looked up at Owen. 'Does Archbishop Thoresby think I murdered Will?'

'And left the evidence in your room? No, His Grace says you are no such fool. But he hopes you can help us find the murderer. That you might know why someone would want Crounce dead. And who that might be.'

Ridley ran a dimpled hand over his forehead where the band of his felt hat was already dark with sweat. He took another drink. 'Want Will dead?' He shook his head, looking down at his boots. 'I cannot say. Will had prospered, though you'd never guess it to see him. He dressed humbly, as he always had. But he did carry a money pouch. He always did, old Will. Prepared for the unexpected bargain, he would say.' Ridley smiled sadly and took another swig.

'You'd best go easy on your drink. You've a way to go to Beverley.'

Ridley straightened and returned the bottle to the pack.

'Your friend had no money pouch on him when we found him,' Owen said.

'So he was killed for the money. Greed. The deadliest

sin, to my mind, coveting thy neighbour's goods.'

Owen fought a smile at those words coming from such a tempter of thieves. 'Crounce met a woman outside the tavern. Did he have a lady friend?'

'He said nothing of meeting a woman,' Ridley said.

'I understand Crounce was a widower . . .'

Ridley nodded. 'And popular with the ladies, Will was.'

'Anyone in particular?'

Ridley took off his hat, wiped his brow, frowned down at the stained brim. 'Last night was our first chance to talk in a long while. But I would guess his current favourite was Kristine de Melton, a widow with a bright young boy Will meant to sponsor in the guild. It's not the sort of thing one does for a mere acquaintance.'

Owen found that an interesting connection. 'The boy's name is Jasper?' Ridley squinted at Owen as he put his hat back on. 'How do you know his name?'

'Jasper de Melton witnessed the murder. It was Jasper who told the Archbishop of the hooded woman who waited for Crounce outside the York Tavern.'

'So it *was* Mistress de Melton?'

'Not likely. Archbishop Thoresby says the boy was sent to fetch Crounce to Mistress de Melton's sick-bed.'

Ridley sighed. 'A mystery woman then.' He shook his head, then looked Owen square in the eye. 'How was Will killed? Was it only the hand they hacked off? They did not dismember him, did they?'

'His throat was slit.'

Ridley crossed himself and bowed his head to murmur a prayer. Owen waited in silence. He knew the rush of bile that choked a man when he learned the details of a friend's death. Ridley's eyes were wet when he looked up. 'He did not deserve such an end, not Will. He was a good man. No saint, but a good man.'

'The hand was something the murderer did afterwards,' Owen said. 'Can you think why?'

Ridley shook his head.

'Someone noted that he wore a signet ring on that hand. Was it on the hand when you found it?'

Ridley winced, thinking back to the hand on the floor. 'God grant him rest.' He shook his head slowly. 'I think if the ring had been on the hand, I would have noticed it. Might even have guessed it was Will's—' He dropped his head, covering his eyes with his jewelled fingers.

'They cut off the right hands of thieves,' Owen said. 'Could someone have felt Crounce had robbed them?'

Ridley made no sign that he heard the question.

Owen repeated it.

Ridley shook himself. 'Sorry.' He wiped his eyes sheepishly. 'I never heard Will called a thief.'

'You can think of no one who might have believed himself cheated by Crounce? No business venture gone sour? Someone who thought Crounce had got what was his – or hers – by trickery?'

Ridley shrugged. 'I have worked in London and Calais for many years. Will was my man here. As long as he carried out my wishes, and those of Goldbetter's, I did not ask about his methods.'

'What did you argue about last night?'

Ridley flinched. 'Nothing of import.'

'Perhaps it will prove important.'

'It was a private matter. Drink loosened our tongues and we tripped over them. It can have no bearing on Will's death.'

'I know it concerned your wife and daughter.' Owen,

watching the colour of Ridley's face deepen with an embarrassed flush, knew it was a cruel thing to say, but Owen had to know everything. There was no way Ridley could say this or that had no bearing on his friend's murder – not if he was telling the truth.

'Someone overheard. I should not be surprised. We did get loud. I meant to apologise today, treat Will to a grand meal.'

'Tell me about the argument.'

'I have been an absent husband, absent father. My business kept me away from Riddlethorpe but for brief visits. Will spent more time with my family than I did. He thought I was unkind to my wife, Cecilia. I thought he was perhaps too fond of my wife, to be honest. So the argument got tangled. And then he started on my daughter's husband. The young man was my choice, you see, and he's turned out to be – impatient – with my daughter. Cecilia is unhappy because Anna – that's my daughter – is unhappy. Will blamed me for all of it.'

'That is a heavy burden.'

Ridley nodded. 'But there's much truth to it.'

'Your daughter's husband was a business associate?'

'Paul Scorby of Ripon. Good family. I had some business dealings with them a long time ago. Nothing recently. But they are of good blood. My son, Matthew, lived in their household and learned how to go about with such people. Paul Scorby is ambitious, though perhaps more of a dreamer than a doer. I did not see that then. I thought it a good match for Anna.'

'Had Crounce argued with Scorby?'

Ridley shook his head. 'He would not have interfered like that. No. I cannot see how our argument had anything to do with Will's death.'

Owen shrugged.

'I am sorry I can be of so little help,' Ridley said.

Owen shaded his eye and looked off into the distance. 'By the time we get to Riddlethorpe you might think of something that will help.'

Ridley started. 'You're going to Riddlethorpe?'

Owen nodded. 'I offer you my protection.'

Ridley frowned. 'What need have I of protection?'

'A good friend and business partner has been murdered, Master Ridley. For unknown reasons. Will Crounce might have had a chance encounter with a robber, but he might have been murdered by someone he knew. And that someone could also know you, and be after you at this very time.'

Ridley took off his hat and mopped his forehead. His hair was matted down with sweat. 'Sweet Mother of God.'

'You must look to your safety.'

Ridley regarded Owen more closely than he had until now. 'You look more like an outlaw than a protector.'

Owen touched the patch. 'You are not the first to say so.'

'How did you lose your eye?'

'In the service of the old Duke of Lancaster. A French campaign. I caught someone murdering our prize prisoners.'

'And now you're in John Thoresby's service?'

'From time to time.'

'Owen Archer, you said?' Owen nodded. 'Captain of Archers, were you?'

'A good guess.'

'To tell the truth, I've heard you called Captain. And with that West Country manner of speech.' Ridley shrugged. 'You married Nicholas Wilton's widow, I think?'

'I did.'

'Mistress Archer is of noble stock, at least on her father's side.'

'Mistress Wilton, not Archer.'

Ridley frowned. 'And why is that?'

'The guild. The Archbishop coerced them into allowing Lucie both to continue the work she'd begun as Nicholas Wilton's apprentice and to marry me. But they insisted she keep the name to remind me I have no claims to the shop if she dies.'

'Pity she could not use her family name. I know Sir Robert D'Arby. A fine gentleman. In fact, if you wish to check my character, your wife's father would vouch for me.' Ridley said this with pride.

'My wife's father?'

Ridley nodded. 'I procured some horses for Sir Robert during the siege of Calais. He can attest to my good character, I assure you.'

'How did you come to know Sir Robert?'

'You know how wars are waged. Deals among the nobles. They also make deals with local merchants, and vice versa. We knew trouble was coming, and it would affect us particularly, we who traded over there. I knew it was important to make a good impression on the man who might become governor of Calais, and at the time it looked to be Sir Robert D'Arby.'

Owen did not want to discuss Lucie's family.

'Master Ridley, considering the unpleasant item left in your room, I think it wise I check your packs.'

'For what?'

'Something equally unpleasant. Or harmful to you.'

Ridley blanched. 'I cannot think who would want to harm me.'

'May I examine your packs?'

'Please do.'

Ridley watched Owen's search from a comfortable spot. Owen could sense the man's uneasiness, but could not tell whether Ridley feared what Owen would find or knew of something he did not want Owen to see. It must have been the former, because there was nothing suspicious in the pack.

Ridley looked relieved. 'Perhaps the hand was just the prank of a madman.'

Owen nodded. 'We should move on if we're to reach Beverley by dusk. Will you accept my company?'

Ridley looked at his servants, idly lounging by the pack-horses. One young, one grizzled with several teeth gone. Neither trained to fight. Ridley looked back at Owen, tall, broad-shouldered, threatening. 'Oh, aye. I'll be glad of your company, Captain Archer.'

The road to Beverley wound through flat countryside rather than moorland, with little to distract the traveller but talk. Ridley rode close to Owen, reminiscing about his friendship with Crounce. Owen recognised Ridley's need to talk of his friend, part of the ritual of mourning.

'I had looked forward to spending time with Will, now that I've handed the Goldbetter and Company business over to my son, Matthew.'

'You are generous to your son, giving him your business.'

'It is just part of my business.'

'Why that part?'

Ridley was quiet a while. Then, at last, he said in a voice almost drowned out by the horses, 'I felt the years settling in my bones. I had built a grand house and I wanted some time to enjoy it.'

Owen believed him, but doubted that was the whole reason.

*

Bess tapped Lucie on the shoulder. 'You've not had supper, have you?'

Lucie straightened up and rubbed her eyes. She'd been working on the ledger since she had closed the shop, hoping to finish a neat copy of the list of herbs, roots, powders, and other ingredients in the shop that she'd made since returning from her Aunt Phillippa. 'This should have been finished weeks ago, Bess. If I let it go, there's always a danger that I will be caught without something in an emergency. People's lives depend on my records.'

'And why did Owen not make up the list while you were away?'

Lucie sighed. 'He's still learning, Bess. It was enough for him to watch the shop. And he did well. I have no complaints.'

Bess gave a disapproving sniff. 'A fine time for him to take off on an adventure for the Archbishop.'

'It was not Owen's choice.'

'Well, never mind.' Bess pushed a trencher of hard bread heaped with stew in front of Lucie, then poured ale into a large cup. 'Now then, do your best with that.'

Bess poured herself a cup and sat down opposite Lucie to watch that she ate. Lucie laughed and dipped a spoon into the stew.

'The shop was uncommonly busy today, I thought,' Bess said, resting her strong arms on the table, her sleeves still rolled up from a day's cleaning and cooking.

Lucie nodded. 'People are using any excuse they can dream up to come in and ask about the murder. They know Owen was called to the Archbishop's palace. Which is good; Owen wanted me to find out more about the boy who witnessed the attack.'

'So what do you know?'

'That his mother, Kristine de Melton, died today. And Jasper de Melton has disappeared.'

'Why?'

'I would guess that the boy fears the murderers will come for him. Just in case he saw something.'

'In the dark?'

'If you had murdered someone, Bess, wouldn't you take any precaution to erase your steps?'

Bess sighed. 'Poor lad.'

Lucie was quiet for a time, enjoying her friend's cooking. 'I hated asking. All those years in the convent being told over and over that gossip was a sin. I cannot do it with an easy conscience.'

Bess sniffed. 'I cannot see why gossip is considered a sin. How else is a body to know what's going on?'

Lucie smiled.

'So did anyone have an idea where the poor lad might be hiding?' Bess asked.

Lucie shook her head. 'But the man I met on the road – you know, the one who helped me free the cart from the mud when I was coming back from Freythorpe Hadden – he has offered to look for the boy in the places where such orphans usually wind up.'

'The man Owen had such a fit over? The stranger with the nice voice?'

Lucie laughed at what Bess had chosen to remember. 'You know, the man had mentioned Will Crounce to me on the ride that night. Told me to watch for Crounce in the Mercers' play. At least he had a reason to ask about the death. He must have been a friend of Crounce's.'

'You didn't ask him?'

'I did, actually, but all he said was, "Boroughbridge is a small town".'

'He's a foreigner, you said?'

'His accent is odd, not quite like my mother's, not Norman French, but more like hers than anyone's here.'

'A Fleming, perhaps? Like those weavers who settled here under the King's protection?'

'I've never spoken with them, so I couldn't say.'

'What's his name?'

'Martin.'

Bess winced. 'Unfortunate.'

Lucie shook her head. 'It is a good name, Bess. I cannot mourn my baby for ever.' Lucie and her first husband had lost their only child, Martin, to the plague.

'Owen should give you a child,' Bess said.

'It's not for want of trying that we are not yet blessed.'

Bess shrugged. 'So you don't know where this Martin is from?'

'I didn't ask.'

Bess disapproved of so much mystery. 'You invited him into your house?'

'He came into the shop, Bess, not the house.'

'What about the ride in the cart?'

Lucie looked closely at her friend. 'What is this, Bess? Why all the questions? What about all the other people who asked about Will Crounce today?'

'This Martin knew Crounce before. He's a mysterious stranger. He could be the murderer.'

'Bess, that's nonsense. Why would he risk coming here if he were the murderer?'

'Like a moth to a flame, Lucie, my child. He wants to hear what folk have to say about his crime.'

'Why would he offer to look for Jasper de Melton?'

'I don't know. What did he say?'

'He was out on the streets at about that age.' Lucie shoved the trencher out of her way and replaced it with the ledger. 'I am busy, Bess. I have no time for any more gossip.'

Bess shook her head. 'You will work yourself into an early grave, Lucie.'

Lucie looked up with a smile. 'So will you, Bess.'

Bess snorted. 'Aye. And I must get back to check on Tom.'

After Bess left, Lucie found it hard to focus on the ledger. It was true she felt Martin was hiding something. So why did she trust him? The question spun round and round in her head and made it impossible to work.

'Perhaps it's time for bed,' she said to Melisende, who was napping near the hearth, resting up for the night's hunt. Lucie closed the ledger, damped the fire, and scooped up the cat, who complained.

'It will be cold up there without Owen,' Lucie told Melisende as she determinedly carried the squirming Queen of Jerusalem upstairs.

It was after dark when Owen and Ridley rode through a stone gate and into the yard of Riddlethorpe. From the size of the house and how long they had ridden since Ridley announced they were on his land, Owen surmised that Ridley had made a respectable fortune in Goldbetter and Company. The house was stone below, half timbered above. A tall woman waited up the steps in the doorway, in the light of a lantern held by a serving girl. Other servants helped Owen and Ridley to dismount, then led the four horses away.

'My wife, Cecilia,' Ridley said as they approached the woman in the doorway. 'Cecilia, this is Captain Archer. One of Archbishop Thoresby's men.'

Cecilia Ridley ignored Owen and asked her husband, 'Is there trouble, Gilbert?' Large, dark eyes in a narrow face gave her the look of a frightened deer. In white wimple and veil and a russet wool gown she was plainly dressed, without any of her husband's ostentation. There was a quiet nobility in her posture.

'No trouble for me as such,' her husband replied, 'but Will Crounce has been killed.'

Cecilia Ridley frowned as if she did not understand. 'Did Will not come with you?'

'Did you hear me, woman?' Ridley snapped. 'Will is dead. Murdered.'

The shock registered on Cecilia's face, making her eyes even more dominant, drawing the skin even tighter along the bones. 'Will? Dear God.' She crossed herself.

'Perhaps you should sit down inside,' Owen said gently.

Cecilia Ridley clutched at her stomach and nodded, her eyes fixed on some spot beyond her husband's or her guest's faces. 'I cannot believe – He was here just four days ago.'

'Cecilia,' Ridley said in a warning tone.

The woman started, glanced at Owen, then her husband, and stepped aside for them to enter the hall. 'Forgive me. You will want something to fortify you after your journey.' It was a toneless recital of ritual. As her husband passed her, she touched his arm. 'Did it happen while you were there?' she whispered.

Ridley nodded and pushed past her, striding into the hall with an air of irritation. He sank down on a bench near the hearth, and a boy helped him out of his travel-stained boots. 'Will was murdered after spending the evening with me. His throat was slit wide.' The boy, who was helping Owen now, sat back with a gasp.

'That's a good boy, Johnnie,' Cecilia Ridley said, shooing the boy out of the hall. She shook her head at her husband. 'You'll have the servants deserting us if you speak of such things in front of them.' All said in the toneless voice of habit.

Ridley shrugged. 'That's not the worst of it, anyway. Someone cut off Will's hand and put it in my room while I slept this morning.'

Owen watched Cecilia Ridley, ready to help her to a seat. But Ridley's comment seemed to snap her out of her shock. 'How uncomfortable for you, Gilbert.' She said it softly, but it bit all the same. She glanced at Owen, then back at her husband. 'Does Captain Archer attend you because he suspects you of the murder?'

'Dear God, no, wife.' Ridley gave Owen a pained look. 'She always suspects the worst. Such a gloomy woman.' He looked back at his wife. 'Get us some refreshment and leave us.'

Cecilia Ridley left after pouring them some wine. The girl who had held the lantern brought them cold meat, bread, and cheese.

Ridley noticed Owen examining the surroundings. With his one good eye, Owen was obvious in his curiosity, moving his whole head to see all around him. 'You wonder at the simplicity, when the manor itself is so grand,' Ridley guessed.

Considering Ridley's rings, Owen had expected tapestries and embroidered cushions, all the trappings of a family proud of its wealth. But the great hall was almost bare. Its wooden floor was scrubbed, the few chairs and benches pushed back against the walls, out of the way, but for the two chairs and a table set for the master and his guest. The few tapestries were unremarkable and were positioned to keep draughts from the area near the hearth. The only sign of Ridley's taste was a set of shelves against the far wall on which polished silver plates and cups were displayed, and, Owen guessed, never used. They had been served on wooden plates, in pewter cups. Owen concluded that Ridley's wife resisted the ostentation her husband no doubt wanted. Owen approved. 'The house is quite new,' he said. 'You have storage cellars below this?'

Ridley beamed with pride. 'Wine, dried meats and fruits. I have learned much in my travels. I will show you in the morning. Another woman would show it off, but Cecilia hates all that. In fact, I complained about her just last night to Will. He defended her, arguing that she is virtuous in preferring simplicity. Is it a sin to enjoy what God has granted? All the cloth I brought for her, the jewels, the silver – you see how she displays the plate, as if it's to sell, not to eat on.' Ridley shook his head. 'I know what you think, she must come from common stock. Not in the least! She is a bishop's niece. Her father was a knight.'

Owen did not wish to offer an opinion. 'You will not object to a few more questions?'

'That depends.'

'About your business, nothing personal.'

Ridley shrugged.

'What was your working relationship with Will Crounce? Are there any other associates who might know something?'

Ridley seemed to think it a reasonable line of questioning. 'When John Goldbetter decided he needed me in London and Calais rather than York and Hull, I looked around for a younger man who already knew something of the wool trade and found Will Crounce. His wife's father, Jake Stephenson, was in the guild in York and was teaching Will the trade, but he'd had some set-backs and was happy to recommend his son-in-law.'

'You are certain Stephenson did not resent this transaction?'

Ridley looked surprised, then nodded. 'I see. You wonder whether Jake Stephenson is somehow involved in his son-in-law's death? Impossible. He is dead. Almost the entire family died of plague. One of those families that seems to live under a curse. But even so, I always had a good relationship with them.'

'So Crounce looked after your interests in York and Hull?'

'Goldbetter's interests, truth be told. We all work for Goldbetter.'

Owen gestured around the hall. 'You've done well.'

Ridley nodded. 'I've been a loyal associate through good times and bad. Goldbetter trusts me.'

'How did he feel about Crounce?'

Ridley considered the question. 'I'm not sure he ever met Will. It was enough for John Goldbetter that I was pleased with the arrangement.'

'Did Crounce work with anyone else?'

'Occasional clerks. They come and go.'

'How did you communicate?'

'Messengers.'

'Any particular one?'

Ridley swirled the wine in his cup. Owen had the distinct feeling that the delay was not to search his memory, but that Ridley found the question uncomfortable and was deciding how much to say. Owen watched him. This was a part of questioning that Owen did well. An archer was trained to wait, watch, motionless but ready to strike. He had trained himself to observe the person silently while waiting for the answer, not repeating the question. This let the person know that he knew they had heard the question the first time, a tactic Owen had learned by observing Bess Merchet. It was a nice way to put his old skills to work.

'He is not the most savoury character is why I hesitate,' Ridley finally said. 'But he would have no cause to murder Will.'

'Still, I would talk with him. He may know something useful.'

Ridley rubbed his double chin and frowned. 'That's a problem. I have no idea how to find him.'

'You cannot be serious.'

Ridley shrugged. 'He just appeared at regular intervals and took his orders. And now that I've handed the business over to my son, and Will is gone, I doubt that I'll see the man again.'

'A surprisingly inefficient arrangement.'

Ridley sighed and threw up his hands. 'You must understand. With our on-and-off war with France, it is impossible to find someone both honest and capable to run messages across the Channel. Wirthir was willing enough and exceptionally reliable, for good pay, of course, and so I did not ask questions. But I suspect he did some pirating or smuggling on the side.'

'Wirthir?'

'Martin Wirthir. A Fleming. He must have stayed with someone in York while Will prepared his response, which sometimes entailed completing transactions before he could reply. But I have no idea where Wirthir stayed.'

'Your son will not use him?'

Ridley shook his head. 'My Matthew is an innocent. My fault for leaving him in the care of his mother so long. I should have sent him to the Scorbys sooner. But he will learn. His greed will teach him. For now

Matthew believes that business can be successfully carried out in complete honesty. He never approved of Wirthir.'

'Your son is in Calais?'

Ridley nodded. 'He will travel back and forth between Calais and London as I did.'

'And how is it that you felt comfortable crossing the Channel?'

'John Goldbetter has all sorts of connections.'

'Ah.'

When the two men had finished their repast, Cecilia Ridley returned to show Owen up to a small, private chamber. 'This is my son's room when he is at home. I thought you would be comfortable here. I thank you for escorting Gilbert.' Cecilia's face had some more colour now. 'Please.' She touched his arm. 'Can you tell me anything else about Will's death?'

'It may have been robbery, though it was violent for that. A ring he wore on his right hand is missing. You knew him well. Could you describe the ring?'

'It was a signet. He used it for sealing his letters. Nothing unusual. Not like Gilbert's rings.'

'You were good friends?'

Cecilia Ridley's hand fluttered to her neck. 'Will was kind to me. He helped me set up the accounts. Found a steward when ours died of plague. Always came with presents for the children's name days.'

'This question will seem unkind, but forgive me, I must ask it. Can you think of anyone who would want to kill Will Crounce?'

Cecilia shook her head. 'He was a gentle man, Captain Archer. I cannot imagine anyone hating him so.'

In the morning, Ridley showed Owen the ground

floor, the stores of wine from Gascony, the stone-floored room in which all estate records were kept. Owen was most impressed by a curing room, where food was dried, smoked or salted. A small hearth and a large stone sink with a drain made it cleverly convenient. Owen had never seen the like. Ridley was pleased. And Owen, seeing the man's genuine pleasure in his house, could not help but like him a little more.

All the same, Owen was grateful to leave Riddle-thorpe. There was a tension between Ridley and his wife that made Owen feel in the way. And surely they had much to say to each other about the murder of their friend and business associate.

As Owen told Lucie over supper, 'The oddest part was how Cecilia Ridley's face changed if her husband was present. It darkened, became stony. That, my love, is an unhappy marriage.'

Lucie considered all he had told her. The elaborate house, Cecilia Ridley's simplicity, the subject of the argument between Crounce and Ridley the night of the murder, what Cecilia Ridley had said about Crounce. 'It sounds to me as if Cecilia Ridley had far more affection for Will Crounce than she has for her husband.'

Owen turned his good eye on her. 'I had the same thought.'

Lucie bit her lip, thinking. 'There is nothing surprising in that, Gilbert Ridley having lived away for most of their married life, but if it's so apparent to us, what must it be like for Ridley?'

'You mean, did he kill Crounce for stealing his wife's affection?'

Lucie started to nod, then sighed and shook her head. 'No. It does not fit your description of Gilbert Ridley. His only passion is wealth. Not his wife.'

'What have you learned about Jasper de Melton?'

'He has disappeared. His mother died, and Jasper vanished.'

'Just as I feared. The boy is afraid that the murderers will come for him.'

'Or they already have,' Lucie said, though she hated saying it aloud.

Owen rubbed his scar.

Lucie took a deep breath. 'The stranger who helped me on the road from Freythorpe has offered to search for the boy.'

Owen's fist slammed into the table. 'And what was he doing here?'

'Did you hear me? He has offered to help.'

'I don't want his help.'

Lucie's eyes flamed. She jumped up, knocking her stool backwards. 'Oh, indeed? I humble myself *and* risk my immortal soul gossiping with the citizens of York for you, and you reject the help I found? How gracious you are.' She stormed out of the room.

Owen felt a hypocrite for criticising Ridley's marriage.

Four

An Impertinent Lady, a Humbled Man

Martinmas. One of Thoresby's least favourite feast days. As the Archbishop grew older, he disliked November more and more, the beginning of a long darkness. He especially disliked November in York. He usually managed to stay in Windsor until spring, but this year Thoresby had several archdeacons misbehaving and he thought it wise to make his presence felt among them. Trouble with his archdeacons had an unpleasant tendency to involve murder.

But the feast was not entirely gloomy. Gilbert Ridley had made a most generous bequest to the minster's Lady Chapel, one of Thoresby's contributions to the glorious cathedral, and the one closest to his heart. Considering the size of the gift, Thoresby could do no less than invite the man to dine with him.

The Archbishop was worried about the dinner; it was the first time he would be speaking to Ridley since Will Crounce was murdered, and it must be obvious to Ridley that Thoresby had made no effort to find Crounce's murderers beyond the initial inquiries made by Archer. Gilbert Ridley might require an explanation.

But Ridley could not be too angry if he had donated all that money for Thoresby's Lady Chapel . . .

And after all, Archer had come up with nothing. Even the go-between for Ridley and Crounce, Martin Wirthir, had eluded Thoresby and Archer. Martin Wirthir appeared to have vanished.

Thoresby paced. It was no good. He had to admit to himself, if to no one else, that it was the situation at Sheen that had turned his thoughts away from Will Crounce's murder.

When Thoresby had arrived at Windsor, there were orders – worded as a request, but from the King – that Thoresby was to go to the royal castle of Sheen and escort Queen Phillippa to Windsor. Having a deep and abiding love – courtly, to be sure – for Queen Phillippa, Thoresby had been happy to oblige.

But a new lady-in-waiting had ruined the occasion for Thoresby. An impertinent upstart from a family grown rich in trade, seventeen-year-old Alice Perrers offended Thoresby by her mere presence in the same room as Queen Phillippa. Bold of eye, blunt of tongue, with a laugh that shattered the peace of lovely Sheen, Alice Perrers had inexplicably become Queen Phillippa's favourite.

And once the entourage arrived at Windsor, Thoresby discovered to his disgust that King Edward delighted in Alice Perrers' undisguised attempts to woo him. But that was nothing to what Thoresby discovered next.

On his second evening at Windsor, Thoresby was invited to sup with King Edward in his chambers. Alice Perrers was also invited. She wore a low-cut gown of soft, thin, clinging wool. And as she turned and curtsied to the King, Alice Perrers' silhouette and the way her hands hovered over her stomach revealed to Thoresby that she was with child.

Thoresby was stunned. The young woman was a nobody. Not even a beauty. Plain as the Queen herself, but with none of the Queen's sweet nature to compensate. And yet by the fawning attention the King paid her it was clear that Alice Perrers was a favourite. Such a common woman, invited to sup with the King, allowed to flaunt her bastard – for Thoresby knew she was unmarried.

Thoresby made it his business to find out what he could about Alice Perrers.

Which was very little.

She was a plague child, as they called those born during the first visitation of the Death in England, and had been orphaned by that same pestilence. Her uncles had paid a merchant family to raise her. And then a few years ago the uncles decided to bring Alice back into the bosom of the family and to train her to be a courtier. Alice had a little money – enough to attract a respectable husband; more learning than was good for her – Thoresby was outraged by her impertinent comments; and a defensiveness that betrayed her upbringing in a merchant household. Thoresby despised her.

He could not very well ask courtiers how Perrers' uncles had bought the Queen's favour, but as Lord Chancellor, Thoresby had access to all legal and financial records. He had his chief clerk, Brother Florian, scour the records for two names, Crounce and Perrers.

Brother Florian reported that Crounce had indeed been a minor member of Goldbetter's company; he was mentioned once, as a source of a letter presented by Ridley to a Crown court in defence of Goldbetter. Perrers was in no Crown records.

'However,' Brother Florian said with a smirk, 'it

is common knowledge in London that this Perrers carries King Edward's bastard.'

'Sweet Heaven.' Thoresby stared at Florian in disbelief. 'How could he choose such a creature? And to humiliate the Queen with such— It is impossible. Are you certain?'

'My best sources confirmed it.'

Thoresby felt as if the world had just turned upside down. And with Perrers on his mind, and having found that Crounce was such an insignificant member of Goldbetter and Company, Thoresby had lost interest in Crounce's murder and recorded it as a case of robbery.

But had that satisfied Ridley?

When Michaelo showed Gilbert Ridley into the hall, Thoresby stared at the merchant in confusion. Thoresby remembered Ridley as a barrel of a man, rather like a boar. But the man before Thoresby was pale and anything but round. Emaciated, with the slack flesh and bad colour of someone recovering from a serious illness.

'I had no idea you'd been ill,' Thoresby said.

Ridley shook his head and sat down at the board. 'No, no, I have not been ill. Well, nothing that I consider an illness. I—' Ridley sighed, passed ringed fingers across his brow. 'It has been difficult accepting my friend's death. You remember. Will Crounce. Murdered right here, near the minster. Butchered.' Ridley shook his head.

Thoresby nodded. 'Of course I remember what happened to Will Crounce.' Noting that Ridley's hands trembled as he lifted a goblet of claret to his mouth, Thoresby thought to reassure him. 'I am sorry our investigation turned up nothing. Will Crounce left little record of his life and apparently had no enemies.'

'I know you did your best. I was unable to help your man Archer. I assure you I was most grateful for your help at the time.'

Ridley gave the Archbishop an oddly sweet smile. By God, it was as if the man had found God through the death of his friend, Thoresby thought. Found charity and humility, two graces he'd most sadly lacked before. 'We did what we could,' Thoresby said.

Ridley nodded. 'Will and I had— You know about our business partnership. We were young and hopeful and thought we might do well for ourselves. And we did. We did that. It could not have happened without Will. He had a way with people that I never had. A gentle voice, a manner that reassured.' Ridley took a long drink of the wine. Tears shone in his eyes.

'We had no luck finding the Fleming who worked as your go-between, Martin Wirthir,' Thoresby said. 'We suspect he goes by another name in York.'

'It is unlikely that Wirthir comes to York any more. He has no reason for doing so.'

Thoresby nodded. 'And no one would come to the North Country by choice. It is a place one must be sent.'

Ridley shook his head. 'I disagree. I could not wait to come home to the moors, the heather, the silence of the winter snows, the first frost that crunches underfoot.'

'My dear man, to speak in such poetic terms of this wasteland . . .'

'It is no wasteland to me. You speak like a Southerner. But you were born in the Dales, were you not?'

Thoresby frowned. 'I do not recall speaking to you about my family.' He did not like people getting too familiar.

Ridley bowed his head in apology. 'I am offering you a large sum of money for what I hear is to be

54

your tomb. I wanted to know everything I could about you, to make sure that this is how I wished to thank the Lord for my good life.'

They were quiet as Lizzie, the serving girl, arranged the food before them.

Thoresby watched Ridley take a pouch out of a pack he'd brought with him and add a small amount of powder to his wine. Lizzie gave it a curious sniff as she passed and wrinkled her nose.

'What is that you mix in your wine?' Thoresby asked.

Ridley drank it down and shuddered, then wiped his mouth. 'A tonic my wife doses me with. She has been giving it to me since midsummer. Foul tasting, but she hopes it will calm my nerves and settle my stomach. Recently she has softened the taste a bit. Still wretched. But I humour her. I must confess to some alarm as the fit of my clothing gets worse and worse.'

Lizzie set a second flagon of wine near Ridley, glancing down at his waist where his tunic was gathered tightly by an ornate belt.

Thoresby followed her gaze and nodded. 'A costly condition. Perhaps you should talk to the apothecary next to your inn. Lucie Wilton is very knowledgeable.'

Ridley shook his head. 'Cecilia would not take it well.'

'Even if it helped?'

'There is no guarantee of that.'

Lizzie disappeared.

'Well, eat hearty,' Thoresby told his guest, 'you need more fat on you for the winter months.'

Ridley chuckled and poured himself more wine. 'Even my goldsmith has benefited – I had him make all my rings smaller.'

Thoresby glanced down at Ridley's beringed fingers, remembering Archer's comments about Ridley's foolhardy magnificence on the road. 'I trust you do not display your jewels when abroad in the city or travelling?'

Ridley lifted his left hand and wiggled his fingers. The pearl and the moonstone were large, their gold settings heavy. 'Captain Archer thought me a dangerously foolish peacock on the road. I have since been more prudent. But here in the city it is important to look splendid. Good for business.'

'Not on the streets, I should think.'

Ridley shrugged.

They ate in companionable silence for a while, then Ridley began to prod the Archbishop for news of the court. 'They do say there is a new lady-in-waiting who has captured the King's heart.'

Thoresby flinched. Even here the upstart Perrers cast a pall over his mood. 'I have kept to myself of late,' Thoresby said, 'except for my duties as Chancellor.'

Ridley gave up the effort.

After dinner, as they sat before the fire with brandy-wine, Thoresby opened the business. 'This is a large sum of money you offer for my Lady Chapel, Ridley. So much money would buy a beautiful stained-glass window. Two, in fact. That is the more common donation when the sum is so large. An appropriate saint's story with your face and perhaps that of your wife on figures in the window, your family crest in the corner, or your name and guild affiliation, that sort of thing.'

Ridley shook his head. 'I particularly did not want to bring attention to myself with this gift. I want the Lord to know it is from my heart, not a bribe of any kind.'

Thoresby sat back and considered this changed man. 'Why such generosity, Ridley?' he asked quietly.

Ridley reddened. 'You do not wish to accept my donation?'

'That is not it. But such a large sum. And I detect – forgive me for mentioning it, but there is such a change in you – something has subdued you. This is not a penance, is it? Something troubling you?'

'Good heavens, Your Grace,' Ridley exclaimed, rising. 'If I had known my money was so suspect I never would have offered it!'

'Please, my friend, sit down. You must forgive me. But this chapel is important to me. I will be buried there. And I want it to be clear of any criticism. I want no blood money put into it.'

'This is not blood money. If you will, it is a symbol of my devotion, my realisation with Will's death that I have had a blessed life and it can end all too soon. I must make those provisions I most want to make before death catches me unawares.'

Thoresby could certainly understand that. 'Please. Forgive me.' He offered Ridley more brandywine. Ridley accepted with pleasure.

'I regret many things in my life, Your Grace, but I know that money to the Church cannot undo them.'

'What sort of regrets?'

Ridley was silent a moment. Then he sighed and said, 'I gave my daughter to a man who I now realise is the devil incarnate. I would that I could undo that.'

Thoresby smiled. 'Fathers often feel that way about their daughters' husbands.'

Ridley reddened. 'Do not make light of my honest confession.'

'Forgive me again,' Thoresby said. 'Is there any hope of annulment?'

'No. The marriage has definitely been consummated.' Ridley passed his ringed hands over his eyes, a weary gesture. 'My son-in-law also appears to be a bragging fool. He tells all that he will soon be knighted. But the simpleton's done nothing to earn a knighthood. He's been neither diplomat nor soldier. The only battles he's fought are with my daughter.'

'I am sorry.' Thoresby studied Ridley's trembling hand, the pain in the man's eyes. 'No, I am more than sorry. I am grieved for you and your family.'

Ridley sipped his brandywine, took a deep breath. 'So your tomb is to be in the Lady Chapel,' he said, changing the subject. 'How did you come to choose that?'

Thoresby did not answer at once, caught off balance by the shift. 'How did I choose it? Ah, well, it was a prayer to Our Lady that brought the sign I needed to know that I was called to the Church.'

'You were not a second son?'

Thoresby smiled. 'Yes, but I had made myself quite useful at court and was rising with pleasant speed. I would have had a position at court for certain.' Thoresby stared into the fire. 'Although these days being a rising star at court is not such an honour – it has become too easy.'

'Perhaps there is hope for my son-in-law then, eh?' Ridley said, smiling. Then he burped rather loudly.

Thoresby glanced up from his dark study of the fire.

Ridley reddened. 'Pardon me, Your Grace.' He burped again.

'Was it something in the supper?'

'Nay. 'Tis every night like this. For months now.'

'Even with your good wife's tonic?'

Ridley nodded. 'You know, I sometimes have the uncharitable suspicion that some of the symptoms have worsened with her ministrations, not improved.

But we have struck a delicate balance in our affections of late, and I will do nothing to upset that.'

'The brandywine should help you digest your food.'

'It is most soothing. Most soothing.' Ridley made a little face as he masked another burp. He rose. 'Your Grace, I think it time I returned to my room at the York Tavern. It is a long journey tomorrow, and as you see I am not as strong as I used to be.'

Thoresby accompanied Ridley to the door. Lizzie brought Ridley's cloak.

'Would you like my secretary, Brother Michaelo, to accompany you to the inn?' Thoresby offered.

Ridley looked embarrassed. 'No need. Really. I am quite used to this. And the inn is so close.'

Thoresby regretted his easy acquiescence next morning when Archdeacon Jehannes stumbled upon Ridley's body in the minster yard. 'I have heard a slit throat described as the hideous grin of Death,' Jehannes said, his face grey, 'and that is exactly what I thought. The eyes, staring up, the lips blue, and below them, another, unholy set of blood-red lips —' he shivered. 'And a raw stump where his right hand should be.'

Thoresby led Jehannes to a chair. 'Sit down. Michaelo is bringing some brandywine. Forgive me for making you speak of it. But on Ridley's left hand — Were there two rings?'

Jehannes nodded.

Later that morning, masons working on the Lady Chapel found a bloody rag, but no hand, no jewelled rings.

Thoresby did not like it. Impossible to consider it a coincidence. Obviously Crounce's hand had been delivered to Ridley's room last summer as a warning. So to whom had Ridley's hand been delivered now?

Thoresby sent for the mayor. All the bailiffs, all the guards of the city must be alerted. They must send word of any news of the hand, even rumours. He would not make the mistake of letting the murderer escape a second time.

And then the Archbishop sent for Owen Archer.

Five

The Ridley Women

W hen Brother Michaelo came to the apothecary this time, Owen woke to the pounding alone. He tried to think why Lucie might have risen early, but his mind was muddled with sleep. Owen marched downstairs and dispatched Michaelo with promises to be along soon, then went in search of his wife. He found the serving girl, Tildy, fussing with the kitchen fire.

'Have you seen your mistress this morning, Tildy?'

'Out back,' Tildy said, without looking up.

Owen could tell by the girl's abruptness that she did not want to say more, that even that answer was more than she'd cared to say. Owen knew what that meant.

Outside, a wet snow fell. Owen guessed from the depth of his footprints on the stone path that it had been snowing for a few hours; but there were no earlier footprints in the snow. And yet there was Lucie, her russet cloak billowing out in the brisk wind as she knelt at her first husband's grave. The Archbishop himself had consecrated the small plot in the back of the garden. Nicholas Wilton had been Master Apothecary, and this garden had been both his master work and his passion. It had been the day of the first snow two years ago when Wilton was struck down with a palsy from which he'd never recovered. Lucie had been remembering Wilton lately. She said it was the time of year. Owen had tried to be patient. He had agreed to the guild's requirement that Lucie keep the name Wilton as long as she was an apothecary. He had agreed to the papers they'd asked him to sign, giving up any claim to the shop if Lucie should die before him. Those had been administrative noise, nothing to do with his love for Lucie or hers for him. But her grieving for Nicholas tried his patience. And this was nonsense, to kneel out here for several hours in the snow.

'Lucie, for pity's sake, what are you doing?'

She looked up at him, her eyes red-rimmed. 'I could not sleep.'

'You've noticed the snow, have you?'

'Of course I have.' Her eyes challenged him to say more.

He knew better. He changed the subject. 'I've been called to the Archbishop's palace. Another murder in the minster yard.'

'Then you must go to him.' Lucie's voice held no affection, no regret that he must go out so early, on an errand that would no doubt mean he must soon go away.

Owen did not have fond memories of Lucie's first husband. He did not understand Lucie's continued affection for the man. Nicholas had not deserved her.

Not that Owen felt himself worthy of Lucie's love, but he trusted he was more deserving than Nicholas.

'Will you come in with me and share some ale or hot wine before I go?'

Lucie nodded, crossed herself, rose to accompany Owen back into the house. As they walked back through the garden, Lucie caught Owen's elbow. 'I do not mean to hurt you.'

Owen pulled her to him and hugged her hard. It was enough to know that she cared how he felt.

Archbishop Thoresby sat at a polished table, a scroll curling beneath his hands. 'A generous gift to my Lady Chapel. But my benefactor was murdered last night, Archer. I need you again.'

'I do not like to leave Lucie at this time of year, Your Grace,' Owen said. 'This morning she was kneeling in the snow at Wilton's grave. I curse the day you agreed to consecrate that grave in the garden. It stirs up morbid humours.'

Thoresby shrugged. 'Wilton's grave is not heavy on my mind at the moment. Ridley's murder is. He was my guest last night. He left here feeling ill and I let him go alone. He was murdered exactly like Crounce. It was no accident. Someone waited for Ridley. This was planned. And this time we must find the murderer.'

'Have you learned something new? We came up with nothing last time.'

'There is one thing. Ridley had changed since Crounce's death. His body had gone from barrel-like to skeletal, his disposition from arrogant to humble.' Owen thought about that. 'Fear can rob one of sleep and appetite.'

Thoresby shrugged. 'Poison can have a similar effect.'

Owen nodded.

'Perhaps Cecilia Ridley will know something,' Thoresby said. 'She was dosing him. I want you to go and tell her of her husband's death. Before she has had time to talk to anyone else. Ask her who might have killed her husband.'

'A churchman should tell her. Not a soldier.'

'You are no longer a soldier.'

'I look like one. With this patch and scar—' Owen shook his head. 'I am not the person for this job.'

'I would send Archdeacon Jehannes, but I cannot spare him at the moment. Besides, Cecilia Ridley has met you.'

'Aye, and bad news it was I brought that time. She'll think me the messenger of Death.'

'Does that disturb you?'

'That is not what most disturbs me.'

'And what is that?'

'Leaving Lucie right now.'

Thoresby waved the argument away with brusque impatience. 'Perhaps your wife would like the privacy to mourn Wilton.'

That stung. 'She has all the privacy she wants.'

'Marriage is not the Heaven you imagined it.'

'I have no regrets, Your Grace,' Owen said.

The eyebrows raised. 'Indeed? Then you are most fortunate. In any case, I want you to go to Beverley. Cecilia Ridley has met you, she did not seem unfriendly towards you, you are precisely the person who should go. I have written a letter of condolence to Cecilia Ridley. Michaelo will give it to you. Two of my men will accompany you.'

'Two men? Most generous, Your Grace.'

'You are becoming arrogant, Archer.'

'I am beginning to find the routine tedious.'

Owen took two days riding to Riddlethorpe. He wished he might have done it in one, but the weather and the short days prevented it. By the time the manor's half-timbered gatehouse was in sight, Owen was sorely tired of his companions and their offensive prattle. He wondered whether he and his comrades-in-arms had been like them, or whether Alfred and Colin were particularly oafish. They ached for a fight, bragged about every scar and broken bone, referred to women by their private parts. If this is what Owen had been like when he first rode into York, it was a wonder that Lucie had ever talked to him. He began to understand why she had such an abiding distaste for soldiers.

When the elderly gatekeeper waved them into the yard at Riddlethorpe, Owen dismounted and left Alfred and Colin to see to the horses. 'Then find the kitchen and stay there,' he ordered. He could not risk their upsetting Cecilia Ridley. The news he brought was itself too awful.

Fear shone in Cecilia Ridley's eyes as Owen crossed the hall to where she stood by the hearth. 'Captain Archer.' She glanced behind Owen, checking to see whether she was mistaken and he was not alone. But he was. 'Something has happened to Gilbert?'

'Please, Mistress Ridley, sit down.' Owen motioned for a servant to bring wine.

Cecilia Ridley caught the gesture and folded her tall frame into a chair with the clumsiness of one suddenly disoriented. She placed her white hands one on top of the other in her lap, and then looked up at Owen, her eyes frightened. 'Something has happened to Gilbert,' she said again.

'Your husband is dead.'

Cecilia jerked as if Owen had hit her. Then she made the sign of the cross and bowed her head. 'He had been ill,' she said softly. Without a word, the servant placed a cup of wine in her mistress's hands.

'He did not sicken, Mistress Ridley. He was murdered.'

She looked up at Owen, shook her head. 'No. He has been ill.'

'He was murdered in the same way as Will Crounce. The throat, the hand.'

Cecilia's eyes widened at that. 'The same as Will? It was not illness?' She lifted the cup to her lips, paused. 'Are you certain of that?'

'Quite certain.'

She drank. 'But he *had* been ill.'

Owen was familiar with shock from his life at war. Cecilia Ridley's insistence on her husband's illness was a sign of it. The Archbishop had said Ridley was ill, and that Mistress Ridley had been dosing him. Perhaps she had not wanted her husband to go on the journey.

'He had dined with the Archbishop,' Owen said. 'Someone waylaid him in the minster yard.'

Cecilia Ridley frowned. 'But it is guarded.'

'The gates to the minster close are guarded, as they were when Crounce was attacked. But many people live inside the walls. Others come and go so regularly the guards think nothing of letting them pass.'

'Gilbert carried a large sum of money.'

'That had already been left with the Archbishop.'

Cecilia Ridley studied Owen's face. 'So you think that someone set out to murder both Will and Gilbert?'

'Yes.'

She looked down at her hands and was quiet for a few minutes. 'Gilbert's finding Will's hand was a warning then.'

'Or a threat.'

'Who—' She swallowed. 'Who found Gilbert's hand?'

'No one so far.'

She nodded, still keeping her eyes down. 'Where is his body?'

'Archbishop Thoresby has arranged for it to be brought to you under guard.'

She nodded.

'Mistress Ridley, this illness of your husband's, how and when did it strike him?'

Her deep-set eyes widened, her hands played with her keys. 'When? Well, I' – she shrugged – 'I could not say.'

'The Archbishop said your husband took a physick you had prepared.'

A nervous hand flew to her neck. 'Gilbert told His Grace about that?'

'When did he start taking this physick?'

She frowned. 'I cannot remember.'

'He blamed his illness on Will Crounce's murder.'

Cecilia Ridley stared at Owen for a few minutes, as if her thoughts were elsewhere. Owen was about to repeat his last comment when she said, 'Yes. Will's death was a great shock to Gilbert. He – well, yes, I suppose his illness stemmed from that.'

'What were you giving him?'

'I'm not entirely certain. My mother used to give it to us. Something to calm his nerves. He was not sleeping.' She dropped her head for a moment, as if hiding emotion.

'Mistress Ridley?'

She raised her eyes, brimming with tears, to meet his. 'What am I to do without him, Captain Archer?'

Now what? Owen was no good at comforting. Besides, what comfort could he possibly offer? Her husband was dead. Nothing would undo that. 'Is there any family I can send for?'

'No.' She wiped her eyes. 'No. They would be no use.'

Owen stood up. 'I should leave you alone for a few minutes. I could go out to the yard, see to my horse.'

Cecilia took a cloth from her sleeve, dabbed her eyes, then lifted her head. Her eyes were red, but tearless now. 'There is no need for you to go out in the cold. I must go up and see to my daughter. Then we will have something to eat.'

Owen watched Cecilia's departing back. She held herself erect, tense. An admirable woman.

'More wine, Captain Archer?' a servant asked.

Owen nodded, held out his cup. 'Is there illness in the house?'

The young woman glanced up at Owen and blushed to meet his eye. 'Yes, sir. Mistress Anna, she's here for her mother's nursing.' She poured the wine and hurried away.

As Owen sat brooding over his gloomy mission, he heard raised voices out in the yard, then running footsteps, dogs barking. The fine hunting dog drowsing by the hearth perked up, began to bark. Owen got up to investigate, glad for the diversion. He went down the passage between the buttery and the pantry and out back to the kitchen, rounding up Alfred and Colin, who grumbled to leave the warm fire.

'You two have ached for a fight since we began this journey. Be grateful, for pity's sake.'

'A fight?' Alfred's eyes went from half closed to wide open with anticipation.

A freezing fog was settling down over the land as the light faded. Owen squinted through the murk and saw a light bobbing out in the direction of the gatehouse. He led his men towards it with caution. As he drew closer, Owen heard an angry voice cry out, 'The devil take you! How can you deny me entrance?

I am her husband! If any harm has come to her, it is my place to comfort her. What right had you to bring her here?'

'Peace, my son.' The second speaker was this side of the pedestrian archway, a priest. A servant held a lantern, revealing the priest's back.

Owen wondered if he'd made a mistake coming out without his longbow. He strode up to the priest. In the doorway, blocked by one of the servants holding two huge dogs that strained at their leashes, stood an angry-faced gentleman, who kept just beyond the reach of the dogs. Motioning to Alfred and Colin to stay by the priest, Owen mounted the stairway to the upper window to see who accompanied the man. Two armed men sat their horses, looking nervous. Owen relaxed. They should have no problem holding the gatehouse against the small party. He returned to the priest.

'I merely carry out her mother's orders,' the priest was saying. 'No one is to enter while Mistress Scorby is in this nervous state.'

'Nonsense.' The angry gentleman gestured towards the servant who held the lantern. 'Jed, tell my father-in-law that I am here.'

'I am afraid he cannot do that,' the priest said.

'Bugger he can't. Then you do it, Father. Get Ridley out here.'

'He is not here, Master Scorby.'

So it was the ill-favoured son-in-law. Owen studied him with interest. Scorby had travelled here expecting trouble, judging from the mail shirt visible beneath his cloak. His face, even in the poor light, flickered with emotion.

'And who is that standing behind you?' Scorby said, catching Owen's intense look. 'Did you bring in cut-throats to keep me away?'

The priest, surprised, glanced back to see who had joined him. 'He's come from the Archbishop of York,' the priest said. 'He's no cut-throat, but he has two armed men with him who do not seem averse to fighting, should we need them.'

Owen knew from the look on Scorby's face that the priest had said the wrong thing.

'So you're fixing for a fight? Men!'

With a clatter of metal, Scorby's men were behind him, knives ready to hand.

Scorby pushed Jed aside. The priest stood firm. 'Move aside, Father,' Scorby warned.

Owen stepped in front of the priest. 'Go inside, Father,' he said quietly. 'Assure Mistress Ridley that we have the matter in hand.' Alfred and Colin joined Owen.

Scorby drew out a dagger.

'Why does the husband of Ridley's daughter Anna come here prepared to break the peace?' Owen asked, keeping his voice quiet, unemotional.

'Because that cursèd priest brought her here without my permission.'

Owen glanced back at the retreating priest, a small, slender man, then back to Scorby. 'Surely the priest did not overpower you in your house?'

Scorby snorted. 'I'd like to see him try. No, the coward waited until I was away.'

'Then perhaps you have misinterpreted his actions. I will speak with Mistress Ridley, see what this is all about. Meanwhile, I suggest that you head towards Beverley and lodgings.'

Scorby lifted his dagger. Owen grabbed the wrist that held the weapon and twisted. Scorby cursed and the dagger fell to the ground. Owen grabbed Scorby's other hand. The man was not weak, but he could not break out of Owen's strong grasp, though his face grew red with the effort. A bull-headed man who could not size up his opponent and withdraw with grace. Owen had met his type before. Scorby would be trouble. Owen let him go. Keeping his eyes on Scorby, he said, 'Alfred, hand the gentleman his dagger. Then we'll escort these three to their horses.'

As Alfred walked towards Scorby, one of Scorby's men came at him with a knife. Colin yelled to Alfred, who used his mail-clad head to butt the attacker in the stomach and send him sprawling. Scorby's right fist came up towards Owen's blind side, but Owen, catching the motion, grabbed the upraised arm with his left hand and punched Scorby in the stomach with his right fist.

'Now, as I said, we will escort you to your horses.'

Which they did.

As Scorby wheeled his horse round he yelled, 'I'll be back. Tell that bitch I'll be back.'

Owen turned to Alfred and Colin. 'Thank you, lads.'

Colin grinned. ''Twas our pleasure.'

'Pleasure?' Alfred snorted. 'They gave way too soon for my taste.'

Owen nodded. 'They might double back. Stay out here tonight. Upstairs. Shouldn't be too uncomfortable. I'll have some ale sent out to you, but see you stay awake.'

He walked back to the hall wondering what had possessed the priest to admit that the master was away.

Cecilia Ridley stood just inside the door. '*Deus juva me*, I did not expect he would come so soon upon their heels.'

'Scorby's wife lies abed upstairs?'

'Yes.'

'An unusual arrangement.'

71

'I hope for the sake of all mothers and daughters that it is unusual.'

'Well, my men can hold the gates against Scorby tonight.'

'Thank you.'

'What is going on here, Mistress Ridley?'

The dark eyes looked affronted by the blunt question. 'I am certain it has nothing to do with my husband's death.'

'And how do you know that?'

'Gilbert is' – Cecilia shook her head, – '*was* Paul Scorby's champion. Gilbert chose Paul for Anna. I never wanted the match.'

'Why did he choose Scorby?'

'Our son, Matthew, lived with the family for a few years. When he left, the family suggested the match between Paul and Anna. Gilbert saw it as an ideal arrangement, wealth on our side, connections on theirs, and the young man ambitious, hardworking.'

'So how does your daughter come to be here without her husband?'

'Anna was attacked, went to Father Cuthbert and begged him to bring her here. Paul was away.'

'Attacked by whom?'

Cecilia Ridley glanced back at the servants. Seeing them with their heads together by the hearth, no doubt discussing the commotion out at the gate, Cecilia invited Owen to sit down on a bench beside the door.

'We have told the servants it was thieves who broke into the house.' She clasped her hands tight and kept her eyes downcast.

'Your daughter is badly hurt?'

Cecilia nodded, but did not look up.

'So this is why you dislike your son-in-law so much. Because he beats your daughter.'

72

Owen heard Cecilia take a deep breath. She looked up, tears in her dark eyes. 'It is not that I think Paul a bad man, Captain Archer. He is just the wrong husband for Anna. My daughter wanted to join a religious house. Another man, one with more patience, might have convinced her that marriage could be a joyous state, might have won her over. But Paul —' Cecilia shook her head. 'He goes into rages over Anna's fasts. And as she retreats, he gets angrier. I could see the impatience in his character. I warned Gilbert.'

More shouts were heard outside.

Cecilia looked up at Owen, her eyes frightened. 'How long do you think your men can hold the gates against him?'

'Scorby and his men are not the trained fighters we are. But we cannot stay here indefinitely.'

'I should go and speak with Paul.'

'Perhaps if he saw her condition?'

She gave him a surprised look. 'He did this to her. How could he not know her condition?' She spoke in a quiet voice, but behind it quivered controlled emotion.

'What do you intend to do?'

Cecilia Ridley shrugged. 'Keep him away from her somehow.'

'May I see her?'

She gave Owen a searching, not entirely friendly look. 'Why?'

'I am an apprentice apothecary. I might be of help.'

'I thought you were the Archbishop's man.'

'That, too.'

'Your life is rather complicated, Captain Archer.'

He grinned. 'You do not know the half of it, Mistress Ridley.'

'What could lead a captain of archers to apprentice to an apothecary?'

Owen tapped his patch. 'A reminder of how easily death creeps up on us.'

Cecilia stared at Owen a moment, then, seeming to decide something, she rose and indicated for him to follow her upstairs.

The room was next to the one Owen had used when he had come in summer. A brazier kept the room warm. A young woman lay in the bed, the hand outside the counterpane bandaged. Her face was bruised and swollen, one side of the mouth cut. She watched them with one eye; the other was blackened and too swollen to open.

'Mamma?' Her voice was ragged, frightened.

Mistress Ridley crossed quickly to the bed. 'It is all right, Anna. This is Captain Archer. He is an apothecary, though he looks nothing of the sort. He thought he might be able to help.'

Owen wondered how Cecilia Ridley managed to sound so calm with her daughter so badly hurt, her husband murdered, and her son-in-law yelling at the gate. But it was good that she could manage it, for her daughter looked terrified even without knowing all that was the matter. Owen knelt beside Anna and asked, 'The hand is broken?'

'A finger,' Cecilia said. 'We pulled it straight and splinted it.'

'And applied a salve of boneset?'

Cecilia nodded.

'Is anything else broken?'

'No. The rest are bruises, her face and her stomach. And the cuts on her mouth.' She told Owen what she had done for her daughter.

He motioned to Cecilia to step out of the room with him. They stood on an open landing looking down onto the hall.

'Some valerian in wine would calm her,' Owen said. 'You say her stomach was bruised. Was there bleeding?'

'Yes. But it has stopped.'

'Do you think she could keep down some wine with valerian?'

'She has kept wine down.'

'Keeping her calm, that is important.' Owen rubbed the scar on his left cheek. 'Jesus Lord, what sort of man would do that to his wife?'

'He says he has needs and she denies him. That it drives him mad.'

'If there is anything else I can do, Mistress Ridley . . .'

She took his hand and squeezed it. 'You are a good man, Captain Archer.' Her eyes swept over his face, lingered on his mouth.

She seemed too close. Too intent on him. Owen resisted the urge to back up a step.

Cecilia smiled through tears, smoothed down her skirt, sighed. 'And now I must go out to confront my son-in-law.'

Owen lay in the room next to Anna's. He jerked to attention at every sound in the house. Cecilia Ridley felt Scorby would stay away for the night, that she had convinced him to sleep at an inn – Beverley was a large enough town to have several comfortable inns – but Owen could not rest. He tossed and turned on the pallet as he listened to Cecilia Ridley pacing anxiously back and forth in her daughter's room.

The footsteps in the next room suddenly changed in character, moving decisively to the door, then outside. There was a knock at Owen's door.

'Come in.'

Cecilia Ridley held an oil lamp to her face. 'Forgive me for disturbing your sleep.'

'I've been unable to sleep.'

She came in, closed the door behind her, placed the oil lamp on a small table next to Owen, and proceeded to pace back and forth at the foot of his pallet, her hands behind her back.

'What is it?' Owen asked.

'You must help us. Anna must not stay here.'

Dear Lord, the woman was panicking. 'I want to help, Mistress Ridley. I cannot sleep for thinking of your poor daughter. But she cannot be moved. Not with the bleeding.'

'It has stopped.'

'If she sits a horse it might begin again.'

Cecilia whirled round and sat down at the side of Owen's pallet. 'Worse will happen to Anna if she does not get away. You must see that.' Her eyes were dark, huge, and wild in the flickering light.

Owen understood what she feared. Was it not what kept him awake, listening for sounds of the man breaking into the house? But Anna was in no condition to travel. 'I cannot understand how Anna bore the trip here,' Owen said. 'To travel again so soon . . .' He shook his head. 'No, you cannot mean it.'

'Merciful Heaven, there is no other solution.' Cecilia leaned towards Owen, as if with her body she could convince him how serious this was. 'You said she needed calming. How can she be calm if she fears he will come take her back there? There is not enough valerian root in all the kingdom to wipe that fear out of her heart.'

True enough, and Anna did need to stay calm to heal. A shower of hot needle pricks across his blind eye warned Owen that he was getting too involved in the Ridleys' problems. He lifted a hand to his scar and discovered that he wore no patch. Of course not, he'd thought he was going to sleep. Amazing that Cecilia Ridley could stare at him with such intensity and not wince at the ugly, puckered lid that would not completely close over the sightless eye. The light in the room was not dim enough to conceal it. Owen reached for the patch on the table beside him.

Cecilia Ridley took it as a sign that he was dressing, that he had decided to help. She stood up. 'Good. I'll prepare her.'

'For pity's sake, I have agreed to nothing. I merely wished to spare you the sight of this eye.'

Cecilia sat back down. 'But it is just that about you, the scar, your suffering, that made me think you would help. Could you rest anywhere near the person who did that to you?'

'I killed the person who did this to me.'

That made her hesitate. She clutched her hands in her lap and studied them for a long moment.

Something in the terrible effort put forth to keep that back so straight, those hands so still, put Owen in mind of Lucie. 'You remind me of my wife.'

'Oh? And what would Mistress Archer do in my place?'

Owen did not correct the name. He thought it best that Cecilia have no idea of any imperfection in his relationship with Lucie. But what *would* Lucie do? Owen thought back to the night that Thoresby, Archbishop of York and Lord Chancellor of England, had given Lucie an order and she had refused. She had decided what was best for her husband, Nicholas, and nothing in Heaven or Hell could move her to change her mind. Cecilia Ridley's back looked that stubborn.

'Lucie would confront Scorby with what he has

done,' Owen said. 'Bring him up here to see Anna's condition. No doubt Scorby left right after he'd beaten her. He may not realise how far he'd gone.'

Cecilia's eyes opened wide with disbelief. 'Are you mad? Anna is terrified. What if he attacks again?'

'I will be there in the room. I will watch his reaction and I will be ready to protect her. But I suspect that Paul Scorby will go away quietly when he sees his wife's condition. He has nothing to gain by forcing her to travel.'

Cecilia shook her head. 'No. I cannot put Anna through that.'

'But you could put her through another journey?'

'Just to St Clement's nunnery outside York.'

'She cannot travel.'

'I cannot let him near her.'

'No matter what you feel, Anna is married to Paul Scorby. He has a right to see her.' Owen did not like the pain in the woman's face. He did not like disappointing her. But he must. To take Anna Scorby on horseback through the snow might kill her. But Cecilia Ridley still did not seem convinced. 'Do you have any reason to fear Paul Scorby will do more than beat her?' Owen asked.

'Isn't that enough?'

'You misunderstand. I am asking if you have reason to think Scorby means to kill Anna.'

Cecilia looked uncertain. 'I never thought that. But look how he hurt her. I don't think he can control himself.'

'Let us try this, eh? See if being forced to face what he did, and in front of others, might teach him something.'

'Perhaps . . .'

'I am curious. How did the priest get involved?'

'Anna begged him to bring her here, hoping her father would . . .' Cecilia looked stricken. 'Dear God, I had forgotten Gilbert for a moment. How could I?'

Owen took her hands. 'You have much to bear right now. You are wonderfully strong.'

Cecilia gave Owen a weak smile.

'You know,' Owen said, 'although I am honoured that you offer me the role of champion, I cannot risk it. You must remember that I am here on the business of John Thoresby, Archbishop of York and Lord Chancellor of England. He would not take it well if I were to break the law for you, Mistress Ridley. Neither would my wife.'

Cecilia Ridley flushed, withdrew her hands. 'I did not think . . . No, of course you must not break the law.'

Owen nodded. 'So when your son-in-law returns in the morning, let him in. I will come upstairs with you.'

Cecilia rose, picked up her lamp. 'I will do so.' She walked slowly to the door, turning just before she reached it. Her eyes were dark in the lamplight. 'I pray God you are right, Captain Archer.'

With that, she left Owen to toss and turn till just before dawn, when he fell into a fitful sleep.

Six

Goldbetter & Co

Owen dreamt of Cecilia. She stood in the doorway of his mother's house, a bowl cradled in one arm, wooden spoon in hand, and asked Owen if he would be home before dark. He retraced his steps and kissed her forehead, then walked away only with a great effort, hating to leave her.

Owen woke confused. Why would he dream of Cecilia as his wife? Did he desire her? Had she suggested in any way that she desired him? The tenderness of the moment when he looked into her eyes and kissed her forehead lingered with him still. He had to admit to himself that Cecilia Ridley's eyes haunted him, her strength impressed him. But that did not explain why he would dream of her as his wife.

Owen dressed and rubbed some salve into his scar before putting on the patch. He told himself that he was tired in mind and body, and this weariness had confused him. He told himself that what the dream really meant was that he missed Lucie.

Nonetheless, Owen wished he could slip away without seeing those dark eyes again.

But that was impossible. He must help Cecilia deal with her son-in-law, then he must question her some more before he could return to York. Owen left his room reluctantly.

Downstairs, the hall was dark but for a cocoon of golden light near the hearth. Two oil lamps sat on a small table. The fire had been stoked and was burning brightly. A young woman stirred something in a pot.

Cecilia sat at a table set up near the hearth. Her snow-white wimple and dark veil lay on the table. Her midnight hair fell in a thick braid down her back. She looked up and greeted Owen with a tired smile, motioning him over. Her hand then dropped to the table, coming to rest on the wimple. 'Sarah! My head-dress.' Cecilia touched her bare head. 'Forgive me, Captain Archer.'

The servant abandoned the pot and, with an embarrassed nod to Owen, she proceeded to undo her mistress's braid, then loop up the heavy hair, a coil on either side of Cecilia's face.

Owen eased himself onto a bench opposite Cecilia. She managed to lift the pitcher and pour a cup of ale for him without moving her head. The wimple and veil were soon in place.

'Ah,' Owen sighed after tasting the ale, 'this is welcome this morning.' He was glad that long black hair was now covered. He must not be distracted.

'You cannot have got much sleep,' Cecilia said. 'I am sorry for that after your long journey.'

Good. A safe topic. 'I feel a stiffness in my joints from the ride yesterday. Was a time I would not have noticed it.'

The dark eyes watched him with sympathy. 'Do you miss your soldiering days? I should think you would miss your companions. My father used to talk about his comrades-in-arms as if they were dearer to him than his brothers.'

'Aye. When you've fought for your lives side by side . . .' Owen stopped himself. If he began to tell Cecilia about his old comrades and she listened with such sympathy, he would be in danger. Lucie hated anything to do with soldiers. Cecilia's sympathy was as tempting as her hair. The dream, Owen now saw, had been a heaven-sent warning. 'It is best not to remember the days that are past.'

Cecilia frowned, puzzled. But she changed the subject. 'Where are you from? Your speech is different. Softer than ours.'

'Wales.'

'Of course. A captain of archers would be Welsh.'

'Nay. 'Tis not always the way of things. In fact it's a rare man like the old Duke, Henry of Lancaster, who would trust his judgement of a man enough to let a Welshman have so much power.'

'I trust you. And Anna does, too. She said you had warm, dry hands and an eye that did not hide its thoughts.'

Owen did not want to discuss himself. He did not wish to hear compliments. 'Any sign yet of Paul Scorby?'

Cecilia shook her head. 'The men at the gate know to escort him in this morning.' She sighed. 'I would rather Anna were long gone from here, but this morning her fever is high and the bleeding has begun again, so I know you are right. To travel at present would be dangerous for her.'

Father Cuthbert joined them, giving them a blessing. 'May I come with you when you take Master Scorby up to your daughter? I feel responsible for Mistress Scorby's being here. Perhaps I should not have given in. She might have stayed at home. She knew she could not make it alone.'

'You should not blame yourself,' Cecilia said. 'It is best that she is here. The servants are afraid of Paul. They would have given her little sympathy.'

They did not wait long for Paul Scorby. He strode into the hall and right up to Cecilia, demanding to know what she had meant, keeping him out last night.

Cecilia rose to face her son-in-law. As she was as tall as he, it was a clever move. Paul Scorby could no longer glower down at Cecilia, but must step back to meet her eyes. Owen mentally applauded Cecilia's courage.

'My daughter must be kept quiet, Paul. You will understand when you see her. She has suffered extensive injuries.'

Paul Scorby glanced at Owen and the priest. 'Injuries?'

Cecilia picked up a lamp. 'I will take you to her now.'

Owen and Father Cuthbert rose.

Paul Scorby frowned. 'I will see her alone.'

'No, Paul,' Cecilia said quietly. 'You will not see her alone.' With that she made her way to the stairs.

Scorby followed, and behind him, Owen and the priest.

When they entered the bedchamber a serving girl was bent over Anna, blotting her forehead.

'Thank you, Lisa,' Cecilia said. 'You may leave us and have something to eat while we speak with Mistress Scorby.'

The young woman scurried out.

Owen watched Paul Scorby's face as the man approached his wife. Anna's injured eye was still swollen shut. As Paul approached, Anna hid the bandaged hand and pulled the covers up to hide the bruised mouth.

Paul Scorby flushed a deep crimson. His eyes slid over to his mother-in-law, then back to his wife.

'Anna has internal injuries as well as those you see,' Cecilia said in a tight voice. 'Her stomach is dark with bruises that bleed within.'

Scorby turned on Father Cuthbert. 'How could you let her travel in such condition?' he demanded.

The priest, young and inexperienced in the world, was so astonished by the man's behaviour that he opened his mouth but could make no sound.

'God forgive you, husband,' Anna said.

Scorby wheeled round with a look of surprise. 'Forgive me?' He knelt beside her. 'What are you saying, Anna?'

She turned away from him.

Scorby looked up at Cecilia. 'She has a fever?'

'Yes,' Cecilia took care not to look into her son-in-law's eyes.

Paul Scorby reached a hand out toward Anna's chin.

'Don't touch me!' the injured woman cried, and tried to move out of her husband's reach.

'What do you want me to do, Anna?' he asked, his voice breaking with emotion.

A good actor, Owen thought.

'Leave me to myself,' Anna whispered.

Scorby stood up. 'Well, of course I cannot stay here and you cannot travel.' He looked at his mother-in-law. 'You will keep Anna here until she is healed?'

'She wishes to go to St Clement's nunnery when she is well enough to travel,' Cecilia said.

Scorby's mask dropped momentarily. He rolled his eyes, disgusted. 'That again.'

Father Cuthbert found his tongue. 'It will help both of you if Mistress Scorby is at peace with her Saviour before she returns to you.'

Scorby smirked at the priest. 'Oh yes, I smell the rat of pious counselling in this. Are you permitting her to eat these days since she is suffering in other ways?'

'Paul!' Cecilia barked. 'I will not have a priest insulted in my house.'

Paul Scorby spun round on his heel and marched out of the room.

Cecilia knelt beside her daughter, smoothed the damp hair from her face and kissed her on the forehead. 'Rest now, love. He will honour your wishes, I will make certain of that.'

They found Paul Scorby standing by the fire drinking ale. He was a handsome man if one looked at the features and imagined them without the petulant expression in the eyes and the pouting mouth. Even the shoulders suggested a self-pity that was unbecoming. Such a man was dangerous. Owen wondered at Gilbert Ridley's judgement, to have married his daughter to this man.

Cecilia picked up the pitcher of ale, offered Paul Scorby more. He let her fill his cup. Cecilia put a restraining hand on Paul's, holding the cup from his lips for a moment. 'You will honour her wishes, Paul?'

His upper lip curled in a snarl. 'Of course I will. It would be a sacrilege if I refused, I am sure. Any day now the Pope himself will come on pilgrimage to pray at my wife's feet.' Scorby downed the ale in one gulp and stormed out of the hall.

Father Cuthbert took a deep breath. 'God was with us.'

Cecilia and Owen exchanged a glance.

'I should like to go and sit with Mistress Scorby and say morning prayers,' Cuthbert said.

'That would comfort her, I am sure,' Cecilia said.

*

Cecilia motioned for Owen to sit. She poured two cups of ale, put one in front of Owen, took a sip from the other. 'My son-in-law behaves like a spoiled child.'

'But he is not a child. He is an angry man.'

'I know. I'm not a fool.'

'I did not think that for a moment. I just want to make sure you realise how dangerous he might be.'

Cecilia sighed. 'You will be relieved to get away from here. We are an unhappy household.' She rubbed the back of her neck.

'You are tired.'

'Very. I sat up most of the night with Anna. But it was not in vain. While I sat there staring at my daughter's ravaged face, I thought of something that might – I cannot say how, for I know so little about it – but it could perhaps have some bearing on the ... deaths.'

Owen sat forward. 'Anything you can remember might help.'

'Gilbert spoke little business around me, but this incident I know about. It was thirteen years ago. A long time for someone to wait for revenge. But if they had been in prison ...' With her eyes, Cecilia asked Owen's opinion.

'Indeed. Prison gives a man much time to gnaw on bitterness.'

'Have you been in prison?'

'No. But I've been captain of men who have. It can twist a man until his soul is wrung out of him and he's more animal than man.'

Cecilia held Owen's gaze with her dark eyes, luminous in the pale, thin face. 'So. I had best tell you about the incident.'

'Why did you sit up with Anna last night? You

had thought she was better.'

Cecilia shrugged. 'I could not sleep.'

'It's a curse, isn't it, the restlessness that comes when you most need the forgetfulness of sleep? My wife sent along something to calm you. She was widowed a few years ago and remembers how impossible it was to rest.'

'I will gladly take it a few nights hence, when I know that Anna is truly on the mend and Paul is back in Ripon.'

Owen nodded. 'Do you want me to go out and check that he is gone from here for now?'

'Please.'

Owen was glad for the chance to stretch his legs and empty his bladder. He could smell the ocean in the driving wind. Another storm approached them from the North Sea.

The man at the gate assured Owen that Paul Scorby had ridden off.

'When do you think the storm will find us?'

'Soon, by the smell of it. 'Twill be over by midday.'

Owen hoped the man was right about the storm, although he'd meant to be back on the road before midday. The wind whipped Owen's cloak about him as he returned to the house.

Cecilia Ridley paced before the hearth.

Owen sat down and helped himself to another cup of ale. 'Now tell me what happened thirteen years ago.'

Cecilia sat down again. 'You know that Gilbert and Will were members of John Goldbetter's company?'

'Aye.'

'The companies of wool merchants financed King Edward's war with France, did you know that?'

'I can't say I ever wondered.'

'Chiriton and Company were the organisers, and Goldbetter and Company, about twenty years ago, lent them money for the King. They all expected to get rich by it in the end, of course. But the King did not gain so much by the war as he had expected. He tried to put them off, tried to satisfy them with customs privileges. And then, just as the privileges began to pay off for them, the King took them away from his own merchants and gave them to the Hanseatic League merchants, a trading federation of German towns that is very powerful. The King proved to be an inconstant friend to his own subjects.'

'I did not think the King so unwise. To betray people in their pockets is dangerous.'

'More foolish than dangerous, it seems. The merchants found a way to get their money despite the King. Chiriton and Company decided to win back their losses by illegal exporting. But they were caught. The Crown offered to forget their transgressions if they would provide a list of businesses who owed them money; the Crown would call in the loans and make a profit.'

'Chiriton and Company were expected to betray their associates?'

Cecilia smiled. 'I see why Gilbert, God rest him, said soldiers made bad merchants. You have a strong sense of honour. Gilbert never had soldiers working for him, except for a man called Martin Wirthir, and Wirthir had little to do with the actual deals.'

That name again. 'Did you ever meet Martin Wirthir?'

'No.'

Owen dropped that line for now. 'So Chiriton and Company betrayed their associates?'

'Yes. But the company had played so much with

their books, it was difficult to interpret them, and the Crown called in some associates in error. John Goldbetter was one of them. He was accused of still owing on bonds and letters of account. With Gilbert's help he was able to produce documents proving he'd settled the debts years earlier. Goldbetter then made a countersuit, claiming that Chiriton and Company owed him over £3000. They settled out of court. Gilbert was even more extravagant than usual on my name day that year. I do not know the details of the settlement, but money obviously changed hands.'

Owen thought about this. 'And do you think that Chiriton and Company may have offered your husband something other than the money? Perhaps names?'

Cecilia shrugged. 'That occurred to me. As did many other possibilities. I merely point out that Gilbert's business dealings might have involved some dishonesty. Some betrayals.'

'Something that would make someone angry enough to murder?'

'Greed can be quite a passion with some. There is more. Three years ago, John Goldbetter was again brought before the Crown and was outlawed. A year later he won a royal pardon, at the request of the Count of Flanders. I presume he'd made some sort of deal with the Count. And possibly also the Crown. But something about it disturbed Gilbert. He turned the business over to our son Matthew and came home.'

'Right before Crounce's murder.'

'Yes.'

'Did your husband personally testify?'

Cecilia nodded. 'He was proud to appear before so august a company. He boasted of it.'

'Did he meet the King?'

'Much to his regret, no. Gilbert was presented to

the Black Prince, however, and that appeased him somewhat.'

'The Count of Flanders requested Goldbetter's pardon, eh?'

'The wool trade is the life blood of Flanders.'

'True. Did your husband know the Count?'

Cecilia shrugged. 'He did not boast of it, but he was secretive about anything across the Channel, so he might not have boasted of that.'

'And you think all this may have something to do with the deaths of your husband and Will Crounce?'

Cecilia looked down at her cup, which she pushed back and forth between her hands. 'When I was betrothed to Gilbert, I was angry. Humiliated. He was a merchant. In trade. I was the daughter of a knight and niece to a bishop. My grandfather fought with our King's grandfather, the just Edward.'

Owen did not like the direction this was taking. He was a commoner married to the daughter of a knight. 'What does this have to do with your husband's death?'

Cecilia looked up, saw the expression on Owen's face. 'Forgive me, I do sound as if I've wandered, but there is a point. You see, I hated the idea of being married to someone whose purpose in life was to collect wealth. A greedy man.' She rubbed the bridge of her nose wearily. 'I was a simpleton. It is not only the merchants who are greedy. Gilbert was no worse than any of the others involved in this war with France. Even the King is in it for the wealth the double crown of England and France would bring him. They all guard their wealth more jealously than they guard their wives.'

'What are you saying?'

Cecilia Ridley suddenly went white. A hand came up to her mouth. She shook her head. 'Nothing. I —

Just that Gilbert and Will were probably murdered by a business associate. Greed is obviously the most common reason for murder.'

Owen studied her. She had covered well with the comment, but he'd seen that realisation, that she had almost— What? Betrayed herself? Said too much? 'That is all you meant to say?'

She kept her eyes averted. 'I am sorry I took such a long way round. I am tired.'

Well, that was true. But it bothered Owen as he went upstairs to pack.

Seven

A Bloody Treasure

Rain pounded against the minster. It drummed down on the paving stones and the supporting columns where the roof was unfinished. The wind played every opening in the stones, wailing, shrieking, moaning, humming. But the sounds did not frighten Jasper. They comforted him. He was curled into a ball and tucked into a small opening in the Lady Chapel wall, inside, near the choir, where he was protected from the rain by the scaffolds of the masons. The masons and carpenters, members of his father's guild, let him stay there; they tried to protect Jasper. But he could not stay long. He must not stay anywhere too long or the accidents would begin. Even here.

Jasper had thought at first that he had become clumsy, what with his mother's death and the horror of watching Master Crounce get murdered and his thoughts being on them all the time, but the River-woman told him that it was dangerous for him to blame himself, that he'd best watch his back.

'Thou'rt the only one can point a finger at the

men who murdered your good Master Crounce. Thou sayest it was dark, thou couldst not see faces, but their fear and guilt will make them certain thou sawest, and they will fear thee. They will want thee dead, Jasper. Magda does not like to think of thee wrapped in a shroud like her dear Potter. Watch thy back and come to Magda when thou canst, show her thou'rt alive.'

The Riverwoman was strange and frightening, with her piercing eyes and bony but strong hands, her clothes made of many colours, sewn together from others' cast-offs, her sudden movements, so unexpected in a person her age, her weird house with the Viking ship upside down on the roof, the sea serpent hanging upside down to greet the visitor with a leer, and her scent – smoke, roots from deep in the earth, river water, blood. But Jasper trusted the Riverwoman as he trusted no one else. His mother had told him that Magda Digby was the only person in York who owed no one, and so she was free to be trustworthy; no one could wring a secret from her. So Jasper had gone to her when he'd broken his arm falling off a roof he was helping thatch, and again with bruises and cuts he suffered when he fell in a stable and grazed his side against a plough that had been half buried in hay.

After the stable incident, Jasper decided to listen to the Riverwoman's warning. And his caution paid off. As soon as the folk he worked for began asking questions about Master Crounce's murder, Jasper disappeared. And the accidents stopped. Now and again he would return to the protection of the masons and carpenters at the minster, but even that was not safe for long.

So his comfortable cranny in the minster was

a temporary home, one he appreciated at the moment with the storm beating against the stones. He curled up in a tighter ball and went back to sleep. But something woke him. A footstep, a sense of someone near. Jasper squirmed to the edge of his cubbyhole and looked out, wondering if he had pushed too far back into the darkness and had missed the dawn. He always tried to wake at dawn so he could relieve himself in private before the masons arrived.

At first Jasper could see nothing. It was still dark except for a pre-dawn greyness where the roof stopped. But he heard something. It sounded like the hem of a cloak or skirt dragging on the paving stones. And there was a scent. Lavender water. His mother used to wear lavender water when Master Crounce visited. Jasper wondered if it was his mother's ghost come searching for him. She would come to comfort him if she could. He would like that. He would like his mother to hold him and stroke his hair and tell him stories of his father.

But Jasper's several months on his own had taught him to be wary. If he was wrong, if it wasn't his mother but someone trying to make Jasper feel safe enough to reveal himself, he could be killed. So Jasper held his breath and listened.

'Blessed Peter, where's the stone?' someone muttered. A woman's voice. 'Five hands from the corner, six stones up, they said.'

She was close enough now that Jasper could hear her quick breaths. There was a scratching sound. Then something snapped. Jasper jumped at the sound, he was so tense.

'Cheap knife,' the intruder muttered. 'She's such a miser. Sharpens knives until they're parchment thin— Ah, ha!'

The sound of stone sliding against stone.

Jasper could see her shadow now as the greyness brightened into a feeble dawn. She faced the wall just beyond Jasper's hiding place, crouching down, pulling at something. A stone, from the sound of it. She'd hidden something behind a loose stone, he guessed.

He shivered. He did not wish to witness anything he might be sorry for. He wiggled back from the edge of his hiding place. His stomach growled and Jasper held his breath, certain that the growl had echoed through the minster. But she did not come. Jasper relaxed and began to twist himself around so his pale hair would not stick out and give him away. Then the rags he wore would be mistaken for a pile of mason's rags. But as Jasper moved, he stirred up dust, and his nose betrayed him with a mighty sneeze, which so surprised him that he bumped his head.

'Who's there?' the woman demanded. She reached in and pulled Jasper from the hole, scraping him along the rock and dumping him on the stones three feet below. She was surprisingly strong. Jasper landed on his right side, his arm and leg bent beneath his weight. The pain left him breathless.

She kicked him. 'Little sneak.'

'I was sleeping,' Jasper cried, terrified. He thought his arm and leg might be broken. He could neither protect himself nor run.

She grabbed him by the cowl of his tunic and dragged him towards the light, then took his head in her hands and studied his face. 'Why, it's Jasper de Melton. Well, you've followed me for the last time. He's after you, you know. He plays with you and brags about it. But he's lost track of you. You're a smart one.'

Dark eyes, a large mouth, large hands. He could

not see much more. Jasper thought he'd seen her before, but he could not remember where. 'How do you know my name?' he asked.

'Everyone in York knows your name. And outside the city gates your fame has spread all the way to—' she laughed. 'But that would be telling.'

Jasper painfully wriggled out of her grasp. She lunged for him, dropping what she'd been clutching in her other hand, a bloody bundle. It fell to the ground. Jasper kicked it away, hoping she would go after it. It rolled out into the rain, the cloth unwinding to reveal a human hand.

Jasper screamed.

The woman pulled a knife from her cloak and raised it above him.

Jasper threw his hands up over his head, shielding himself.

She laughed. 'Not to worry, Jasper. The point broke off in the stone and I've no stomach to poke you to death with a blunt knife.' She picked him up by the cowl again. 'But from now on I'll carry a sharpened knife with a very good point. And if I hear you've said one word about what you've seen, or describe me to anyone, I will kill you. Or he will.' She laughed again.

Jasper knew her now. He remembered that laugh from Corpus Christi day. The woman who had laughed at Master Crounce.

She dropped him, grabbed up the hand and stuffed it under her cloak. 'Remember,' she said, with a glint in her eye that made Jasper think she looked forward to stabbing him, and then she ran out.

Jasper pulled himself up to his knees and said a prayer of thanksgiving for his deliverance. When he tried to stand, a sharp pain ran up his right leg.

He clenched his teeth and stood up straight. His right arm hung useless. The pain in the arm was a dull throbbing. He wanted to curl himself into a ball and cry. He wanted his mother. He wanted things to be as they once were, his mother waiting for him, Mistress Fletcher yelling at him not to run up the stairs because it gave her a headache. Jasper felt hot tears on his cheeks.

But things were not as they once were. Jasper was alone. The riverwoman had been right. He had enemies. Master Crounce's murderers. Jasper must disappear. He limped out of the minster.

One of the city bailiffs stomped into the shop, cursing the weather and then apologising as he noticed Lucie standing at the counter. 'Forgive me, Mistress Wilton, but it is a godforsaken world out there today, all this rain and wind.' He shivered and set a damp pack down on the counter before her. 'I took the liberty of pausing at the York Tavern and asking if Mistress Merchet might come here.'

Lucie eyed the leather pack curiously. 'What is this about, Geoffrey?'

Bess came bursting in the door. 'So you've found a pack under Foss Bridge you want me to identify, eh?'

Geoffrey doffed his cap. 'Mistress Merchet, I need you to tell me whether you recognise this pack, and then Mistress Wilton must identify the contents of a pouch within it.' Geoffrey nodded to the travel-stained saddle pack on the counter. 'It was found under a pile of rocks near Foss Bridge.'

Bess touched the damp leather. 'May I look inside?'

The bailiff nodded.

Bess opened the flap. Inside was a leather wineskin, empty, a change of clothes, several drawstring pouches, a small account book, a knife and spoon, and a pair of soft, impractical shoes in bright red. 'Gilbert Ridley's, no doubt about it,' Bess proclaimed. 'See the stone set in the spoon handle? Those shoes. The colour of the jerkin.' She nodded. 'Gilbert Ridley's.'

The bailiff looked pleased.

'And I am to identify the contents of which pouch?' Lucie asked.

The bailiff handed her a leather one, greasy with handling. 'Take care opening. 'Tis a powder.'

Lucie opened it gingerly, sniffed, touched a finger-tip to the powder, which was damp from its sojourn under the bridge, touched the powder to her tongue, stood with her eyes closed for a moment, tasting it, sniffed the powder again, poked at it with her finger, feeling the grain, seeing the different colours. 'Well,' she said when she finally looked at those awaiting the verdict, 'this is a dangerous powder. It is an assortment of things, mostly healthy. But then there's the arsenic. Not enough to kill at once, or quickly. It would kill gradually, over a period of time.' She tested the weight of the pouch in her palm. 'I would guess this amount would have lasted Ridley more than a fort-night, considering the concentrations of the other ingredients. Or Ridley's victim, I suppose. But if you look at the pouch, it was once much fuller. Twice as much again. So I would say it was his, since he had been in York but two days.'

Bess crossed herself. 'Lord have mercy, why would anyone have done that to Gilbert Ridley? He was a proud man, but he did no harm.'

The bailiff looked uncomfortable. 'You say this would kill gradually, Mistress Wilton?'

Lucie nodded. 'This would be administered by someone looking for a slow, painful death, not the death that Ridley finally suffered. You said he was ailing, didn't you, Bess?'

'Indeed,' Bess said. 'Stomach complaint. So bad he had become a shadow of himself.'

Lucie nodded. 'This "tonic" would do that over time.'

'Then I will deliver this up to you for Captain Archer,' the bailiff said, 'as the murder of Master Ridley occurred in the liberty of St Peter.'

Lucie took the pack and set it down on the floor behind the counter.

'And there is something else that will be of interest to the Captain,' the bailiff said.

'More?' Lucie said. 'Your men have been busy.'

'This had naught to do with us, Mistress Wilton. 'Tis the artisans at the minster. They say Jasper de Melton, the lad who witnessed the first murder, disappeared this morning without his cloak. There was blood and signs of a struggle. They are afraid for him.'

'I don't understand,' Lucie said. 'I thought the boy was missing.'

The bailiff nodded. 'As did we. Now they say the boy's been taking shelter in the minster now and then, and they've been keeping it secret in memory of his father, who was a carpenter, you see. And this morning the boy's gone. Out into the storm. Without his cloak. I thought the Captain ought to know, Mistress Wilton.'

When the bailiff had gone, Lucie stared down at Ridley's pouch of poisoned tonic, which she turned round and round in her hands. Her eyes were sad.

'What are you thinking, Lucie?' Bess asked, touching one of Lucie's hands to quiet it. 'Are you disturbed about the boy? Or that Ridley had two enemies?'

Lucie let the pouch lie, but still she stared down at it. 'Both. I thought this was a simple matter of robbery at first. Then I thought perhaps revenge upon a false business partner. But Gilbert Ridley was also being poisoned. Slowly. Ridley had told His Grace that his stomach complaint came on him after Crounce's death. He said his wife made a tonic for him. Something noxious. He said he sometimes thought that his complaint had worsened since he'd taken the tonic. But he took it because he knew his wife had his welfare in mind.'

Bess studied her friend's face. 'And you think the arsenic mixture was that tonic?'

'It is a horrible thing to contemplate, a wife slowly poisoning her husband, no matter the reason. And yet Owen once suspected me of that.'

Bess snorted. 'I cannot believe Owen suspected any such thing. He thought you might have poisoned Montaigne, and accidentally Fitzwilliam, but not Nicholas – did he?'

'He did, Bess,' Lucie said, her voice almost a whisper.

'Well, it all turned out in the end,' Bess said lamely.

Lucie smiled up at her friend. 'We have yet to be sure, but I think it turned out, yes. And now I must write all the facts down for Owen. He will be angry about the boy. He told the Archbishop the boy was in danger. I must send a messenger to Beverley with this pack and the letter.'

'My stable boy can take it,' Bess said.

Lucie was glad of the offer. 'Thank you. I trust John to get it there safely.'

While Owen put his few things in his bag, Cecilia Ridley paced the room.

When he could ignore her pacing no longer, Owen asked, 'What is it?'

She would not look him in the eye. 'Could you and your men stay another night?' She glanced up, looked away as if embarrassed. 'I keep thinking, if Paul is going to change his mind and come back, it will be today or tonight. So if you could stay that long, in case I need you . . .'

Owen wanted to leave. He missed Lucie and worried that she would be out there in the rain, praying over Wilton's grave. 'What about your men? They will be here. Your steward should be aware of your concern.'

Cecilia shook her head. 'Jack Cooper? He's no fighting man. None of them is. One night is all I ask. I do not like to ask at all, but it would make such a difference to me.'

Owen had to admit that he was rushing with his duty, and besides, it was already midday. At this time of year that meant he would not get far before twilight.

'One more night. We will leave early tomorrow.'

'Thank you. I will not forget this.'

'But I will make use of the time,' Owen said. 'I would like to speak with your steward.'

'Why?'

'He might know something about your husband's business that you do not know.'

Cecilia bristled. 'Indeed.'

'Forgive me. I did not mean to insult you.'

'I know. And you might be right. Jack Cooper's house is behind the great hall. At the stream. There's a path beyond the stables. You will see it. But he may be anywhere on the land at this time of day.'

'I will find him.'

Owen went out the back, past the ovens and the building in which the serious cooking was done. He checked in the stables. His horse was groomed and quiet. Three children knelt over a sleeping dog.

Owen found the path and was at the cottage in perhaps fifty strides. Trees would shade it in summer, but now the trees surrounded it like skeleton sentinels. Owen knocked at the door. It was a comfortable looking cottage with two shuttered windows, one on either side of a door that was fitted well into the doorway and looked to be heavy oak. Ridley had been generous with the quarters for his help. Owen knocked again, and had turned to leave when the door behind him opened.

A rumpled looking man with a pockmarked face and greying hair stood in the doorway, blinking at the daylight, meagre though it was. 'Ah. You're the Archbishop's man came last night. I'm Jack Cooper.' He held out his hand.

Owen shook it. 'I am glad to find you here. I had resigned myself to walking across this entire estate looking for you today.'

The man frowned. 'Why would you be looking for me?'

'You have heard about Master Ridley's murder?'

'Oh, aye. Terrible thing, that was. Highlanders, I'd bet. No one disliked Master Ridley enough to do that to him.'

'Can I come in?'

Cooper thought about that, then shrugged. 'You're used to better, coming from the great hall, but you're welcome, to be sure. I was having a rest. Stood watch out at the gate last night.'

'But my men were there.'

Cooper nodded. 'I thought we should have some men from the household there, just the same. Master Ridley would have wanted it.'

Inside, the house was smoky and warm, a fire burning well in the middle of the room. A pallet was pulled up near the fire. A cup beside it.

Cooper saw Owen's eye take in the scene and was quick to explain, ''Twas a night for neither man nor beast, Captain Archer. I was chilled through all my clothes. Thought I'd never stop shivering. Made the fire, stripped out of my wet things, put a hot poker to some spiced wine, and lay down close to the fire as I could get without burning myself.'

Owen looked around the large room. The walls were whitewashed to brighten it, there were fresh rushes on the floor. A woman's touches. 'Wives are always good at undoing a chill, eh?' Owen said.

'Aye, but Kate's away,' Jack said. 'Tending her sick mother,' he added in a nervous tone.

'Are you recovered enough to talk with me?' Owen asked. 'Answer some questions about your late master?'

'I've warmed up just right. Come,' Jack pulled a bench out from the wall and placed it within the fire's light. 'Could you drink some ale?'

'I could at that, Master Cooper.'

'Oh, Jack is fine, Captain Archer.'

Owen nodded. 'Then I'm Owen to you.'

They settled down with two tankards of ale. Not as fine as Tom Merchet's, but acceptable. Jack Cooper stretched his stockinged feet out to the fire, toasting his toes. The cottage was quiet.

'Are your children with your wife?' Owen asked, making conversation before he launched into questions.

'Nay. They're out in the stables watching over a sick dog. Keeps 'em out of my way and makes 'em happy.' Jack took another drink. 'So what is it you'd like to know about the master?'

'Did you ever meet any of his business associates?'

'Aye. Master Crounce, God rest his soul,' Jack crossed himself.

'Other than Crounce?'

Jack screwed up his face and thought. 'Nay.' He shook his head. 'I don't remember meeting any others.'

'How did you get along with Master Crounce?'

An odd look flickered across the man's face. 'He was a big help to Mistress Ridley. And always fair in his dealings with us who work the estate.' Jack shrugged. 'Cannot say much more than that. Is it true you lost your eye to a Saracen?'

Owen grinned. 'Wish it had been a Saracen. If I'd killed him, I would have been forgiven all my sins. But it wasn't on crusade. The King's war, that's where I lost the eye.' Owen took another drink. The ale improved with time. 'What is it you didn't like about Will Crounce?'

Jack looked surprised. 'I said nothing about not liking him.'

'What didn't you like?' Owen asked softly.

Jack looked down at his simmering toes. 'It doesn't

make me the murderer of Master Crounce and my master.'

'I never thought it did.'

Jack took another thoughtful sip of his ale. 'Master Crounce should have married again.'

Owen thought about that response. 'You mean he needed a woman?'

Jack nodded, still watching the fire.

'He got too friendly with Mistress Cooper?'

Jack closed his eyes. 'I never caught them at it, but a man knows.'

'Did you speak with him about it?'

Jack faced Owen now. His look said Owen was a fool to ask that question. 'He was master when my master was away. I could not accuse him. Besides, it was Master Crounce recommended me to Master Ridley. I could not be ungrateful.'

'Did he make free with other women here?'

Jack glanced back at the door, as if to make sure they were alone. 'I don't like to tell tales, but I wondered about him and Mistress Ridley, if truth be told. Something in the way they caught each other's eye, something feeling too much like husband and wife.'

'I wondered about that myself,' Owen said, 'so you haven't betrayed your mistress, Jack. I thank you for being so honest.'

Jack nodded and squinted up at Owen. 'I'm no fool. You don't become steward by being a fool.'

'That's why I wanted to talk to you. The steward sees into the heart of the estate.'

Jack smiled. 'Couldn't've said it better.' He was quiet a moment. 'So how did you lose the eye?'

Owen was tired of the story, and he needed to get out in the fresh air. The smoke was making his eye water and any blurring of the good eye made him uneasy. He was as good as blind when his right eye failed him. But he owed Jack Cooper something for his hospitality and honesty.

So Owen told the steward about the Breton jongleur he'd rescued from his companions and set free, only to catch him a few nights later slipping through the camp slitting the throats of prisoners whose ransoms would be most valuable to King Edward. As Owen attacked the jongleur, the jongleur's leman had attacked Owen. Owen had killed both of them, but not before the bitch had opened his eye.

Jack listened with a face shifting between wonder and regret. 'I would have liked the life of a soldier, I think.'

'Perhaps. But by now you'd have more wounds on your body than you could count, if you were still alive. And you might be missing a limb or two.'

'But I would have done something I could tell my boy about.'

Owen shrugged. 'If you even had a boy.'

'No children yet?' Jack asked.

'No. But I've been married a year is all.'

'Well,' Jack said, 'children will come, most like.' He nodded. 'And you'll have good stories to tell them.'

Owen stood and stretched. Rubbed his eye. 'God bless you for your hospitality, Jack.' Owen held out his hand.

Jack jumped up and shook it heartily. 'I wouldn't be thinking a jealous husband could be the murderer. Crounce was one for the ladies. But not Master Ridley. Not that I could tell. So what was the motive?'

'That's the question, Jack.'

'You know, you asked about business associates besides Master Crounce. There was Master Goldbetter. He came once, and such a fuss they made over him. An impressive man, with fine clothes. But no rings that could match my master's.'

The rings. Owen had forgotten about them. He wondered how many of Ridley's rings were missing with the hand.

'How did Goldbetter act towards the master and mistress of the hall?' Owen asked.

'Oh, it was a good visit,' Jack said. 'His jokes made the ladies blush. He praised everything set before him. A most genial man.'

'Thank you, Jack. I must be off now. God be with you.'

Owen walked back to the house, deep in thought.

Cecilia met him, her face tear-stained and pale. 'They have brought Gilbert's body,' she said, one hand pressed to her middle, one near her mouth. 'It is unholy, what they did to him.' She looked deep into his eyes, asking for comfort.

Owen stood there woodenly, resisting the temptation to take Cecilia Ridley in his arms to comfort her. He recognised the hunger in her eyes and did not believe himself saint enough to resist it. He must do something to calm her. He had the powdered valerian root in his belt pouch that Lucie had suggested the widow take to sleep. He called for wine, slipped some of the powder in, and sat quietly watching Cecilia Ridley drink the mixture. He waited for the colour to return to her face. Cecilia had found the wounds on her husband's body a shock, even though Ridley had been cleaned and wrapped in a shroud with sweet-smelling herbs.

'There was no need for you to look,' Owen said.

'Of course there was need. I had to make sure he was prepared properly. Now I am reassured.' Cecilia sipped some more.

'Can you describe all the rings your husband was wearing when he departed?'

'Rings? What do I care about rings?' Cecilia cried.

'If some are missing, we might find your husband's murderers by searching for the rings.'

'Oh!' Cecilia gave him an apologetic look. 'Of course.' She rubbed her eyes. 'I should be able to tell you what Gilbert wore that day ...' She put her head in her hands and thought.

Owen hoped he had not put too much of the powder in the drink. He had not wanted it to take effect so soon.

But Cecilia finally lifted her head and nodded to Owen. 'That day Gilbert wore the rings he usually wore to impress. He said Archbishop Thoresby was a proud man. And as this gift was for the chapel in which the Archbishop meant to be buried, Gilbert wanted the Archbishop to be proud to have our money. He wore four rings. A pearl, a ruby, a moonstone, and one hammered gold with no stone.'

Owen remembered how Ridley's rings had glittered in the summer sun. 'Quite a fortune to wear on the road.'

Cecilia shrugged. 'Gilbert was foolishly proud of his success. But I think he rode gloved.'

Owen motioned for the servant Sarah, who waited nearby. 'Now you should sleep,' he said to Cecilia. He would check for the rings on Ridley's remaining hand and in the pack Ridley had left at the York.

Cecilia stood up and stumbled. Sarah caught her,

letting her mistress lean on her shoulder for support. Cecilia said to her, 'I'm suddenly so dizzy. Thank you for the shoulder.' Cecilia looked up at Owen. 'Gilbert also carried a small pack with him everywhere. Money and other important things. I did not see it among the things they brought.' She rubbed her forehead. 'What did you put in the wine?'

'Valerian root,' Owen said. 'You will sleep a while. It is important that you rest.'

'I would have preferred to choose my own time,' Cecilia said, but she let Sarah lead her up the stairs.

Owen waited until they were out of sight before he began his search. Ridley's pack contained little. A pair of sturdy boots, a fur-lined hat with a long cloth drape to protect the neck, a wallet that held a twist of thread, a needle, and a small pair of scissors, another wallet with a comb, a piece of polished steel, a chunk of rose-scented soap wrapped in oiled cloth, a small bottle of rose-scented oil, a razor, and an ivory toothpick. The travelling apparel of a dandy, for certain. A plain pair of leggings and a soiled shirt completed the contents. There was no jewellery of any kind.

Owen turned to the corpse. Cecilia had not rewrapped the shroud, but just draped it over her husband. For that Owen was grateful. He would much rather lift a sheet than unwind it. It seemed less disrespectful, though he did not know who he thought would be offended, the corpse or God.

The left hand lay palm up. Owen tried to shift the rings around on the fingers, but the swelling made it impossible. He knelt down and lifted the hand. A pearl and a moonstone. So the ruby and the hammered gold rings had probably been on the severed hand. Owen doubted they would still be on the hand if it was ever found.

Eight

Down by the River

T he guard at Bootham Bar paid no attention to the boy who hobbled along beside the dung cart. Jasper had hidden in bushes near the Archbishop's palace until he caught his breath and decided where to go. Now outside the city walls, he whispered a prayer of thanksgiving that no one had been waiting for him. He had only to follow the abbey wall to St Mary's Tower, and then around to the river. The Riverwoman's house was easy to find. Jasper could force himself that far.

But his right arm throbbed, and with every step he fell more heavily on his right leg. Although the rain had dwindled to a drizzle, Jasper was already soaked through. In his terror, he'd left his cloak at the minster. He reached St Mary's Tower and rounded the corner of the abbey wall, heading down towards the river. The closer he got to the river, the colder he felt. His head hurt and his stomach rumbled. He had not eaten in a day or two; he could not remember exactly how long it had been. That frightened Jasper, to forget when last he'd eaten. He always remembered his food.

The ground became uneven as he passed among the flimsy structures of the vermin city, and Jasper kept stumbling in the rutted mud. Babies cried, brush fires burned smokily in the damp, dogs barked incessantly and sniffed at Jasper as he passed. Icy rainwater puddled everywhere. Jasper looked at no one, just trying to keep his footing. He was cold enough with his feet so wet; he did not want to fall and get himself even wetter. The wind had picked up and the river was rising. It must be raining or snowing hard up on the moors. Jasper groaned, knowing that meant he would probably have to wade out to Magda's hut, which stood on a muddy rock at the water's edge of the flood plain.

Indeed, when he'd battled his way to the edge of the huts he could see the Riverwoman's strange home rising out of the swelling river. The water surrounding her hut did not look too deep yet, but crossing it would completely soak Jasper's feet. He hesitated, wondering what would happen if she wasn't there. But even as he stood, the water continued to rise. Jasper must cross now or find another refuge, and he could think of none.

He strode in. The water was deeper than he'd guessed, soaking him halfway up his calves, and with his injured leg it was hard work keeping upright in the current. By the time he climbed the slope to face the serpent's head above the doorway, Jasper could not stop his teeth from chattering. The sea monster leered at him, and Jasper imagined he saw its tail flicker at the back of the hut. He closed his eyes and stepped up to the door, banging on it so that the Riverwoman would hear him above the wind. No answer. Jasper stepped back and checked the roof. Smoke curled out, so her fire was lit. He knocked again. Still no answer. He pushed on the door, too desperate for the heat of that fire to be polite.

The smoky hut was dark but for the fire in the centre. Jasper took a few steps in and closed the door behind him. Something brushed his forehead, giving off a dusty scent. He stood still, letting his eyes adjust. All along the rafters bunches of herbs were hung to dry. A few tables and benches were scattered around the room, and there were two curtained corners where Magda Digby must have beds. Jasper checked them. No one was there. The beds looked inviting. Maybe he would take off his wet clothes and nap until she returned. He pulled a bench close to the fire and laid his clothes along it so they might dry. They were all he had. As he tucked his torn shoes at the edge of the fire circle he noticed a bowl of broth simmering on a stone. He reached over and stuck a finger in. A green, bitter taste. No meat or fat of any kind in it. Some sort of herbal infusion. Not very appealing. But it was hot, and he was so cold. Jasper took a small bowl from a stack and poured himself a bit of the broth, drinking it down quickly. He shuddered as his tongue discovered its bitter taste. But it warmed him inside, and for that he was grateful. He dropped down on one of the beds and was asleep in moments.

Severe stomach cramps woke him. Jasper clutched his middle and got out of the bed, not wanting to mess it. He was giddy and could not get his balance. He sat down hard in the rushes and bent double, retching. He crawled away from the mess, but it felt as if fire and knives were ripping his stomach out. Jasper curled up on his side and moaned as his stomach cramped again. He was frightened. People died from pain like this. He tried to pray, but his thoughts would not stay on the prayer. That frightened him even more. If he could not pray, how could he die in grace? He drifted in and out of a dream that he had shrunk to the size of a mouse and was drowning in a bowl of bitter green broth that he must not inhale or drink. In another dream, a brown-robed friar carried Jasper's mother to one of the curtained beds in Magda's hut and told Magda to see to the boy first. 'No!' Jasper cried. 'Save my mother. Don't let her die again!'

Then someone was bending over him, smelling of river and earth and fire. 'Jasper, open thine eyes. What hast thou eaten, Jasper? Magda must know. Was it the green broth?'

He nodded weakly and closed his eyes against the light from the oil lamp Magda held up to his face.

'Foolish boy. That was not for thee. That was for the lass who must rid herself of her lord's babe. How much didst thou drink, Jasper?'

'Little bowl.' He pointed feebly in what he thought was the direction of the fire. 'My mother?'

'Not your mother, poor lad. Just the lass whose physick you sampled,' Magda said.

Jasper closed his eyes against the tears that exposed his disappointment.

Magda laid him down gently, went over to the fire and picked up the small bowl lying beside the broth. She sniffed, considered the size of the bowl. He had not been greedy, but it was far more than she would administer. 'Oh Jasper, my pet, thou mayest have killed thyself. Magda must hope thy belly purged itself before the poison took hold. And now Magda must give thee pain while she sets the arm and wraps the leg. Thou art lucky the leg did not break.'

Jasper whimpered as the brown-robed man from his dream bent over him, holding him down.

'Friar Dunstan brought the lass whose physick thou hast sampled, Jasper. He will help thee hold still while Magda straightens thy arm.'

When Magda pulled at Jasper's arm, he passed out with the pain.

She was glad of that. The boy had had enough pain for his eight years. She did not like giving him more. When she had splinted his arm, poulticed and wrapped his bruised hip and knee, Magda made up a pallet for Jasper as close to the fire as she dared, piling blankets and hides on top of him to make him sweat. Now she must wait to see if the poison had been too long inside the boy and had taken hold.

While Jasper slept, Magda saw to the young woman, but her thoughts were with the boy who lay there by the fire so still and pale. She did not want to be responsible for the boy's death. He was a favourite of hers. He had a quick mind and a good heart. Magda had considered taking him in when his mother died, but she had thought better of it. If he could make it on the streets of York, he would be better off. To become associated with the vermin city, as the fine folk of York called the pathetic tumble of huts along the river, was to be doomed to a life of begging or thieving.

The boy cried out, and Magda hurried over to him, cradling his thin body in her arms, splint and all. His breathing was laboured, but not a death rattle. Perhaps he was out of danger. He had not fallen into the stupor that led to death. Magda rocked Jasper and hummed softly until the boy slept quietly.

Soon the young woman slept quietly, too. Magda turned to the friar. 'And how wilt thou pay Magda, eh, Dunstan?'

'I thought to humble myself before my brother and ask for money,' the friar said. 'Unless you would accept prayers said for your soul every day until I die?'

Magda snorted. 'Prayers of a sinful friar? Even if Magda shared thy faith she would not count thy prayers worth much. And as for thy brother's money . . .' She rolled her eyes. 'Magda says thou shalt carry out a task for her. Thou shalt go to the apothecary, Mistress Lucie Wilton, and ask her if she would take this boy into her house until he is out of danger. *All* of his present danger, mark thou sayest that, Dunstan. She will understand.'

Ambrose Coats, one of York's town waits, or musicians, hurried down Footless Lane with his instruments wrapped in a cloak and held close to his chest, though the overhanging buildings went far to protect him from the rain. He was humming the new piece he'd just rehearsed with his fellow waits and did not notice the bundle in front of his door until he stumbled on it. He grabbed it up, eager to get in the door to a warm fire. Inside, he dumped the bundle near the brazier, then carefully unwrapped his rebec and crowd and two bows and hung them on pegs far enough from the fire that they would not feel an extreme change in temperature. That done, he bent to the bundle, which gave off an unpleasant odour.

Ambrose decided to leave his gloves on until he unwrapped the damp bundle. He was compulsive about protecting his hands from chills that would stiffen them. He had seen many a good musician lose his skill because his fingers stiffened and became clumsy on the strings. Ambrose sat down on a stool and leaned over, unrolling the cloth.

'*Deus juva me*,' Ambrose whispered, staring at a severed human hand.

His first thought was that the neighbour's pig had been digging again and left this behind. But the hand had been wrapped. No then, not the pig. That damnable creature would have disturbed the wrapping.

So whence came this horrible thing? Sweet God in Heaven, what was he to do with it? Ambrose gingerly rolled the thing back up in the cloth. If it hadn't been the pig, then . . .

The hand. Of course – the two murders. Had they ever found the hands? More importantly, had they ever found the murderers? For if not, everyone was suspect, and Ambrose did not care to make himself conspicuous. Not with his friend's questionable connections.

But what to do with this thing? If he buried it in the garden, that damnable pig might come snooping and dig it up. The pig was always on the loose, which was illegal in the city. Ambrose should report his neighbour to a bailiff. Should have done so long ago. But he'd refrained because he was afraid his neighbour would retaliate by spreading rumours about him and his friend. Especially his friend. The city folk did not like foreigners.

Ambrose sat glumly by the brazier, pondering his dilemma, all the joy from his rehearsal gone.

Late in the evening Magda heard the scratch and thump of a boat being pulled up onto the rock. She put Jasper down gently and went for her knife. She hoped it was Friar Dunstan bringing Lucie Wilton's response, but it was best to be prepared for trouble. Magda had not worked so hard over Jasper only to have him murdered. She crouched by the door and waited, holding her breath.

The door opened slowly. Magda gripped the knife.

'Mistress Digby? It's Friar Dunstan with the apothecary and her serving girl.'

Magda straightened up. 'They have come here?' She tucked the knife back in her belt and lit an oil lamp.

Lucie took off her wet cloak and knelt to look at the boy. 'You have purged him?' she asked.

Magda bristled at the question, but calmed herself. The apothecary was brave to come to a strange place at night in a storm to rescue an injured child. 'Magda has done all that can be done at present. Come. Sit by the fire and warm thyself.'

Magda held the oil lamp up to Lucie's face as the apothecary turned to her. 'Thou art much like thy mother, but with a stronger spirit.' Magda grinned. 'Magda thanks thee for coming.'

Lucie motioned to Tildy to come sit by her. 'I don't understand. Why did you ask me to take the boy in if you have the skill to take care of him yourself, Mistress Digby?'

'Well might thou ask,' Magda said, nodding. 'But come. Sit thee down. Drink some of Magda's fine brandywine. Crossing the flood has chilled thee, Magda knows.'

Lucie took the cup gratefully.

'Thou art more trusting than thy husband. Bird-eye will not drink with Magda.'

Lucie laughed. 'He hates that you call him that, you know. As to trust, I know that you assisted my Aunt Phillippa at my birth. I have nothing to fear from you.'

Magda liked this wife of Bird-eye. 'Thou art just the person Magda hoped thee would be. She needs thee to take Jasper into thy house, nurse him, protect him. Canst thou do this?'

Lucie glanced over at her serving girl. 'Tildy says she is willing to take on the work of caring for him.'

'This young chick?' Magda said, eyeing Tildy.

The girl had been staring down at Jasper with a melancholy look. Now her face lit up. 'I've nursed all my brothers and sisters many times. And he reminds me of my brother Alf who was killed up on the moors. I would like to nurse him.'

'I know Owen is concerned for the boy,' Lucie said, 'so I am willing to take him in. But why not keep the boy here? The friar said Jasper made his way to you. He must feel safe with you.'

Magda looked down at the boy. 'Magda wishes she could keep Jasper by her. But he needs protection, someone to be near him at all times. Magda lives alone. How can she do this?'

'If he is to come home with me, I ought to know what you know about him,' Lucie said.

Magda nodded. 'Thou'rt right to ask it. So. What does Magda know? His father was a carpenter, like thy St Joseph. Died when Jasper was six. His mother was an embroiderer. The Mercers' Guild hired her to pretty up their pageant costumes and make a new guild banner. Will Crounce was responsible for approving her work. One thing led to another, and he meant to marry her. To prove his good faith he planned to sponsor Jasper in the guild. First step was the job Jasper took on, greasing the pageant wagon.'

'That was the day his mother took sick?' Lucie asked.

Magda nodded. ''Twas Will's child Kristine de Melton carried. But the gods took the child in the womb. It often happens that such a thing poisons the mother.' Magda shrugged. 'There is little else. Thou know'st the boy witnessed Crounce's murder and went into hiding. He has survived attacks before, and come to Magda for care. It is the second time he has broken that same arm. Poor lad. Magda can do so little to protect him.'

Lucie looked down at the sleeping boy. 'How old is he?'

'Almost nine.'

'Do you have any idea from whom he's hiding?'

Magda shook her head. 'The boy thinks to protect Magda by saying naught. Canst thou imagine?' Her laugh was more like a bark.

'Do you think it's the same person who keeps finding him?'

Magda thought about it. Shrugged. 'Magda thinks this is the first time Jasper has faced his attacker. Something has changed. Perhaps the attacker is more desperate. That is not good.'

'Should we take him tonight?' Lucie asked.

Magda nodded. 'It is best.'

Magda and Lucie woke the boy and explained where he was going, but he did not seem to comprehend. He whimpered as they wrapped him in blankets and clung to Lucie when Dunstan tried to lift him.

'I will carry him to the boat,' Lucie said. 'It is not far.'

Lucie and Tildy held the boy on their laps in the boat while Friar Dunstan rowed the short distance. The wind blew bitterly and Lucie hugged the boy to her to protect him. Friar Dunstan carried Jasper up the muddy bank despite the boy's protests. Up there, one of Tildy's brothers waited with Bess's donkey and cart.

The city gates were already closed for the night, but the gate warden at Bootham Bar had agreed to let them back through. With Jasper moaning and shivering in the cart, Lucie felt the warden took an eternity to answer their ringing, but he finally came. It was very late when they got to the apothecary.

'Do you need a bed for the night?' Lucie asked the friar.

'Bless you, but no, the friary is not so far from here,' he said.

'This is a hard night's work,' Lucie said. 'Why have you done this? Do you know the boy?'

Dunstan bowed his head. 'No. I do this in payment for Mistress Digby's night's work.'

Lucie frowned. 'Her night's— The young woman in the curtained bed, you mean?'

The friar nodded.

'It was your child she carried?'

'My sweet Lord have mercy on this sinner,' Dunstan said, striking his breast. 'I will leave you now. God's blessing on this house.' He went out the kitchen door.

Lucie found herself smiling at Magda Digby's exacting penance for payment. There was a comfortable logic to the Riverwoman that appealed to Lucie.

Nine

Tonics and
Waits

O wen had just come downstairs to the warm
fire, his mind still muddled with sleep, when
Alfred and Colin burst into the hall with a
bedraggled traveller in tow. Blast, Owen thought, Paul
Scorby is the last person I want to see this morning.
Anna Scorby had cried out with fever dreams in the
night, and Owen had worked over her, bringing down
the fever. Cecilia had been too drugged with the valerian to rouse. She was with her daughter now, having
come to check on Anna in the early morning when the
root wore off. It would be the Devil's timing for Scorby
to arrive now.

'Captain Archer, this lad says he comes with messages from your wife,' Alfred said as he roughly pulled
back the captive's hood.

'John!' Owen said.

'Aye, Captain Archer. 'Tis only me, not a High-
lander.'

'You know him?' Alfred asked.

Owen slammed his cup down on the table. 'Where
did the Archbishop find you men? Do you attack

anyone who comes to the gate?'

''Tis early in the day for an honest traveller to arrive,' Colin said in a whining voice that irritated Owen even more.

'Early in the day?' Owen repeated angrily. 'Is there an ordinance against arriving at certain hours, then?'

Colin shrugged.

'I rode hard, Captain,' John said. And he did look it, wet and spattered with mud, his nose red and his eyes bloodshot.

'Surely you didn't ride through the night?'

'Nay, I don't know the countryside well enough for that. I found an empty hut.'

'Didn't Mistress Wilton give you coin for an inn?'

'Oh, aye, Captain, but I'd as lief stay away from other travellers.'

Owen knew little about the stable boy, but he did know that John did not like to explain himself, so he accepted his odd answer without further question. 'Good lad. When you've given me your message, these two louts will show you to the kitchen, where you'll be well rewarded.'

John handed Owen the pouch and the letter. 'That pouch is Master Ridley's, may he rest in peace. Mistress Wilton said to read the letter first.'

'Is she well?'

'Oh, aye, Captain. All is well at the shop. This has naught to do with shop matters.'

'Good. I will look at these. Now off to the kitchen with him, men.' Owen, satisfied to hear their polite request that John follow them, turned at once to the letter.

What he read disturbed him. A poisoned tonic. And Cecilia Ridley so vague about what Ridley had been taking. Owen did not like this. Could he have been so wrong about Cecilia Ridley? Or was there someone else in the household who had hated the Master?

Sweet Heaven, how was he to approach this? 'Mistress Ridley, were you poisoning your husband for any particular reason?' Blast. Jehannes would be better at this than Owen.

Owen read on, about Jasper's disappearance from the minster and the evidence of a struggle. Damn Thoresby. Owen had told him the boy would be in danger.

'What's amiss?' Cecilia asked.

Owen started. He had not heard her come down to the hall or approach him. She wore a kerchief to hold back her hair and her sleeves were pushed up.

'How is your daughter this morning?' Owen asked.

'Cool. She took a little watered wine, and I've come down to see what Angharad might fix for her.' Cecilia sat down by Owen. 'I heard voices.'

Owen nodded. 'A messenger from York with your husband's other baggage – the pack you said was missing, most like. We will look at it later, after you've seen to Anna.'

'Other baggage?' her voice was nervous.

'Nothing to worry about,' Owen lied.

'The messenger has gone out to the kitchen?'

'Aye. Shall I go out and speak with the cook about a broth for Anna while you have a cup of hot wine?'

Cecilia looked anxiously towards the back door, then sighed and nodded. 'I am in need of something warm.'

Owen left her there, taking the letter with him, but leaving the pouch. When he returned a while later, followed by the servant, Sarah, carrying a bowl of broth, Owen noted a flush on Cecilia's face. And the pouch had been moved. So she had examined it.

That did not necessarily mean she feared there was something incriminating in it, but it could. Owen did not like the complexities that he'd begun to see in this family.

In the morning, Jasper seemed out of danger. He understood what Lucie said to him and managed to swallow some broth. Lucie and Tildy fixed up a bed for him in Tildy's tiny room behind the kitchen. It shared the chimney with the kitchen, and he could stay warm there and yet be out of sight of any visitors. Melisende circled the boy's pallet, sniffing and considering, then jumped up on his chest and stared at him for a while. When Jasper reached out and gently stroked her between the ears, she gave her approval, turned three times round and settled on the boy's stomach, purring. Jasper fell into a healthy slumber. Lucie and Tildy were just sitting down to some bread and cheese when the shop bell rang.

'Lord have mercy, what now?' Lucie muttered as she went to answer the door.

A youthful looking man in the colourful livery of a town wait stood without. 'Ambrose Coats,' he said with a bow. 'Are you Mistress Wilton?'

'I am.' Lucie stood aside for him to enter, noting he carried a bundle. She lit a lamp by the counter and studied her visitor. His green eyes were large in a slender, bony, but not unhealthy face. He looked worried or frightened. 'How can I help you, Master Coats? It is unusually early . . .'

'Forgive me, I could wait no longer. A friend advised me to bring my trouble to you.' Ambrose Coats smiled shyly and took off his felt hat. Dark blond curls tumbled into his eyes and he pushed his hair back with a gloved hand.

'What trouble?'

Ambrose set the bundle on the counter. 'It is this — I apologise for bringing such a hideous thing into your shop, but I could not think what else to do. I understand that Captain Archer is helping the Archbishop look for the murderers of the two mercers. I — Oh dear, perhaps if I just —' He unwrapped the bundle.

Lucie crossed herself and whispered a prayer. 'Gilbert Ridley's hand?'

'That is what I fear, Mistress Wilton. It was on my doorstep yesterday. I thought perhaps my neighbour's pig had dug it up somewhere and had left it there.'

'It was just sitting there, unwrapped?'

'Yes.'

Lucie noted that his voice changed with that answer. Ambrose Coats was lying. About what?

'Why not take it to a city bailiff?'

Ambrose looked down at his boots. 'I — I prefer that no one know. I am employed by the city. I must not be connected to any scandal.' He shrugged.

'Why do you assume this is Gilbert Ridley's hand? Pigs are outlawed in the city because of their habit of digging up graves. It could be anyone's hand, gnawed off any corpse.'

Ambrose grimaced. 'But the wrist. It was done with a sword or axe, don't you see? Not a pig's teeth.' He was shifting from foot to foot now, and his voice slightly breathless, as if —

'Are you going to be sick, Master Coats?'

'Oh dear me,' he passed a gloved hand over his forehead, 'I think not. But it is not easy to speak of it.'

'It could be the hand of a thief cut off and buried outside the gates.'

Ambrose shook his head. 'Too far for the pig to carry.'

'You are rather set on its being the pig's treasure.'

'I suppose I could be wrong.'

'Did you know Will Crounce or Gilbert Ridley?'

'I knew Master Ridley only to nod to. I knew Will better. Because of the pageant. We had rehearsed together. Yes, I knew Will. A gentle, talented man.'

'Is it possible that someone left this on your doorstep as a warning?'

The green eyes widened in alarm. 'A warning? How could it be? I knew Will, but how could I be connected with Master Ridley?'

Lucie took his answer to mean that he had thought about it. And again, she felt that if he was not lying, he was at least not saying everything that was on his mind. She had a thought.

'Do you live alone?'

'I— Yes. I live alone.' Ambrose nodded too eagerly, as if convincing himself.

'Please, Master Coats,' Lucie said with rising irritation, 'if you did not want to be honest with me, why did you bring your trouble here?'

'What else could I do?'

'Rebury it?'

'But the pig, you see.'

'Why does it concern you what happens to the hand, Master Coats?'

'I thought it might help Captain Archer to see it. To know that it was in the city.' Ambrose shook his head. 'I don't really know what I thought. I just wanted to get it out of my house.'

That sounded honest enough – who could blame him? Lucie relaxed a little. 'Who advised you to bring it here?'

'A friend.'

'Someone I know?'

'You are the apothecary. Everyone knows you.'

'That is not an answer. Who is your friend?'

Ambrose looked down at the cap in his hand. 'I cannot say, Mistress Wilton.'

Lucie sighed. 'I do not appreciate your giving me half the truth, Master Coats. It makes me wonder what you are hiding. Whether you have good reason for not going to the bailiff.'

'I am sorry I bothered you. Would you like me to take it back?'

'No, of course not. But you might give me more information. Have you nothing more to tell me?'

Ambrose shook his head.

'Then let me get this out of my shop and get back to my breakfast.' Lucie came round the counter and opened the door.

'God be with you, Mistress Wilton.' Ambrose Coats whisked past her and disappeared into the foggy morning.

Lucie rewrapped the hand and took it out to the potting shed, scrubbed the shop counter, and washed her hands before she returned to her bread and cheese. She decided to put the bundle in a large stone jar and bury it in the back of the garden until Owen returned. At least their garden was walled in. No pigs would dig it up and present it to another innocent neighbour.

But was Ambrose Coats innocent? He hid something from her, and yet he had brought the hand. The murderer would not have done that. And if Ambrose felt he might be the next victim, would he not have admitted that?

Lucie wished Owen were home.

Ten

Forebodings

lthough cold and grey, the afternoon was dry.
Owen was out in a field behind the manor
house shooting at a makeshift target. It was
the best way he knew to relax, emptying his mind
of everything but the bow, the arrow, the target, his
arms and sighting.

Owen had spent the morning helping Cecilia bleed
Anna to rid her of the humours that kept bringing on
fever. The young woman slept now, and Cecilia had
gone to rest for a while. John had left for York in
the morning, carrying a letter from Owen to Lucie.
Owen wrote that he missed Lucie. He thanked her for
sending John so quickly with the new information. It
did, however, mean he must stay longer; how long he
could not say. He explained the situation with Paul
and Anna Scorby.

It had felt good to write down his thoughts, though
Owen could not include everything just in case the
letter fell into the wrong hands. Indeed, as he rested
against a tree, Owen wondered whether he had been
wise to mention Paul Scorby in the letter. The man
disturbed Owen. Out in the field, his type meant

trouble because they were unpredictable, reacting with violent anger to something that had been acceptable the day before. Owen could not tell from his brief observation what Scorby was after. He might be watching the manor. And if so, might Scorby not waylay John and search him to see what messages were being sent away?

It was little details like this that made Owen's work for the Archbishop frustrating. If one waited until confident that everything was considered before making a move, one would never move. And yet it was the little details that could prevent disaster. Life had been so much simpler as a soldier. Someone attacked, he shot him. Simple as that.

Owen cleared his mind and went through another round of arrows. Tonight, if Anna Scorby still rested quietly, without fever, Owen would mention the poisoned tonic to Cecilia. He must be clear-headed for that.

Father Cuthbert was sitting with Anna, praying with her, and Alfred and Colin were on guard at the gatehouse. So Owen and Cecilia were to dine alone. Cecilia wore a peaked head-dress draped with a sheer, black veil that fell softly over her dark hair, coiled on either side of her face. No wimple hid her long, white neck. Owen wondered how Ridley had dared leave his wife alone most of their married life. She dressed simply, but the style became her. Became her very much indeed.

Owen told himself he must put aside such thoughts and concentrate on his business, which was not to endear himself to Cecilia Ridley. He permitted himself to keep to pleasant topics until they had finished their food.

Then Owen put Ridley's pack on the table. 'As I told you, Mistress Ridley, this was found under Foss Bridge. We believe it is Gilbert's. I hoped you might look through it and tell me if that is so. And if it is, perhaps you can tell whether anything's missing.' Owen pushed the pack across to Cecilia.

She touched it cautiously, as if afraid to open it.

Was it possible that she had moved it yesterday, but not looked inside? Was she afraid what she might find? Or was she afraid that she would give something away in how she behaved about the pack? 'I have looked inside,' he assured her. 'The hand is not there, if that's what frightens you.'

'The leather is damp.' Her voice was tense. She did not look up at Owen, but kept her eyes on the pack.

'It would be, yes.'

Cecilia opened the pack. When she drew out the shoes, her eyes filled with tears. 'These are Gilbert's.' She blinked, hugged the shoes to her.

Owen thought with a shiver how he would feel if they were Lucie's shoes and she were lying dead in the chapel. It was the everyday things that would most remind him of her, particularly her shawl and her hair combs. 'Take your time,' Owen said gently. 'Try to remember what Gilbert usually carried in this pack.'

Cecilia placed the shoes on the table. 'I do not know how helpful I will be. Gilbert packed for his trips himself.' She took out one of the pouches, opened it. Empty. 'He carried money in this one, I think. So they did take his money.'

'Would he have been carrying a lot of money? Was he doing any business besides his business with the Archbishop?'

Cecilia shook her head. 'I think not. He had been — He had handed most of the business over to our son, Matthew. I think this visit was only for the donation to the minster.'

'Why did he hand the business over to Matthew?' Owen had never been satisfied with Ridley's explanation.

Cecilia played with the string on the empty money pouch. 'Do you want to know the reason Gilbert gave me, or what I think?' Now she looked Owen in the eye.

Considering his dissatisfaction with Ridley's explanation, Owen said, 'I would like to know what you think.'

'I believe Gilbert had criticised John Goldbetter once too often. He felt Goldbetter was giving in to the King too much. Matthew worships the King and Prince Edward. He will be far more accommodating.'

'Did you and Gilbert talk about this?'

Cecilia shook her head. 'Will told me,' she said softly. She set the money pouch aside and reached for another item. One at a time, Cecilia picked up the small pouches, opened them, looked inside, closed them, piled them to the side. Her hands trembled. When she had checked them all, Cecilia sat with her hands clenched together on the table before her.

'This spoon,' Owen said, picking it up, 'is the stone valuable?'

Cecilia glanced at it. 'Not really. Gilbert thought it pretty. He had a London silversmith set it in the handle for him. When he was going to sup with Prince Edward.'

Owen nodded. 'You have seen it all. Is anything missing that you can think of? Anything you know Gilbert carried that was neither in the pack they brought with his body or in this pack?'

Cecilia shook her head.

Owen reckoned he deserved the failure. He had tried to trick her and it was not working. He must get to the point. 'Mistress Ridley, there was another pouch that has been removed. It was half filled with a powder that appeared to be a physick of some sort.'

She looked up, her eyes guarded. 'A physick?'

'I presume the one your husband took when he dined with the Archbishop. The one he said you made up for him.'

Cecilia shook her head. 'I have told you that I'd stopped making the tonic when it did no good. Gilbert worsened.'

'And what was in that tonic? You said it was to help him sleep?'

'Yes. And to calm his digestion. Mints of various kinds, and anise, raspberry leaf, a small amount of comfrey, some barks that my mother collected long ago ... Is that anything like the tonic you found in his pack?'

If she was lying, she was being clever, describing something completely unlike the incriminating powder. 'No,' Owen said. 'What we found was a tonic meant to thicken the blood and keep the mind sharp. Not something for the digestion.'

Cecilia shook her head. 'That is not what I had made for him.'

'Where else might he have gone for something like this?' Owen asked.

'I cannot say. But Gilbert was feeling unwell, and he was wasting away. I can understand why he would try someone else's skill.' Cecilia frowned down at the pack, then up at Owen. 'You say the powder was removed. Why?' She studied Owen's face, then suddenly stood up, her right hand to her throat. 'Are you playing a game with me? What are you after?'

'It was a perfectly harmless powder, except for one ingredient.' Owen paused, watching Cecilia's reaction. It seemed forced, as if she were acting. And she would not look him in the eye. 'The ingredient was arsenic,' he said.

'Arsenic,' she whispered, her eyes on her hands. 'Dear God.' The long, slender hands pressed into the table.

'It was a small amount. Your husband was dying slowly. It would not have been a fierce pain, but dull and constant.'

'Gilbert,' Cecilia whispered.

'I must ask you, did you fix the physick I have described for your husband?'

At last she raised her eyes to Owen and stared at him without blinking for a long moment. 'Captain Archer, I told you I stopped making my mint concoction when I saw no improvement.' She took a deep breath. 'I do not understand this. You said Gilbert's throat had been slit. Like Will's. Did you lie? Why would someone also poison him?'

'Your husband died as I told you he did. I do not think whoever slit his throat was the same one who was poisoning him. That would make no sense.'

Cecilia Ridley said nothing, just stared at Owen.

He wished more than anything to escape from those dark eyes full of pain, but he must persist. It would be worse to return to it later. 'Then this powder your husband carried in his pack was not anything you had prepared for him?'

'I do not see how it could be,' Cecilia said quietly. She remained regarding him with those disturbing eyes.

The answer bothered Owen. Because he did not believe her, or because it still felt evasive? He could not say. He managed to return her stare steadily for a time, wishing he were a better student of people. Could someone stare like she did and be lying? Or was a liar better able to do that than someone caught off guard, an innocent confronted with a horrible suspicion? Owen did not know why in Heaven's name the Archbishop trusted him in such business. He was too ignorant of people.

Cecilia stood up. 'I must go and tell Lisa to take some food up to Anna.'

'Forgive me for asking such questions,' Owen said. 'I could think of no way to ask them without hurting you, and I had to ask them.'

'I understand,' Cecilia said without emotion. 'I have not for a moment forgotten why you are here.' She left him.

Owen's back and legs ached as if he'd not moved throughout dinner. He stretched his legs out and poured more wine. He did not believe Cecilia, not about the physick. Why? He'd believed her tears when she held her dead husband's shoe. But there was more that disturbed him. When he'd come to Riddlethorpe the first time, he'd sensed in her a great unhappiness. She had not struck him as a woman who easily hid her emotions. But now she was subtle. She answered carefully. She used tears at the right moment. And she used those mysterious eyes and that silken hair to distract him. But, damn it, distract him from what?

He lifted his cup, drained it, and caught himself about to dash it to the floor. This business twisted all his muscles into tight bundles that wanted to spring loose. He wanted action. He wanted to take someone's head and drive it into the wall.

But not Cecilia's. He could not imagine doing harm to her.

And she knew it. She had made it so.

Bess had invited Lucie to come sup with her when she'd closed the shop for the day. Tildy supported the idea with enthusiasm. 'You must, Mistress Lucie. Mistress Merchet always cheers you up.'

With the disturbing item buried in the backyard and the frustrating meeting with Ambrose Coats on her mind, Lucie was in need of Bess's good sense and cheer. She went over.

They sat in the kitchen, close to the fire, Bess and Tom and Lucie, eating in companionable silence. Then, over cups of Tom's ale, Lucie told them about her odd visitor.

'Blessed Mary, Mother of God,' Bess said, 'what a thing to drop in your lap.'

'That is not what bothers me,' Lucie said. 'I think Coats lied about something, but I cannot make out what. What do you know about him?'

Bess shrugged. 'He's a talented musician and a gentle man. He never over-indulges when he's in the tavern, never gets noisy.' Bess looked at her husband. 'There is little else to tell, eh?'

Tom considered that. 'Nay. Except that he's a private one. Not unfriendly, mind you. A good listener. And folk do say he's a generous friend. Just quiet about himself.'

'Who are his friends?' Lucie asked.

'Well, you see, that's it, isn't it?' Tom said. 'I could not say who his friends might be. I suppose his fellow waits, he seems friendly enough with them, but then again, they might know as little about him as I do.'

'Speaking of one who keeps his story to himself, our stable boy, John, has been showing an interest in the ladies of a sudden,' Bess said.

Tom and Lucie exchanged a puzzled look.

'What's this to do with Coats?' Tom asked.

'It's naught to do with him. It's to do with John and Tildy.'

Lucie sat up. 'Tildy?'

'The girl's temperature rises at the sight of John, if you haven't noticed, and he fans the flame just enough to keep it going. Wicked lad. When all the while he's bedding down with a woman of experience.'

Tom almost choked on a mouthful of ale. 'How do you know that? Are you spying on the boy?'

Bess rolled her eyes. 'I've no need to spy. It's a scent he's got about him. And a swagger that says some woman's turning his head. Telling him he's a man.'

Lucie stood up. 'Poor Tildy.'

Bess nodded. 'That's why I mention it. You'll have your hands full when her feelings aren't returned.'

As Lucie left her friends, she resolved to speak with Tildy. But in the kitchen, she discovered John and Tildy sharing a cup of ale. Jasper's pallet had been moved out by the fire. The boy sipped some broth and listened to them sleepily.

'He was a great war-horse,' John was saying as Lucie entered, 'and I was warned that he let only Sir Thomas touch him. But he was gentle as a lamb with me.' As the draught from the open door reached him, John turned, instantly on guard. When he recognised Lucie, he bobbed his head. 'God be with you, Mistress Wilton.'

Lucie nodded to John. 'It looks like your company combined with Tildy's has cheered Jasper. I thank you.'

John nodded, his eyes disturbingly direct. Something had definitely changed since he'd travelled with Lucie in the summer.

Tildy took Lucie's cloak and hung it on a peg on the wall. 'Jasper does look better this evening, doesn't he?' Her cheeks were flushed and she looked pretty.

Lucie did not ascribe that to Jasper's condition. Bess must be right. Lucie had seen just now how Tildy hung on John's every word with a look of adoration. Merciful Mother, Lucie had not realised that Tildy had lost her heart to John.

She could not imagine Tildy knew much about the boy. John kept to himself. Even the nosy Bess had never got much out of John about his life before he showed up in the York stable, burning with fever and his hand crushed. Three fingers on his right hand had had to be amputated, leaving John with the thumb and the little finger. But he'd healed quickly under Bess's care, and he'd proven to be an honest, hard-working and resourceful young man. Four years later, Bess and Tom still had no idea how John had crushed his hand or whence he came. Lucie wished Tildy had chosen someone more predictable.

Owen woke early and crept past Anna's door, glad that she slept. Downstairs, the fire had just been stoked and had not yet warmed the air near the hearth. Owen stepped outside into a biting wind with a chill to it that promised snow. He headed out back to the kitchen to get warm.

The kitchen was a one-room stone building with a large hearth and two baking ovens. Her sleeves rolled up to show strong arms, Angharad, the ruddy-faced cook, basted a haunch of venison while she talked with a younger woman who huddled close to the fire. Next to the younger woman lay a wet, mud spattered travelling cloak. The woman held her hands and feet as close to the flame as possible, and Owen noted that her boots were crusted with mud. She seemed absorbed by a tale the cook was weaving. Owen stood in the doorway and listened. To his delight, it was a tale from his childhood, and Angharad's voice had the soft accent of Wales.

It was from the story of Branwen, daughter of Llyr, about Evnissyen maiming the horses of Mallolwch, King of Ireland. 'When King Bran heard of it,' Angharad said, 'he was as dismayed as was Mallolwch, for to my countrymen a horse is a noble beast, deserving as much care as our own babes.'

'Really?' The young woman's eyes followed the cook's movements.

'As close to the truth as a good storyteller ever gets,' Owen said, laughing.

The two women turned startled faces in Owen's direction. The traveller's face was interesting – square jaw, wide-set brown eyes and a generous mouth. When the brown eyes met Owen's, there was a moment of interest, then alarm. Owen's mood sank. The scar and patch again. He would never be allowed to forget it. The woman stood up with a abruptness that knocked her cloak on the floor. She was an unusually tall woman. Large-boned. Strong, but not ungraceful.

The cook greeted Owen. 'I was telling Kate the story I told her little William to make sure he cared well for your horse, Captain Archer.'

'It is good to hear the old tales,' Owen said. He turned to the younger woman. 'I see you've been travelling. How did you escape being escorted from the gate by my men?'

'Oh, she's Kate Cooper,' Angharad said. 'Steward's wife. Came in through the fields.'

'Yes. I came in through the fields.' Kate Cooper kept her eyes focused on the floor. 'I should be going.

The children will be wanting their food.' She turned to get her cloak, seemed confused when she did not see it on the bench.

Owen picked it up from the floor and offered it to her.

'Thank you.' She still did not look directly at him, which was a challenge since they stood eye to eye. 'I — I must have knocked it down.' She seemed oddly flustered as she took the cloak, almost dropping it again. Owen did not think it was his charm that flustered her so. She'd hardly glanced at him.

Perhaps if he were friendly. 'So your mother is improved?'

Kate Cooper frowned, then nodded. 'God has spared her once more, yes.' She glanced at him while she adjusted her cloak, but looked quickly away when she caught his eye.

'Going so soon?' Owen could tell by the surprise in the cook's voice that Kate's departure was unexpected.

'Must see to the children, Angharad.' Kate Cooper hurried out the door.

'A fine-looking woman,' Owen said as he sank down on the bench Kate Cooper had vacated.

'Oh, aye, she is that, is Kate. And she knows how to trade with her looks, that one does. I'm surprised she didn't go to work on you. Are you wearing some sort of charm your wife made to keep you true?'

'Perhaps she does not care for the patch.'

'Nay, I'm sure it wasn't that.' Angharad put a tankard of ale down in front of Owen and eased herself down on a bench beside him. 'Where did you hear about her mother?'

'From Jack Cooper.'

She nodded. 'Didn't think the Mistress would have told you about that.'

'Why not?'

'Mistress never took to her. She could see what Kate Cooper was about from the start and she almost didn't take Jack as steward because of it.'

'Kate's a wandering wife?' Owen wanted to make sure he understood what the cook was hinting.

'Aye, and the Mistress doesn't believe that Kate goes off to nurse her mother.'

'That must make it difficult for Jack Cooper.'

'He never mentions her to the Mistress. As he puts it, why remind her of the thorn if the wound's gone numb?'

'What wound, Angharad?'

'I'd best not say. It's enough to say that the Mistress was quite right about Kate. And that's why I'm surprised you're sitting here with me instead of out in the stables with her.'

The servant Sarah hurried in from the hall. 'Mistress Ridley is down, Angharad.'

The cook sighed and eased herself up. 'Well, Owen, there's work to be done out here and she'll surely be wanting you in the hall. I'll send in something to fortify you just in case Kate changes her mind.' She winked at Owen and turned back to her cooking.

Cecilia Ridley stood with her hands on her hips, her eyes snapping with anger, watching Owen cross the hall to her. 'I hear you've been out to the kitchen to meet the harlot.'

The venom in Cecilia's voice stunned Owen, even with the forewarning from Angharad. 'I went out to get warm,' he said. 'I did not know Kate Cooper would be out there.'

'So what did she say about me?'

'About you? Nothing. In fact, she said precious little to me at all. Took off as if she thought me a leper. What should she say about you?'

'She has stayed away from me since I found her with Will Crounce. In the stables.'

Owen could tell by the passion in Cecilia's eyes what she'd found them doing. So that was the thorn that Angharad would not define. He decided to take the leap. 'That must have been painful for you, considering your feelings for Will.'

Cecilia opened her mouth, closed it, turned her head away. 'My feelings?' Her voice was tight. 'How did you — I mean.' Her eyes flared again. 'What has that harlot been telling you?'

'Nothing. No one had to tell me. I guessed it the first time I came, when I brought news of Crounce's murder.'

'Sweet Jesu.' Cecilia crossed herself and sat down, her pale face even paler. 'Was I that obvious? Do you think Gilbert knew what a Mary Magdalene I'd become?'

'I do not think one indiscretion makes you a Mary Magdalene. In any case, your husband did not seem a particularly sensitive man, Mistress Ridley. I noticed because it is my business to study people when I am working for the Archbishop.'

Cecilia dropped her head and made a great business of smoothing her skirt. Owen guessed she hid tears. Her voice, when she spoke, verified that. 'Will Crounce was a gentle, loving man.' She took a deep, shuddering breath, still with her head bowed. 'We were thrown together so much. He was kind. Always ready to help. He was what I had thought Gilbert would be. He was more my husband than Gilbert ever was.'

'I am not here to judge you.'

Now she looked up. Her dark eyes shimmered with

tears in the light of the fire. 'But the last months, after Will died, Gilbert became a husband. He took Will's death hard. It transformed him, as if somehow God's grace moved from Will to Gilbert. Had I known Gilbert could be so kind —' Cecilia shook her head. 'I never knew him. I was his wife for twenty-years, but I never knew him. I regret so much.' She buried her head in her hands and wept, the sobs coming from deep within her, a sound painful to hear.

Owen sat quietly.

'Please,' Cecilia suddenly rose, wiping her eyes. 'Excuse me.' She ran up the stairs, to the confusion of Sarah, who had just come through the door with a tray of food.

Owen hated himself for forcing Cecilia to reveal such intimate feelings. It explained her guarded behaviour. She suffered because she'd betrayed her husband with his best friend, a wrong she could never undo. Owen did not think it possible now that Cecilia had prepared the tonic.

He ate and then went out to the steward's house to find out why he made Kate Cooper so nervous.

No one answered his knocks. He stepped inside, saw no signs of a traveller just arrived. Perhaps Kate Cooper had already tidied up. Owen left the house and headed for the stables. He met Jack Cooper on the way. The man looked angry.

'So you've been to my house? Did you see Kate? Is it true she's back?'

'I saw her in the kitchen this morning. I just went up to your house hoping to speak with her, but there's no one there.'

'Kate's not there?' Jack started to walk quickly towards the house, burst through the door as if trying to catch someone who was eluding him. He spun on his heel and faced Owen angrily. 'So where's she got to, that's what I want to know.'

Owen wanted to know that, too. And why Jack was so angry. 'When she left the kitchen this morning she said the children were waiting for her.'

Jack shook his head. 'I've just taken the children to the kitchen for some food. Angharad asked me how many meals the children wanted to eat today. She thought Kate had come back to the house to feed them, just as you say. But Kate's not here. There's no sign of her, is there?'

Owen looked around. A large pallet in the corner looked as if it had just been left, rumpled blankets and all, when the children and their father got up this morning. There were no travelling packs in evidence. Nor did Kate Cooper's cloak hang on the wall. 'I'd say you're right, Jack. Not a sign of her anywhere. Where had she been?'

'With her mother.'

'How far away?'

'York. Just like yourself.'

'Your wife was in York? Did she travel there when Gilbert Ridley went?'

'Oh, aye, they went together, those two.'

'But that could be important.' Owen was excited. 'Why didn't Mistress Ridley tell me that, I wonder?'

'That's easy enough to answer. We didn't tell her. I've learned it's best to let the Mistress forget Kate.'

'But your wife was stranded in York when Ridley was murdered. Surely you were worried. I wonder you didn't mention it to me.'

'Nay, not stranded.'

'What do you mean?'

'Kate did not expect to travel back with Master Ridley. Thought she would be gone longer – her mother was that sick, you see. Kate would find a way back. Or has, I guess. Where could that woman have got to?' Jack had closed the door to the house. Now he turned about as if deciding where to head.

Owen tried to piece things together. Cecilia had caught Kate with Crounce, whom Cecilia loved. Kate went to York with Ridley. Ridley and Crounce were murdered. Someone had been poisoning Ridley. Owen could not fit all the pieces together yet. But something about Kate Cooper bothered him.

'How often does your wife travel to York?' Owen asked.

Jack Cooper shrugged. 'I don't suppose I should complain. Her mother's alone. Kate's all she has for family.'

'How often, Jack?'

'Well, let's see. This Martinmas. Last Corpus Christi — '

'She was there for the Corpus Christi procession?' Owen thought of Crounce's cloaked companion.

'Oh, aye. And I was with her. But that time wasn't so much for her mother. A family wedding up in Boroughbridge. We took her mother up.'

Owen tried to keep the excitement out of his voice. 'How many days did you spend in York at Corpus Christi?'

'Well, let's see. We would have been there a day before Corpus Christi and a day after.'

'So you left the night Crounce was murdered?'

'Well now, no, we left the morning after. But we didn't hear about it till at the wedding. He was from Boroughbridge, you know, so word got up there quick.' Jack frowned. 'Why all these questions?'

'I'm just trying to place who was where at the time of the murders, Jack.'

'You're not accusing us of anything?'

'Not so long as you don't seem to be hiding anything. Why should I?'

Jack shrugged. 'It's just all these questions.'

'How did you and your wife feel about Crounce's death?'

'Kate and I were grieved, you can be sure. 'Twas a terrible thing to happen to as good a man as ever lived. Well, he was no saint, as I've told you – about him and the Mistress.'

'Were you apart from your wife at any time during your stay in York, Jack?'

'Nay,' Jack said, then shrugged. 'Well, there was the night Kate felt sickly, you know, and I went to a tavern. Being in York and all. I couldn't just sit and watch her mother work all evening.'

'And what night was that, Jack?'

Jack squinted at Owen. 'Why do you want to know?'

Owen thought fast. 'Crounce was in a tavern, the York Tavern, right before he was murdered. If you were there that night, you might have heard something. Seen someone approach him?'

'Well, it was that night, but not the York Tavern, so I can't help you. How would you and your men like to help me track down Kate, Captain Archer?'

They searched for Kate Cooper all day, but found no trace of her.

Owen took his leave of Cecilia Ridley and Anna Scorby the next morning. He asked Anna to send word when she arrived at St Clement's nunnery. He might need to speak with her.

He made a last visit to Jack Cooper, hoping that Kate might have returned during the night. The man was glumly dressing his three children.

'What is Kate's mother's name, Jack?'

'Felice. Fancy name for an embroiderer, eh?'

'Embroiderer? In York?'

'Aye. Mostly vestments and altar cloths, you know the sort of thing.'

'Does she live in the minster liberty?'

'Inside the gates, aye. Very humble is Felice. For all that fancy name of hers.'

Owen had slept little the night before, trying to get the facts about Kate Cooper to fall into a neat pattern. And now this. Someone who could easily come and go through the minster gates. But Owen could not think why Kate Cooper would murder the two men. He threw his things together in a hurry, eager to return to York and talk this all over with Lucie. She often saw connections that he didn't see.

Cecilia came out as Owen tied his pack to his horse. She offered him a stirrup cup. 'Have you learned what you need to know?' she asked as he drank.

'Not yet.'

'And the poisoned tonic?'

'Forgive me for questioning you about that last night, Mistress Ridley.'

'You had to.'

'But I am sorry.'

Cecilia smiled and, reaching up and pulling Owen's head down to her level, kissed him on the mouth. 'I forgive you with all my heart, Owen,' Cecilia whispered in his ear.

Thank God he was leaving. Owen straightened up, noting how Alfred and Colin grinned. He was determined to leave on a more official note. 'This Martin Wirthir who worked for your husband. You said he was a soldier?'

She gave him a puzzled look. 'Martin Wirthir?

Yes. Gilbert wanted me to have nothing to do with him. What he said was that Wirthir had the habits of a life of soldiering. I'm not certain what he meant by that.'

Owen glanced back at Alfred and Colin. 'Perhaps I do. Did your husband say anything else about him?'

'He thought Wirthir acted as a liaison between French prisoners of war in England and their families on the continent. A dangerous business.'

'You never met him?'

Cecilia shook her head. 'I wanted to. Gilbert and Matthew both called Martin Wirthir a dangerously charming man, but I was never given the opportunity to judge him.'

'Are ye ready, Captain?' Alfred called.

'Aye.' Owen mounted his horse.

'God go with you.' Cecilia touched his gloved hand.

Owen felt Cecilia's eyes on him as he rode out of the yard. He prayed that he did not need to return to Riddlethorpe for the Archbishop.

Lucie exclaimed at the state of Owen's cloak, stiff underneath, where it had frozen when it was still damp, and covered with a crust of snow. She insisted that his first business was to thaw out and get his fingers and toes warm. He was quite warm now, his legs stretched out towards the fire, a cup of Tom Merchet's ale in his hands.

As Lucie dished up the stew she had kept warm for Owen, she told him about Jasper, pleased to have such a surprise for him.

'Thank God the boy's safe,' Owen said. 'Where is he? I have questions to ask him.'

Lucie smiled at Owen's relief. 'He's sleeping at the moment. You can wait till morning.'

But Owen was already frowning. 'Who brought him from Magda Digby's?' It was the tone that usually led to an argument.

Lucie wanted no arguments. She nodded at the stew. 'Eat that. You've been riding for two days. I am sure you have not eaten well in that long.'

Owen ignored the stew. 'Did you go down to Magda Digby's to get Jasper?'

Lucie sighed. 'I wish you would eat before we talk. You know your temper when you're hungry.'

'Did you, Lucie?'

'I did not go alone, Owen. Don't treat me like a child.'

'It is dangerous down there. And with all the rain and snow, it must be flooding.'

'I said I was not such a fool as to go alone. A friar, Tildy and one of Tildy's brothers accompanied me. We had the use of a boat and Bess's donkey cart. We were quite well prepared.'

'Did you take care to keep Jasper concealed?'

'Of course I did.' Lucie was getting angry.

'You went at night, didn't you?'

'Yes, Owen. And now you're going to tell me how foolish that was.'

Owen banged his fist on the table. 'Do you realise how dangerous it is to row across a flood in the dark?'

'Sweet Jesus, what would you have me do, Owen? Leave the boy down there? It was you who cursed John Thoresby for not protecting Jasper.'

'And who's protecting you? Whenever we're separated, you take risks. Last time you travelled, you returned with a stranger. Now you've risked your life rowing across a flooding river at night. What am I supposed to do with you?'

Lucie stared at Owen. 'What are you talking about? You were worried about the boy. He turned up at

149

Magda Digby's, and she sent the friar to ask if I could take the boy in. I brought him here safely. He is recovering. I did it for you. Now instead of thanking me, you're looking for an argument. I don't understand you.'

'You did not have to go yourself.'

'I wanted to.'

They stared at each other, both angry, for a long, quiet moment.

Then Owen closed his eye, shook his head. 'Forgive me, Lucie. I am tired, disappointed in the results of my journey, aching from the ride, and my stomach is in turmoil from a greasy stew I ate on the way.' He caught Lucie's hand. 'Damn it, we always ruin homecomings with an argument.'

'It is you who have ruined it, not I. I gave you what I thought – what any sensible person would think – good news.' Lucie pulled her hand from Owen's and stood up. 'I'm going up to bed. You will digest your food better if I am not in the room.'

Owen pushed his bench away from the trestle table and pulled Lucie down on his lap.

She kept her head turned from him and stared at the fire.

'You were on my mind all the time, Lucie.' Owen stroked her hair. 'I did not like leaving you when you were so sad. Please forgive me. And forgive my ingratitude.'

Lucie had to admit that was a step towards apology. 'I cannot deny I had misgivings about going, Owen. But I took precautions. You go on as if I were a child.'

'So how do I dig myself out of this?'

'You finish eating your stew and then come up to bed.' Lucie tried to wriggle out of Owen's grasp, but he held tight.

'God allows even the greatest sinners a chance to redeem themselves. Will you not grant the same?'

Lucie could not help it, her humours betrayed her. She felt the corners of her mouth twitch, and she turned away to hide her smile.

'*Mea culpa, mea culpa, mea maxima culpa.*' Owen pressed his head to her chest.

Damn the man. He was too good at being charming. 'You know I will forgive you. I always do.'

Owen hugged Lucie. She turned and put her arms around him, burying her face in his wiry hair.

'I am not as hungry as I thought,' he said, getting his arms under her and beginning to rise.

Lucie lifted her head. 'Then go on up. I will tidy up down here and follow.'

Owen let Lucie stand up. '*We* will tidy up. What am I going to do up in that cold bed waiting for you?'

'Contemplate your sins?'

Owen snorted.

Lucie laughed and gave him a kiss. 'I did miss you, you scoundrel.'

He held her tight, and she could feel his heart pounding. 'This is what I thought about all the way back.' Owen's voice was different now, soft and affectionate. 'Why does it always take so long to get to this point?'

Lucie said nothing. She wondered the same thing. It was as if their humours were opposite. They could turn the simplest conversation into an argument. She worried about it.

Eleven

The Wool War

B y the time Owen reached the Archbishop's house it was midday. Brother Michaelo sniffed at Owen's timing, but he returned in a moment to extend Thoresby's invitation to sup with him.

Owen was shown into the hall, a lofty room hung with tapestries almost as lovely as the ones in Thoresby's chambers in London. The floor was tiled. A huge fireplace promised warmth; in front of it, a cloth-draped table was set for supper. A servant was pulling up an extra chair, setting out another plate and cup, and a spoon.

Thoresby stood in a simple black cassock, hands behind his back, staring into the fire. Owen paused halfway across the tile floor, puzzled by this un-accustomed glimpse of the great man. No chain of office, no scarlet robes, fur-trim. Owen was surprised to see how slender Thoresby was for his age and importance. John Thoresby turned and caught Owen studying him. He motioned for Owen to join him.

'You wonder about the dress?'

Owen nodded.

Thoresby looked down at himself. 'It *is* unusual. And I find it difficult to explain. I went to St Mary's this morning to help with the food distribution to the poor. Can you imagine that? I woke with a desire to do something unselfish. Charity. God's work.' Thoresby smiled. 'You should like that. You once suggested that I had lost sight of my duties as a man of God.'

'Aye, so I did.' Owen did not know whether to grin or steel himself for trouble. The Archbishop's behaviour was so odd.

Thoresby moved to the table. 'Sit. I am in need of food and wine at the end of that experience.'

'Gladly.'

They filled their cups. Lizzie brought in a fish soup and bread to begin with. Owen cleaned his knife on a piece of cloth.

Thoresby tasted the soup. 'Tell Maeve her cooking is a gift from Heaven.'

Lizzie bobbed and hurried away for the next course.

Thoresby took another spoonful of soup. 'This would be a feast to be remembered for those folk I saw today. Only this, the soup and bread. The wine would be an unimaginable delight.' He did not have his usual comfortable demeanour.

'I do not mean to sound impertinent, Your Grace, but you do not seem yourself. Are you well?'

Thoresby frowned down at his soup for a moment, then burst out laughing. 'That is what delights me about you, Archer. You are not in awe of my ring and my chain of office.'

'You wear no chain today,' Owen reminded him.

'Indeed. But the chain has never stopped you from saying your mind to me. I am humbled by my experience, a state in which you have never seen me.'

Owen feared there was danger in being too bold

with the Archbishop. 'I meant that you looked uncomfortable. Pale, Your Grace.'

Thoresby seemed taken aback by this. 'Pale?' He thought about it, shrugged. 'Perhaps God is warning me that my time is passing quickly.'

'Gloomy thoughts, Your Grace.'

'Sinfully self-absorbed, that is my problem of late.' Thoresby drained his cup and filled it. 'So. What did you learn in Beverley?'

Owen, realising Thoresby did not wish to discuss his mood further, described the dramatic relationships at Riddlethorpe. They were cutting into the roast when Owen came to the information Mistress Ridley had offered about Goldbetter and Company.

'Ah. I am not at all surprised that's coming round again to haunt the Crown,' Thoresby said.

Owen was surprised the name Goldbetter was so familiar to the Archbishop that he had not even paused to recall it. 'Is it true?' Owen asked. 'Is wool financing the war?'

Thoresby sighed. 'Yes and no. Let us finish this fine meal, then I will tell you about King Edward's war financing. I cannot think about it while I eat or I will never digest this much needed sustenance.'

They ate in silence for a few minutes, but Thoresby was not in a mood to continue so for long.

'This daughter, Mistress Scorby. What do you think of her?'

Owen tasted his wine and considered how to put it. 'Anna Scorby is in love with God, not with her husband. I think perhaps she truly has a vocation. But she was the only daughter, and Gilbert Ridley wanted a liaison with the Scorbys – he seemed impressed by their bloodline. According to Mistress Ridley, her son-in-law has been as patient as his character will permit, which is not very patient. She believes that Paul Scorby made an unfortunate match. A gentler man might have wooed Anna away from the spiritual life.'

'Some time at St Clement's nunnery might convince her that her life has not been so dreadful.'

Owen shrugged. 'They are Benedictines. I do not think they deny themselves much.'

'All the better. She will see that even in a convent the world is difficult to put aside.' Thoresby chuckled at his own joke. The food and wine had brought him back to himself. Owen was relieved. He did not want to like the Archbishop too much.

When Lizzie brought out a hard cheese, more bread, and more wine, Thoresby pushed his chair back from the table and sighed with pleasure. 'Now I can think about the court. But first, I must give Michaelo an assignment.'

He rose and crossed the tiles. Owen took the opportunity to seek out the back door and a privy. He returned through the kitchen, a warm, savoury-smelling place. Maeve smiled at him. 'You're a pleasure to cook for, Captain Archer. A good soldier's appetite, you have.'

'Believe me, the pleasure was all mine.'

'I'll give you some wastel as you leave. For you and Mistress Wilton. She has eased my bones with that salve she made me. As God is my witness, you would find no better apothecary in London.'

Owen knew Lucie loved the white loaves that Maeve baked. Wastel was the second highest grade of bread, but in Maeve's hands it was transformed into the finest pandemain. 'She will be most grateful, Maeve. And so will I.'

Owen was seated and pouring another cup of wine before the Archbishop returned. Thoresby surprised him by coming in from the kitchen. 'Now. We shall not be interrupted. I would take you to my chambers, but that fire was just lit. It cannot have warmed the room yet. And I had a most chilling morning.'

'Do you think this Goldbetter business could have bearing on the murders?'

Thoresby sipped some wine, then tilted his head back and contemplated the rafters. At last he looked back at Owen, nodding. 'It might well have something to do with it, though I cannot say what at this point. When Edward began to play with the wool merchants, I warned him. You play them one against the other and you destroy all loyalties, all the honour that keeps commerce civilised. And uncivilised merchants are more dangerous than an army of mercenaries. Especially the wool merchants, men who control a commodity critically important to all the nations involved in Edward's war.'

'You speak so plainly to the King?'

'I have ever done so. But these days I am uncertain that is wise.' Thoresby looked down at his hands, resting on the arms of his throne-like chair, lifting the finger on which he wore his Archbishop's ring, letting it catch the light. He seemed lost in his contemplation of it, his face sad.

'Do you know this John Goldbetter?' Owen asked, pulling the Archbishop back to the present.

Thoresby shook his head as if to clear it. 'Although we have never met, I know something about him. He is much like William de la Pole in his respect for law, and I know de la Pole. In fact, it was de la Pole who first mentioned Goldbetter to me. He pointed out that Goldbetter had done much the same as he, and yet Goldbetter was not being brought up in Chancery. I assured de la Pole that I knew many were guilty, but on such a smaller scale than he that it was not worth our time.'

'You enjoy your power as Lord Chancellor.'

Thoresby shook his head. 'Not often. The power is a heady wine, but of inferior quality. It brings on nausea and headache as it sours in one's belly.'

'You would stay away from the Court?'

'If that were possible.'

'Because of the war?'

'Sadly, because of the King.' Thoresby's deep-set eyes were fixed on Owen. 'This is why I made sure that we had no ears about, especially Michaelo's. Whenever one criticises his King, one speaks treason. I trust you to understand the difference between disaffection that might lead to overthrow and that which is merely an expression of disappointment, but I do not trust Michaelo.'

Owen was not comfortable with this direction, but it was unlikely that Thoresby would excuse him from the task he had set for him. 'You can trust me, Your Grace.'

Thoresby nodded. 'There are precious few I can trust.'

'Why do you keep Michaelo as your secretary?'

'On what unsuspecting soul would I thrust him? I have come to see Michaelo as my hair shirt.'

The image of the elegant Brother Michaelo as a hair shirt amused Owen. He laughed.

Thoresby nodded as he reached for more wine. 'Well might you laugh over my foolishness,' he grumbled, but his eyes smiled. He poured his wine, cut off a piece of cheese and dropped it in his mouth, savouring it, then drank some wine. 'When all is said and done, this is the reward of rank, not the power that comes with it. So much danger rides with the power.' The

Archbishop shook his head, serious once more. 'And so. On to the business. When the King set his mind on claiming his birthright to the crown of France, he needed a great deal of money to realise his ambition. He listened to some crafty explanations about how he might obtain higher revenues than usual with wool by manipulating the supply and raising duties. The merchants and lawyers who suggested this were no doubt in the pockets of the earls who feared the war expenses might somehow come from their pockets.'

'Or the Church?' Owen suggested.

'No, it was not the Church's scheme to avoid taxes.' Thoresby sipped his wine. 'At the time, the wool merchants had the largest cash resources of any group of men in the kingdom. And wool was,' he shrugged, 'perhaps remains, the most valuable product of our fair isle. And so very important to the Flemings, who have such a changeable allegiance, sometimes to us, sometimes to the French King.' Thoresby sighed, shook his head sadly. 'Golden Edward. Tall, kingly, bull-headed. I was not the only counsellor who reminded Edward that the King of France could just as easily lavish gifts and level threats at the Count of Flanders.'

'The King does not welcome criticism?'

'Not when to his mind he has invented a brilliant scheme. So he met with the merchants in the ninth year of his reign and declared an embargo on the export of wool. He meant this to persuade the merchants to accept an increased subsidy, and to coerce Flanders into siding with him. What it actually did was cause a glut of wool and low prices here, a scarcity of wool and high prices in Flanders. The Flemings were alarmed. Our wool merchants were delighted. They agreed to increased duties and a list indicating the highest prices wool producers could charge, which would ensure the merchants of profits despite the rise in customs rates.'

Thoresby absently crumbled the cheese on his bread, then poured himself more wine. 'Such a muddle. As with everything in this scheme, the purpose of the price list has varied over the years, sometimes serving the producers, sometimes the merchants. No one feels the King is truly on their side. I thought it was a mistake from the beginning, but it was one of those things so difficult to see clearly at the time that it was impossible to know if my misgivings were valid.'

'The King does not think it a muddle?'

Thoresby touched his fingertips together and stared at the fire. 'It is a painful thing, to watch a warrior age.' His voice was pensive. 'Edward was a tall, golden lion of a man. You have seen him before a battle, riding down the lines, inspiring feats of astounding courage in mere mortals. You have heard his men cheer him, haven't you, Archer?'

Owen nodded. 'Many a time as I sat with my arrows stuck in the ground beside me, waiting for the French to appear.'

'Edward was regal. Resplendent. But off the battle-field,' the Archbishop shook his head, 'he has not always been wise. This war. Oh, there is precedence, he does have a claim, and a better one than Valois, but it is mostly to satisfy a kingly ego.'

Owen's scar began to prickle. 'I do not want to hear this, Your Grace. I don't want to hear that I lost my eye, and so many men, on a whim of the King.'

'Ah.' Thoresby moved his gaze from the fire to Owen. 'I should not digress. I have probably drunk too much wine. Do you know, Archer, I think I begin to feel my mortality.' Thoresby glanced down at the piece of bread in front of him, then pushed it aside.

Owen stayed silent, made increasingly uncomfortable by the Archbishop's mood.

Thoresby nodded. 'I disturb you. I disturb myself these days.' He rubbed his eyes. 'Where was I? Oh yes, the merchants could not be sure of the King's support. He paid no heed to the edge in their voices. In the tenth year of Edward's reign, the merchants agreed to lend the Crown £200,000 and pledged to pay the King half of the profit on 30,000 sacks of wool. In return, the merchants would receive a monopoly; only those merchants who agreed to the terms of the bargain would be permitted to export wool. They were promised that their loan would be repaid by splitting the customs receipts with the Crown, and the customs were raised to forty shillings a sack. The wool was to be sent to Dordrecht in three shipments, and the King was to be paid in three instalments. A substantial number of the monopolists were members of the English Wool Company, which was led by a small core that included Reginald Conduit, William de la Pole and John Goldbetter.'

Owen sat forward. This began to sound like what Cecilia Ridley had told him. 'I cannot see why any wool merchants disagreed. At least it permitted them some trade.'

'By now many did not trust the King. In fact, it was those with enough power and money to hope to twist this to their increased profit who agreed, not the smaller merchants. They hoped to continue trading by hiding their shipments with the help of . . . unofficial shippers.'

'Pirates?'

Thoresby nodded. 'The powerful merchants were hiding shipments, too. A bit above board, a bit below board. And thus the King was disappointed in the results. The shipments were slow and the profit slender. He had the government seize what little wool arrived in customs, about 11,500 sacks, and put it up for sale. Merchants were given receipts of bonds for the wool. They could either redeem them directly at the Exchequer or use them in the future to ship wool duty free. But as the Crown was so short of money, redemption was unlikely. And, of course, the merchants had found another way to ship duty free. The King's scheme collapsed, and the wool collection halted.'

'The merchants have no allegiance to the Crown?'

'To be fair, they were given little cause.'

'But he is their King.'

Thoresby smiled at Owen. 'You have not completely lost your innocence, Archer. I am glad of that.'

'You have a gift for making me feel a fool for my years of service.'

'Years of service,' Thoresby repeated in an oddly sad tone, then shook his head. 'I digress again. The King was disappointed. And yet, against all reason, he continued to pursue his plan the following year. Another 20,000 sacks were to be seized and the producers given royal bonds promising payment out of tax proceeds. Even less wool was collected. More and more sacks were hidden away, then smuggled overseas and sold. Admittedly, production was lower in those years, but it could not have been as low as the customs reported — there was too much trade in Flanders for it to be so. I suspect that Goldbetter's trouble with the Crown had something to do with such activities.'

'I had no idea finance could be this confusing.'

Thoresby sighed. 'It is one of the more creative aspects of government.'

'As Lord Chancellor, why do you allow such dishonesty?'

'It is difficult and costly to catch thieves of this calibre, Archer.'

Owen rubbed his neck. 'It seems the King reigns on quicksand.'

'All our mortal lives we totter at the edge of a bog, Archer. The higher we sit, the deeper we sink when we lose our footing.'

Thoresby sat forward, hands on knees. 'Unfortunately, I must go to Windsor to be with the King for Christmas. I leave shortly. But I will not be idle. While there I shall go down to London for a few days on business and I will see what I can find out about Goldbetter.'

'And my task?' Owen hoped he might now be relieved of his duties until the Archbishop returned.

'Continue asking questions. My Lady Chapel becomes more precious to me every day. I would like to use Ridley's money.'

Owen sighed. 'I do not relish the task.'

'I know. But you will do it.'

Owen took his leave of the Archbishop with a troubled mind. For a while, as Thoresby explained the King's folly, he had seemed himself again, sardonic, assured. But the dark mood had returned. Owen did not like Thoresby in that mood. He worried that in such a mood Thoresby would confide in him. And the more Owen knew of Thoresby and his peers, the less he wanted to know.

Not that the merchants seemed any more admirable. Goldbetter and his associates served the King only if it benefited them. Were soldiers the only fools who served without question?

Enough of this. Better to concentrate on what he'd learned from Thoresby. While seeming to co-operate with the Crown, the wool merchants had hidden much of their wool and used pirates to transport the wool to Flanders. Gilbert Ridley had probably played a dangerous dual role in Calais. And Martin Wirthir, former soldier careful to stay in the shadows – was he a pirate? Cecilia had said that Ridley suspected Wirthir of acting as a liaison between prisoners of war in England and their families in France – but could Ridley have fabricated that suspicion to satisfy his wife's curiosity without implicating himself?

And what was the agreement that Goldbetter reached with Chiriton and Company that brought such a profit? Cecilia had suggested that Gilbert Ridley's business dealings had involved dishonesty and betrayals. No doubt. Owen was now certain that Thoresby's inquiries about Goldbetter and Company would turn up something in that vein.

Twelve

A Gleeful Conspirator

Weighed down by his gloomy thoughts, Owen headed down Petergate and through King's Square towards the Merchants' Hall. A man locked in the pillory on Pavement was being pelted with mud by two small, dirty boys. It put Owen in mind of the boy who was staying in his house. When would Jasper be free to roam the city without fear again?

Last night's snow had not melted much, and as the sun made a brave effort to shine forth, the icy roofs glistened. It was a welcome sight in this dark city. From the first day he had arrived in York, Owen felt the gloom here, the buildings huddled close together, the upper stories jutting out over the lower. Daylight rarely lit the narrow streets. Having only one eye, Owen disliked shadows. They could be deceptively deep or shallow. Without both eyes it was difficult to tell. Not that other folk liked the dark streets any more than he did. People sought out the squares and the churchyards for a bit of sky.

The Merchants' Hall had a nice border of grass around it, a glistening blanket of white at the moment.

Owen tried not to think about the dishonourable deals that might have funded this building as he walked up and knocked on the heavy door. A clerk answered. 'Ah, Captain Archer. What can we do for you?'

It amazed Owen how well known he was, all because he supervised the townsmen's practice at the butts. 'I am on business for the Archbishop, Master Clerk. Can you spare me some time?'

The man nodded and led Owen up the stairs. On the ground level the area was used as a hospital for the aged members of the guild and their wives. Up the stairs was the great hall with wooden partitions marking off some small rooms to the sides. The clerk led Owen to one of the side rooms, a tiny area lit by a casement window open to let more light in than the expensive greenish glass would allow. There were shelves for documents and a writing desk cluttered with pens and inkpots. A tiny brazier generated little warmth in the room, merely taking some of the damp chill out of the air from the open window.

'You have come about Masters Ridley and Crounce, I'll wager,' the clerk said, looking officious.

'In a sense, Master Clerk. I ask two things of you, the names and whereabouts of the actors who performed with Crounce last Corpus Christi, and where I might find Martin Wirthir, a Fleming who worked for Ridley.'

'Wirthir? Martin Wirthir?' The clerk shook his head. 'Not a guild member. I know all the names.'

'Have you ever heard the name before?'

The clerk shook his head again. 'But then there would be no cause, you see. If not guild business —' he shrugged. He was a little man, thin and oddly wizened for his age, which Owen guessed was not much past five and twenty.

'And the actors, Master Clerk?'

The clerk nodded enthusiastically. 'That I can give you. Can you read?'

'I am an apprentice apothecary. God help my customers if I cannot.'

The clerk flushed. 'Pardon, Captain Archer. I think of you down at St George's Field, showing us how to shoot. I forget that is not your daily trade.'

'So you will write the names and addresses down for me?'

'That I will do, yes, Captain. Though — Well, I should know why.' He looked embarrassed to be asking.

Owen thought it a sensible query. 'Since Crounce was murdered the day after he appeared in the pageant, I thought perhaps — if I'm very lucky — someone might have noticed something odd.'

The clerk brightened at that explanation. 'Oh, indeed. An excellent thought.' He screwed up his already wrinkled face. 'But it will take a moment. Have you seen our beautiful hall? Would you like to look around while I do this?'

Owen appreciated the chance to stretch and move about. 'Where do your members keep their bows? It is a good time for me to inspect them.' Owen was to check at random the longbows of the townsmen to see that they were made properly. He had precious little time to spend on this, so he welcomed this opportunity.

The clerk pointed out the door. 'The guild's bows are in a cabinet all the way on the other side of the hall. You are welcome to inspect them, Captain.'

Owen left the tiny cell and went back out into the light, high-ceilinged great hall. It bespoke the wealth of the members with its huge oak beams and white plaster. The floor was new wood, recently laid down. An odour of stale food and humanity came from below, and the damp smell of the River Foss and the King's Fish Pond nearby came from the windows. But this area was clean, well lit, and one could forgive the odours for the joy of real windows with pale green glass.

Owen found the cabinet and examined the bows. Only one was too short, even for the clerk, and the wood improperly prepared so that it might snap at any time. When the clerk scurried out with his list, Owen pointed this bow out to him.

The clerk nodded. 'I will tell the guild warden. He will speak with the owner.' He handed Owen the list. 'It is terrible about Ridley and Crounce. Some of the guild members worry that it's a plot against the guild.'

'I think not. Crounce and Ridley were clearly business partners. And friends.'

'So there's no hope it was just a coincidence?'

'What do you think, Master Clerk? Do you think that's likely?'

The clerk shook his head. 'This Wirthir you asked about. Do you think he might be guilty? Or might be next?'

'Guilty?' Owen shook his head. 'Of course I cannot know for sure, but I would say he might be the next victim. Unless he has disappeared from this part of the kingdom for good, he would have been foolish to murder two men so linked to him, don't you think?'

'Hatred drives men to do silly things,' the clerk said sagely.

Owen nodded. 'I will keep that in mind, Master Clerk. Now this list. Who would you seek out first?'

The clerk considered. 'Stanton,' he said. 'He knew Crounce best.'

Owen thanked him.

*

Stanton lived in a substantial house on Stonegate. Owen was lucky to find him inventorying stock in the ground floor cellar, a stone vaulted room that ran the length of the house. The man shook the dust off his hair and jerkin. 'Come up to the hall,' he said, leading Owen up the outside stairway. 'I welcome the excuse to wash some of the dust down with wine. You will join me?'

Owen agreed.

'We will not be interrupted,' Stanton said. 'My wife has the household out in the kitchen making candles.'

The hall was furnished with a heavy table and two high-backed chairs. Benches were pushed back against the wall. A simple tapestry hung on the wall furthest from the fire. Stanton invited Owen to sit at the table, which was beneath one of the two windows. He poured wine from an interesting pitcher.

Owen admired it.

'Got it in Italy, the one time I ventured so far. It is my pride and joy,' Stanton said, pleased. 'Well. So you're looking into Will Crounce's death, are you? A terrible thing. He was a good man, Captain Archer. A charitable soul. And our best actor. If his voice had been deeper, he most assuredly would have been our God in the play. He always remembered his lines, never stammered, never rushed.' Stanton played with the pitcher, turning it this way and that to admire it while he talked. 'His wife's family hated it, you know.'

'Hated what?'

'His taking part in the plays. Being an actor.' Stanton shook his head. 'Such a bother about something he did once a year. And for the Lord Jesus Christ.' He shook his head again.

'Was there anything unusual about Crounce's performance this year? Any sign that he was troubled? Distracted?'

Stanton took his hand off the pitcher and sat back with his cup of wine. 'Nay. He was good, was Will. It transformed him. I think the Lord Jesus inspired him, that's what I think. Folk always commended us for his Jesus. I cannot think who will take his place.' Stanton looked sad.

'So you noticed nothing out of the ordinary that day?'

'Nay. Nor did the others. We've all talked about it, you can be sure.' Stanton took a drink, frowned, then gave Owen a thoughtful look. 'Now that I think of it, John de Burgh did notice one thing I had not. Mistress de Melton was led away as Will spoke his last lines. She was a widow, mother to the boy Will was to sponsor in the guild. We all assumed Will meant to marry again. As the pageant wagon began to move, Will jumped off to find out what had happened, but no one knew aught but that she'd taken ill.'

'And it did not affect the rest of his performances?'

'You do not seem to understand. The performance is worship. What better way for Will to intercede with God on Mistress de Melton's behalf than to play the Christ better than he ever had before? Which he did, on that day, I must say.'

They both drained their cups. Owen rose. 'I should not keep you from your work. But one last question, Master Stanton. Did Crounce have any enemies that you knew of?'

'You mean someone who might want to kill him?' Stanton shook his head. 'As I said, he was a gentle soul. I could name a baker's dozen whose murders would have been less surprising.'

'Enemies who would not necessarily have wished to kill him?'

Stanton looked around him, though no one had disturbed them in the hall, then pulled his chair closer to Owen and leaned forward conspiratorially. 'I do not like gossip as a rule, Captain Archer, but there was the situation between Will and Mistress Ridley that we all wondered about. Gilbert Ridley was a man with a temper, and how he and Will never fought about Mistress Ridley I do not know. I can only assume that they were such good friends that Will meant more to Ridley than his wife did.'

'Are you saying that Crounce and Mistress Ridley were lovers?'

Stanton lifted his eyebrows and shrugged as if to say he did not know.

'But you assume.'

'Not me. Everyone.'

'There was talk? In public?'

'Only among members of the guild, to be sure. We do not share our problems with the townsmen.'

'Are there guild rules against such behaviour?'

'Not as such, but we pledge to obey the commandments.'

'And yet no one officially spoke to Will Crounce about his behaviour with Mistress Ridley, another guild member's wife?'

Stanton looked uncomfortable. 'Will was never caught in the act, you see. And there was Mistress de Melton. It looked as if Will meant to reform his ways.' Stanton shrugged. 'Then again, it might be just gossip. And I've insulted the dead.' He crossed himself.

Owen noted the man's discomfort and let the topic drop. 'Did you ever meet a business associate of Crounce's by the name of Martin Wirthir?'

Stanton screwed up his face, thinking, then shook his head. 'Name means naught to me.' He looked eagerly at Owen. 'Might he be the murderer, then? This Martin Wirthir?'

Owen shook his head. 'If he were, he would be a fool and easy to find. What do you know about Ridley? Did he have any enemies?'

Stanton sat back and chuckled. 'He was a brusque man, Captain Archer. And impressed with himself. God help me, but many a time I wished to put my fist through Ridley's teeth.'

'Would you have killed him?'

'Nay!' The merchant straightened up and pulled at his sleeves. 'I would never kill any man except to protect my family. Though I play a Bad Soul in the pageant, I am not a violent man.'

Owen wondered if Stanton appreciated how fortunate he was to be able to choose non-violence. No one had ever ordered Stanton into battle. 'Do you think any of the more violent guild members could have been driven to kill Ridley?'

Stanton shook his head.

'So Ridley was irritating, pompous, but not the sort of hateful that gets a man murdered?'

'Right,' said Stanton. 'And he was away so much, no one had to put up with him for long.'

'Oh!' The guild clerk raised an ink-stained finger and his eyes widened as a memory interrupted his copy-work. Should he go after the captain and tell him? It seemed a small point, but there might be something to it. Perhaps on his way home he would stop at the apothecary. He could use a soothing wash for his eyes. They were giving him trouble lately. So tired.

*

Owen had just returned and wearily stretched his frozen toes towards the fire. 'Has your mistress been busy all day?' he asked Tildy.

'Oh, aye.'

'I will work in the shop tomorrow so she can catch up on other things.'

'That would be nice, Captain. The horse-radish root has dried, and we should put it up.'

The beaded curtain rattled as Lucie came through. 'There's a man here to see you, Owen.'

Owen groaned. 'Who is it?'

'A clerk, from the ink on his fingers. He says he spoke with you this afternoon.'

'Oh, that clerk.' Owen rose and stretched, feeling his shoulder muscles crinkle. Questioning people was no work for a man. It crippled the body. He went out to the shop.

'Captain Archer.' The clerk smiled. He wore a cloak of fine wool, but well worn. A cast-off from one of the guild members, Owen guessed. 'I thought of something after you'd gone,' the clerk said, 'may be nothing of importance, but as I needed an eyewash I thought I'd come by and see you.'

'What's the trouble with the eyes?'

'By vespers I do not see so clearly.'

'You use your eyes in close work and little light all day, Master Clerk. It is a common complaint amongst such as yourself. Mistress Wilton has a soothing wash. A flask is a halfpenny.'

The clerk nodded. 'I'm willing to try it. And to tell you this, what I remembered when you'd gone. There was a man who sometimes came on business for Masters Crounce or Ridley. His speech was much like that of the Flemish weavers. He did not come often, and not lately. But here's something else. I once needed to send something on to him, and he directed it to the lodgings of Ambrose Coats, one of the town waits. I was to say it was for "the foreigner".'

Coats. Lucie had told Owen about the musician's visit. And what was now buried in the garden. 'Ambrose Coats? Are you certain?'

The clerk nodded. 'He plays the rebec and the crowd. You might say he's a bowman like yourself.' The clerk laughed at his joke.

'He is a friend of Martin Wirthir?'

The clerk got serious again. 'A friend? That I cannot say. I do not even know if Coats would remember aught about the foreigner – he may have stayed there the once only – but it might be worth a visit.'

'I thank you.' Owen handed the clerk a small clay bottle. 'I must enter your name in the ledger, Master Clerk. Mistress Wilton is keen on records.'

'I am John Fortescue,' the clerk said, and spelled it for Owen. 'I'll wager you're thinking it does not fit, eh?' He grinned.

Owen made an apologetic face. 'You sound a Yorkshireman through and through.'

'Oh, I am, Captain, through and through for many generations. But long ago my people came with William the Bastard, and though we are a poor branch, we carry the name with pride.'

'So your ancestors built the castles of York?'

'Aye, they did so, Captain. They did so.'

Owen thanked Fortescue again, and the clerk left a little taller for pride.

'An odd man,' Lucie commented when she returned to help Owen close up for the day.

Owen was thoughtful. 'He puts me in mind of Potter Digby.'

'Oh, no, never!' Lucie had never liked the summoner,

no matter how helpful he had been to Owen. 'This man was clean and looked trustworthy. What can you possibly see of Digby in him?'

Owen shrugged. 'I cannot say. Just a feeling he brings with him. Of gleeful conspiracy.'

Lucie raised an eyebrow. 'I am not certain I would find that pleasant.'

'He is pleasant, so I am saying it poorly, as usual.'

'You have a honeyed tongue,' Lucie said. 'It's my own lack of humour that is the problem.'

'Do you know what he came to tell me? That a foreigner who worked for Crounce and Ridley – Martin Wirthir, I'm guessing – stayed at least once with a town wait named Ambrose Coats.'

'Sweet Jesu. So the hand was left for Martin Wirthir as a warning, just as it was for Gilbert Ridley?'

'Perhaps. And perhaps the musician's friend was not Wirthir. There are other foreigners in York. I will go and talk with Coats tomorrow morning, before I open the shop.'

'You are opening the shop? What will His Grace say about that?'

'Thoresby is off to Windsor for Christmas. Besides, I owe you some time in there I should think. I am your apprentice, after all.'

Lucie's hug and smile made Owen feel well rewarded.

He stood up. 'I'll go and meet Jasper now.'

Lucie stayed him with a hand on his arm. 'Would you just welcome Jasper at first, ask no questions for a day or two? He's been through so much, I want him to feel welcome and safe.'

It was difficult to agree when Owen wanted so much to describe Kate Cooper to the boy and see if she had been the cloaked woman, but Owen saw the concern in Lucie's eyes. 'Whatever you think best. I will wait until you give me leave to question him.'

Owen was glad of his forbearance when Lucie kissed him. He would wait till Hell froze over to question the boy if it made Lucie that affectionate.

Thirteen

Liaisons

Ambrose Coats's address was Footless Lane, across from St Leonard's Hospital. Not enticing. Owen set out after fortifying himself with some ale and bread to see if Ambrose Coats remembered Martin Wirthir.

'You don't know that he will be awake at dawn,' Lucie warned. 'A musician might well sleep late if he performed last night.'

'Let's hope he is a reasonable man so that I can keep my promise to you to open the shop.'

The house was part of a row, this one distinguished by a large orange tabby wailing at the door. A slender man with dark blond curls opened the door just as Owen lifted his hand to knock. The blond smiled down at the cat and let it glide into the house, then glanced up. 'Forgive Merlin, sir. It is his nature to become hysterical when his routine is broken. I am late opening the door for him.' He smiled apologetically, but as he studied Owen's face his expression changed. 'Captain Archer?' There was a tension in his voice and face that had not been there a moment ago.

Owen silently cursed his scarred face that put people on guard. 'You must be Ambrose Coats, Town Wait?'

The man nodded. 'I am.' He stepped aside. 'Please, Captain, come in. The least I can do is offer you hospitality after leaving that horrible thing with Mistress Wilton.'

'I am surprised you know me, not being down at the butts on Sundays,' Owen said as he entered the small house. As a town wait, Ambrose had not to practise the longbow but to save his hands for his music.

'You are a noticeable man,' Ambrose said.

Owen reached up to the patch. 'Aye, that I am.'

Ambrose smiled. 'It adds a suggestion of danger in an already arresting face.'

Owen did not know how to respond to that. If the words had been spoken by a woman, he would have turned on his charm. But what could Ambrose Coats mean by such a remark?

Ambrose Coats's large, deep green eyes watched Owen nervously. 'Please, sit down.' Ambrose pulled the one chair in the room up to a brazier. 'Would you share my morning ale with me?'

'If you're offering.' Owen sat down.

Ambrose poured two cups of ale and pulled up a stool. 'I told Mistress Wilton what I could about the hand. I don't know what else I can tell you.'

'A neighbour's pig left it on your doorstep, is that what you think?'

'I cannot imagine how else it got there.'

'I can. I was told you might help me find someone. But I think someone else has discovered that he is a friend of yours, too.'

'Find someone? A musician? For a gathering?'

'No. I need to tell this person he may be in danger.'

Ambrose sat up even straighter than before. 'And who might this person be?'

'Martin Wirthir.'

The chin clenched and looked more prominent than ever.

'You do know him?' The man's expression made it clear that he did.

The musician thought about it, then shrugged. 'I know Wirthir. But I have not seen him for a long time. So perhaps that is why he does not come, because he is in danger?'

Ambrose Coats was clever. Quick. 'I doubt that Wirthir knows of his danger if he has not been in York of late,' said Owen. 'But it is important to get the message to him.'

'He was never one to announce his visits. Perhaps you could tell me what this is about, and if he shows up . . .'

'Your friend worked for Will Crounce and Gilbert Ridley, did you know that?'

'I know nothing of his business.'

'But you recognise the names, and you knew that Gilbert Ridley's hand was still missing. Do you also know that Will Crounce's hand was left with Ridley? As a warning that he was next, it seems. So now Gilbert Ridley's hand is left with Martin Wirthir.'

Ambrose fidgeted on the stool. 'This is not Martin's home.'

Owen shrugged. 'Crounce's hand was not left at Ridley's home, but in his room at the York Tavern. I understand Martin Wirthir has stayed here . . .'

'What do you want?'

'To speak with Wirthir. Tell him about the danger. Ask him what business deal might have spawned such grisly deaths.'

'Who are you working for?'

'The Archbishop.'

The green eyes widened. 'Truly.'

'The murders occurred in the minster liberty.'

'So they did. And you think someone knew Martin once stayed here and put the hand on my doorstep to warn Martin?'

'It seems likely. Do you have a better explanation of the odd coincidence of the three being business partners?'

'As I said, I did not know Martin worked with those men. How can I be certain that the Archbishop doesn't want to accuse Martin of the murders?'

'It would be a foolish murderer who would leave that hand to be discovered,' Owen said. 'From what I have heard of his activities, Wirthir is no fool.'

Ambrose played with the cup in his hands. 'There's a boy who witnessed one of the murders, isn't there? Whatever happened to him?' He kept his eyes down, his voice quiet, but Owen could tell it was not an idle question, that Ambrose was anxious for an answer.

'You must mean Jasper de Melton. I'm afraid he's disappeared. Poor boy. I'm sure he's in danger. Why do you ask?'

Ambrose took a drink. 'I wondered. He's disappeared, you say? Someone should have watched out for the boy.' The green eyes looked sad.

'I urged His Grace to do something to protect the boy, but he thought it unnecessary.' Owen drained his cup. 'Well, I will keep you no longer. Please send word if you see your friend.' He walked to the door, then turned back. 'There is one favour you might grant me.'

'What is that?'

'You could tell me what Martin Wirthir looks like.'

Ambrose shrugged. 'I can see no harm in it. Tall,

straight-backed, devil in his eye.' He cocked his head to one side, studying Owen. 'Dark hair. Like yours only straight.' He shook his head. 'No, lighter hair than yours. But dark. Lovely, deep voice. You will not find him if he does not wish to be found.'

'I can but try.' Owen opened the door, paused. 'I wonder. If your neighbour's pig bothers you so much, why have you not complained to the council?'

Ambrose met Owen's eye, did not flinch. A defiant look. 'There is no point in starting a feud with a neighbour.'

Owen studied the man. Lucie was right, there were things Ambrose did not say, and yet Owen had the feeling that what he did say was true. 'What is your relationship with Wirthir? How do you come to know a foreigner?'

Ambrose reddened. 'I meet all sorts of people in my work, Captain Archer. Martin is a delightful man, he needed a place to stay . . .' the musician shrugged.

Owen believed it, as far as it went. But there was much more to it, he was sure.

As he walked back to the shop, Owen mulled it over. Protective. Like his comrades-in-arms had been of each other. But Wirthir was a pirate, Coats a town wait. What was their bond?

Lucie scrubbed horse-radish roots and handed them to Tildy to grind. The pungent root had Lucie wiping her eyes every few minutes, but Tildy hardly seemed to notice. She frowned over her work and muttered to herself.

'What's troubling you?' Lucie asked when she could ignore the behaviour no longer.

Tildy hunched her shoulders. ''Tis naught, Mistress Lucie.'

'How is Jasper this morning?'

'He does better every day. It's good that he's here.'

'I see you made fish cakes this morning.'

Tildy nodded.

'Is Jasper ready for such food?'

'No, this is for you and Captain Archer. For being so good to Jasper. Not everyone would take him in.'

'So what is troubling you?'

The girl bit her bottom lip and turned towards Lucie. 'Is it a sin to swear an oath that has naught to do with God?'

Lucie did not have an immediate answer to that. She hoped that Tildy and John had not pledged their troth.

'What sort of oath, Tildy?'

'A secret. You know, never telling anyone else. That sort of thing.'

'You mean a secret a friend has told you? Or a secret oath?'

Tildy frowned. 'I'm not sure.'

'Did someone tell you something about himself and you promised not to tell anyone? Or did someone ask you to take an oath – perhaps you swore never to eat fish cakes again – and made you swear that you would tell no one?'

''Twas the first.'

Lucie was relieved. 'A secret like that is fine, Tildy, so long as it doesn't hurt anyone.'

Tildy was quiet, still biting her bottom lip. She'd begun to sniffle as the horse-radish root piled up beneath the grinder.

Lucie opened the kitchen door for air. 'It seems to me that you are rather fond of John. Am I right, Tildy?'

Tildy blushed and ducked her head.

'I don't mean to pry, but I can't help but wonder if your mood this morning has something to do with your feelings for John.'

'Oh no. John is fun to talk to and he's so nice to Jasper. No, I – I just feel so sorry for Jasper. So many awful things have happened to him.'

'Well, I'm glad to hear that John isn't breaking your heart.'

Tildy smiled through tears. 'He would never do that to me.'

Lucie coughed. 'This horse-radish root is about to choke me.'

'Your eyes are very red, Mistress Lucie.'

'So are yours. Why are we standing in here like fools?'

They laughed and rushed out the door, dissolving into coughing fits that turned into giggles. Lucie realised how fond she was of Tildy and hoped Bess was wrong about John. There was no way to protect Tildy from a broken heart if Bess was right. Tildy seemed firm in her affection.

Fourteen

The King's Mistress

Sleet drummed on the hood of Thoresby's cloak as he hurried down the path to the riverbank. He could already feel the freezing water seeping through his hood and hat to his head. Two servants tottered behind him, balancing a trunk full of papers and gifts on their shoulders. Ned, Thoresby's squire, carried a basket with food and wine for the journey; it was not a long barge trip upriver from London to Windsor, but Thoresby had been too busy to eat since early morning, and it was now mid afternoon. He cursed as his new boots sank into the mud on the riverbank. The bargeman looked surprised to hear such words coming from the mouth of the Archbishop of York.

'The sorry truth is, I'm more of a Lord Chancellor than an Archbishop,' Thoresby said.

'Your Grace?' the bargeman said with a blank face.

'Never mind.' Thoresby stepped aside to let the servants past with the trunk. 'Let's see if you can get me to Windsor before I freeze to death.'

'Yes, Your Grace.'

Thoresby took consolation in the thought that sleet down here in London likely meant snow in York, so he was still the better for being here, wet and cold though he was. He ducked under the canopy. Ned placed a cushion on the throne-like chair in the centre of the small enclosure, and Thoresby sat down, arranging his cloak around him for maximum warmth.

'Would you care for some wine, Your Grace?' Ned asked.

'Not yet. Try to get the mud off these boots first, Ned.'

While the boy worked at the boots with a stick and a rag, Thoresby sat back and reviewed his business in London. He had met with the second son of an old friend and advised the youth that if he truly wished to retreat as far from temptation as possible – he had been caught in bed with two cousins at once, both married women – he should have his father write to the abbot of Rievaulx, a Cistercian abbey up on the moors. Once up there, the youth might never see another woman as long as he lived. Thoresby had also put his most efficient and trustworthy clerk, Brother Florian, to work searching for records pertaining to Goldbetter and Company. Florian was intrigued to hear that his purpose was to uncover a murderer. In the midst of all that, in just one day Thoresby had ordered three tuns of wine to split between his cellars in York and London, and acquired the boots that were now just damp, no longer muddy.

'God bless you, Ned,' Thoresby said, examining his boots. 'These cost me as much as your entire wardrobe. Now I can enjoy my wine.'

The sleet still came down as they eased up to the dock at Windsor. Thoresby emerged from under the canopy reluctantly, but at least here he stepped off the barge onto wooden planking, blessedly free of mud. On the knoll above rose the castle. Thoresby could see that Wykeham was still at work expanding the structure. William de Wykeham's building projects had won great favour with the King. Wykeham was now Keeper of the Privy Seal, a post that typically led to that of Lord Chancellor. Thoresby had been Keeper of the Privy Seal. He wondered how long it would be before Edward took the Chancellor's chain from his neck and hung it around Wykeham's. A gloomy thought.

In the great hall, roaring fires and much wine warmed the courtiers, and hundreds of candles burned away all memory of the sleet outside. The flames reflected off jewels and brilliant fabrics. Thoresby had heard stories of Edward's first Christmas courts on ascending the throne – modest, plain, quiet, a necessary economy because Edward's father and mother, King Edward II and Queen Isabella, and John Mortimer, Isabella's lover, had emptied the royal coffers. But now, with victories in France bringing booty and ransoms, Edward let the court sparkle.

After Thoresby was thoroughly dry, he sought out Queen Phillippa. He was sorry to see that her health was still in decline. The Queen's face, which had always been round and of high colour, was now ashen, the flesh sagging. She leaned on a cane to walk about her chamber, a jewelled cane, but a cane nonetheless. The Queen had not been well since a riding accident eight years before, but until now she had managed to mask the limp. Only her finery shone as of old.

Thoresby's heart went out to the Queen. He had always admired her. She had been an inspired mate for Edward, a paragon of all the virtues lacking or weak in the King. Phillippa understood what her subjects wished a Queen to be and fulfilled their wishes, and the people loved her for it. Where Edward was quick to anger, Phillippa reacted with her head, not her heart. Edward held grudges, Phillippa strove to forgive. She had borne Edward twelve children; though some had died young, enough had survived to secure the succession and gain valuable allies with carefully arranged marriages. Thoresby felt he'd known Queen Phillippa all his life, certainly all his life at court. She always welcomed him with what seemed sincere pleasure, and her presents to him were thoughtfully chosen, more personal than opulent.

This afternoon he was not alone with the Queen. By a window sat Alice Perrers, sewing. She wore a gown of pale brown silk that matched her eyes. A babe lay in a basket at her feet. So she'd had the baby and it was still at court. Thoresby had assumed the baby would be sent away to a well-paid wet nurse as soon as it was born.

Queen Phillippa motioned to Thoresby to sit with her. 'I am pleased you have come. I have heard that work has begun on your Lady Chapel. I hope it goes well?'

'I have been blessed with talented and efficient masons so far. I hope that one day you might come see the progress we have made since your wedding mass at the minster.'

Queen Phillippa's eyes were sad as she shook her head. 'I do not think, my good friend, that God means me to make such a journey again.'

What brave, sad words. Thoresby did not waste his breath with polite denials. Hollow reassurance was pointless with such a woman as the Queen. All in all, it was a sad visit, and when Thoresby left Phillippa he was in a gloomy frame of mind.

Fortunately, Alice Perrers had not spoken to him. He had not known whether he could trust himself to be polite.

Flaunting the baby like that. How could the Queen permit it? How could she allow the King to make a fool of himself with Alice Perrers?

And what an old fool Edward looked, the once glorious warrior, stooping a bit now, his golden hair dull and lank, eyes recessed in reddened, wrinkled skin, cheeks puffed from rich food and too much wine.

That is how Thoresby saw Edward when he entered the King's great chamber for dinner. Already seated at the table, Phillippa to his right, Alice to his left, the King greeted Thoresby with affection. The Queen smiled sweetly, but said little. They both looked ancient beside Alice Perrers, who was now gowned in crimson, pearls about her neck and in her hair. The gown was cut sinfully low to show off a long, pale neck, softly rounded shoulders, and high, youthful – and at the moment lusciously swollen – breasts.

Thoresby tried not to stare at those breasts as he took his seat. Alice might not be beautiful, but she knew how to emphasise the youthfulness of her body.

'Your Grace,' Alice said to Thoresby, 'I understand that you are adding a Lady Chapel to the great cathedral of York Minster.'

The crimson gown accentuated the whiteness of Alice Perrers' skin, but did an odd thing with her pale brown eyes, giving them a crimson glow. A succubus might have such eyes, Thoresby thought.

'I have begun on the Lady Chapel,' Thoresby said.

A thin eyebrow lifted, a smile played at the corners of the generous mouth. 'To what do you attribute the recent resurgence of devotion to the Blessed Mother?'

Thoresby did not know what to make of the question. Was it rehearsed, something the King had suggested Alice ask, or was there an intelligence at work? He decided on the safest conversational ploy, turn the question back to her. 'As it is so uppermost in your mind, I think it would be far more interesting to hear your thoughts on the subject.' He said it politely, with a courteous bow.

The King smiled and nodded, pleased with Thoresby's response.

Alice Perrers sat back in her seat, her eyes momentarily on the cup in her hand. Thoresby noted spots of colour on her cheekbones and collarbone. Did the woman take his response as a slight? If so, there was intelligence here indeed.

While Thoresby was still watching, Alice put her cup down on the table and lifted her eyes to his. 'My opinion is possibly ill-formed, Your Grace, but I have not had the benefit of education. For what it is worth, I think the people yearn for an intercessor during frightening times, someone beloved of God the Father, who will ask Him to remember that they are but sinful children and although imperfect they are trying. Mary, Mother of God, is the perfect intercessor.' Alice dropped her eyes again, but not before Thoresby had seen a challenge in them.

Or a bravura. Was he imagining such sophistication in the woman, or was it really there?

'Are these frightening times?' Thoresby asked.

Alice looked surprised. 'Forgive me, Your Grace, but you know these are frightening times. I am a child of the plague years. I have lived with the fear of its return all my life. And it does keep returning. We are told that its visitations are punishment for our sins. There was the bad harvest two years ago, and this year. And a war, although blessedly it is fought in France, not here.'

'Mistress Alice's points are well conceived, are they not?' Queen Phillippa said with an indulgent smile.

The King beamed.

Thoresby had had enough of the upstart. 'Indeed they are. And appropriate for one who was orphaned by that dread disease.'

Alice did not try to hide her amazement. 'You have made a study of me, Your Grace?'

'Not really, Mistress Alice. But one hears these things . . .' He gave her his most benevolent smile. 'It is widely held that children of the plague years are more robust and are great survivors, did you know? Some say that God grants this strength to prove that He has not forsaken mankind, that the Death is but a warning.'

'How remarkable,' the King said, rising. 'But now we must allow the ladies to rest while we get down to business, John.'

Thoresby watched Alice gracefully rise and walk out of the chamber with a straight back and high head, supporting Queen Phillippa with one arm. There was an assurance about Alice Perrers that disturbed Thoresby's sense of propriety. She did not know her place. She played Queen. A commoner such as she could never rise to be Queen – a commoner who would bring nothing to a match to further the interests of the realm. But Alice Perrers affected a regal air. An arrogance. She was dangerous.

When the King and his Chancellor were alone but for a few trusted servants who were to keep the wine flowing and the fire hot, the King said to Thoresby, 'You have seen Mistress Alice's child, eh, John? Mistress Alice is an extraordinary woman. She bore that boy and missed hardly a day of service to

Phillippa. For a Christmas gift to Mistress Alice for her attention to duty, I would like to settle some London properties on her.'

'London properties?' Thoresby suppressed a groan. 'But surely her annuity and the clothes, the jewels, the honour of living at the court – surely all this is more than generous already.'

'And I mean to be more than generous, John. You know that Mistress Alice is dear to me, second only to Phillippa, my dearest Queen. The child is mine, you know. I hope it does not shock you. As my bastard son, he must want for nothing – though of course I can never publicly acknowledge him as mine.'

Thank the Lord for that, but the rest was disappointing enough. Thoresby wanted to shake the King, demand how he could insult Queen Phillippa in her illness, with such a common, scheming creature. But the Chancellor knew the limits of his sovereign's affections. He might not survive such an outburst.

'I am not shocked to hear of new proof of Your Grace's remarkable fertility,' Thoresby said in what he hoped was an affectionately teasing voice.

Edward fell back in his seat and roared with laughter.

Praise be to God, Thoresby still could dissemble convincingly.

'You never disappoint me, John. You never preach.' The King sobered. 'Did Mistress Alice tell you the child's name?'

'No.'

Edward's face lit up in an expansive smile. 'He was christened John. After you, for your friendship.'

Dear God, make it not so. Surely the boy had been named after Edward's son, John of Gaunt, Duke of Lancaster. Yes, Thoresby was sure that was the case. This was simply a ploy to endear the child to Thoresby.

'I require no reward but your friendship, my King.' Thoresby raised his glass. 'Let us drink to the young John.'

Edward beamed. 'I knew you would be pleased.'

Thoresby took a long drink. 'As to the gift of London property, if you are determined in this, I would advise that the gift be made in private.' Thoresby chose his words with care. 'Your affection for Mistress Alice is already noted at Court. To call more attention to her special standing might cause her difficulties. And the child might in later years bear the brunt.'

The King frowned into his cup. 'Mistress Alice is a remarkable young woman. To what could they possibly object?'

That was not a question that Thoresby could answer truthfully, much as he yearned to.

'It would be so with anyone. Your courtiers are jealous of your affection. It is their great love for you that makes it so.'

Edward finished his wine, waved away the servant who hurried to pour more. 'It is late. I am weary.' He studied Thoresby's face for a long moment. 'You are a good friend to me, John, and I thank you for it. But you need not coddle me. I know that Mistress Alice offends with her sharp wit and canny business sense. My Queen has these abilities, but they are softened by a nurturing *gentilesse* that makes the people love her.'

So Edward was not so blind. Thoresby was relieved. 'And Queen Phillippa was born to a noble family, my King. That is important to the people. Mistress Alice comes from nowhere.'

The King nodded. 'Which makes her all the more admirable, John.'

'You are a wise man who can see that, Your Grace.

The people are not so wise.'

'Indeed.' The King rose. 'We will talk more about the gifts. A list of the properties will be brought to you.' Edward began to depart, but turned, with a softened expression, to say, 'Phillippa and I are most glad to have you here, John. My Queen is unwell, as you can see. We need the comfort of good friends about us.'

'I am most honoured to be here, Your Grace.' Thoresby left after the King, exhausted from his journey and his efforts to be civil to and about Alice Perrers. It would be a long December.

Brother Florian arrived at Windsor on the third afternoon of Thoresby's visit. He was soaked through, having shared a barge with a group of jongleurs who had contrived to fill the enclosed area with their gear and persons before the clerk boarded, forcing him to make the trip as unprotected as the bargeman. Fortunately the sleet of the previous few days had subsided to a chill mist and occasional drizzle, but it was enough moisture to weigh down Florian's cloak and his mood.

'Might one ask, Your Grace, why these papers could not be entrusted to Brother Michaelo, your secretary, who sits so cosily in your chambers in London? Can he really have so much to do with the ordering and shipping of supplies to York that he could not be spared for this journey?' Brother Florian, white-haired and confident from years of experience, was not one to mince words.

'You have asked, Brother Florian, and I am happy to answer.' Thoresby smiled. 'I do not entrust the papers to Brother Michaelo because I cannot be certain that he will not trade their contents for some of the luxuries he finds irresistible. Whereas Michaelo is very good at the tasks to which I have set him, because he knows that he will share in the enjoyment of these items if they reach my houses in Yorkshire. It is all actually quite tidy. Do you not enjoy being indispensable?'

Brother Florian snorted. 'Had I been truly indispensable you would not have passed me over when looking for a secretary to replace Jehannes, Your Grace. It is no doubt Brother Michaelo's Norman wealth that is truly indispensable.' Florian raised his cup to his lips, discovered it was empty, and thumped it down with a growl.

'I see that your river voyage chilled your soul, a penance out of all proportion to your simple sins.' Thoresby pushed the flagon of wine over to the monk. 'We will dine well tonight. That should cheer you.'

When Brother Florian had gone away to improve his disposition with prayer and a nap, Thoresby opened the packet of notes and documents and settled back to read. He was pleased to find that Florian had done his usual thorough job.

According to court records, just as Chiriton and Company had informed on Goldbetter, Goldbetter had informed on business associates who smuggled wool to Flanders to avoid customs fees. Various Goldbetter and Company agents had provided a list of smugglers in exchange for a blind eye to their own less questionable but still not quite legal activities. Ridley and Crounce had been among the agents who provided names, but it was not recorded who had informed on whom.

Florian had included a list of the smugglers who had been sent to the Fleet prison, annotated with information gained at the prison itself. Excellent Florian, to take the time to visit the prison. Most of the smugglers had been released after a brief stay, two were still there because of later information brought against them to compound their sentences, and one had died in prison. This last had been one Alan of Aldborough.

That interested Thoresby. Aldborough was near Boroughbridge, where Will Crounce had lived. Crounce might have been privy to local gossip about Aldborough's business transactions. It was possible that someone in Alan of Aldborough's family was avenging the man's death.

Brother Florian had discovered another interesting fact about Aldborough. After two cups of brandywine the jailer confided that he had been most surprised when Aldborough sickened and died in two days. He had been remarkably healthy and optimistic up to that point.

The next day Thoresby found a courtier who was sending a messenger north and added a letter to Owen Archer to the messenger's load.

Fifteen

Nightmares

Wind rattled the shutters and sent draughts dancing through the house. Lucie woke to the sound, realised it was just the wind, and curled up against Owen's warm back. And then she heard the scream. And again. The second one woke Owen.

'What the Devil?' he grumbled, sitting up and rubbing his scarred eye.

'It's Jasper again. I'll go and see if Tildy needs me.' Lucie threw on her shift, then a shawl.

Owen caught Lucie's arm. 'Let it be. Tildy likes comforting him. You need rest. You've been so pale. If you get up every night for Jasper's dreams you will sicken, and then I'll have him out of the house.'

Lucie sat on the edge of the bed. 'Owen, please. He's just a boy. I had bad dreams after my mother died. I know how frightened he is. I remember.'

'You've taken him in. You've done that for him. And Tildy's down there right now rocking him and crooning, you know that. Let it be. She's done wonders with the boy.' Owen grabbed Lucie's shift and dragged her over to him, holding her tight.

'He's frightened, Owen. He needs to feel welcome. A part of the household. Then he'll feel safer. He keeps apologising for being here.'

'I will talk to him in the morning. I will not let you lose more sleep over the boy. There is no need.'

When Owen went down to the kitchen in the morning, Jasper was sitting beside the fire clutching a cup of steaming liquid. He was a handsome lad with expressive eyes and golden hair.

Owen pulled up a stool and sat down beside Jasper. 'I'm glad to see you mending, lad. We're all grateful that the Lord did not mean to take you just yet.'

'Thank you, Captain Archer.' Jasper's eyes were wary.

Owen poured himself some ale. 'How old are you, Jasper?'

'I will be nine this winter.'

'Nine years.' Owen nodded, took a drink. 'A good age to begin to build the strength for the longbow, it seems to me. What do you say, Jasper?'

The boy shrugged and looked away, but Owen saw the glitter of a tear sliding down Jasper's cheek. 'My arm's still bandaged.' The boy lifted his right arm.

'It's healing well, I hear. We can work around it at first. Besides, a strong lad like yourself must find it hard to be stuck indoors. After you've broken your fast, would you like to go out with me and start strengthening your left arm?'

Jasper turned back to Owen with a friendlier look, but then frowned. 'I cannot be seen.'

'So much the better that we have a walled garden. Mistress Merchet at the York Tavern has no guests staying in the room with the window that looks down into the garden, and no other buildings around us are tall enough for anyone to see in, unless they climb atop roofs to do so. And scaling a roof, well, we would notice that, wouldn't we, lad? So you've got a bit of space outdoors to walk about in.'

The boy's face brightened a little, but he still looked uncertain. 'Why are you being so good to me?'

Owen grinned. 'Now, that's a good question, Jasper. You know that Mistress Wilton is a Master Apothecary?'

The boy nodded.

'So we have the expertise here to get you well. So does the Riverwoman, but she has no space that's private like this. We do not invite strangers back into the house. All in all, it seemed a good place for you.'

'But why are you helping me?'

'Because it is the Christian thing to do?' Owen grinned as Jasper shook his head. 'You are right to distrust such an answer, Jasper. The whole city knows of your trouble, and there are doubtless some murderers looking for you.'

Jasper looked down at the cup in his hands. 'You've heard that I watched them murder Master Crounce.'

'A terrible thing to watch, a friend being attacked.'

'I didn't help him,' Jasper whispered.

So that was part of the boy's problem. He felt guilty. 'That is nothing to feel bad about, Jasper. What could you do against armed men? A soldier is wise to know when it is best to keep quiet, stay alive, and go for help. Which you did.'

The boy looked up at Owen. 'Really?'

Owen nodded. 'I have also heard that your mother died afterwards. That is what the city at large knows.'

'Did Mistress Digby tell you anything more?'

Owen wondered where the boy was going with that question. He wanted to be as honest as possible with the boy without telling him how involved he was in finding the murderers. That would surely make the boy nervous.

'Would it bother you if Mistress Digby had spoken to us about you?'

Jasper shrugged. 'I wondered, that's all.'

'We know what Mistress Digby knows.'

Jasper tried a smile. 'If the Riverwoman trusts you, then I do, too.'

'Thank you. Well.' Owen stood up. 'You finish what you're drinking and have a bit of bread and cheese, too, for it's cold outside. Then we'll go out in the garden and see how strong you are.'

Tildy took her cue and bustled Jasper over to the food she'd set out for him. The boy bolted down his food and declared himself ready.

Low, grey clouds threatened snow, but so far the day was dry. Last night's windstorm had scattered some debris from the trees about the garden.

'You might pick up the branches and take them to the back of the garden later,' Owen suggested.

'I will, Captain Archer.' Jasper seemed pleased to be given a task.

Owen had a bow slung over his shoulder. When he and the boy reached the woodpile, Owen shrugged off the longbow and held it up to the boy. The seven-foot bow was several feet taller than Jasper, though he was tall for his age.

'My father's bow was decorated,' Jasper said, eyeing the plain wood.

'They're beautiful when they're painted, aren't they?' Owen said, though he preferred his plain. He liked a clean sweep of wood. 'Do you have your father's bow hidden somewhere?'

Jasper dropped his head. 'I had to leave it when I went into hiding.'

'That must have been hard for you. You've had to be a brave lad. I doubt I would have survived so well when I was your age.'

'Tildy says you're from Wales.'

'Tildy's right about that. I'm a long way from home.' Owen held the bow out to Jasper. 'Do you know how to hold this?'

'I've watched them practising at the butts.'

'Show me.' Owen kicked a wide plank of wood over to the boy. 'Keep the bottom of the bow on that so that it doesn't dig into the mud. The string would be no use to me then.'

Jasper took the bow, an unwieldy thing being so tall for him, and managed to reach his left hand to the middle. With his right he touched the string. He looked up at Owen for approval.

'Excellent. Now pull back with your right hand.'

Jasper looked down at his splinted forearm. 'I can't.'

'See what you can do. We need a marker to see where we began. Then you can track your progress.'

The boy took a deep breath, clenched his jaw, and managed to pull the string. The movement was tiny and brought sweat out on the boy's forehead and upper lip, though the day was cold.

'Enough!' Owen said.

The boy let his breath out as he let go the string. Owen caught up the bow and slung it over his shoulder again.

'Now we'll begin to work on the left arm. You must grasp the bow strong and steady with your left hand, and a strong, steady arm is what makes that possible. So,' Owen picked up a round, smooth stick he'd brought along and handed it to the boy, 'hold this out in front of you in your left hand, arm straight and stiff, and don't move.'

'How long?' Jasper asked, raising his arm.

'Until you cannot hold it out there any longer. Your arm will feel as if the stick has become a lead ball or a rock. That's what you want. That makes you strong.'

Jasper took a deep breath and held it as he stood with his arm out, his hand grasping the stick.

Owen smiled. 'You must neither talk nor squirm, lad, but you must breathe. It does you no good to get light-headed.'

In a few moments, the boy began to wobble.

'Begin again, and this time stand with your feet a bit apart.' Owen showed Jasper. 'It helps to steady you.'

The boy shook his arm out, planted his feet about a foot apart, and lifted his arm with a look of grim determination.

Owen moved around Jasper, adjusting the boy's arm, feeling his back and easing it upright, pushing his head so that it rested straight on his neck. Owen knew how much pain an awkward posture could cause.

Jasper held the stick steady. He lasted longer than Owen had expected, considering the boy's weakened condition.

'Excellent, Jasper. That's enough for today. Tomorrow we'll do that again.'

'Thank you, Captain Archer.' Jasper looked happy for the first time.

Owen nodded. 'It's nice to have someone to train from the beginning. I can make sure you have the right habits from the start.'

'Tildy says Welshmen are born knowing how to shoot the longbow.'

Owen laughed. 'Not true, Jasper. We must learn. Practise. It's hard work being an archer.'

'I'll work hard, Captain.'

Owen looked at the earnest face, the glow in the cheeks from the outdoors and a bit of exertion. 'You've shown me that already. Was your father an archer?'

'Just for sport. He was a carpenter. But he was a good bowman. Folk said so.'

'A carpenter? I thought you were going to apprentice to the Mercers' Guild.'

The boy nodded.

'Did you not want to apprentice as a carpenter?'

Jasper bit the inside of his mouth and shrugged. 'Dad fell from a scaffold working in the castle.'

'Ah. So your mother thought she'd like you safe as a merchant.' Owen nodded. 'It makes sense.' Though considering the fates of Crounce and Ridley . . .

Jasper cocked his head to one side and looked up at Owen. 'Could I try it again?'

Owen grinned and handed Jasper the stick.

The boy took his stance with a determined set to his shoulders, lifted his arm and eased it into position, adjusting his shoulder just as Owen had shown him.

He would do well.

Owen walked away from Jasper for a moment, looking about, checking the rooftops around them. When Owen turned back, Jasper still stood. Owen sat down and waited. The boy's arm trembled slightly, but not badly. Sweat beaded on Jasper's upper lip, darkened the hair that fell over his forehead. At last, with an explosive sigh, the boy dropped the arm. He'd lasted almost three times as long as on the last try.

'So. Today, whenever you notice that shoulder, move it around like this.' Owen showed Jasper how to bring the shoulder forward, up, back and around. Jasper tried it. 'Good. That will keep it from getting too stiff to go on with your training tomorrow. That is, if you want to go on.' Owen gave the boy a questioning look.

'Oh yes, Captain. I do want to go on.' Jasper smiled.

'You're strong for your age. I suppose it takes some strength to keep the wheels of a pageant wagon greased, eh? Were you tired after a day of that?'

The boy nodded. 'My back hurt. And I got some bruises when I missed my footing.'

'No doubt. How did you train for that?'

'They showed me the day before as they moved the wagon to Toft Green.'

'Did they pick you for your strength?'

Jasper shrugged. 'Master Crounce just told me I was to do it. I don't know if they even knew who I was.'

Snow had begun to fall softly. Owen stood up. 'You'd best get to work picking up the branches that fell last night before they're buried in the snow. Then get inside and have Tildy give you something to warm you. I don't want you getting a chill.' Owen patted Jasper on the back. 'No doubt you'll sleep more peacefully tonight.'

Jasper grew red at the mention of his troubled sleep. 'I'm sorry if I wake you and Mistress Wilton.'

'I'm sorry you still have bad dreams. You're safe with us, you know.'

Jasper bent down to pick up some sticks.

'What is it you dream about, Jasper?'

The wary look returned to the boy's eyes. 'It's naught.'

Owen could see that he'd overstepped the boy's carefully guarded boundaries. He would wait and try again another day.

Sleet pelted against the casement beside the table the King had provided Thoresby with for his work.

Thoresby sat with his left elbow on the table, his hand supporting his head, as he looked up, idly watching the icy water run down the glass, meander round the imperfections, seeking the sill, where it no doubt puddled and overflowed.

Though he watched the rain, his thoughts were on Alice Perrers, how cleverly she had insinuated her way into the royal household, how she had mastered plucking the strings of the King's affections until they sang at her touch. Thoresby had observed her bend and sway with the King's moods, pry and prod to discover their causes, then side with the King whatever his desire, whatever his complaint – most of the time. So that when she suggested an alternative path, the King listened, for it was so unusual for her to express a contrary opinion that it must be important when she did. Was there ever such another manipulator as Alice Perrers?

Beneath Thoresby's hands lay several documents describing properties in London owned by the King, properties that should rather go to one of the King's children than to Alice Perrers. What did the King see in her? Thoresby remembered the crimson glow to her eyes his first night at Windsor. Might she have a pact with the Devil? It was not impossible. Now that he thought of it, how else could such a plain, outspoken, immoral woman take over the King?

Woman. Thoresby snorted. More like a girl. She was but seventeen.

And already she had such power – and knew how to use it. Her uncles must have realised her intelligence and seen their opportunity. But how had they got her to Court? Thoresby could smell a rat, or a pack of them – but he needed proof. His most damning evidence against them so far was the lack of evidence. A family that had climbed to prominence so recently must have done so through business deals and court suits, leaving a trail of paper and vellum. But he could find no such trail behind the Perrers family. They had taken care to cover it up. Damn them. He must have a clear case before he approached the smitten King.

Thoresby looked down at the papers and pushed them aside, reaching instead for the flagon of wine that a pretty maid had brought him. Why couldn't the King satisfy his lust with a girl like the maid, unassuming, happy to be noticed by her lord and master? If she bore the King's child she would not demand properties in London. She would be happy to be sent away to wed a farmer, while the child would be raised in a suitably noble household.

Sent away. Now there was a thought. What if he suggested such a clever match for Mistress Alice that the King could not resist? Someone rich and important to the King.

Failing that, what if she should die suddenly? In mysterious circumstances.

Sweet Mary in Heaven, he was the Archbishop of York and Lord Chancellor of England. He should not waste his time plotting the death of the King's mistress. She was trivial. Unimportant.

No, that argument did not work. The King had made Alice Perrers important. Her uncles might have placed her at Court, but it was the King who kept her there. What Thoresby wanted to know was why the King had chosen her. Perhaps she was indeed the Devil's handmaiden.

Thoresby straightened as he heard a commotion outside his door – the rattle of weapons, an angry footfall. It would be the King, irritated that Thoresby dawdled over the deeds. Thoresby gathered the documents in front of him. As the King entered, the Chancellor was bent over his work. Feigning surprise and confusion, Thoresby glanced up, then rushed to stand. 'My Lord.' He made a flustered bow.

High colour and dark eyes verified Thoresby's guess that the King was angry.

'Why is my Lord Chancellor asking about the wool smugglers I sent to the Fleet?' Edward demanded.

Thoresby was caught so off guard he could think of no instant answer. Who had told the King?

'Do you dare disapprove?' the King demanded.

'Disapprove? No, Your Grace. Not at all.'

'I will not be told how to finance this war.' Edward pounded his fist on the table.

Thoresby lunged for his cup of wine as it began to topple. He managed to prevent most of the spillage. 'Your Grace, please let me explain. My clerks were set to gathering background information concerning two murders in York. I would not think of criticising your decisions, my Lord.'

The King sat down opposite Thoresby. 'What murders?'

'Two members of the Mercers' Guild. Both murdered within my liberty of St Peter. Both in the same manner, their throats slit and their right hands cut off.'

Edward grabbed the cup of wine and drank. 'So someone thought they were thieves. A deal gone wrong. These merchants are wont to cheat each other.'

Thoresby shrugged. 'Perhaps, Your Grace. But I desire facts. And since they were agents for John Goldbetter, I thought the records would suggest some motive, and perhaps even the murderer's identity.'

'Why do you care about those Northerners, John? Haven't you enough to do as my Chancellor? I did not expect you to neglect your duties as Chancellor when you became Archbishop of York.'

'Forgive me if I have offended. Perhaps I am giving too much attention to this. But you see, one of the victims, Gilbert Ridley, had just delivered to me a large sum of money for my Lady Chapel. I do not want to use it on the chapel if the money was stolen.'

The King threw back his head and laughed. 'Good God, man, if it's money earned in trade, it's bound to have been stolen from someone.'

'Please, Your Grace, I want to please our heavenly Father and the most Blessed Virgin Mary with this chapel.'

'You think to buy your way to sainthood? You're no saint, John. You'll fool no one.'

'I am quite earnest, Your Grace. I wish to make reparation for my sins.'

The King gave his Chancellor a long, searching look. 'You know, John, you begin to take your post in York too seriously. Have you no Dean of the Chapter? No archdeacons?'

'Yes, of course, but —'

'There you are. They are to do the work for you. You go up there too often. They will begin to depend on your being there. It makes them lazy.'

Perhaps before Thoresby murdered Alice Perrers, he should study her technique. He was handling the King clumsily.

Edward took out a jewelled dagger and poked at something in the palm of his hand, then reached over with the dagger and poked the papers in front of Thoresby.

'What is taking you so long, John? I asked you simply to choose the property that would be best for Mistress Alice.'

Thoresby pressed his thumbs into the muscle between his eyebrows. The pain calmed him. He faced the King. 'What is best for Mistress Alice in what way? Do you wish her to be inconspicuous? Then you should choose a site well away from London. Do you wish her to be close at hand? Then it would be best to keep her as your Queen's lady of the chamber. A house in London will keep her away from you. Do you wish to provide a comfortable home for the boy? Again, choose a house well away from the Court.' Thoresby threw up his hands. 'You see my dilemma. I find it inadvisable to give such a gift at all.'

'*Merde*. All argument, no substance. You sound more like a cleric every day. You disappoint me, John.'

Those words might be the beginning of the death knell for Thoresby's career. But rather than anxiety, he felt a perverse twinge of relief. He was not himself. He must be unwell.

Unwell. That could be useful. 'Your Grace, I confess to not knowing myself of late.' Thoresby used his sincerest, humblest voice. 'This morbid fascination with the murders, my obsession with the Lady Chapel, my tomb. Perhaps I should leave the court for this joyous season, retreat to York. I am not healthy company —'

'No!' the King thundered. Then, in a quieter voice, 'I will not allow it.' The veins stood out on the King's large hands, belying his gentle tone. He was angry. 'I need you here to arrange the deed of trust for Mistress Alice. I will not have you running off to the North Country to play with your murders and tombs. The moors have made you choleric, John. That is the problem. The worst thing for you would be to spend the solstice up in that darkness.'

'But if I cannot make a good decision, Your Grace —' Thoresby held his hands out, palms up in supplication. 'You do not need me for a deed of trust. Any lawyer can draw it up for you.'

The King toyed with the dagger, turning it this way and that. A dangerous quiet had descended on the room. Only the crackling fire and the sleet tapping against the window dared break the tense silence.

Then the King sighed. 'One might almost think that you disapprove of Mistress Alice, John. But we are old friends. You have served me well and faithfully. I will not take up such suspicions.' The King rose.

Thoresby rose.

'We will talk again tomorrow.' The King's voice was still quiet, controlled. 'You will have a decision for me then.' Edward turned and marched from the room.

Thoresby shivered. He had not handled that well. Not at all well. Perhaps Mistress Alice had put a curse on him.

Sixteen

Uncomfortable Encounters

W ind whipped around Thoresby as he stood on the battlements of Windsor Castle, watching the dying embers of a fire that had caused a moment of excitement in early evening, way out at the edge of the town's fields. The sleet had stopped as a freezing wind came down from the north. The frozen limb of a tree had fallen on a woodcutter's hut while the family huddled around the supper fire. The hut had ignited, then a pile of wood outside the hut. Two children had survived, faster to run from danger than their parents.

It seemed a random accident, not an act of God. What could man learn from such a death? Not to live at the edge of the forest? Not to have a fire in one's hut? Would their parents dying in such a way, and an infant sibling, make better Christians of the children who survived? Or was all death pointless? Was Thoresby's obsession with the purpose behind the murders of Crounce and Ridley just a search for an antidote to his fear of dying?

Thoresby turned away from the glowing embers,

crossed the icy stones and descended into the castle, to warmth and light. He paused in front of his chamber, considered going to the chapel to pray for the souls of the woodcutter, his wife and their babe. But Thoresby's toes were numb and his hands stiff with cold. He would first warm himself with fire and brandywine.

His selfishness was punished at once. He entered the room to find Alice Perrers seated at the fire, sipping from her own jewelled goblet. Ned shrugged in response to Thoresby's questioning glance.

Alice rose respectfully as Thoresby approached.

'Your Grace,' she murmured, curtsying neatly. She raised her eyes to his. The fire turned her light brown eyes into cat's eyes.

Thoresby found his heart pounding.

'Please.' He motioned for Alice to resume her seat. 'You looked so comfortable there.' He would not let her see how he loathed her. 'This is a most unexpected pleasure, Mistress Alice.'

Ned came forward with a chair for the Chancellor, then poured him some brandywine. Thoresby nodded. 'You anticipate me, Ned. God bless you.'

Alice watched Thoresby get settled.

He took his time, letting Ned hold his cup of brandy-wine while he rubbed his hands over the fire, ensuring that they warmed up enough so he could hold the cup without mishap. Thoresby then took his brandywine and asked Ned to remove his damp boots and replace them with dry shoes.

All the while the cat eyes watched. When Thoresby at last seemed settled, and Ned had retreated to his post in the shadows, Mistress Alice smiled. 'Please forgive my intrusion, Your Grace, but I did not want to wait till morning. At table this evening, the King spoke of your concern over murders that occurred in your liberty.'

Thoresby sipped, watching the long, pale face over the rim of his cup. He said nothing.

Mistress Alice did not squirm under his close regard. Indeed, she seemed to preen in it. The cat eyes shimmered in the firelight. 'I said that I thought your concern was to be admired, and that your duties as Archbishop are far more important than my Christmas gift.'

What did this woman possess that made her so self-assured, so bold before the Lord Chancellor of England, Thoresby wondered. 'The King spoke of the murders?' He tried to concentrate on her words and not her slender neck, which would be so easy to crush, or her white breasts, which brought on quite a different thought.

'I once attended the Corpus Christi plays in your city.' Alice smiled. 'The King says that one of the victims was the man who played the Christ in *The Last Judgement*. I remember him. Perhaps because it was the last play of the day, perhaps because of his performance. He was so excellent in the part I remember thinking that he must truly be a good man to be able to play that part so movingly. You must find his murderer.'

You must. Sweet Saviour, how was he to bear this? Thoresby did not look in her eyes, knowing that his were burning with fury. But the tightness in his voice betrayed him. 'It is gratifying to hear you say so.'

Silence. Ash whispered in the hearth as a log settled. Thoresby could hear the wind far up at the top of the chimney. He glanced at Mistress Alice. The cat eyes searched his face. The pale cheeks were flushed.

'Forgive me,' Alice said. 'I can see that I overstepped. Please, Your Grace, I did not mean to offend. I hoped to —' A cloth was drawn from a sleeve, dabbed at the lips. 'The King regards you as one of his most trusted administrators. I would be your friend. But I have been awkward.'

Thoresby did not for a moment believe she wanted friendship. But there was nothing to be gained by bullying the woman. 'Let us begin again, Mistress Alice. You have heard of the murders in my liberty. You understand my concern. You remember Will Crounce. You feel this is all more important than your Christmas gift. Is that what you wished to say to me?'

She was not such a good actress that she could hide the flush that came to her pale face at his curt summation. But her voice was smooth, meek. 'That is simply the background, Your Grace. What I wished to tell you is that I have prevailed on the King to permit your return to York. And I hope that you might take with you a letter to my cousin in Ripon in return for my intercession. It is a small thing to ask, is it not?'

Thoresby could not deny that it was little to ask. He was free to go, to escape this impossible situation. And to carry a letter for the woman relieved him of any future indebtedness to her. Yet it was odious to him to do anything for her.

'Ripon, you say? That is some way north of York.'

'But surely you have a messenger you could send from the city?'

'As surely as you have messengers you could send from Windsor.'

The cat eyes met and held Thoresby's. An energy passed between them that would surely have felled most wills. Thoresby was shocked to feel himself sexually aroused.

She suddenly broke the hold and smiled secretly to herself as she smoothed her skirt. 'Your Grace,

I asked such a favour in good faith, having learned of your kindness to a former favourite of the King – Marguerite.' The eyes rose to his once more.

Thoresby hoped his face did not betray his shock. Marguerite. How in God's earth had the trollop discovered Marguerite? They had been so careful – so fearful the King would discover them. Marguerite. If he denied it, the woman who stared at the world through those chilling eyes would find a way to ruin him with the King. She was quite a player. He must back away. This must be Thoresby's penance for those exquisite nights suckling the rosiest nipples in God's creation. He must give in to Alice Perrers.

Thoresby nodded. 'I send missives to my bishop in Ripon, so it is no trouble. Who is this cousin?'

The cat eyes lit up with triumph. 'Paul Scorby.'

Scorby. The name was familiar, but Thoresby could not place it. 'Is he a guild member in York? You said you had seen the pageants.'

'I was not there as Paul's guest. One of my uncles had business in York and took me with him to act as hostess.'

'Ah. Well, the name is not foreign to me, but I cannot place him.'

'So you will carry the letter?'

Thoresby gave a small, acquiescent bow, his stomach churning. 'I can hardly decline such a trivial request when you have freed me to pursue a problem that weighs so on my mind.'

When Mistress Alice was gone, Thoresby resisted the urge to slam his cup into the door. How dare she intercede for him with the King? How dare she presume that her influence over the King was greater than his? How dare she ask him to be her messenger? How dare she speak Marguerite's name? Trembling with rage, Thoresby paced to calm himself. When he felt more in control, he went to the chapel.

There, in the quiet, Thoresby admitted to himself that in the end Alice Perrers had done him a favour. And herself. By leaving Windsor, Thoresby would escape any more such encounters. His response to Perrers disturbed him. She aroused him, but in a savage way. He wanted to throw her down on the floor and ravish her. Tear at those white breasts with his teeth. Devour her. Perhaps he had been without a woman too long. Or perhaps she was a witch. How else could she resurrect his passions with such violence? When Marguerite died in childbed, Thoresby had thought his carnal lusts were stilled for ever. Alice Perrers had proven that untrue. Only his gentleness had been buried with Marguerite.

Jasper, obsessed with his preparation for using the longbow, begged Owen to take him to one of the Sunday practices on St George's Field. No matter how Owen argued that it was dangerous for Jasper to go out in public, the boy persisted. At last Owen took pity on the boy and agreed – as long as Jasper went in disguise.

On the promised morning, Tildy held a polished steel mirror up for Jasper to see his blond hair now bright red. Lucie had used henna on his hair and eyebrows. Tildy had taken Owen's old leather vest and leggings and cut them down for Jasper. With a little padding added to change his shape, and a short cape with a hood to throw shadow on his face, Jasper was indeed difficult to recognise.

He was elated. He had gradually steadied and strengthened his left arm, his right arm was no longer splinted, and he was now carving a small bow. It was not finished, but the purpose of today's excursion was not actually to practise, but to watch, to listen to what Captain Archer said to the men, to prepare himself for the day, coming soon, when he would draw his own bow.

Lucie watched Jasper with a worried frown.

'I will be careful,' Jasper said.

Lucie smiled. 'I do not fear that you will be reckless, Jasper. But I wonder if you are ready for this. Do you feel well enough to spend such a long while outside? It is much chillier down by the river than in the garden here.'

'I feel fine,' Jasper insisted.

Owen laughed when he came down to the kitchen and saw the red hair. 'And who might this fiery-headed lad be?' he teased, slapping Jasper on the shoulder.

Jasper admired Owen. He looked every inch a soldier, with his height, the longbow and quiver of arrows hanging from his broad shoulders, the patch on the left eye with the bit of scar that showed beneath it. And the ear-ring. Jasper hoped that someday he could have an ear-ring. He had another friend who wore an ear-ring with a precious stone that Jasper admired.

As they passed the friary, more sky was visible overhead and Jasper was happy to see that the sun shone. He knew that no practice took place in rain because the bow strings were not to get wet. 'Look at the sun, Captain. It is a good morning for practice.'

'The sun is not always the friend of an archer, Jasper,' Owen said, striding along. 'In practice we can adjust the butts so that we do not shoot with the sun in our eyes. But in battle, that is not possible. You must hope that your commander is in control of the battle formation and the sun will not be shining in your face, but will be behind you, blinding the enemy. That worked to our benefit at Crécy.'

They passed the castle, then St George's Chapel, and walked out onto St George's Field, a triangular plot of land that lay between the Ouse and the Foss, coming to a point where the rivers converged. For all that the sun was warm, the wind caught at Jasper's short cape, whipped it about him and blew back his hood. Jasper secured the hood as his ears felt the first pains from the damp wind.

'This wind will give an added challenge today,' Owen said.

Jasper looked around him. Men of all sizes were gathered there, stringing their bows.

Owen put his hand on the boy's shoulder to guide him through the crowd. 'It's nothing like a trained company of archers in the lord's livery. That is a sight. An orderly company, disciplined, none of this idle chatter. And see that man's eyes? He's embarrassed already and he hasn't even shot. No one trained him as I'm training you. He has no idea what he's doing and he knows that.' Owen shook his head. 'I don't know what the King's thinking. Few of these men could help him win a battle.'

As the men noticed Owen's presence, they settled into quiet groups, organised about the string of butts, a group for each of the targets. Each group had a man in charge who arranged the order in which the men would shoot. The practice began.

Owen moved among the men, making suggestions to those in charge of the groups. Jasper had orders to stay close to Owen, but now and then he fell behind to watch the men shoot. It was at one of these times, when he realised Owen had gone on and Jasper was straining to see what direction Owen had taken, that the boy noticed someone familiar moving at the edge of the crowd. It was Jasper's friend Martin, the man who had helped him out with food and hiding places on many occasions. The man noticed Jasper at about the same moment and hurried over to him.

'Jasper? Is it you?' Martin said, a look of incredulous joy on his face.

Jasper looked around to make sure that no one was listening. 'You're not supposed to recognise me. I'm in disguise.'

'Not good enough. Not for someone looking for you. You are lucky that I'm the one who recognised you and not your enemies.'

'Captain Archer thought it was a good enough disguise.'

'Archer?' Martin jerked his head, looking behind him. His ear-ring sparkled in the sun as he turned back to Jasper. 'What does Archer have to do with it?'

'He brought me today.'

'Is that where you disappeared to? Is he hiding you?'

Jasper nodded.

'Good. I am happy that you are safe with him. But you must stay by him. I do not know what he was thinking, bringing you to such a public place and letting you out of his sight.'

Jasper looked around nervously. 'You're scaring me, Martin.'

'Perhaps I know you better than the men you're hiding from, but you cannot be sure. You must be more careful.' Martin's dark eyes swept the crowd. He pointed towards a knot of men. 'There is your captain. Come.' He took hold of Jasper's hand and led him through the crowd. When they were within hailing distance of Owen, Martin whispered, 'God be with you,' and disappeared into the crowd.

Jasper stayed right behind Owen for the rest of the practice. When they were on their way home, Jasper told Owen about seeing his friend.

'He gave you good advice. But he must know you well to have recognised you in the crowd, for on my honour that is a good disguise.'

Jasper shrugged. 'Martin's used to looking out for me. Maybe that's why he saw through it.'

'Why did he not bring you right to me? I would like to meet him.'

'He is in hiding, too. I suppose he didn't even want you to meet him.'

Owen crouched down to be eye to eye with Jasper. 'This Martin is in hiding? Why?'

'I don't know.' Jasper was frightened by Owen's sudden seriousness. 'He told me he's from across the Channel and that folk around here don't like foreigners. He's not a bad man, Captain. He's been good to me.'

'You said his name was Martin and he's a foreigner?' Jasper nodded.

'What does he look like?'

'Dark eyes and hair, tall like you, but not so strong. And he wears an ear-ring.' Jasper bit his lip. 'Why?'

'Is he from Flanders, Jasper?'

'I don't know. What's the matter, Captain? Do you know Martin?'

'He may be someone I've been looking for. He may be in danger and not know it.'

That was different. 'What kind of danger?'

'Do you know where he lives, Jasper?'

'I don't think he lives anywhere. He hides around the city, like I did. What kind of danger is he in, Captain?'

'Some people may be looking for him.' Owen glanced around.

'Maybe he knows already and that's why he's hiding.'

'That could be, Jasper. Let's hope so. Does he ever use the name Wirthir? Has he ever called himself Martin Wirthir?'

'Not to me. So maybe he's not the person you're looking for?'

'Perhaps not.' But the frown stayed on Owen's face as he straightened up and searched the crowd.

Owen had made light of the incident to Jasper, but it bothered him. Was it mere coincidence that someone who sounded so much like Martin Wirthir was in hiding? But what was his connection with the boy?

He told Lucie about the incident when they went up to bed.

Lucie sat up in bed and looked down at Owen. 'Do you know who that sounds like?'

'Don't tell me you know this man.'

'It sounds very much like the man who helped John and me get the cart out of the ditch on my way from Freythorpe Hadden.'

Now Owen sat up and stared at Lucie in the dim light from the spirit lamp. 'Are you telling me that you've known Martin Wirthir all along?'

'I knew him only as Martin. And this is the first time you've described him. It sounds so much like him, Owen. And he knew Will Crounce, remember? He told me to watch for him in the pageant of the Last Judgement.'

'If that's true, he's been in York since the first murder.'

'I don't understand.'

Owen shook his head. 'Neither do I.'

Sleep eluded them both for a long while.

Seventeen

Jasper's Quest

'Stop squirming,' Tildy cried, digging the wooden comb into Jasper's scalp to make him hold his head still.

Jasper sighed and closed his eyes. His head throbbed from Tildy's attempts to comb through his hair after washing it. 'Why do you hate me?'

'I don't hate you, you nit. I'm doing this to help you.'

Jasper rolled his eyes, which made his head move, forcing Tildy to dig the comb into his scalp again. 'Ouch! You're giving me a head full of splinters. My mother had a comb made of horn. It didn't have splinters. And it was smoother and didn't catch on my hair.'

'Well this is the best I've got.'

'If you hadn't rubbed my hair so hard with the cloth it might've been wetter and it would've been easy to get through the tangles, even with that comb.'

Tildy snorted. 'You remind me of my brother William. Always full of opinions on things he knows nothing about.' She jabbed at Jasper's hair.

Jasper gave up the argument. 'How many brothers

and sisters do you have?'

'Living? Four brothers, three sisters.'

'What's it like to have brothers and sisters?'

'Noisy. And there's never enough food. The boys eat it all.'

'Still, I'll bet you were never lonely.'

Tildy laughed. 'No chance of that, to be sure. Captain Archer had a house full of brothers and sisters too. He says that one of his brothers decided to be a monk because he heard that in a monastery each monk had his own little cell. He thought he could stay in his cell all the time and think in peace. When he found out he had to spend most of his time in church, praying with all the other monks, he ran away without taking his vows.'

Jasper was fascinated. 'Captain Archer told you about his family?'

Tildy tugged and smoothed away the last snarl. 'There,' she said with satisfaction, and sat down beside Jasper. 'Yes, Captain Archer talks to me a lot, just like I was part of the family. He's a kind man.'

Jasper nodded. 'I wish I were his son.'

'You could do a lot worse than have him for a father, to be sure.'

Behind them, the door from the garden opened. Jasper saw Tildy blush as she turned towards the door. He knew even before he turned that it must be John.

'Well, now, what a cosy couple you make.' John brushed snowflakes from his shoulders and moved a stool close to the fire. 'I saw the Captain and the Mistress over the tavern supping and thought I might come round.' He smiled, showing the gaps in his teeth. He looked at Jasper's wet hair, the comb in Tildy's lap. 'So you're making him pretty, are you, Tildy?'

Jasper flushed at such a comment from his new friend.

Tildy giggled. 'Nay, John, you troublemaker. Mistress Lucie put henna in Jasper's hair to disguise him so he could go out yesterday. But now he's got a rash on his scalp, so she had me wash his hair with rosemary water to soothe it. If you'd take a look at Jasper's face you'd know he wasn't happy about it.'

John squinted at Jasper and nodded. 'Poor lad. And all for naught, I'd say. I told you to trust no one. Captain Archer's a good man, but he's the Archbishop's man first. I think he's using you to lure the murderers. He knew they'd recognise you even with the hair. That was to comfort you. And now they know you're to be found near the Captain.'

'What do you mean?' Jasper asked, confused. 'I asked the Captain to take me.'

John nodded. 'And you gave him the idea, see?'

'What're you about, John?' Tildy demanded. 'What are you accusing the Captain of?'

John grinned at Tildy's tone. His eyes were teasing as he faced her. 'So you've lost your heart to the Captain, have you, Tildy?'

'I never!'

John shrugged. 'You know the Archbishop left Captain Archer in charge of finding out who killed those two merchants, Will Crounce and Gilbert Ridley. That's why they have Jasper here. To protect him from the murderers. But maybe to lure them too.'

Sweet Jesus. Jasper had never thought — Would the Captain betray him?

Tildy looked irritated with John. 'Captain Archer wouldn't let anything happen to Jasper.'

'No,' Jasper said in a tiny voice. 'He's been good to me.'

'And besides, Mistress Lucie wouldn't let the Captain put Jasper in danger.' Tildy squeezed Jasper's shoulder to reassure him.

John stretched his long legs out towards the fire. He smelled of stables. 'I'll be more than happy to be wrong in this. But I told you to trust no one, Jasper. That's the only sure way of being safe.'

Jasper suddenly had an awful thought. 'You didn't tell them my secret, did you, Tildy?'

Tildy looked askance at Jasper. 'Of course I didn't tell them. Mistress Lucie told me a secret's all right to keep as long as it doesn't hurt anyone.' She glanced over at John to see if he believed she'd betray Jasper.

John had his eye on a jug of ale on the table near him.

'Go ahead,' Tildy said, 'have some.'

John got up to get a cup.

'I'm glad you didn't tell, Tildy,' Jasper said softly.

'I promised you, didn't I? Though I still think it might be better to tell the Captain everything.'

'If John's right, I'm glad I didn't.'

Tildy gave Jasper a hug. 'The Captain would never let them hurt you. I don't understand why John's stirring you up.' She said it loud enough for John to hear.

John sat down again, pouring himself a cup of ale. 'I meant no harm, Tildy. Just wanted Jasper to understand that he must be careful. And that going out yesterday was foolish.' John leaned towards Jasper. 'But since you went, tell me about it.'

Jasper frowned up at John, not so sure he was such a good friend after all. 'Why don't you go with us next time? I don't see you practising of a Sunday. You're old enough. Older'n me.'

John held up his right hand, displaying the stubs of his middle three fingers. 'Can't hold the arrow right with this mess, else I'd be there. I'd like to shoot a bow.' He was not smiling now.

Jasper didn't know what to say. He'd wanted to challenge John, not to hurt his feelings; he'd forgotten John's hand. 'I'm sorry. I wasn't thinking.'

John shrugged. 'No matter. The Lord God set me in the way of honest work. I've nothing to complain about.' He took a drink of the ale. 'So. Tell me about St George's Field.'

Jasper thought a moment, deciding where to begin. 'They bring the butts out from a lean-to next to the chapel, and they set them up so the sun's not in your eyes. That's important. And Captain Archer walks around and tells them what they're doing wrong. Some can't shoot right even after he tells them what to do. He says it's because they were never trained. But they try, and no one argues with him. Everyone respects him. He's a great man.'

'You don't have to tell me that, Jasper,' John said. 'I like Captain Archer well enough. I'm just warning you that Archbishop Thoresby's a powerful man. He's not just the Archbishop, he's the Lord Chancellor of all England. And if he tells the Captain to find some murderers, the Captain had best do it no matter what. And if the only way's to lure the murderers with you, since you're the only one saw them, well . . .' John closed his eyes and tipped back his head to drain his cup.

Jasper said nothing. He didn't want to believe that the Captain might put him in danger.

John set the cup down and leaned over to Jasper. 'I've been thinking about how you had to leave your father's bow behind, and how it was special because he painted it.'

Jasper shrugged. 'I'm too small for it anyway.'

John snorted. 'Well you won't always be, Jasper

de Melton. You're growing every day. So what I'm thinking is we go see early some morning if it's still there.'

Jasper frowned. 'But you just told me how stupid I was to go out yesterday.'

John nodded. 'Parading you around like that, sure. But this'd be just you and me, sneaking out, taking the alleyways. Who's going to notice us? And wouldn't you like to get your father's bow if you could?'

Jasper folded his arms and frowned down at his stockinged feet as he thought about it. 'I don't know that I should go. But you could go over and ask Mistress Fletcher. It's her house. She would have the chest it was in if she's got new tenants. And no one's looking for you, John.'

Tildy nodded. 'That sounds like a better idea. I could even go.'

John rolled his eyes. 'So why should Mistress Fletcher give me, a stranger, your things, Jasper?'

'You could give him a note to give Mistress Fletcher,' Tildy suggested.

'Mistress Fletcher can't read. Nor can any of her family,' Jasper said. Nor could Jasper or Tildy or John for that matter.

'Right,' John said. 'So we'll go and see what's what. Even if someone's watching you, who's going to be on the look-out early in the morning, Jasper? And if we don't find the bow where you left it, then maybe Tildy can go ask Mistress Fletcher. She'd probably trust Tildy.'

Jasper studied John's face. His eyes were burning as if he were about to embark on a quest.

'Why do you want me to do this?' Jasper asked.

'Because I wish I'd gone back. Seen to things. That's all.'

'That doesn't seem like much of a reason,' Tildy said.

John groaned. 'Girls don't understand such things. You haven't had any experience to know what it's like.'

Tildy opened her mouth as if to speak, then froze like that, her face red, angry tears glittering in her eyes. 'You're wrong, John,' she finally said. 'You're going to get Jasper in trouble just because you want an adventure. That's what you don't understand.' She threw down the comb and stomped out of the room.

'Girls,' John sighed.

Jasper didn't understand, but that was nothing new. He didn't understand a lot of what went on between Tildy and John. They had a peculiar friendship. They smiled while calling each other unpleasant names and taunting each other. But this seemed more serious. 'Maybe you should make up with Tildy. You hurt her feelings.'

John grinned. 'I'll go and talk to her. She's just going to be out in the shop, pretending she's busy. But first, what do you think? Should we sneak out tomorrow morning and see if we can get your father's bow?'

Jasper shrugged. He didn't want to seem a coward. And he very much wanted to see if his things were still there. But what if Tildy was right?

'Well, what do you say?' John squinted at Jasper.

Jasper looked down at John's right hand, the stubs that had taught him how dangerous the world was. John wasn't stupid. John had been out there and survived. Jasper nodded. 'We'll do it. Tomorrow morning. Now go apologise to Tildy.'

Jasper found John asleep in the stable of the York Tavern, wrapped in several blankets and nested in hay. Matins had rung a while before and Jasper, who could not sleep, had judged it a good, dark time in which to have their adventure.

John was hard to wake up. And when Jasper roused him and told him that matins had been rung perhaps an hour past, John declared Jasper crazy. 'What would the Fletchers think to hear us clunking up the steps in the middle of the night? They're sure to think we're thieves and come after us with clubs.'

'But we are being thieves. Even in daylight, we'd be thieving to sneak up to the room.'

'Give it more time.' John opened his blankets. 'Come on, snug up with me and sleep a bit more.'

'You just want to go back to sleep. You never meant to go with me.'

'That's not true. But I tell you, I know what I'm talking about. We must wait till just before dawn.'

'Then I'll go alone.'

John grabbed Jasper as he started to get to his feet. 'No you won't go alone.' He sat up beside Jasper, rubbing his eyes. 'Is it still snowing?'

'No, it's stopped for now.'

'Well, that's one blessing. Why do you want to do this in the middle of the night?'

'In case someone's watching the house. Or the apothecary.'

John yawned and stretched. 'You're probably right.' He stood up. 'So. We stick close together, stay in the shadows, and keep as quiet as possible. We creep up the stairs. Does the door creak?'

Jasper closed his eyes and thought about opening the door. It seemed so long ago since he'd been there. 'No, it doesn't creak, but it doesn't hang right, so it drags on the floor.'

'Then you open it – you'll know how to hold it up.'

Jasper nodded. His stomach felt fluttery, now that

227

he was really thinking about doing this. 'What if someone's sleeping in there?'

'We'll know soon enough, and we just get away as fast and quiet as we can.' John held up the cloak he'd been about to put on. 'Maybe we should leave these. They get caught on things in the dark.'

Jasper was already cold. 'My teeth will chatter too loud if I have no cloak.'

'It'll keep you moving fast. That's good.'

Jasper didn't like the excitement in John's voice, but it seemed too late to back out, and just because of a feeling. Jasper reluctantly shrugged out of his cloak.

They stayed close to the buildings, creeping past the inn, past the apothecary, then crossed the street where the shadow was deepest, and rounded the corner. The new snow made walking treacherous, hiding the icy patches. John slipped once and landed on his behind with a disgusted grunt. Then they both flattened themselves into a doorway as a nightwatchman strolled by. Jasper had been right, his teeth chattered so loudly that John could hear them and jabbed him with an elbow. When the watchman was out of sight, John signalled Jasper to move on. Jasper must go first. He knew the way.

Mistress Fletcher's house was dark. They crept around to the side steps and climbed. Eleven steps, narrow and high.

'Lord,' John whispered, 'this is more like a ladder than stairs. We can't carry a chest down this way in the dark.'

'We'll just get the bow. And maybe my jerkin,' Jasper whispered back.

He tried the door. It moved. Not bolted shut. Good. He lifted it slightly and pulled it towards him, just far enough to slide in. John slid in after him. Jasper opened the shield on the little lantern he carried. The light was weak, but good enough to show him that the chest stood just where he remembered. He knelt down in front of it, opened it. His heart sank. It was empty. He could smell his mother's lavender, but there was nothing in the chest.

Behind him, John made a funny noise, as if he'd bumped into something.

'Sshh,' Jasper whispered as he turned to tell John what he'd found. Sweet Mary in Heaven, the blade of a knife hovered just beyond Jasper's face.

'So I was right. You came back for your things.' It was the voice of the woman in the cathedral, the woman who'd hidden the hand.

Jasper could just see John's feet by the door. He was lying down. No blood was visible, but that didn't matter, his friend was lying very still while a woman held a knife at Jasper. That meant John was at least knocked out.

Still holding the knife at Jasper, the woman leaned over and picked up the lantern. She held it up to Jasper's face. He turned away from the light, but the knife guided his chin back so that Jasper was looking into the woman's eyes.

'Well, little boy,' she said softly, 'what am I going to do with you, eh? He wants you dead, you know. You were foolish to tell anyone what you'd seen. If you'd just run away that night, said nothing to anyone, your life would not be forfeit.'

'I didn't see faces.' The knife had cut Jasper under the chin and the cut burned. His knees were wobbly where he knelt on the rough wood floor. He felt a splinter digging in.

The light flickered across the woman's face. She studied Jasper.

'I knew you were behind us that night, did you know?' Her voice was calm, as if this were an ordinary conversation. 'I saw you waiting with me at the tavern. I felt you turn to follow. Such an earnest boy.' She caressed his cheek with the knife blade. 'I heard later that your mother was dying. The beautiful Kristine. Will Crounce meant to marry her, you know. I was just trifling with him so that when the time came I could lure him to the ambush. Like I used John to get to you.'

Jasper gasped.

'Yes, your friend and I play together. He thought he was bringing you to be initiated. But I had other plans.'

Jasper tried to see his friend through his tears. So John wasn't so smart. 'Is he dead?'

The woman chuckled. 'What a fool I would be to kill my pet, don't you think? I suppose you could be my pet, too.' She caressed his cheek with the blade again. 'You could have stayed silent, boy. I was not going to tell him you'd seen. What did I care? I didn't kill poor Will Crounce. His own greed killed him. He was not as brave as you, Jasper. Not nearly as brave.'

She moved the lantern so close to Jasper he felt its heat. When he jumped, she laughed and pulled it away.

'Such pretty curls.' She flicked a curl with the point of the knife. 'Such a sweet boy.' A frown replaced the laughter. 'How could I hurt such a sweet child?' she whispered as she touched the tip of the knife to Jasper's cheek. He felt the prick and the wetness. 'I told you the next time I would have a sharpened knife with a good point, didn't I?'

Jasper lifted his hand to his face. It was not a big cut, but it bled a lot. 'Are you going to kill me?' he asked.

230

'What do you think I ought to do, my love? I am as guilty as he. Neither of us raised a hand to kill them, but we set their deaths upon them.' Her eyes moved down Jasper's body. The knife followed, hovering at his groin, picking at the material. 'We had such delicious fun planning this. He is a big man. I wonder if you'll be a big man like him someday?'

Jasper felt a rush of wetness. Not blood, but urine. She either saw the dark stain or smelled it, because she laughed. 'Fear is so humbling. We should have asked Will before he died whether Jesus wet himself on the cross. I'm sure after all those years playing Jesus, Will would have known. Wouldn't you like to know that?'

Jasper shook his head. 'It's blasphemy to talk like that.'

She knelt down to him, placing the lantern on the chest behind Jasper. Grabbing his shoulders, with the knife terrifyingly close to his ear, she peered into his eyes. 'I frighten you, don't I, Jasper? But tell me this. Don't you hate us for killing Will Crounce?'

Jasper nodded.

'Imagine that hate festering over the years. While you watched boys who had the life you would have had. Envy would fill you like a poison, burning through you from the inside out. That's how much I hated Will Crounce and Gilbert Ridley. I prayed for their suffering. They destroyed my father. And God answered my prayer with Ridley in such a mysterious way. Ridley the boar dwindled to Ridley the frightened, frail little man.' She flicked Jasper's ear with the point of the blade and laughed when he flinched. 'Your blood is so red, little boy, so healthy.'

Out of the corner of his eye, Jasper saw one of John's feet move. *Oh please, God, let him wake up.* Jasper did not know what John could do. He didn't think John had brought a weapon. But perhaps if John just scared her . . .

She clenched Jasper's shoulder with the hand that held the knife, and leaned over, closing the lantern shade.

All was dark. She pressed Jasper to her, fiercely, digging her fingers into the small of his back and his shoulder. 'I don't want to kill you, my pretty baby,' she whispered in the darkness, 'but I must. Or I'm much afraid he will kill me.' The hand that held the knife eased off Jasper's shoulder. She pulled back to thrust the knife. Jasper held his breath, waiting for death.

But she toppled sideways, dragging Jasper down with her. The knife slit his face, then his side as they fell.

'Run, Jasper,' John hissed in the darkness. 'Run!'

Jasper squeezed out beneath the woman as she thrashed. He lurched to his feet and stumbled to the door, knowing the room well enough to find his way without thinking. Halfway down the stairs he doubled over, coughing, which made his side burn. He stumbled, then fell the rest of the way, landing in a trembling heap at the bottom of the steps. He crawled into the shadows, his heart pounding, whimpering in pain. He must get to Captain Archer and bring him back for John. But the steps and the building and the snow swam around Jasper. If he closed his eyes for just a moment, everything would settle.

Jasper closed his eyes.

When he opened them, snow was coming down thick and heavy. He shivered uncontrollably and yet his side burned, his cheek felt ripped wide, his head felt hot. He was sheltered from the brunt of the storm by the overhanging second storey, but his feet were wet with melting snow. He tucked them under him and reached to pull his cloak around him. No cloak. He remembered. John. He must go to help John.

People were coming down the steps, a halting, heavy sound. 'Merciful Heaven,' Mistress Fletcher said, 'whatever was this young man doing up there? Who attacked him up there while we slept? God has forsaken us. Ever since the pestilence. We will none of us die peacefully. None of us sinners. Sweet Mary, he's a heavy one.'

'That's why they call it dead weight,' Master Fletcher muttered. 'We should have called the coroner and bailiff before we moved him, you know.'

'And who knows when they would come? We must take him below in case he's not dead. Come on. Let's get him by the fire.'

'I know a corpse when I see one, Joanna,' Master Fletcher said.

Jasper was alert enough to understand. John was dead. And it was Jasper's fault. He'd left John up there with the woman and she'd killed him. No one could ever forgive Jasper this. And she would be more determined than ever to kill him. She would come wherever he was. He must get away. He must trust no one. He had trusted John, and John had led him to her. Had he known who she was? *Oh John, is that why you told me to run but you stayed?* Jasper's head swam and he wanted to vomit, but he forced himself to stay still until the Fletchers were inside. Then he managed to stand up against the wall. He emptied his stomach and the pain in his side from the spasms made him gasp and crumble against the wall. But he must move. Must get inside. Somewhere dark. Where there were no eyes. Where there was no snow. The sky was white with snow, but it wasn't dawn yet. Time to hide.

Eighteen

Tildy's Secret

When Tildy went to wake Jasper, he wasn't there. Only Melisende slept on the cleverly mounded covers.

Tildy checked outside in the snowy garden. Jasper wasn't out there, either. It was no use looking for footprints, it was snowing too hard. She ran back in, went out to the shop hoping against hope that he was in there, tidying for Mistress Lucie perhaps. He did that some mornings.

But Jasper was nowhere. Jasper and John must have gone to Mistress Fletcher's. Unless Jasper had just gone to talk to John about it.

When Lucie came downstairs, Tildy was taking off her shawl.

'Where were you so early?' Lucie asked. Then she saw Tildy's face. 'What's the matter? What's happened?'

'Oh, Mistress Lucie, Jasper's gone. He's not in his bed or the shop or the garden. And John's not in the stable. And Jasper's cloak —' Tildy held it up to Lucie and started to cry.

'Where did you find Jasper's cloak, Tildy?' Owen asked, coming into the kitchen.

Tildy tried to stop crying. 'It's John's fault. He got him all excited about getting his father's longbow.'

'Where was Jasper's cloak, Tildy?' Lucie asked.

'The stable where John sleeps.'

Lucie took Tildy by the shoulders and led her to a chair. 'Sit and calm yourself.'

Tildy took some deep breaths and dabbed her eyes with the corner of her shawl.

When Tildy was reasonably calm, Lucie asked, 'What's this about John and Jasper and a longbow?'

Tildy told them about the chest Jasper had left behind at the Fletchers' and John's idea that he and Jasper should go to see if it was still there.

'I went there once looking for the boy,' Owen said. 'It's close. I'll go and see what's happened.'

'I'm sure it's too late,' Tildy cried. 'She got him. She got both of them. Oh, sweet Mary, Mother of God, why did Jasper listen to him?'

Owen turned around at the door. 'Who are you talking about, Tildy? Who is "she"?'

Tildy's eyes opened wide. She shook her head.

'Tildy, you must tell us,' Lucie warned.

'I can't tell you, Mistress. I swore.'

Swore. Lucie remembered their conversation over the horse-radish. 'Tildy, I told you that it was all right to swear if the secret hurt no one. But you know something about the danger Jasper is in. Something Captain Archer should know before he goes out there.'

Owen knelt down in front of Tildy and took her hands. 'Jasper is the only one who saw what happened to Will Crounce, Tildy, and the murderers must know that – all the city knows it. If I were a murderer, I would want to get rid of anyone who might recognise me and tell someone what I'd done. Wouldn't you do anything to save your own life, Tildy?'

'But he didn't see who did it.' Tildy did not want to believe Jasper could be in such danger. And John. Dearest John.

'I know that Jasper says he could not identify the men,' Lucie said, 'but they might not want to risk that, Tildy.'

'I promised,' Tildy said in a weak, uncertain little voice.

'Right now, keeping the secret might hurt Jasper,' Lucie said gently, 'if we can't find him, if those men find him first.'

Tildy hated this. She was confused. She had thought that keeping Jasper's secret would help him. But Mistress Lucie and the Captain said differently. They were smart people. So perhaps she should listen to them. She knew that they would not hurt Jasper. It was Jasper who didn't trust them, even though he wished he was the Captain's son.

'Will you tell him why I told you, Captain Archer?'

'I promise you I will, Tildy. Just tell me what you know – quickly.'

'There's a woman he saw on Corpus Christi, talking with the second man who died. Jasper saw her again when he was sleeping in the minster. She had a bloody bundle. It fell and it was a hand. Sweet Lord, deliver him.' Tildy crossed herself. 'And then she told Jasper she'd kill him if he ever told. And she said something about someone else, the murderer Jasper thought, who wanted him dead. And oh, the woman was the same one, he thinks, who was walking with Master Crounce when he was murdered. So you see, she's after him.'

'Did he describe her?' Owen asked.

Tildy thought about it. 'He said she was pretty.

And strong. She dragged him in the minster.'

Owen and Lucie exchanged worried looks; then Owen was off.

The bailiff and the coroner were already at the Fletchers' house. Owen, prepared to find Jasper dead or wounded, stared with confusion at John.

'So what was the stable boy from the York Tavern doing up there?' the bailiff asked.

Owen went over to the family huddled by the fire. They looked dazed. 'Was there another boy up there?' Owen asked them. 'Younger? Blond – no, red hair?'

Joanna Fletcher shook her head. 'We saw someone running down the alley. Such a commotion. It's what woke us. And when I realised the noise was up there, in that empty room, I woke Matt and we went up together. With sticks. And there was this lad by a spilled lantern. Lord knows the house might have burned down around us if I hadn't heard 'em and jumped up to set that right. The lad's face was burned, like you see, and there was all that blood —' she broke off, staring down at John's bloody body.

'But you did not see Jasper de Melton?' Owen asked.

Joanna Fletcher looked back up, surprised. 'Jasper? Is that what this is about? Was this lad after the boy? Was he the murderer?'

'No, Mistress Fletcher. He was Jasper's friend.'

'So what did they want up there in the middle of the night?'

'They'd got some silly idea to come and look for a longbow that Jasper's mother had kept in the chest up there.'

'But it's down here, waiting for Jasper,' Joanna cried. 'Why'd he not come to me?'

'I don't know, Mistress Fletcher. I wish I did.'

'The poor lad. Where's he got to, then?'

'This person you saw running,' Owen said, 'could it have been Jasper?'

Joanna Fletcher stared over Owen's head, considering. 'Nay. The person was taller than Jasper. And didn't run like a lad.'

'"Twas a woman, is why,' Matt Fletcher said.

Joanna snorted. 'It was never a woman did that to this strong young man.'

'I swear to you, Captain Archer, that's what I saw. 'Twas a woman running away.' Matt nodded to emphasise his certainty.

The woman again. Owen would give a year of his life to find this strong woman who hounded Jasper. And had perhaps killed John. 'I thank you for this information. If you remember anything more – or if you see anything else suspicious, please let either myself or the bailiff know.'

With great solemnity the Fletchers vowed to do so.

Owen went back to the bailiff. 'The body should be taken to the Merchets. They will want to bury John.'

'Where are you off to?' the bailiff asked.

'I must see if there are any signs of Jasper. The boy could be injured. Or just frightened. I would like to go up and see if I can learn anything from the room.'

The bailiff nodded. 'As long as you let me know what you learn.'

'I will.' Owen paused over John's body, said a silent prayer. There would be much grieving in the two houses this day.

With the snow still falling, Owen did not expect to find much to help him outside, but he had to try. With the aid of a small lantern, he examined the ground beneath

238

the stairs and found a bloody handprint on the wall –
the size of a child's hand, and blood and the contents
of someone's stomach on the ground. He was able to
follow the trail of blood for a few feet, then picked it
up a few more times down the alley, but he soon lost
it completely as the alley opened up in a small square
where the snow fell freely. Disappointing, but a hopeful
sign. Though wounded, Jasper might be alive.

Retracing his steps, Owen climbed to the room
where Jasper and Kristine de Melton had lived. Beside
an old chest the floor was scorched where the lantern
had fallen. The floor in front of the chest was smeared
with blood. A puddle of blood was near the door. But
there was no sign of Jasper.

If the boy was badly injured, he had probably crawled
into some cranny. If Jasper was able to walk the
distance, Owen suspected he would go to Magda Digby's,
where he'd gone before when he was in trouble. Owen
wrestled with the idea of returning first to tell Tildy
and Lucie what had happened, but he should get to
Magda's. The Riverwoman had eyes and ears throughout the city. She would alert her people to Jasper's
danger.

And if Owen was very lucky, Jasper would be
sitting by Magda's fire.

Owen made his way through the quiet city, cursing
the snowflakes that had to be blinked away and his
bird-like sight that required his turning his head this
way and that to watch his footing on the snow. If he
pulled his hood far enough over his face to ward off the
flakes, the hood covered what little peripheral vision
he had. The going was slow.

Magda pulled the curtain around a patient in the
corner bed, then invited Owen to have some ale.

'Customer gave it to Magda last night. Bird-eye will find it suitable.'

'I'm wishing that's Jasper de Melton you hide in the corner,' Owen said. He'd taken off his boots and now sat cross-legged by the fire holding his hands out to the warmth. 'If Jasper's out in the snow and injured, I've little hope for him.'

'Jasper? Nay, 'tis not the boy who lies there. What's amiss with the lad now?'

Owen told Magda what had happened. 'He came to you in need before, I'd hoped he'd done it again.'

Magda frowned over her ale. Her eyes were shadowed.

'You look tired. Is the patient very ill?'

'A night of fever dreams. Magda is aged enough to have passed through the need for much sleep, but a little is a good thing, and she's had none for two days.'

'I am selfish to come here with my problems, never thinking of yours.'

Magda smiled. 'Thou dost not come with thine own problems, Bird-eye. Thou art a good man. And thou shouldst not despair yet.'

Owen protested.

'Nay, Magda sees the darkness descending over thine eye. Injured limbs move slow. Jasper might still come.'

'Would you spread the word among those you trust? And tell them Jasper's hair is red at present. With henna.'

Magda's tired eyes opened wide. 'Henna?' She snorted. 'Didst thou think to hide him with bright colours?'

'If I'm searching for a blond boy, a red-haired boy might not catch my eye.' Owen felt defensive about the business – perhaps with reason. It had seemed so

240

sensible at the time, but it sounded foolish in Magda's terse summation.

Magda drank down her ale, wiping her mouth on her sleeve with a brusque motion. 'Past is past. Magda will put forth the word, and thou shalt hear as soon as may be. What dost thou know so far, Bird-eye?'

He told her about Jasper and the woman, and also his suspicion that Jasper's friend Martin and the stranger Lucie had befriended were both Martin Wirthir, who sometimes stayed with the town wait Ambrose Coats. He also told Magda about Coats bringing the hand to Lucie.

'Poor Ambrose lives in fear his hands will stiffen so he can't make his music. Was it a cruel joke?' Magda laughed, then turned serious. 'Ambrose's Flemish friend is this Martin Wirthir? Magda may know him.'

Owen was amazed. 'You know Martin Wirthir?'

Magda rubbed her eyes and shook her head, as if waking herself up. 'Magda must rest tonight. There is naught else for it. Aye, Magda thinks she knows this man. Pirate is what she calls the rogue. Sounds like him. Watches out for Jasper, though he's not so good at it, being in hiding himself.'

'Who does he hide from?'

Magda shrugged and yawned. 'He has come to Magda because she does not ask such questions. It is good that Pirate is the one. He cares about the boy. Word will reach him. Not as soon as thou wouldst like, but there is no remedy. He protects Ambrose Coats by never letting the poor man know where he is to be found.'

'Why do you call him "Pirate"?'

Magda shrugged. ''Tis something about him. Speech. Flemish, Magda guessed before thou didst say it. Like the weavers under the King's protection. So what does such a man, not a weaver, want in York, Magda asks herself. And why does he hide? Ah, she thinks, perhaps he smuggles the wool that the King wants to steal from the merchants for his war.'

Owen was amazed. Magda, not Owen, should work for Thoresby. She even knew about the King's war finances. Owen gulped the rest of his ale. 'Has this Pirate ever mentioned the name Martin Wirthir?'

Magda wrinkled up her face in thought. 'Nay. But 'tis the sort of name he might have.' She nodded. 'Thou art clever in thy bones, Bird-eye. Thou hast put much together.'

Owen felt ridiculously pleased by her praise. 'I begin to think I should watch Ambrose Coats's house.'

'Like Magda says, Pirate is careful for Ambrose. They are secretive about their friendship.'

'Why? Because Wirthir is Flemish?'

Magda shrugged.

'How do you come to know Wirthir? Did he bring his leman to you? An unwanted child?'

Magda chuckled. 'Nay, Bird-eye. Pirate is not the sort to bring a lady to Magda's hut.'

'He is a loyal friend, concerned about Jasper, and does not bring you compromised women. A paragon of virtue. So why does he come here?'

Magda burst into one of her barking laughs. 'Magda hears what thou thinkst of her. Well, hear this with surprise, Bird-eye. Martin Wirthir is a friend to Magda Digby, simple as that. He likes to talk with her.'

Owen made his way slowly home through the still falling snow. He dreaded bringing to Lucie and Tildy the news of John's death. After such news, how could he assure them that Jasper was probably hidden somewhere, wounded but alive? He did not know whether he believed that himself.

Owen stopped in the minster to pray for Jasper's

deliverance, then went among the artisans and asked if any had seen the boy. He particularly asked the carpenters, those men of Jasper's father's craft, who would want to help one of their own. They had not seen Jasper since the morning of the storm, when the boy's cloak was found in the unfinished Lady Chapel. But they promised Owen they would look out for Jasper and get any news to him as soon as they could.

Archdeacon Jehannes caught up with Owen in the unfinished chapel.

'Why so glum, my friend?' Jehannes asked.

Owen told him.

'May God guide him to a safe harbour.' Jehannes crossed himself. 'The boy lives under a cloud of misfortune. I left him some food once in a while when he was sleeping in the hole in the wall here. I discovered that if he guessed someone was pitying him, he disappeared, so I could not do it often without frightening him away.'

'I had hoped he would trust us enough to return to us if he was in danger.'

Jehannes shook his head. 'The boy has learned that it is best for him to trust no one. No amount of goodness on your part can change that for him. It will change only when the danger is past.'

'Do you know an embroiderer named Felice? A widow who lives in the liberty?'

Jehannes thought about it. 'No. But I have little to do with the embroiderers. Shall I ask about her?'

'No. She must not suspect anyone is interested in her. I just thought you might know whether she had a daughter visiting her.'

'I will keep my ears pricked for the name. Something to do with the murders?'

'Perhaps. I am no closer to finding the murderers

than when I began. I am not the man for the job.'

Jehannes patted Owen on the back. 'You have said that with every job His Grace has given you, and always you have satisfied him. You will find the sinners, Owen, and you will deliver them. Perhaps there is one line of the riddle that you have yet to hear.'

'You have an overabundance of faith, Jehannes.'

Jehannes laughed. 'A priest can never have too much faith, my friend.' He grew serious. 'But do not think I am not concerned for the boy. I would mention it in chapter, only I hesitate, since whoever committed the murder Jasper witnessed had some connection with this liberty. I do not like to think one of our chapter could be guilty, but even if one's only sin is to know the guilty ones, a word in the wrong ear could be fatal to the boy.'

Owen agreed.

'But I almost forgot. A Father Cuthbert from Ripon came to mass this morning. He asked if I could get a message to you. Mistress Anna Scorby is at St Clement's nunnery. He said you would want to know.'

'Thank you, Jehannes. I will go to her when I can. At the moment I must go deliver the news of John's death to those who loved him.'

'God give you strength in your dreadful task.'

Nineteen

Grief

B ess opened the kitchen door to a nightmare. Her John, a boy as dear to her as her own children, slung between two of the bailiff's servants. Blood stained John's smock and leggings. An angry burn had already begun to pucker the right side of the boy's lovely face.

'Sweet Saviour, this is an evil day.' Bess caressed John's left cheek with her hand. 'God bless you for bringing him home. Put him inside.' She walked past the servants to the bailiff. 'Tell me what happened.'

'Your neighbour Captain Archer will do better with that, Mistress. He will be along soon.' The bailiff gave her the bare facts.

'So Owen hunts for Jasper?' Bess looked out into the falling snow. ''Tis a hard day for such a pastime.' She gestured to the bailiff to enter the kitchen. 'Sit yourself down, Geoffrey. And your two boys who carried such a grim burden.'

She poured them all some spiced wine, watered down for the morning.

The bailiff took a drink and tipped his hat to Bess. 'We think the young man might have been dead from the wounds before his face was burned, Mistress, which is to be hoped.'

Bess crossed herself and wiped her hot eyes on her apron.

The bailiff cleared his throat and asked without looking at Bess, 'Now this lad that Captain Archer says was with your John, was he staying here, too?'

Bess shook her head. 'He was under Captain Archer's protection. And Mistress Wilton was treating him. The boy has had one horror after another come upon him.'

'Were John and this Jasper de Melton friends?'

'John took an interest in poor Jasper. I'm sure there was something in the boy's misfortunes that reminded John of the dark time in his past.'

'Ever know how your John lost the fingers?'

'Not the how or why. The fingers were crushed and in an awful state when we found John sleeping in the stables in a high fever. Master Wilton, God rest his soul, sent for the barber, who removed the pitiful things, then Master Wilton treated the wounds and the fever. We none of us asked any questions, except whether any kin were to be notified. He told us he had none living. Not any more. And that was that. If he had wished us to know, he would have explained. He seemed most grateful that we did not ask.'

The bailiff nodded. 'Could last night's attack have been aimed at John, do you think?'

Bess looked down at John's mutilated body. 'It's most likely to do with Jasper's troubles. Where exactly are John's wounds?'

'A knife slit him down the middle. That bleeds a lot, that kind of wound. The rest are bruises and one head cut that might've knocked him out. Looks like he struggled a good bit.'

'A strong assailant,' Bess said.

'That's what's odd, Mistress. Matt Fletcher thinks it was a woman they saw running away down the alley. Can you imagine a woman that strong?'

Bess rolled her eyes. 'Just because we can bear children and be as loving as the day is long doesn't mean we can't also be strong and vicious. Well,' she stood up, 'I'd best clean the poor lad up before Mistress Wilton's girl Tildy sees him and shows the whole city of York how strong and vicious a woman can be when given cause.' She went over to John. 'A woman, you say? We'll just have to find her, won't we, Geoffrey?'

'Aye. We'll do our best.'

'We all will,' Bess muttered to herself as she poured water from the heavy kettle into a shallow basin.

Lucie's throat tightened when she saw Owen's face. 'Sweet Jesu, what is it? Jasper is dead? Injured?'

Owen sank down on a stool in the shop. 'Tildy can't hear?'

Lucie tiptoed to the beaded curtain and listened, returned to her husband shaking her head. 'She is making enough noise with the water on the hearth-stones to mask anything we might say in normal voices.'

'John is dead.'

Lucie sat down, too, crossing herself. 'And Jasper?'

'Jasper is injured, I think, but he has disappeared into the city again.' Owen ripped off the patch and rubbed his scarred eye. 'I don't know how to tell the girl, or Bess and Tom – though the bailiff has probably already delivered John's body to the York Tavern.'

'Who has done this?'

'I believe it is the woman Jasper told Tildy about. She must have watched his old home, hoping to catch him sneaking back.'

'Foolish boys. It was so unnecessary.'

'I have a suspicion, Lucie. You say Bess thought John had a woman?'

Lucie nodded.

'This is what I'm thinking.' Owen raked his hands through his hair. 'Kate Cooper, wife of the Ridley's steward, she's one for the men. And she's strong enough, I think, tall and large-boned, to overpower John. She might have discovered he knew Jasper and somehow got John to deliver Jasper to her. When John realised she meant to harm Jasper, John attacked her, but she was too ready for him. And Jasper escaped.'

'It fits together in a tidy package, but why would Kate Cooper do it?'

Owen sighed. 'That's the problem. I don't know. A favour for a lover?'

'That is not likely. Just because Kate's morals are questionable it does not follow that she has no sense – nor a mind of her own. No. She would have to be somehow involved herself.'

Owen fiddled with the patch. 'I know too little about her. I cannot guess how she might be involved.' He sank back against the wall, his eye closed. 'I cannot believe John is dead.'

Lucie sat quietly, waiting for Owen to go on.

He finally opened his eye, took Lucie's hands in his.

'We did our best to protect Jasper,' Lucie said.

Owen nodded.

He looked so defeated, Lucie wanted to gather him in her arms and hold him safe. But it was not the time for that.

At last Owen put the patch back on and straightened

up. 'Jehannes says that Anna Scorby is at St Clement's nunnery. I will go talk to her. Ask her what she knows about Kate Cooper. The woman accompanied Gilbert Ridley to York at Corpus Christi and at Martinmas.'

'Do you really have any hope that John's murderer will be found so easily?'

'Easily? No. If Kate Cooper is this strong woman who has killed a young man and injured another, not to mention killed two grown men, she is desperate and clever. She will not be easily found.'

'Is there any danger that she has taken Jasper?'

'I don't know. The Fletchers thought a woman escaped alone. I hope that is true. I did not come sooner because I went to tell Magda Digby what had happened. I asked her to keep her ears open. I confess I'd hoped Jasper might have gone there again.'

'He still might.'

'That's what Magda said.'

'Owen, I've been thinking about Martin Wirthir.'

'So have I.' Owen told her what Magda had told him.

Lucie tried to perk up. 'That is all helpful, isn't it? I think I should go to Ambrose Coats and tell him about Jasper.' Lucie gave Owen a challenging look.

To her surprise, Owen nodded. 'I think perhaps you should.'

Lucie stared at him. 'You are not going to argue?'

'No. Jasper is out there somewhere, wounded, perhaps dead. I must find him quickly. I am not in a position to refuse help.'

Lucie touched Owen gently on the cheek. 'You are not to blame. The boys went out of their own accord. Tildy has made that clear.'

Owen shrugged and looked down at his hands.

'There's been a message from the Archbishop,' Lucie said, hoping to distract him. She handed him the letter.

'I took the liberty of reading it. It kept me occupied while waiting for you.'

'Is there anything useful?'

'Perhaps. If we could piece it all together.'

Owen scanned the letter. 'Alan of Aldborough. That's near Boroughbridge. A possible connection with Will Crounce. We have so many little pieces. But none of them fits.'

'I'll go to see Ambrose Coats when you've returned from St Clement's,' Lucie said.

Owen nodded, then pounded his knees with clenched fists and stood up. 'And now I must tell Tildy about John.'

'True. There's no hiding it from her. She will read it in our faces.'

'How do I soften something like this?'

'Tell her that he probably died defending Jasper. Tildy is at an age when heroism appeals. It will at least help her see it as a noble end. Meanwhile, I should go see Bess.'

Tom Merchet sat on a stool beside the table where Bess had laid John to clean him. Tom stared at the ragged wound that traced a line from near John's left breast to his navel.

Bess looked up from her determined scrubbing. At the sight of her good friend's face Bess's reserve crumbled. 'Oh Lucie, look what they've done to our John,' she cried, and stumbled over to Lucie to bury her face in her friend's shoulder. Lucie hugged Bess as she fought her own tears. She should say something comforting. But what good were words? She just let the tears come and held Bess tightly while the woman sobbed.

*

Tildy frowned down at her wet hem, then back up at Owen. 'Why would someone kill John?' Her voice, a mere whisper, trembled.

'Perhaps John was defending Jasper,' Owen said.

'I must see him.'

'He would want you to remember him in life, Tildy.'

Tildy picked up the bucket of ashy water, hugging it to her, then suddenly threw it into the hearth. The water turned to billowing steam.

Owen jumped to pull the bucket out before it caught in the few flames left.

Tildy looked around, fists clenched, searching for something else to throw.

Owen grabbed her shoulders and guided her to a chair, where he sat her down and told her to wait while he got a cup of wine for her.

'I don't want wine, I want my John,' Tildy said flatly, her hands still clenched. She glared down at the floor.

'John is dead, Tildy. The Lord has claimed him. Now you must be strong for Jasper. When we find him, he will need your nursing.'

'Who was it, Captain Archer? Who killed John?'

'We don't know, Tildy,' Owen said.

'It's that woman. She was bedding him. That's why he was so full of himself all of a sudden.'

'That may be so, Tildy, but we don't know who she is.'

'When I find out, I will kill her. And I will take unholy pleasure in it.' Tildy smiled.

Owen handed Tildy the wine and ordered her to drink.

As the wine took effect, Tildy's nose and cheeks reddened and the tears began. Owen knelt in front of her and held her as she sobbed John's name and cursed in a vocabulary that astonished him.

*

The bell of St Clement's rang for nones as Owen approached. He slowed his steps, knowing that he must wait half an hour before the women would be out of church. The snow had stopped and sunlight reflected off the fresh snow, making it sparkle like stars in a white heaven. Owen paused in one of the orchards that surrounded the nunnery wall. The bare branches still held delicate ridges of snow. A line of small indentations revealed the pathway of a neighbourhood cat. Behind him, a bargeman called to another on the river. Owen turned to look at the muddy water, receded from the previous flood but ready to rise again as soon as the snow began to melt up on the moors. He thought of Potter Digby drowning in the Ouse, another victim who had died without cause. At least this time Owen did not carry the burden of responsibility. Lucie was right about that, but Owen found little comfort in it.

As he wandered aimlessly through the winter orchard, Owen grew conscious of an uneasiness that made him spin round to check behind him several times. Along with the shower of needle pricks he felt across the blind eye, it was a sign of danger. Someone watched him, so good at the task that Owen could not catch him – or her – at the game.

The next time he felt it, Owen spun round and ran full tilt towards the source of the feeling. Suddenly two men appeared running along the riverbank, slipping in the icy mud. With Owen's limited vision he was no more nimble-footed than they, and he soon lost them. Well, he'd given them a scare, that was something. He went into the nunnery.

Wearing the garb of the Benedictine sisters, Anna Scorby entered the receiving room. She kept her head down, each hand tucked in the opposite sleeve.

'You look at home here, Mistress Scorby.'

She looked up at Owen and her face broke into a shy smile. The swelling was gone; pale bruises were all that marked her face now. 'I am glad it is you, Captain Archer. I have wanted to thank you for making it possible for me to stay at Riddlethorpe until I healed enough to come here. God bless you. I pray for you daily.'

'Have you had any more trouble from your husband?'

Anna shook her head. 'But I know that he is not done with me. He is not the sort of man to forgive. Even though I doubt he truly loves me.'

'Why do you doubt it?'

She blushed and dropped her head. 'He has another woman. Perhaps more than one.' Her voice trembled.

'So you have loved him.' Owen was surprised.

'Oh yes, I did love him at first.' Anna raised her head. 'Even though I knew the marriage was a business deal. I felt lucky that he was handsome. Clever. But he killed my love with his hatefulness. Do you know what terrible thing I did to deserve the beating? I picked up a letter that had come for him. He found me holding it. Not reading it, just holding it.'

'His temper does seem out of proportion to the deed. Perhaps it was a letter he wanted no one to see. Was the seal broken?'

'No. He said I was to learn not to touch his things.' Anna looked directly at Owen now, her dark eyes much like her mother's, but sad. 'You see, Captain, I am not an unnatural woman. I would gladly have loved him. But he turned my love to hate. And to save my soul from that unforgivable sin, I have thrown my heart into prayer.'

'He had beaten you before?'

She looked away. 'Never so badly. A clout on the head for a late meal or a dropped dish. I feared for any children we might have, how they would be beaten for every misstep.'

'Do you know who the letter was from?'

Anna shook her head. 'But I suspect. There was something about the seal that made me think it was from a woman. And that is why I think perhaps Paul has more than one leman. I doubt that the steward's wife can either read or write, and of course such a woman would not have her own seal, so I think Paul has another leman of some social standing. Perhaps it would cause a scandal. I don't know.'

'The steward's wife? Your steward or your mother's?' Owen asked.

'My mother's.'

Another little connection. 'Kate Cooper is your husband's mistress? Are you certain?' An insatiable woman, she must be.

'Of her I'm certain. Just as my mother found her with Will, so I found her with Paul. Before we were married, and after. When I found them in the stable before we married, I forgave it, thought that young men must satisfy themselves somewhere before they are wed. But after —' Her eyes swam with tears. 'Of course I said nothing. I would never dare accuse him.' She pressed her sleeve to her eyes.

'Was Jack Cooper married to Kate before he came to Riddlethorpe?'

'Oh, yes. She was large with their first child when they arrived.'

'Do you know anything about her past?'

Anna shook her head. 'Nor do I care to.'

'Do you think your mother knows anything about Kate Cooper?'

'Ask her. She is to come visit me here at Christmas.'

'I will.' Owen got up to leave. Paused. 'While you

are praying for me, Mistress Scorby, pray for Jasper de Melton, too. The lad who witnessed Will's murder. He is missing, probably wounded, I hope not dead. And a young man is murdered whose only sin was being Jasper's friend.'

Anna crossed herself. 'I will pray for all of you.'

Ambrose Coats listened to Lucie's account while rubbing the wood of his rebec with an oily cloth. The activity allowed him to keep his head down, his hair hiding his expression.

'I know that your friend Martin Wirthir is anxious to stay hidden,' Lucie concluded, 'but Magda Digby says he tried to watch out for Jasper. So I thought he should know to look for him. The boy is likely weak and feverish. He cannot protect himself in such condition.'

Now Ambrose looked up at Lucie. 'If there were some way I could find Martin and tell him, I would. But I tell the truth when I say that I have no idea where he is, even whether he is in York. He would want to know about this. I pray that he will come here or go to Magda's soon. He does worry about the boy. He says the boy is an innocent victim. He grieves for him.'

'When Martin helped me on the road, I felt he laboured under a great sorrow,' Lucie said. 'He was kind to me.'

Ambrose nodded. 'Martin has his own moral system that defies my efforts to understand. He is one of the kindest, most generous men, but also one of the greediest, most ruthless. It depends on who you are.' Ambrose shrugged. 'I find his strangeness irresistible.' Their eyes met, and suddenly Lucie understood what Martin was to Ambrose.

'Our hearts are rarely wise in whom we love, are they?' she said.

Ambrose laughed. 'Praise God. What would we sing about otherwise?'

Twenty

Desperate Measures

A rat ran across his wounded side. Just an average-sized rat, and yet the pain woke Jasper. His right side and his right cheek throbbed and burned. He had tried to bandage himself, but he could not bandage his cheek properly and still breathe. He slipped in and out of fever dreams. A woman as tall as a house with a knife that glowed with fire bent over him. A string of hands tied to her waist brushed Jasper's face. As the hands touched him they came to life, clawing at him, raking across his right cheek.

When he woke now and then, he tried to make himself sit up. He knew he was in an alley, one of the alleys too narrow for horses or carts. But when the fever was high the opposite wall seemed terribly far away and much higher than any house he'd ever seen. He remembered lying in bed burning with fever and his mother standing in the doorway, looming in the doorway, so large and far away that Jasper had screamed, fearing that God was taking him away from her. She had come to him, come across miles and miles of floor, to gather him up in her arms. And it had been all right then. The room had returned to normal.

His mother was not here now to make everything all right.

But he should be safe here. He knew from his past efforts at hiding that he would be fairly safe in such an alley. The folk who hurried by would leave him alone, or if he'd rolled underfoot they would just kick him out of the way. He could smell that he'd rolled in dung and urine, but he was too weak to care.

Still, he must care. He must eat. He must try to remember what had happened. There was someone in trouble. He could not remember who. His head hurt. He thought he'd fallen, but the wounds in his cheek and side were knife wounds, he was certain. He kept thinking about the giant woman in his dreams. That could not be possible, could it? He was confused.

But he must eat. Maybe if he ate something he could think better. He remembered going to the beggar's door at the abbey and getting food. Someone had asked him how he'd cut himself. He'd run away. He had to hide. No one must know who he was, what he'd done.

What had he done? Jasper tried to get his memories to line up in the right order. He'd fallen down stairs. A woman with a knife. He'd wet himself. John lay so quiet. John. That was it. He'd killed John.

No, the lady with the hands had killed John. All those hands hanging from her belt.

No. She was a dream.

There *was* a woman, though. The woman with the knife. John had betrayed Jasper to the woman. Why?

With effort, Jasper pulled himself up to sit against the wall. That was good. He felt dizzy, queasy, but the feeling passed. He listened to the sounds of the city, trying to figure out what time of day it was. It was too dark in the alley to tell, and all he saw when he looked up was the jutting second storey of the building he sat against. Carts moved through the streets, but it was still quiet. Early morning, he guessed. If he got himself moving, he could get to the abbey for food. And then he could think what to do.

His mother had always said that a body could not think clearly with an empty belly. Jasper was not hungry, but he needed to think clearly. He could not even tell how long he'd been hiding. Days, for certain. But could it be weeks?

He pulled himself up onto his feet, leaning weakly against the building beside him. Holding onto the wall as he went, Jasper stumbled towards the street at the end of the alley. Lop Lane. He was close to the abbey. Praise God. But the beggar's door was on the far wall, outside the city gates.

So much mud. But out in the open the ground was snowy. No wonder he'd been so cold. Why had he not worn his cloak? He closed his eyes and leaned against a building, trying to remember. It seemed important to try to remember everything. It frightened him that there were things he could not remember. Someone jostled him and his feet slipped out from under him. A hand helped him up, then a woman's voice exclaimed, 'You've been sleeping in the alleys. How did you get inside the walls?'

He headed towards Bootham Bar, hoping to hide beside a cart to sneak out the gate, as he remembered now he'd done last time. He did not want anyone to see him. Some of the guards knew him. They would notice.

But there was no cart in sight when Jasper reached the gate. The gatekeeper squinted at him, as if he could not decide whether Jasper looked familiar. Perhaps he was so dirty. Or the cut in his cheek disfigured him enough to disguise him. His head felt much larger on the right side than the left. Maybe that was a good disguise.

A disguise. Henna. To go to St George's Field with Captain Archer. Jasper remembered now. He'd been so happy. That was certainly a thing of the past. Captain Archer would never forgive him for John's death. And how could he make them believe John had led him there?

Jasper hurried through the gate. Instead of going to the beggar's door at the abbey, he could continue on to Magda Digby's house. But no. He must trust no one. He'd learned his lesson.

A crowd already huddled before the door in the north wall of the abbey. Jasper crouched under a tree near a one-armed man and a woman with two babies tucked under her tattered cloak. He'd heard about twins, God's special blessing. But the woman did not look as if she felt blessed. Her eyes were sunken and expressionless, her jaw slack, revealing blackened and missing teeth. Her face was fleshless. Skull-like. She was starving. Why had God given this woman two babes when she was starving already?

No. No, it was not good to question God's justice. It was just Jasper's weakness and his pain that made him think such thoughts.

Jasper's eyes fluttered closed and he dreamed about the sad mother. As her babes suckled, one at each breast, she shrank and shrank, her skin wrinkling and collapsing, as if her bones were being sucked out, too, and then she was gone. The babies screamed.

When Jasper opened his eyes, the babies were screaming, but the sad woman still held them sheltered in her cloak. Jasper looked up. The giant woman stood at the edge of a cluster of people, staring at him from the crowd. Jasper closed his eyes and shook his head, then looked back. She was not there.

Of course not. She was a dream.

But the woman who had attacked him, she wasn't a dream. Maybe it had been her.

Jasper thought about leaving, but the beggar's door had just opened and he saw people grabbing for small loaves of brown bread. He needed that. Maybe his legs would work better if he had some bread. He moved forward with the others.

People had cups and bowls with them. He'd brought nothing. He must have said something out loud, because the one-armed man nudged him and then pointed to a man by the door who had got his loaf and torn it open. As he held up the two halves, one of the monks scooped something from a pot and dropped it on the bread. Jasper thanked the man. The man smiled and opened his mouth. Jasper saw that he had no tongue.

A criminal. Jasper's mother had told him not to speak to criminals. But that was long ago, before Jasper was out on the streets himself. And this man had been kind to show him what to do.

'God bless you,' Jasper said to him. 'May the Lord remember your goodness on Judgement Day.'

After a long while, Jasper made it to the front of the crowd. Once he thought he saw the woman again, but by now the smell of the food had made him remember the sensation of hunger and Jasper could not bear to give up his place. Besides, he told himself, she was just a dream. The bread was hard, and he fumbled getting it torn in half, but at last he saw two pieces of fish, bones and skin and all, dropped onto the halves. He sat down a few steps away and devoured it.

Now he was thirsty. He looked down at the river,

but he knew that people got sick drinking the water. On the far end of the beggar's door stood a monk with a ladle and a large barrel. Maybe Jasper could get enough in his cupped hands, or he could just open his mouth wide. He struggled to stand, then started pushing his way back towards the door.

And there she was, the woman who had attacked him. He knew her now. In his dream she was a giant, but this was the real woman. And she was looking right at him.

Jasper turned and ran. He did not know how he was able to, but he ran, slipping and sliding, sometimes falling and fearing that he would not get up again. But he got up every time. She was not behind him, not that he could see, but he knew for certain that she had seen him. He would not let himself stop.

As he approached the gate he prayed for a cart to be going in that he could hide in, but the gatekeeper, who had had time to think, yelled, 'Jasper? Is it you? The Riverwoman's been looking for you, boy. These two weeks or more.'

But Jasper just ran past him and in the gate, knowing it for a miracle that the man had recognised him in his extreme need. Jasper's side was burning and his breath came in gasps, but still he kept moving down Petergate. Hurry. Hurry. As Jasper turned into Goodramgate, he heard a cart creaking and groaning as it turned the corner behind him. The street was too narrow for both him and a cart. Jasper looked to his right and left for an alley or even a deep door. And then in front of him he saw Martin. The man was waving at him and yelling something, but the noisy cart was too close to hear what Martin was saying. The cart was very close. Jasper turned around and realised that the cart was bearing down on him. He stumbled and screamed. Suddenly someone scooped him up and out of the way.

Jasper pressed his burning face into his saviour's shoulder as the cart trundled past. It was the second time today that God had saved him with a miracle.

'Jasper, quiet. It is Martin. I am going to sit you down for a moment and ask if anyone recognised the man in the cart.'

Jasper clung to Martin. 'It's a woman. She has to kill me.'

'No, Jasper, I saw. This was a man.'

Still Jasper clung to him, terrified to be lost in the alley again.

'I will come right back. I don't want them to see that I have you.' With strong hands, Martin pried Jasper off him.

But no one could tell Martin who had been driving the cart.

'He should have been leading the horse,' a woman said. 'That's why we have that ordinance. So many children have been killed that way.' She shook her head.

A few days before Christmas, word came to the shop that Cecilia Ridley was at the nunnery.

'I will go another day,' Owen said. 'She will surely stay a while.'

Lucie knew he was disappointed. So was she. When the messenger had come, they'd both thought it was news of Jasper. Two weeks he'd been missing. Not a word. But it was important to continue searching for the murderers of Ridley and Crounce. And John.

'Perhaps Cecilia Ridley will know something that will lead us to Jasper. If Kate Cooper has him somewhere.'

'If she has him somewhere, he's probably dead,' Owen said.

'You're not giving up?'

'No. You know I cannot.' Owen considered Lucie thoughtfully. 'Would you go speak with Cecilia?'

'Me? Why?'

'I have asked her so many questions already. She has been hiding something from me. I cannot discover what it is. Perhaps you will have a better way with her. Woman to woman.' Owen shrugged. 'I don't know.'

Lucie climbed up and set the jar she'd been using back on a shelf, descended, wiped her hands, took off her apron. 'If you will watch the shop, I will go right now.'

'You don't have to do that.'

'Why not? Why delay it?' Lucie took Owen's hands. 'I will feel better if I take some action.'

Owen kissed her forehead. 'You made a sorry bargain when you married me.'

'Why do you say that?'

'I involve you in the awful business I do for the Archbishop. We would have a merry Christmas if it were not for him.'

'And how do you know it would be merry?' She put her arms around Owen and tucked her head against him. 'Without you, I do not think I would be very merry. Without the Archbishop's intercession the guild might not have allowed me to marry. And you would be off fighting for John of Gaunt.'

Owen slipped her veil off and stroked her soft hair. 'You do not regret it?'

'Not for a moment, Owen.' She lifted her face to his.

Lucie hesitated at the door to St Clement's, feeling strange to be back here after all these years. She'd returned only once, to Sister Doltrice's funeral, the one sister who had truly befriended Lucie in her miserable years in the convent after her mother died. Her father still thought he'd done the best thing in putting Lucie in the convent. He had no idea what it had been like for her. The sisters had considered Lucie's mother a French whore and watched Lucie for signs of the same behaviour. Nicholas had saved her from this place.

Nicholas. That was why she was here. Lucie had a suspicion about Cecilia Ridley's relationship with Gilbert that echoed Lucie's own unresolved feelings for Nicholas. She must do this. It would help Owen. Perhaps help to find Jasper. And John's murderer. Lucie lifted her hand and knocked.

A young nun answered. 'God go with you, Mistress Wilton. Dame Isobel will be pleased to see you.'

Lucie, remembering Isobel, doubted that. 'I have come to see Mistress Ridley. Is that possible?'

'I will ask. Please, come in.'

The nun left Lucie in the prioress's receiving room. It was not long before a tall, sombrely dressed woman entered. Dark eyes studied Lucie so intently that she felt herself blushing. That would not do. She must be in control for her scheme to work.

'I am Lucie Wilton, Owen's wife.' Lucie hoped her smile was relaxed and friendly. 'I asked him if I might come to speak with you.'

Cecilia Ridley sat carefully at the edge of the bench near Lucie. 'You asked to come? Why?' Her eyes were a little too wide open. Lucie realised Cecilia Ridley was frightened. 'And why are you called Wilton, not Archer?'

'I was made Master Apothecary after my first husband died. The guild insisted that I keep Nicholas's name.'

'So you and Owen are indeed married?'

Lucie found it a strange question. 'Many women do not carry their husband's names.'

'It is a custom that is changing. In France most women now carry their husband's names.' Cecilia Ridley gazed down on Lucie, the fear now gone from her eyes. It was replaced by a chilly glare.

'Please,' Lucie motioned to Cecilia to sit down, 'I came here to speak with you about the murders of your husband and your friend. We must work to find the murderers before more people die. A child is missing, a boy who witnessed Will Crounce's murder and whose life has been threatened by a woman who may be Kate Cooper.'

'Cooper. I always said she would amount to no good.'

'What can you tell me about her?'

'Why did you come? Why not Owen?'

Lucie noticed a warmth in the way Cecilia spoke Owen's name. She pushed that aside. 'I am concerned about the boy, Jasper. I want to help find these people before they harm him.'

'How noble.'

Lucie had not expected Cecilia to be hostile, just secretive. Was she hostile because Lucie had come in Owen's place? This did not bode well. 'Forgive me for intruding on your visit with your daughter. I will try to be brief. Please, just tell me about Kate Cooper.'

Cecilia sat as if perched to depart without warning. 'Kate Cooper. I know little about her. Did not care to know. There is a bitterness, a hatred in the woman that men are blind to. They think her passionate, but she feeds on them. Conquers them because she hates them.'

'Can you describe her to me?'

'Tall. Long limbs. Light brown hair, brown eyes, square jaw, large mouth – like a leech.'

'The woman who attacked Jasper was quite strong.'

'She would be. Her hands are very large for a woman. That's why I noticed how she used them. She lifted her spoon with her left hand. The mark of the Devil.'

'She is left-handed?' Lucie thought of Jasper's injuries, his broken arm, his leg, all on the right, where a left-handed person would have grabbed him if facing him. 'Are you certain?'

The dark eyes stared coldly. 'Why would I say it otherwise? What makes you think she is involved?'

'It is Owen's theory.'

'Ah.' The eyes softened a little. 'He would be more perceptive than most men.'

'I certainly did not think so when I first met him.'

'Really?' The voice expressed interest. 'How did you meet?'

So be it. Lucie could see how this might lead in exactly the direction she must go. 'Owen came to York to look into two deaths at St Mary's. Poisonings. First he flirted with me, then he decided I might be the poisoner. He even thought for a while that I was poisoning my husband to keep him quiet. Much as he suspects you of poisoning your husband.' Lucie watched with interest as Cecilia Ridley went pale. 'Does that make Owen more perceptive than most men?'

Cecilia put a hand to her heart. 'He suspects me of poisoning Gilbert?'

'He does not like thinking it, but he feels that you are hiding something.'

'He believes me capable of such a thing?' Cecilia whispered.

'I know how you feel. I remember how outraged

I was by Owen's suspicion.' Lucie paused. This was not easy to speak of. She reminded herself of Jasper. 'You see, I felt so guilty myself. And I knew I could never explain my feelings to Owen.'

Cecilia brushed an invisible mote of dust from her skirt. 'What do you mean?'

'My husband Nicholas poisoned someone. When I realised what he had done, I hated him for it. And for things that I learned about our marriage. I wanted to hurt him. I did hurt him, but not in the way Owen thought.'

Cecilia Ridley was quietly watchful. 'How did you hurt him?'

Lucie bowed her head, hiding tears. It would not do to appear weak in front of this woman. But this was the hardest part to say aloud. 'I hurt Nicholas in the worst way. As he lay dying, he asked for forgiveness. I refused him.'

The room grew dark with the winter afternoon. The young nun came in, lit a few lamps, shuffled back out again.

Cecilia Ridley stood up, went to a small window, looked out at the darkening garden. Still turned away from Lucie, Cecilia said, 'I do not understand why you are telling me this. Did Owen make this up to catch me?'

'No. I am doing it for myself. It does no good to confess it. I have tried that. I cannot explain. I want you to know that I hated the man I loved, who had been good to me, and in that moment of hatred, I punished him. And I regret it bitterly. It cannot be undone. Ever. I kneel at his grave and beg his forgiveness.'

Cecilia had turned back to Lucie.

'Owen does not understand,' Lucie said.

'How could he?' Cecilia sat down again near Lucie. 'But you love Owen now?'

Lucie nodded. 'I cannot imagine life without him.'

'Is it different from your first marriage?'

'Quite different.'

'How?'

Lucie squirmed under Cecilia's intense regard. But she must finish what she had begun. 'I loved Nicholas in a different way. He was a comfort to me. My love for Owen is darker. More needy. Frightening.'

Cecilia dropped her gaze to her hands, which she clasped tightly in her lap. Lucie worried that she had said too much. Then the dark eyes moved back to Lucie.

'The way you love Owen, that is how I loved Will Crounce,' Cecilia said in a voice tight with emotion. 'I would have done anything to keep his love. When I heard that he was dead, I thought my life was over. I wanted to punish everyone who still lived. And then I wanted to die.

'I watched Gilbert. He'd become secretive. Nervous. Suddenly solicitous of me and the children. I began to put things together. Just before Gilbert went to York at Corpus Christi we'd had an argument. He knew what was between Will and me. Had known it for a while. He said he was home now and it had to stop. I was his wife. Remembering that argument, I decided that Gilbert had killed Will. He had gone to York with that purpose. I hated Gilbert at that moment. I wanted him to suffer. I wanted him to feel the pain of my grief for Will.' She touched Lucie's hand. 'I never meant to kill Gilbert. Just make him suffer.'

The light in Cecilia's eyes frightened Lucie. So it was true, and she had made Gilbert suffer for so long, so horribly, to teach him her own pain. Lucie shivered.

The dark eyes filled with tears. 'I would undo it if I could. Gilbert changed. He became so like Will, thoughtful, gentle. I told myself the suffering purified him.' A sob shook Cecilia. 'I am the Devil. Gilbert was innocent. I should burn in Hell for all eternity.' She put her head in her hands and silently wept.

Lucie moved to the bench beside Cecilia Ridley and put her arms around her. 'How awful you must have felt when Owen brought you the news of Gilbert's death.'

'I felt God had taken him to punish me.'

'To punish you?'

Cecilia looked up, wiping her eyes. 'I can never beg Gilbert's forgiveness.'

Lucie felt she was looking into the eyes of her own pain.

They sat quietly for a long time. Then the prioress arrived, bearing wine. Dame Isobel seemed momentarily startled by the tearful faces. 'It is almost time for our evening meal. Will you join us, Mistress Wilton?'

Lucie looked at Cecilia.

Cecilia took her hand and nodded.

Twenty-one

Martin Wirthir

M artin hid for a while in the alley to see if anyone would return to the scene. If it had been an attempt on the boy's life, the assailant would want to know whether he'd succeeded. Last night, Ambrose had told Martin about Jasper's latest trouble. Two weeks the boy had been on the streets with festering wounds. He must be a strong lad. Even so, a fever burned through the boy's thin frame. Martin judged it best to know who he was up against, but it was difficult to resist getting the boy to safety immediately.

Martin's watch was soon rewarded, but not by the man in the cart. It was a woman's voice he heard, stopping people in the street. 'They say that a boy was hit by a cart in this street,' Martin heard her say, 'I wondered— My son is missing. More than a week ago. He is wounded – his father – it was a terrible argument. The boy they described – it sounded like my son. Can you tell me? Was a boy hit in this street? Do you know where he is?'

Martin peered out to see this excellent actress. The

woman was tall, with a queenly carriage. He could not see the face beneath the hood, but there was something about her that seemed familiar.

Folk could give the woman no information. There had been a reckless driver down the street, yes. And some thought perhaps they'd seen a boy running. But no one had actually seen a boy hit. Eventually she gave up, going off in the direction of the Shambles.

Martin hoisted Jasper over his shoulder and headed for the apothecary.

Owen and Tildy had waited for Lucie to return from St Clement's, but as the hour grew late they decided to eat the stew that Tildy had prepared, then Owen would go out after Lucie. When the knock came at the shop door, they both looked up in fear. Lucie would not knock, but if someone had found her . . .

Owen was at the door in a few strides. When he saw the body slung over Martin's shoulder, Owen feared the worst. 'Lucie! Sweet Heaven, I should never have—'

'Peace!' Martin held up a hand. 'Not Mistress Wilton. This is Jasper. I have found him. Almost didn't find him in time. A man tried to run him over in a cart.'

Martin turned so Owen could see the boy's face with its awful wound, feel the boy's fever. Owen touched the hot cheek. 'I hope you have brought him in time.'

Martin carried Jasper to the kitchen.

'Sweet Mary in Heaven,' Tildy exclaimed.

When Owen saw the extent of the boy's wounds he shook his head.

'This is more than we can deal with here. He needs Brother Wulfstan's ministrations.'

'Where is this Wulfstan?' Martin asked.

272

'At St Mary's abbey. He's the infirmarian.'

'Good. That is not too far. Let us go at once.'

Owen turned his head to get a good look at Martin. 'I take it you are Martin Wirthir?'

The man nodded, shrugged. 'Forgive me. My worry over Jasper has robbed me of my manners. I am Martin Wirthir. I heard that Jasper was missing and in danger. I went looking for him.'

'Thank God you did.'

'We must get the boy to the abbey at once.'

Owen nodded. 'Very soon. You can help Tildy clean his wounds first, get him into dry clothes, and try to get some wine into him. I must go out. Lucie is at St Clement's talking to Cecilia Ridley.'

'She is outside the city walls at night?'

'It was daylight when she left. I cannot think why she is so long returning.'

'Someone must go for her,' Martin agreed. 'I propose that I do, and you take Jasper to the abbey infirmary.'

'No. I go for Lucie.'

'I delivered Mistress Wilton safely before. The boy needs attention now. They know you at the infirmary —'

'Lucie is my first priority,' Owen insisted.

'Be sensible, man. I know my way among the night people of York.'

Owen bristled. 'I did not ask for your approval of my plan. It will be time enough to take the boy after I've found Lucie.'

They both turned as the kitchen door opened, letting in the cold. And Lucie. She looked at Martin with some surprise, then down at the boy lying in front of the fire. 'Sweet Jesus, you have found him!' Lucie rushed over to Jasper. She looked back at the two men who stared at her as if she were unexpected in her own house. 'What is the matter?'

'What kept you so long?' Owen demanded. 'And how did you get back here in the dark?'

'I spoke with Cecilia, and then I ate with the sisters. The dean of the minster brought me back with him. He is the brother of Isobel, the prioress, and had dined there.' Lucie looked from one to the other. 'What were you arguing about?'

'We were discussing how we will get Jasper to St Mary's infirmary tonight,' Owen said.

'St Mary's?' Lucie bent over Jasper, lifted the torn shirt to examine his side, touched his wounded cheek. She crossed herself, whispered a prayer. 'We must get him to Brother Wulfstan at once. Shall I ask Bess for the use of her donkey cart?'

'It will be faster if I carry him,' Owen said.

'Shall I come with you?' Lucie asked.

'No,' Owen said, with more force than necessary. 'You stay here with Tildy and keep out of trouble.'

Martin raised an eyebrow, looked back and forth between Lucie and Owen.

Lucie's face reddened. She clasped her hands behind her back. 'Then go quickly. God be with you.'

Tildy had managed to clean the boy's face without causing much pain, but the water roused him. Jasper looked up into Tildy's concerned eyes and whispered, 'John is dead. Can you forgive me?'

Tildy's eyes brimmed with tears, but she managed enough voice to say, 'There is nothing to forgive, Jasper. He brought it on himself.' She dabbed his forehead.

Lucie knelt down to him. 'Owen is going to carry you to our friend at the abbey, Jasper. He will dress your wounds and make you comfortable. And you will be safe there.'

The boy squeezed her hand.

Wulfstan had been called from the chapel to Jasper's bedside. He shook his head as he studied the boy's wounds. 'In this most sacred of seasons, how sad it is to see what man has become. God give me the grace to undo this.' He looked up at Owen. 'God be with you, Owen. Go home to Lucie now. Henry and I will get right to work.'

Martin had stayed back by the door to the infirmary, keeping out of the way while Owen explained what he and Lucie had noted about the wounds and Jasper's condition. Now Martin came forward. 'You must know that the boy is in grave danger. Someone tried to kill him today. And those knife wounds would have been mortal had not another young man come between the attacker and Jasper.'

Wulfstan nodded. 'The boy will be safe here. This other young man. He was badly injured?'

'He is dead,' Martin said.

Wulfstan and Henry crossed themselves.

When they returned to the apothecary, Martin and Owen joined Lucie by the hearth. Tildy had spiced and heated a jug of wine, and now went to bed to leave them to their talk.

Owen lifted his cup towards the guest. 'You've led me quite a chase, Martin Wirthir. Do not misunderstand, you are welcome here. But I wonder why you have been so reluctant to meet me.'

Martin raised his cup to Owen, then Lucie. 'You are gracious to offer me drink and a fire. I have not recommended myself to you by my secretive manner, but I did not know whether I could trust you. I thought

I could trust Mistress Wilton, but you, Captain Archer, I had doubts about you. And it is such a complicated business.'

Lucie studied Martin, noting that although he dressed like a tinker, in leather and rough wool, there were touches, his cleanliness, the ear-ring, the faint scent of perfumed oil, that contrasted with his disguise at close quarters. 'You are not in the habit of living on the streets.'

'No. I work with wealthy merchants and nobility, Mistress Wilton. But ever since Will Crounce's murder —'

Owen sat forward, fixing his right eye on Martin. 'If you felt threatened by Will's murder, why did you stay in York?'

Martin rubbed his eyes, sighed. 'For many reasons.'

'And these reasons are?'

Martin glanced from Owen to Lucie, who was just as intent, and back to Owen. 'I *can* explain myself. I'd come to York, as you know, shortly before Corpus Christi. I had been near the court and heard that a ruthless family who had no cause to love Gilbert and me were suddenly in favour with the King, so I came up here to tell Gilbert. And to warn Will Crounce that by association with Gilbert and myself he might be in danger.'

'So Will knew of his danger?' Lucie said.

'Yes. Though much good the knowledge did him.'

'Severing the right hand,' Owen said, 'that is usually to mark a thief.'

Martin dropped his gaze to the floor. 'You make a success in trade, someone is bound to call you a thief.'

Lucie glanced at Owen. She could tell by the set of his jaw that he was not satisfied with the response. Neither was she.

Owen shrugged. 'You still do not trust us. I do not know how to prove to you that we can be trusted. My interest in your activities has to do with the Archbishop's wish to understand why Ridley was murdered. I do not intend to use the information for any other end, except of course to protect Jasper and my own household, which is now involved. I have searched for you to warn you that you are in danger.'

Martin jerked his head up. 'The fact that I am a foreigner makes me an outcast here. And other things about my life do not help the matter. Yet you sought me out to warn me. Why?'

Owen sat back, smiling. 'I confess that once I'd warned you I'd hoped to learn more about you and your connection with Ridley and Crounce. Anything that might help me understand why they were murdered, and in such a manner. I thought it a reasonable trade.'

Martin shrugged. 'I appreciate your honesty.' He stretched his arms and yawned. 'I am very tired.'

'So are we all,' Owen said. 'Did you go to Riddle-thorpe after Crounce's death?'

'I did. Quietly. There is an inn I know in Beverley where I could stay and send word to Gilbert. He did not want his family or household to associate with me. For their safety. Considering what has happened, I see how wise he was.'

'And did you notice how Ridley wasted away?'

Martin looked puzzled. 'Ridley? Wasting away? The man loved his food.'

'Not of late, according to Archbishop Thoresby himself.'

Martin stared into his cup, thinking. 'I remember his looking uneasy and weary, but that is all. And he ate well that evening. Why? Was Gilbert ill?'

'He was being slowly poisoned,' Owen said.

Lucie studied the floor, not wanting to reveal in front of Martin what she'd learned at St Clement's.

'*Merde.*' Martin was visibly shaken. 'How could that be? Gilbert had stopped at home. He must have eaten mostly at Riddlethorpe.'

'It was something he believed to be a tonic,' Owen said.

'Horrible.' Martin crossed himself. 'No. I saw no sign of such a thing.'

'How long after Crounce's death did you visit Ridley?'

'A week, perhaps. I did not wait long. Who was poisoning Gilbert?'

Lucie held her breath.

'We do not know,' Owen said. 'Do you?'

'I never met his household, as I've told you, so I do not know what enemies he might have had there.'

Owen nodded. 'So you warned Ridley, returned to York, and stayed. That seems unwise.'

'It was when I returned from Riddlethorpe that I discovered Jasper de Melton on the streets. I had dined with Will the night before Corpus Christi and then walked with him to Toft Green, where they were assembling the wagons. He pointed out Jasper with such pride. "I hope to be a father to him," Will had said. The boy was being instructed in the use of the greasehorn so I wasn't introduced, but I could see he was a lively, bright child. I was happy for Will. He was a sensitive man. He was not happy without a wife, and I knew, though he did not as yet, that Gilbert was coming home for good. Suddenly he would be without Cecilia Ridley.'

'So you knew of their attachment,' Lucie said.

'I did.'

Owen folded his arms. 'What else can you tell us?'

Martin shrugged. 'There is little more to tell. I tried to keep track of Jasper, show him where he might get food. He seemed to be doing well. I went away for a while.' Martin took a drink, his eyes suddenly sad. 'I remember that my first thought when I heard of Will's murder was that Gilbert had killed him, and the hand was for stealing Cecilia. Not that I could really imagine Gilbert doing that, but Will was so uninvolved with our more secret undertakings.' Martin put his cup down, rubbed his eyes. 'It was a short-lived suspicion. It was too dreadful a thing. And anyone who knew Will knew how gentle he was. He couldn't inspire that kind of hate in a friend.'

Owen stifled a yawn. It was getting late. 'It seems Will Crounce was loved by all who knew him.'

Martin nodded.

'What do you mean by "more secret undertakings"?' Lucie asked.

'We took risks, Gilbert and I.'

'And one of them had to do with the family in favour at court?'

'That was mostly my folly. My greed. Gilbert stumbled on it later. But not Will. He knew nothing.'

'What family?' Lucie asked.

'It is too dangerous to tell you.'

Lucie cocked an eyebrow. 'Things are rather dangerous for us already.'

'For now I will not speak their name. And now it is my turn to ask you a question. Do you know who has committed these murders?'

Owen shook his head. 'No.'

Martin sighed. Stood up. 'You are tired. I am tired. I must take my leave.'

'Will we see you again?' Lucie asked.

'Of course. I shall want to know what you learn,

considering I am likely to be the next victim.'

Upstairs, Lucie curled up against Owen and closed her eyes. Owen shook her shoulder. 'Can you think I'd let you sleep before you tell me what you learned at the nunnery?'

Lucie looked up sleepily. 'Have you noted that Jasper's wounds are on his right side?'

Owen feared that her mind was already muddled with sleep. 'What does that have to do with Cecilia Ridley?'

'Cecilia says that Kate Cooper is left-handed. Facing Jasper, she would have most easily wounded him on the right. She must be the one involved.'

Owen grinned. 'That is useful. What else did Cecilia Ridley tell you?'

'Very little about Kate.'

So little information. And he'd been so worried about her. 'Well she must have told you something for all the time you spent there.'

At the angry tone in Owen's voice, Lucie came to attention, propping herself up on her elbow. 'You asked me to go and speak with her. Are you now angry that I did?'

'I am angry that you stayed there to sup and did not send word.'

Lucie touched Owen's cheek, urging him to look at her. He glared. She reached up and kissed him. 'I am sorry, love. Please forgive me. I was so proud of myself for getting a confession from her that I was quite giddy.'

Her smile was so smug. 'A confession? You waited all this time to tell me?'

'We had company, my love.'

'What confession?'

'Cecilia was poisoning Gilbert. She thought he'd killed Will out of jealousy. She did not mean to kill Gilbert, just to give him pain as Will's death pained her.'

'Cecilia said that?'

'Yes.' Lucie held the oil lamp close to Owen's face. 'You find that difficult to believe?'

Owen shrugged. 'I knew she was hiding something. I suppose it is exactly what I suspected.'

'But you don't like her having done such a thing.'

'It is so cruel a thing.' Truth was, he did not know what he felt about Cecilia, but he was disappointed in her.

'It was a passionate act, Owen. She loved Will Crounce.'

'And not her husband?'

Lucie was quiet.

'Well?'

'There was a time when you wondered how I could love mine.'

True enough. Owen decided to change the subject. 'Do you think Martin is telling us the truth?'

Lucie nodded. 'So far as it goes. But he holds much back.'

'I think so, too. Do you think he will come back?'

Lucie put the lamp aside and lay down again. 'The next time the murderer moves, Martin will come to us. Let us hope he does not wait too long.' Owen sighed and lay down beside her. 'It is difficult to wait.'

Lucie pulled herself closer to him. 'It is a chilly night.'

He heard the invitation in her voice and turned towards her. 'When I opened the door and saw the body slung over Martin's shoulder, I feared it was you.'

Lucie kissed him on the nose. 'Forgive me for my thoughtlessness. But I'm here now, safe and sound, and wanting my husband.' She hugged him tight.

'Something is different tonight.' Owen held the lamp over Lucie's face. She looked at peace, smiling. 'What happened at St Clement's?'

'I forgave myself.'

'For what?'

She touched his scar. 'For loving you more than Nicholas.'

Owen put down the lamp and pulled Lucie over on top of him.

Twenty-two

Complications

Brother Wulfstan grumbled to himself as the guest appeared at the infirmary door for the second time in one day. 'He still sleeps, my son. It may be many days before Jasper is strong enough to have visitors.'

'Forgive me, but this time I come for healing.'

'Are you ill?'

'Injured.' The man held up a hand uncalloused by manual labour.

Wulfstan squinted at the white hand. 'I don't see—'

The man wiggled a finger and pointed to the palm.

Wulfstan picked up a lamp and held it close to the hand. 'I am afraid my eyes are weakening at an alarming rate. Is there perhaps a slight reddening?'

'I burned myself. A foolish thing. I was lighting a candle.'

Wulfstan touched the spot on the palm. The man winced. Wulfstan felt blistering. The fingertip was the same. But the wounds were trivial, and, God forgive him, Wulfstan found the man's impatient breath irritating. 'This is nothing at all. Surely you travel with a salve for such minor things.'

'I would if I had a wife to pack it for me, but she took herself off to the nunnery for prayer weeks ago and I have no one to see to such things while she's gone.' He sounded like a petulant child.

Wulfstan told himself that courtesy toward this man could be offered up as a penance. He tried to keep the irritation out of his voice. 'Does your wife pray for something in particular?'

'No. She needs no excuse for prayer. I told her to pray that God cure her of her barrenness.'

Wulfstan wondered whether the man's wife was really praying that her husband might be called to God's side while she was away. Such thoughts. He was not doing very well with this penance. But to be so cold about his wife's childless state. Ah. That was odd. Earlier in the day he'd said that Jasper reminded him of his son.

'Then your son was the product of an earlier marriage?'

The man looked confused.

'The son who looks like Jasper?'

'Oh. Of course. My thoughts are muddled. My hand is beginning to throb. Yes, my son is the child of my first wife, who died in childbed.' He shook his hand to indicate how hot it felt. 'Perhaps if I could come in and sit down. I feel faint.'

Faint from such a superficial wound? Wulfstan did not budge from his stance blocking the doorway. 'What is your son's name?'

The man thrust out his jaw. 'What does that have to do with anything? I came here to have you see to my hand.'

'What is your name, for that matter?'

'John,' the man barked.

'Wait here, John,' Wulfstan said, closing the door.

He did not want the man entering the infirmary. It would be more difficult to get rid of him. The man had made himself a pest the past few days. Ever since Jasper arrived. In truth, Wulfstan did not believe the man's name was John or that this 'John' had a son who looked like Jasper. Wulfstan spooned some burn ointment into a cup and took it back to the man. 'Rub this into the burned areas several times a day. Do not use much or it will get on everything you touch and soil it. You might wrap a strip of cloth around the palm. Go in peace, my son.' Wulfstan bowed his head and closed the door in the man's face. How sinfully delicious.

A while later, Brother Henry peeked in to see if Wulfstan was ready to go to the refectory for the evening meal. 'That man was here again,' Wulfstan said. 'The guest who pouts.'

Henry laughed. 'I do not know when I've known you so to dislike a man.'

'It is not simply dislike. The man is too interested in speaking with Jasper. Says the boy reminds him of his son, but I do not think he has a son. If he did, and he were so fond of him that Jasper's likeness moved him as he says it does, he would not torment his present wife about her barrenness. And he lied about his name.'

Henry moved back to check that the door was closed, then sat down by Wulfstan. 'You think he means the boy harm?'

'I feel it in my bones, Henry. God help me, it is not proof of anything, but the poor boy has been through so much. You saw how putrid the wound was in his side. I am sure he has been lying out in the alleys, pain robbing his wits. And the slice through his cheek – he will look almost as battle-scarred as Owen Archer when he's healed – and he's but eight years of age. I cannot risk something more happening to him.'

'So what do we do? Go to Abbot Campian?'

Wulfstan shook his head. 'No. I will not accuse the man to the abbot on so little evidence. But we must make sure that one of us is with Jasper at all times. He must not be left alone, even for a quick trip to the reredorter.'

Henry nodded. 'I will watch him while you go to the refectory. My hunger will be a prayer that the man means Jasper no harm.'

Wulfstan patted Henry's arm. 'You need not go hungry. I will bring food for you.'

'Should I find out more about him tomorrow? His name, his home?'

Wulfstan shook his head. 'We do not want to alert him to our concern. At the moment, I am a rude, overbearing monk, it has nothing to do with him. That is good.'

Tildy gasped as Lucie brought down from the chest three crystal wine glasses on delicate stems. 'I have never seen such a thing.'

'Don't you remember them, Tildy? We used them at our wedding feast. A gift from my father.'

'There was so much that day, Mistress Lucie. I could not see it all.'

'I thought the eve of Christmas would be a good time to use them.'

'What will they eat over at the York Tavern tonight with the Merchets coming over here?'

'They get cold meats, cheese, a simmering soup, bread. You should not worry about the few guests at the York tonight, Tildy.' Lucie motioned to her to get on the far side of the oak table. 'We'll move this to the centre of the room.'

Tildy hesitated. 'Should we not wait for the Captain?

He must be almost finished with the customer.'

'We are not weak, Tildy. We can easily move it ourselves. Besides, I heard the shop bell jingle again. He will be busy for a while.'

But it proved too much for Tildy, who cried out and dropped her side of the table.

Lucie was amazed. Tildy was a strong young woman. She hurried around the table to her, helped her over to a chair, felt her forehead. Cool. 'What is it, Tildy?'

'I'm just worn down, Mistress.'

'Am I overworking you?'

'No! No, it's never that. But since John—' she shrugged. 'I cannot eat or sleep for thinking of him.' Her voice trembled.

Lucie had noticed the shadows under Tildy's eyes, but had never imagined it was bad enough to affect her health. She hugged Tildy and felt her shivering. But no tears came. 'You must sit right here and eat some apples and cheese while I finish getting things ready,' Lucie ordered, rising to fetch the food.

'You're not going to make me go to bed?'

'And miss Christmas Eve? What do you take me for? But I don't think you should go to the evening service with us.'

'I wanted to pray for John tonight.'

'You can pray here, Tildy. God will hear you.' Lucie sat down by the girl, tucked some stray hairs into the girl's cap. 'Would you like to tell me about him?'

'He just had such a bad time.'

'He told you how he came to be hiding in the Merchet's stable?'

Tildy nodded, nibbled on a piece of cheese.

'Would you tell me?'

Tildy sighed. 'I suppose it can't hurt now.' She wiped her nose. 'His family died of plague. He got sent to his father's brother, a steward at a great house. They never fed John enough, even when the lady of the manor took him as a groom. One day he saw her push away a dish with a few figs left on it. When she wasn't looking, he took them. He thought she wasn't looking, anyway. She got so angry she screamed and her lord came. He took his sword hilt and crushed the fingers that had stolen the figs. When John's uncle saw his ruined hand, he said John was good for nothing and kicked him out.'

'How awful.'

'Can you believe such hatefulness in Christians, Mistress?'

Lucie took Tildy's hand. 'He must have cared for you very much to tell you the story, Tildy. He told no one else in York.'

Tildy sniffled.

'I will pray for him tonight, too.'

'Thank you, Mistress Lucie.'

'Tildy, your weakness. Are you with child by John?'

Tildy shook her head. 'But I wish I was. Then I'd have something left.'

Lucie drew Tildy to her. 'I understand, my love, I do.'

All day the waits had rehearsed for the Christmas festivities at the Guild Hall. It was late afternoon as Ambrose walked home, looking forward to his fire and some hot broth. Footless Lane was dark, but outside a few houses dim lamps cast eerie haloes of light over Ambrose as he passed. Near his own house, his steps faltered. His front door stood open. It could not be Martin – he was much too careful for that. Slowing, Ambrose considered what to do. He knew from Martin that he should be concerned – it was no accident that Gilbert Ridley's hand had been delivered to this very door. Ambrose began to turn round. He would go for one of the city constables But then he heard the unmistakable sound of a snorting pig. That was too much. The pig in his house. Ambrose rushed inside and caught the pig snuffling about in the embers of the cooking fire. It had moved the coals about so much that an ashy smell pervaded the house.

'Get out!' Ambrose shouted.

The pig ignored him.

Ambrose was furious. It was dangerous to attack a pig. But he had put up with enough from the filthy beast. Ambrose climbed the ladder to his sleeping loft. He would put his instruments out of harm's way and then attack the damnable creature. As he neared the top of the ladder, he noticed with alarm that the smell of burnt wood that he had presumed came from the pig's rooting in the embers had got stronger. Nothing but oil lamps and candles were ever lit up there. Ambrose eased himself up into the loft, laid his instruments carefully on his bed, and lit a lamp.

At first he could make out nothing amiss. The chests in which he stored his instruments were all there and intact, the bed, the bedding, Martin's chest of clothes, Ambrose's. And then he walked into it, dislodging something powdery that made him cough and almost drop his lamp. Hanging from a rafter was one of the metal baskets he hung bread in to keep it out of the way of rats. It should be downstairs. The basket swung back and forth gently. Ashes sifted through the metal bands and fell as a silent rain.

Ambrose crossed himself. Whatever had been inside, it was a charred mess, unrecognisable. He sniffed. At least it was not animal. But it was certainly no accident. Nothing Martin might have done while Ambrose was out.

With a shiver, Ambrose realised that whoever had done this might still be around. His heart racing, he examined his little loft, then, taking a deep breath to steady himself, he left the lamp at the top of the ladder and crept down. He remembered the pig. But he heard nothing. Thank God for that, although the pig was no longer his chief concern.

Ambrose closed the front door and held his breath, listening, while he let his eyes adjust to the darkness. When he could make out vague shapes, he walked around the room, touching the few pieces of furniture. No one here. He opened the door into his back garden. Merlin rubbed against his legs and walked into the house. A definite sign that no stranger lurked in the garden.

'Praise be to God,' Ambrose whispered, shutting the door. He stirred the embers of the fire, piled on some extra wood, took a coal from his firebox to rekindle the pile into a hearty blaze. Only then did Ambrose go back up for the bread basket and bring it down to the fire, where in the light he saw white pieces in the ashes. He opened the basket and drew one of them out. An ivory peg. Dear God, one of his instruments. He examined it and suddenly cried out as he recognised the pieces. He hurried back up to his chest of old instruments.

His first crowd was missing, just as he'd feared. Given to him by his first lover, Merlin the Crowder, the finest crowder in London. It was the instrument on which Ambrose had learned to play. He felt sick to his stomach. Who knew him so well to know what it would mean to him?

Downstairs, he poured himself a tankard of ale. He tried to calm himself, reasoning that the old crowd had been on top in the chest. That it was his most cherished piece could not have been known; but that any instrument in a wait's house would be dear was the intention.

How cruel that it should be the gift of Merlin. Ambrose closed his eyes and let the tears fall.

Bess could not wait until they were all seated and eating. While Tom poured the Gascony wine, Bess looked round, caught everyone's eye. 'You'll never believe it. I've discovered who Kate Cooper was before she married. Her mother is Felice d'Aldbourg.'

Her news was received with puzzled stares. Then Owen's face lit up. 'D'Aldbourg. Aldborough?'

Bess grinned. 'Felice came about five years ago to live with her sister, an embroiderer. Felice is an embroiderer, too, but she had not worked for years because she was married to a merchant in Aldborough. And then something happened to him, what no one knows, and Felice came to York to seek work through her sister. Her daughter comes to visit, and that's Kate Cooper.' She sighed, proud of the nods all round, held up her glass. 'Shall we toast the arrival in Bethlehem?'

All picked up their glasses and toasted.

When they were seated, Owen asked, 'You have spoken to Felice?'

'Are you mad? If Kate Cooper is guilty of any of this, her mother would certainly warn her of our interest. I have learned this in bits and pieces from this person and that. It is my Christmas offering to you.'

'And she lives in the liberty of St Peter?'

'Indeed she does. She is presently employed on embroidery for several chapels at the minster.'

Lucie, who had stared into her glass all this time, looked up and said quietly, 'It is a gift accepted with gratitude, Bess. But such a sorry topic for a celebration – the identity of the woman who murdered John and injured Jasper so badly that he cannot be with us tonight.'

It took some time for the mood to rise once more.

By the time Martin arrived at Ambrose's house, two tankards of ale had heated the musician's sorrow. When Ambrose looked up at Martin, he remembered that this misfortune stemmed from something Martin had done. It was Martin's fault. 'You bastard.' He tossed the dregs of ale in his tankard in Martin's face. 'First the hand and now this. I at least deserve to be told what heinous thing you did to bring this on my house.'

Martin wiped his face. 'What has happened, Ambrose?'

Ambrose lifted the basket.

Martin peered at it. 'Burnt bread? Such a temper over burnt bread?'

'No, not burnt bread. The crowd that Merlin the Crowder gave me.'

'How— Ambrose, the crowd would not fit in that basket.'

'It seems that your enemy is more creative than you are, Martin. He thought of smashing it to pieces before putting it in here to burn.'

Martin sat down beside Ambrose, put his arm around him. Ambrose tried to pull away, but Martin held tight. 'For God's sake, Ambrose, tell me what happened.'

Ambrose gave up and slumped against Martin. 'When I came home, the door was wide open, and this was hanging up in my loft. Burnt. While I was out. Someone is watching us, Martin. And you are the one with enemies.' He sat up, took Martin's hand, turned it palm up, and dropped the ivoury pegs into it. 'That is all I have left of the lovely instrument.'

Martin stared down at the pegs in his hand. 'I am sorry. I know that does nothing to make you feel better.'

'I want to know what it is you did, Martin. You owe me that.'

'I have kept you ignorant to keep you safe, truly I have.'

'It did not work.'

Martin clutched his hand tight around the pegs. 'It is time to co-operate with Captain Archer. We must discover the murderer before more happens.'

Lucie was setting out the savoury when she noticed Tildy leaning against the wall, her eyes closed. 'Poor child. She's not used to so much wine.'

Lucie and Bess roused Tildy and tucked her into bed.

The two couples were relaxing by the fire when the shop bell jingled. Tom, used to jumping up at the tavern, began to rise.

'Ignore it,' Owen said. 'We cannot be expected to dispense medicines at this hour on Christmas Eve.'

The bell jingled again. And again. Owen cursed. Then he heard the creak of the garden gate. He was at the kitchen door before the intruders could raise a hand to knock.

Owen yanked the door open. 'Who's there?' he demanded in a voice that he hoped would make whoever it was turn around and leave him in peace.

Martin Wirthir and Ambrose Coats stepped into the light from the doorway. 'Forgive the intrusion,' Martin said, 'but things have gone too far. We must talk.'

Ambrose held up a wicker basket covered with a festive cloth. 'A peace offering.'

Owen stepped aside to let them in.

Ambrose handed Lucie the basket. She looked from

Martin to Ambrose with a puzzled frown.

'The murderer has moved again, I think,' Martin said.

'Sweet Jesus, what happened?'

'This will seem a small thing to you, perhaps,' Ambrose said, and told them about his crowd. 'But you cannot know – one becomes so attached to an instrument. It is like a death.'

Lucie motioned to the two men to sit down at the table. 'It is not a small thing. Someone broke into your house and destroyed something valuable and dear.'

Tom had been examining the contents of the basket. Now he pulled out a bottle and held it up to Owen. 'Gascony wine even older than the one we drank earlier – look at this odd bottle. They have not made these in a long time.' He beamed. 'Three bottles of it. And two bottles of brandywine.'

'It is the time of night for brandywine, I think,' Martin said.

When Tom had poured a round, Owen nodded to Martin. 'Tell us what you know.'

Martin took a gulp of the brandywine. 'What I have told you so far is all true. Believe me. But the rest— I hoped it would not be necessary to tell.'

'We are your allies,' Lucie said.

Martin lifted his glass to her. 'I hope that is still so when I've finished.' He took another drink. 'When I heard Will's murderer had cut off his hand, I thought I knew what old trouble had caught up with me, and that Will had been murdered by mistake. You see, for a long time I'd feared that John Goldbetter had told the King whence came the information that I'd obtained for him to make his peace with your King.'

Owen frowned. 'Why would he reveal his source?'

'It is an unfortunate aspect of my business that I make many enemies, and that my employers are not

294

keen to protect me. So such as myself often become scapegoats.'

'I am not certain that I understand what your business is,' Lucie said.

'I like to think of myself as a negotiator between the continent and your fair isle. An ambassador, albeit a secret ambassador – for wealthy merchants and landed families.'

'Magda Digby calls you "Pirate",' Owen said.

Martin smiled. 'Magda teases me with that name. I do not actually touch the goods. I negotiate for their transport.'

'And the severed hand – it made you think of what old trouble?' Owen asked.

'A merchant I had betrayed. He went to the Fleet prison. He learned of my part in his misfortune and swore that he would cut off my right hand for a thief when he got out.'

'Who was this merchant?'

'Alan of Aldborough.'

'Ah,' Bess sighed.

Martin looked at her. 'You knew him?'

'We have just spoken of him tonight. Or rather his wife and daughter.'

'Why did this man consider you a thief?' Owen asked.

'I had taken money from Alan in exchange for a promise to keep still about something I'd learned about his business. I took the money without ever thinking clearly about what I was promising. I just wanted to escape an uncomfortable situation.'

'An uncomfortable situation?' Lucie asked.

Martin glanced at Ambrose, who sat watching him raptly. 'It is awkward. His son, David, was a passionate young man who had become attached to me.'

Ambrose flinched and looked down at his wine.

'It was David who told me of his father's dealings with the Flemings, how Alan sold wool to them despite the King's ban. When I told David that he should marry the woman his father had selected for him, that he would ruin his life and live in poverty if he persisted in his pursuit of me, David told his father that he had told me everything, that he must go off with me to keep me quiet. Of course his ploy did not work. He was the only son. Alan offered me a tidy sum to disappear and keep my mouth shut.' Martin shrugged. 'But I foolishly told Gilbert Ridley one night when we were in our cups. I did not guard myself with Gilbert. He was my employer. I learned that I should not have been so trusting. When Gilbert wanted to help Goldbetter by giving him a name, he gave Alan's. And named me as the informant when pressed. He was, however, discreet enough not to tell Goldbetter how I had got the information.'

'And yet you came up here to warn Ridley of some other trouble?' Lucie said. 'One would think you would have resented him.'

'We had worked together a long time. Most people employ me once or twice, rarely more. Gilbert provided me with steady work. And in all that time, he had betrayed me only that once.' Martin nodded at Owen. 'I understand he even told you that there was no reason for me to be in York any longer, once Will was dead.'

Owen nodded.

'He knew about Ambrose?' Lucie said.

'Exactly. He knew I would not stay away from York. But for the one indiscretion, Gilbert had been good to me. So I went to Riddlethorpe and told him about your King's new friends, for whom I'd arranged shipments to Flanders and then later reported when they'd paid far less than they'd agreed to pay for such a dangerous enterprise. I feared they would think Gilbert was also a voice to hush. I also wanted to tell Gilbert about Alan's threat. I had no idea whether Alan was out of the Fleet or not, but it seemed likely. That is when I learned that Will's hand had been left in Gilbert's room. We both found that a riddle.' Martin sipped his brandywine. 'And then Gilbert was murdered in the same fashion as Will had been, which made me more confident of my theory. Alan or a hired murderer had mistaken Will Crounce for me, but they got Gilbert right – the one who had offered the name to Goldbetter. I had no trouble believing Goldbetter had betrayed Gilbert. I went down to London to find out if Alan had indeed been released from prison. While I was gone, Jasper disappeared again. And Gilbert's hand showed up at Ambrose's front door. Meanwhile, I could learn nothing of Alan's fate.'

'He died in the Fleet,' Owen said. 'Could it be his son David?'

Martin's expression changed. He closed his eyes and shook his head. 'No,' he said in a voice not much louder than a whisper, 'no, it was not David.'

'How can you be certain?' Lucie asked.

'David took his own life when his father was sent to prison.'

'*Deus juva me,*' Lucie whispered, crossing herself.

The room grew quiet enough to hear the hiss of a damp log on the fire and the rumble of Melisende's purr.

'If it's not the son, what about his wife or daughter, Kate Cooper?' Lucie asked.

Martin frowned. 'Cooper? I know that name. Someone at Riddlethorpe, I think.'

297

'Did Ambrose know any of the family?' Owen asked.

Ambrose shook his head. 'Until this night, I never heard the name.' He looked at Martin, then away.

'Then someone has been watching the two of you, to know to leave the hand with Ambrose,' Owen said. 'And yet you think they mistook Will Crounce for you, Martin?'

Martin sighed. 'As I have said, Will might have been presumed guilty because of our partnership. I don't know. I just wonder how many will die before we discover the murderer. And there's the poisoning. How does that fit?'

Owen glanced at Lucie, who shook her head slightly.

'The poisoner had nothing to do with the murders,' Owen said.

'You have discovered who was poisoning him?' Bess asked.

'It has no significance,' Owen said.

'It might,' Ambrose said.

'No. Lucie and I are both certain of that.'

'I have other sins,' Martin said. 'Gilbert's death made me think it more likely that another family is after me. Except that the hand was so much the mark of Alan.'

'How many enemies do you have?' Ambrose asked. He sounded as if he regretted having instigated his friend's confession.

'I have no idea how many people I have ruined. Or who blame me for their ruin. I confess I never gave a thought to it until Will's murder. Not really. I was good at it. It was like gambling. Thrilling. I don't deny it. I don't apologise for myself, either. I am no worse than any of them.'

'This other family?' Lucie said.

Martin poured himself more brandywine and poured

for the others whose glasses were empty, all but Lucie and Ambrose.

'I will not name names,' Martin said. 'It is too dangerous for the rest of you. But Gilbert and I were involved, and it would seem likely to them that Will was, too. I had arranged for their wool to be smuggled to Flanders, money to be returned. They were a greedy lot, and I despised them when they cheated me. So I got even. I sold their name to Chiriton and Company.'

'Martin!' Ambrose's eyes were wide with amazement. 'How could you?'

'If you knew them you would hate them, too. About twelve, thirteen years ago Chiriton and Company gave John Goldbetter's name to the King as one of their debtors. Goldbetter proved he'd paid the debt and went one better, claiming that Chiriton owed him money. Chiriton settled the debt by giving Goldbetter the information I'd sold them about the family. Enough information for Goldbetter to extract pleasant sums of money from them.'

Owen remembered Cecilia's account of the mysterious settlement out of court. *Gilbert was even more extravagant than usual on my name day that year.* 'So this family is after you for the money you've cost them?' Lucie asked.

'It is worse than that. Suddenly, Heaven knows how, they were in favour with your King. They had power. They turned on Goldbetter, and had him exiled. Goldbetter went to the Count of Flanders, who convinced King Edward to pardon him. They did not interfere. They did not want to draw the Count's attention to them and they knew that Goldbetter would keep quiet. But Gilbert and I, ah, we were under no one's protection; on us they could take revenge.'

'Why do you think this has to do with them? And what part did Ridley play?' Lucie asked.

'They had a small partner in their dealings.'

'Alan of Aldborough?' Owen guessed.

Martin nodded. 'Why were you speaking of Alan's widow and daughter this evening, Mistress Merchet?'

Bess looked over at Owen. 'Ask him. I think perhaps I've become too involved as it is.'

'The daughter Kate is the wife of Gilbert Ridley's steward. She travelled with Ridley to York before both murders. And she disappeared when she discovered me at Riddlethorpe. We believe her to be involved. Probably the woman who lured Will Crounce to his murderers. And being left-handed, she may be the woman who attacked Jasper at his old lodgings and murdered John, the Merchet's stable boy.'

'Sweet Mother in Heaven, could she hate all of you so much?' Ambrose asked.

Martin wiped his forehead. 'Most assuredly. She and her mother would see me as the cause of David's death *and* their father's ruin. She has more reason to hate us than the others.'

Owen was quiet, thinking about the Archbishop's letter concerning Alan of Aldborough. His death had been a surprise to the warden. Poisoning? The suddenly powerful family wanting to silence him as well as Wirthir and Ridley?

'*Merde!*' Martin banged his cup on the table, rousing Owen from his thoughts. 'The woman who came looking for Jasper in Goodramgate. I could not see her face, but there was something familiar. David's sister was tall like her. And she had his way of gesturing.'

Owen nodded. 'Kate Cooper. We must set someone to watch Felice d'Aldbourg.'

Twenty-three

St John's Day

Two days after Christmas, on St John's Day, Thoresby sent for Owen. An unpleasant surprise. Owen had not expected the Archbishop to return from the Christmas Court for at least another fortnight.

'St John's Day.' Lucie looked up from her work. 'He cannot have stayed at Court for Christmas. What could be wrong?'

Owen found the Archbishop glumly staring at the fire. Shadowed eyes and a lassitude in his movement as he raised his hand for Owen to kiss his ring suggested illness. It was too bad, because Owen had intended to point out the Archbishop's role in Jasper's misadventures. But if the Archbishop was ill . . .

'You did not stay for the Christmas Court, Your Grace?'

'No. I held my own Christmas court at Bishopthorpe.' The deep-set eyes were unreadable.

'I hope that the cause was not illness.'

'If I were ill, I would hardly choose Yorkshire over the Thames valley for my convalescence, Archer. Why?

301

Have you made no progress?'

'Progress, yes. But there is still much to sort out.'

'Did the information about the unfortunate man in the Fleet prison help you?'

'Indeed. And I thank you for sending word. It is almost certain that the man's surviving daughter, Kate Cooper, wife to the steward at Riddlethorpe, is involved. She attacked Jasper de Melton twice, by the way, seriously injuring the boy both times. She would have killed him the second time, but was stopped by the boy's friend, my neighbour's stable boy, who died defending Jasper.'

'Another death? What are we dealing with? Lucifer's spawn? And you say it is a woman?'

'I am certain she is not acting alone. But she is violent. And determined.'

'Why is she not in the jail in my palace?'

'She is missing, Your Grace. She disappeared before I knew she was guilty.'

'I am glad that it is not a matter of your falling in love with your suspect again.'

Owen considered how good it would feel to strangle Thoresby with his Chancellor's chain. 'I wish to point out that the death of the young man, and Jasper's injuries, might have been prevented had you agreed at the beginning that Jasper should be protected. But, as I recall, the boy was too insignificant.'

Thoresby closed his eyes and leaned back in his chair. 'It would be more useful if you confined yourself to the facts and left the emotions for your own fireside.'

'Can you discard a young man's life so easily as that?'

Thoresby sighed. 'I do not need someone to count off my sins to me. I am of late too aware of my sins and my mortality for comfort. I sleep little. Have no appetite. And I wonder if my Lady Chapel will be ready in time. Does that please you, Archer? Does that satisfy your desire that I suffer as I've made others suffer?'

'So you are ill.'

'Perhaps I am.'

'Then I will be brief. I have at last made contact with Martin Wirthir.'

'Excellent.'

'He believes the murders are the result of a curse Alan of Aldborough laid on him for betraying him to the Crown. Alan swore he would cut off Wirthir's hand for thieving. Wirthir thinks that Aldborough might have decided Ridley and Crounce were also involved. Wirthir is therefore the next and probably the last intended victim.'

'What is this Wirthir like?'

'He told quite a tale of crosses and double crosses. A rogue, and not entirely repentant, I think.'

'And this Kate Cooper is the one slitting throats and cutting off hands?'

'As Aldborough's only surviving child, Kate Cooper seems to be acting with a man or a group of men. There is possibly another family involved, in favour at Court right now and eager to eliminate all detractors. Because she has disappeared, I cannot question Mistress Cooper. Wirthir leaves for the town of Aldborough today, to discover who was to inherit the estate that is now forfeit to the Crown.'

'This powerful family. What is their name?'

'Wirthir will not say. Claims it is too dangerous for us to know.'

'Hmpf. Probably hopes for money from me. What about Ridley's condition? The stomach complaint? The wasting away?'

Owen had prepared an answer that would not incriminate Cecilia Ridley. Both Owen and Lucie felt

Cecilia's own remorse was punishment enough. 'I doubt that Ridley's complaint had anything to do with this. Unless it was his own sense of guilt.'

'Why was Will Crounce murdered first?'

'Wirthir thinks that the murderer might mistakenly have believed that Crounce was involved. But he really does not know. It appears that Crounce knew nothing of the betrayal. Indeed, knew nothing of Aldborough's business.'

'And you say the de Melton boy was injured?'

Owen told Thoresby about Jasper's two encounters with Kate Cooper.

'It sounds to me as if the second encounter and the death of the young man happened under your ineffective protection, Archer. So how effective do you think mine would have been?'

'You can be certain that Lucie and I feel the burden of guilt.'

Thoresby got up, stood in front of the fire, hands clasped behind him, head bowed. 'I cannot fault you, Archer. You should not blame yourselves. I am merely disappointed. It sounds more and more like Ridley's bequest was conscience money. Blood money. I cannot accept it for my Lady Chapel.'

'To my mind, all money given for charity or to the Church is in some way conscience money, Your Grace. What else would motivate merchants, who work so hard to accumulate wealth, to give it away?'

'In that sense, I agree with you. But it sounds to me as if Ridley found it far too easy to forgive himself for acquiring money at another's expense. Or using others to get himself out of trouble.'

'He offered you the money in good faith. You accepted it. No matter how he acquired the money, he believed he was making amends by offering it to the Church, for God's house – at least partial amends. Is that not enough for you?'

Thoresby stared at Owen for a long while before he said, 'Let us see this to its conclusion if possible, Archer. That is all I ask of you. I do not ask for your counsel, excellent as it may be.' He played with his ring, thinking. 'What of Ridley's son and heir? Matthew, is it not?'

'He is in Calais, managing the business.'

'Curious that he would not come howling back to see that his father's murderer is caught. Would you be so indifferent?'

'No.'

'Most unnatural.'

'I confess, I had not given Matthew Ridley much thought.'

'Perhaps you should have.'

As Owen rose to take his leave, Thoresby held up a hand. 'Aldborough. Do you think I might impose upon this Martin Wirthir to deliver a letter to the Dean of Ripon?'

Owen shrugged. 'I will ask him. Ripon is close enough to Aldborough.'

'Excellent. Michaelo will bring the letter to the wait's house within the hour.'

Owen snarled at Michaelo as he passed him on the way out. His conversation with the Archbishop had left an unpleasant taste of ashes in Owen's mouth. How unlike the Archbishop's almost sympathetic behaviour before he left for the Christmas Court. Something must have happened to cause Thoresby's early return and his present mood. Something that put Thoresby out of humour and made him think of his mortality. That made Owen smile.

*

After the brief nones service, Brother Henry returned to the infirmary to give Brother Wulfstan a chance to nap. It was a dreary afternoon with a chill rain falling, and the infirmary was dark. But it should not be quite so dark. Henry was uneasy as he stepped inside. Wulfstan should have lamps set around his work-table or a reading lamp near his chair. Henry found the old infirmarian nodding in the chair beside Jasper's cot. He lit a lamp in haste to check the boy. Mercifully, Jasper slept. Henry said a prayer of thanksgiving.

But he could see that their plan to protect Jasper would not work without help.

'We must tell Abbot Campian about our problem, Brother Wulfstan. We need assistance. You must admit that you cannot stay alert as long as you must. Perhaps our abbot would allow us a novice to share watches with me.'

Wulfstan rubbed his eyes, looking sheepish. 'You are right, Henry. Arrogance is my sin. I refuse to admit that I cannot protect the boy myself. But I will not compound the sin by ignoring your good advice. I shall go to Abbot Campian at once.'

The abbot sat reading near the fire in his hall, a candle on the table beside him. When he noticed Wulfstan, he closed his book and set it aside. 'Come. Sit by me, old friend.'

Wulfstan settled himself with pleasure close to the fire. Though the arcade had protected him from the brunt of the rain, his toes were chilled by the damp walk from the infirmary. 'God go with you, my Abbot.' Wulfstan kissed the abbot's proffered hand.

Abbot Campian smiled, folded his long-fingered hands in his lap. 'Now, my old friend, are you at last going to tell me what you and Brother Henry have been up to in the infirmary?'

Wulfstan was startled. 'How did you know?'

'For six days I have seen but one or the other of you, never both together, at meals and services. Do you conduct some experiment that must be watched, I wondered.'

'Oh, no, nothing of the sort, no. It is the boy. Jasper de Melton. You know the boy's history? Why he is here?'

Campian nodded.

'Well it seemed to me that a certain guest, he told me his name was John, the one who burned his hand on Christmas Eve, he was too interested in the boy. Kept returning to visit him. So Henry and I set up a watch.'

Abbot Campian frowned. 'John? Who burned his hand? I am not quite— Oh. Would he have a bandage around the palm of the hand? Just a strip of cloth?'

'That would be him.'

'Well now, you will be happy you have at last come to me. You are rid of him. I bid him a safe journey just after the midday meal. A woman came for him. They went off on fine horses. Very fine horses. But why do you call him John?'

'That is the name he gave me.'

'How strange. I cannot think why he would lie to you. Unless he lied to me? The name he gave me was Paul.' The abbot frowned down at his white hands. He did not like disorder at St Mary's. 'I think we must say a prayer of thanksgiving that he has left the abbey.'

Martin and Ambrose stopped in a small, modest inn at Alne for the night. It had been a cold, wet ride, and they were grateful for the fire and hot food. Especially the excellent ale. As Martin unpacked his saddlebag, he noted the name on the letter he carried for the Archbishop.

'Why, what a piece of luck, Ambrose. It's going to Paul Scorby, the husband of Anna Ridley. The Scorby land is this side of Ripon.'

Ambrose rubbed a soothing lotion on his hands and pulled on gloves. The long, cold, wet ride and the stiff grip on the reins was bad for a musician's hands. 'How do you know these Scorbys? More past employers?' His tone was biting.

'Yes. Are you going to hold all of this against me for ever?'

'Would I be here if I were?'

'I can hear the disapproval in your voice.'

'It will pass. What is the point about the letter being addressed to this Scorby?'

'If we deliver it ourselves, we shorten our journey and perhaps he will know something of his father-in-law's affairs that will enlighten us. What do you think?'

'It seems there is everything to recommend it.'

Twenty-four

Connections

Owen stopped to pay his respects to Abbot Campian before going to the infirmary. To Owen's surprise, Campian invited him to share a hot drink made with various herbs. 'It calms the spirit quite remarkably,' the abbot promised.

'Is this one of Brother Wulfstan's remedies?'

'It is indeed. God blessed Wulfstan with a gift for combining the fruits of the earth to heal mankind. But you will never hear my old friend brag of it. He is as modest a man as I've ever known.'

'Brother Wulfstan is one of the treasures of St Mary's.'

Abbot Campian smiled and nodded. 'I understand His Grace is already returned from the Christmas Court. Does that not strike you as odd?'

So that was why Campian was so friendly. Wanting information. 'I was surprised to see him so soon.'

'Does he return in good humour?'

'To be honest, he returned in a strange mood. But ours is not the sort of relationship that allows the questioning of such things. I have no idea what disturbs him.'

'Pity. It is so helpful to subordinates to know the cause of any unusual moods. But in my travels I have had occasion to ride with John Thoresby to the Great Council, and I have found him to be a private man.'

'No doubt he realises that the eyes of the kingdom are upon him.'

Campian inclined his head. 'No doubt.' He put down his cup and rose. 'Now I must detain you no longer. You are a busy man, I know, and anxious to see how young Jasper mends.'

Owen left the abbot with a sense of relief. Although kind and much more a man of God than Thoresby, the abbot watched the politics of York with an eagle eye. Owen always felt uncomfortable when he spoke with Campian, uncertain where the abbot's questions led, unable to circumvent them.

Brother Wulfstan greeted Owen warmly. 'You will be so pleased when you see how Jasper improves.' The old monk led Owen to the pallet where the boy lay staring at the ceiling. Jasper glanced over at his visitor, then back to the ceiling.

'Jasper! Have you no greeting for Captain Archer?'

The boy stared at the ceiling.

'Well, I cannot explain it,' Wulfstan said, turning to Owen. 'He has been so pleasant.'

'Perhaps if we spoke alone.'

Wulfstan nodded. 'I have an errand that will not take long. You sit with the boy and chat.'

Owen pulled a stool up beside Jasper and sat down. 'As Captain of Archers, I found it advisable to tell someone why I was punishing them. It made the punishment more effective.'

Jasper still stared at the ceiling.

'So why are you punishing me, Jasper?'

The boy frowned at the ceiling.

'It is punishment to ignore me like this. I thought we'd become friends. Comrades-in-arms.'

'John told me why you were friendly to me.'

'And you don't like the reason? If that's true, then John, God rest his soul, got it wrong. Because I've never known a young man who did not want to be liked. And that's certainly why we're all so worried about you and anxious to have you back with us.'

'It's not because you like me. I'm to lure the murderers to you so you can catch them.' Jasper still stared at the ceiling.

'Lure the— Sweet Jesus, do you believe we would do that, Jasper? Lucie and I tried to keep your presence in our house secret. Poor Tildy was scolded because she did not warn us that John had been coaxing you to go to your old house.'

'I wanted to go. And I didn't want Tildy to tell.'

'If you had not gone there, you would not have met up with your tormentor.'

'And John would be alive,' Jasper said in a shaky voice.

'True, Jasper. Poor John. I cannot imagine why he was so set on your going there.'

'She talked him into it. She was his sweetheart.'

Kate Cooper – just as Tildy had suspected. 'How do you know this, Jasper?'

'She said so.'

'What else did she say?'

The boy shrugged.

'Please, Jasper. I want to find these people and stop them so you can go on with your life. Don't you see?'

'So I can go back on the street.'

'No. I hope you will come back to us.'

The boy looked over at Owen. 'Why would you want me back?'

'Because we miss you. All three of us.'

'Really?'

'I have no reason to lie to you, Jasper. So, the sooner we unravel this knotty business the sooner you can feel safe. What else did she tell you?'

'She said she hated them – Master Crounce and Master Ridley. As I should hate the men who killed Master Crounce, she said. I don't remember anything else. I was scared. Except she said Master Crounce meant to marry my mother.' Jasper blinked and tears rolled down his pale cheeks.

'Did she say anything about the man who she's working with?'

'Just that he wants me dead. That's why she wants to kill me.'

'Is she tall, Jasper?'

He nodded. 'For a woman. And she's strong.'

'Think about her holding the knife, Jasper. How did she hold it?'

He lifted his right hand, as if holding a knife poised to stab, then shook his head and changed hands. 'Like this. With her left hand.'

Owen leaned down and hugged the boy. 'Excellent. It is just as I thought. We know who she is, Jasper. We are partway there.'

Wulfstan cleared his throat in the doorway. 'I see you two have made up. I am glad. It is so distressing to part with a friend.' He noticed Jasper wiping his eyes. 'It is time to rest again, my son.'

Owen stood up. 'I will come back soon to see if you're ready to come home, Jasper.'

Wulfstan moved a wooden screen beside Jasper's bed to block the light.

The two men went across the room to the work-table, where there was some light from a small window. Wulfstan motioned for Owen to sit close to him. 'I don't want the boy to hear.'

Owen sat down.

'I must confess that I almost failed you, Owen.'

'You almost lost Jasper? Were his injuries that bad?'

'Not lost like that. There was a man, a guest in the abbey. He was far too keen to speak with Jasper. Henry and I stood watch over the boy until the man left.'

'Who was he?'

'Now that's one of the odd things about him. He told me his name was John. He told Abbot Campian his name was Paul.'

'Paul? Describe him to me.'

Wulfstan shrugged. 'Middle height. Brown hair, brown eyes. Not unpleasant looking, except that he had an air about him, pouting. As if the world was a constant disappointment. Otherwise nothing remarkable.'

'Do you know anything about him?'

'He claimed his wife had gone to the nunnery. Which is why he needed burn salve from me, had none of his own.'

'He'd burned himself? When?'

'Christmas Eve. Sometime during the day. Is it important?'

The day of the fire in Ambrose Coats's house. 'It is all important, my friend. I think you speak of Paul Scorby. Though what he has to do with all this I cannot say.' And yet – Anna had told him that Paul Scorby and Kate Cooper were lovers. 'I thank you heartily for keeping Jasper safe.'

'As I said, I almost failed you. God knows I deserve no thanks.'

'Did a woman come to visit this man?'

Wulfstan nodded. 'A woman came on horseback to get him.'

'How long was he gone?'

'Abbot Campian says he is gone for good.'

Damn. 'When did they leave?'

'Yesterday.'

Owen was disappointed. 'Was there anything else? Did he say why he wanted to speak with Jasper?'

'He said Jasper looked so like his son. But I don't believe he has a son.'

'Why?'

'He said something later about his wife being barren. So I asked if his son was by his former wife. He seemed confused, as if he'd forgotten the first lie.'

'What else did you notice about his manner besides his being disappointed with the world?'

'Impatient. Nothing that he said, but his breath told me. You know, you can hear the impatience in the way some people breathe.'

'Does Abbot Campian know more about the man?'

Wulfstan shook his head. 'He did not seem to know which of the names we'd been given was correct, if either.'

Owen stood up. 'I thank you, Brother Wulfstan. If the man should return, which I doubt that he will do, please get word to me at once.'

As Owen hurried out the abbey gate, past St Leonard's Hospital, he thought of Ambrose Coats. He stopped at the house in Footless Lane to describe to the wait the two people he must watch out for. But there was no one at home. A large orange cat mewed at the door. Owen headed home, anxious to talk this all out with Lucie.

But she was busy in the shop when he arrived. Owen paced impatiently by the door. When the last customer had gone, Lucie turned to Owen, hands on hips. 'Do you want to force all our custom away, pacing like that, making them nervous? You might have helped.'

He might have. He had been so wrapped up in the connections he was trying to piece together, he had not thought about his duties. 'Forgive me. But we must talk. I need your thoughts on all that I've learned today.'

'Well it must wait. I have an order from Camden Thorpe, our guildmaster if you recall, and I must fill it before I can sit down and chat. One of his sons is waiting in the back. Tildy's with him.'

'This is important, Lucie. People's lives may depend on my thinking this through.'

'People's lives? What do you think I deal with?'

'Forgive me again. I see there is no pleasing you. I will go back in the kitchen and wait.'

'You will not. You will go upstairs and get the powdered emeralds.'

'Powdered – The guildmaster can afford a physick made with emeralds?'

'It's for Mistress Thorpe. She's lost a near term babe and her spirit seems to be draining with her every breath. So, you see, someone's life does depend on it.'

'Poor Camden. I'll get the powder.'

After they had sent young Peter Thorpe off with the medicine, Lucie sank down in a chair by the kitchen fire. Owen asked Tildy to pour them some ale.

'You do have the strength to lift a tankard of Tom's ale?' Owen asked Lucie.

She gave him a weary smile. 'It will be nice to

have some while we talk about the connections you're trying to piece together.'

'You were listening, even though your thoughts were on Mistress Thorpe.'

'Of course I was. Now tell me.'

Tildy hurried over with filled tankards. 'Could I ask quick, Captain Archer? Is Jasper healing?'

'He's much improved, Tildy. And I've told him we're waiting for him to come home.'

Tildy smiled happily. 'I'll look forward to that, Captain.'

Owen toasted Lucie. 'To the best apothecary in Yorkshire.'

Her eyes were sad. 'I hope so, Owen. But it did not sound hopeful. Tell me what Jasper and Wulfstan had to say.'

When Owen had recounted it all, Lucie stared into the fire for a while. 'Paul Scorby and Kate Cooper. Both connected to Ridley's household. How did Kate Cooper come to Riddlethorpe?'

Owen thought back over what seemed a sea of information. 'Crounce. Cecilia said that he had found a new steward for her.'

'Will Crounce lived in Boroughbridge, which is close to Aldborough, and both are close to Ripon. It is all tidy in that sense, but I cannot think what Paul Scorby would hope to gain. He would not inherit Ridley's business unless Matthew Ridley died.'

'Thoresby pointed out yesterday that Matthew has been strangely quiet for the son of a murdered man.'

'And Cecilia told you that Matthew was taking over the business because he was more discreet about the King?'

'Something like that.'

Lucie sighed. 'It seems important, but I don't know

what it might have to do with all of this.'

Owen shrugged. 'I think we're still missing some important pieces.'

Lucie nodded. 'We had better eat before I fall asleep.'

They had finished their meal and sat in front of the fire when someone knocked at the kitchen door. Lucie crossed herself. 'Pray God it isn't bad news of Mistress Thorpe.'

Tildy opened the door. 'Goodwife Digby!'

'Captain and Mistress at home?'

Owen got up to show Magda to a chair. She yanked her elbow from his solicitous grasp. 'Magda needs no help to walk across a room, Bird-eye. Whence came such a notion?'

'A lunatic strain in my family line, to be sure.' Owen poured a small cup of brandywine and handed it to her. 'To take off the chill. I trust you will not reject this.'

'Nay, Magda's neither old nor foolish.' She sipped, nodded her approval, looked at the waiting faces. 'Mistress Thorpe will mend. They sneaked Magda into the city. Thou sent her a good tonic, Mistress Apothecary. It will do her well. But Magda comes about other business. Not so pleasant. Felice d'Aldbourg's girl, Kate Cooper, was brought in on the tide this evening.'

'Drowned?' Lucie whispered.

'Nay. Not like Magda's Potter. Though like in that it was no accident she was floating in on the tide face down. Her throat had been slit and much blood drained before she hit the water.'

Owen went to Thoresby in the morning to tell him of Kate Cooper's death.

'It's a bad business, Archer. Are you any closer

to naming her accomplice? Her murderer, I suspect.'

'Does the name Paul Scorby mean anything to you?'

Thoresby looked puzzled. 'The name was familiar when she asked me to carry the letter, but I could not place it. Had you mentioned it?'

'Of course I did. He's married to Gilbert Ridley's daughter.'

Thoresby stood up abruptly. 'Dear God.'

'When *who* asked you to carry *what* letter?'

'The Queen of Hell, Dame Alice Perrers. To her cousin, Paul Scorby of Ripon. The letter Martin Wirthir carries to my dean, who will send it on to Scorby, I trust.'

'Perrers? My father-in-law spoke of the family at our wedding. Nobodies who'd suddenly found favour with the King.'

Thoresby sniffed. 'Found favour? That is an understatement. But Wirthir had spoken of a family . . .'

Owen nodded. 'Scorby is in the wool trade,' he said, more to himself than to the Archbishop. 'Wirthir told me he'd double-crossed a powerful family. He did not give the name because he said it was too dangerous, they were too favoured at court at the moment. Could it be the connection I've been looking for? The Perrers family?'

'It is too likely to ignore.' Thoresby paced back and forth.

'I doubt that Wirthir knows of Scorby's connection with the Perrers family. He would have mentioned it.'

Thoresby was shaking his head. 'I am such a fool. I handed the man his doom. We must ride to Ripon. Make sure that the dean says nothing to Scorby about who carried the letter. Then we must go to Aldborough and warn Wirthir.'

Owen stared at the Archbishop. '*We* must ride? You and I?'

'Who else at such short notice? Besides, it is my fault. Yes, damn it. You and I.'

'But you are ill.'

'In spirit, Archer, not in body. I will not let Perrers win this one. Come. We will ride this afternoon.'

Twenty-five

Wirthir's Doom

A bright though chilly morning sun cheered Martin and Ambrose on their way. 'I enjoy travel when the weather is so cordial,' Ambrose said. 'I can admire the countryside instead of hiding my face from the rain.'

'At this time of year it's colder when the sun is out. I think I prefer the rain.' Martin nodded towards Ambrose's gloves. 'And I hate wearing those things.'

'And hats, I see. No wonder you're cold.'

Martin reined his horse in; Ambrose did likewise. Martin studied his friend's face. 'Why are we talking about the weather?'

'I am trying to be civil today since you thought me unfriendly yesterday.'

'Oh.'

'So today you're the one who's glum.'

'I have been thinking about the future.'

'And it's gloomy?'

'If I'm not to continue in the career I've fashioned for myself – which I was very good at, by the way – then what am I to do?'

'You enjoyed what you did?'

'Would I have been good at it otherwise? When a man plods at his work it's because he hates what he does. For the rest of my life I will be a plodder.'

'You can find something new. Captain Archer did.'

'I have watched him down in St George's Field, training the townsmen. Though he speaks to them patiently, his hands are clenched so tight his knuckles are white. And he seems to detest the Archbishop. The only joy he has found is in his marriage.'

'Ah. The fair Lucie Wilton. I admire her. She is skilled, wilful and beautiful.'

'I'll bet there's marvellous sport in that bed.'

They laughed and spurred their horses on, friends again.

The Scorby lands were more extensive than Ridley's, complete with a village and church. The house was older than Riddlethorpe, with a moat and drawbridge, but not as welcoming or as lovely. Though Martin had never been a guest at Riddlethorpe, he had managed to ride across the land and study the house – in case he needed to contact Gilbert in a hurry. Looking at Scorby's house, Martin guessed that money was less freely spent here. Perhaps less available.

Martin and Ambrose rode up to the gatehouse and stated their business.

The gatekeeper was a scarred old man who sported two daggers at his waist. Not a comforting type to meet with. 'Masters Wirthir and Coats.' The gatekeeper motioned towards Ambrose. 'You wear the livery of the city of York. A bailiff? Or a constable?'

'Neither. I am a town wait.'

'A musician. Good. We want no trouble here. But why not give me the letter and be off?'

'We would speak with Master Scorby, if he is at home,' Martin said.

'He is indeed. I will just get Tanner to lower the drawbridge and take you to the master.'

A younger, but equally scarred man led them into the house. Three men sat by the hearth in the great hall, hunting dogs lying at their feet. One of the dogs, a black-faced giant, growled as Ambrose and Martin were announced. A brown-haired man, by his dress the master of the house, motioned them over. Martin noted that Paul Scorby's companions looked as battle-scarred and unfriendly as Tanner and the gatekeeper. He wondered whether he had been so clever to come here after all. One of the companions placed a bench near Scorby. Martin and Ambrose sat.

'I understand you carry a letter for me,' Scorby said. He was a handsome man, good features, though there was a wildness about the eyes that made one look again and proceed with caution. He carried his trim figure with a weary arrogance. He was not a fighting man by the look of his face and hands, though one hand was bandaged. The costly fur on his tunic and long, curling toes on his shoes spoke of one who enjoyed luxury and let others do the dirty work.

Martin handed Scorby the letter. 'I hoped to ask you about your recently deceased father-in-law while I was here.'

Scorby glanced at the seal on the letter and grinned, then turned his attention back to Martin and Ambrose, looking them up and down. 'I've heard your name in connection with my father-in-law, Wirthir. But you, Coats? What was your business with Gilbert Ridley?'

'I am travelling with my friend. I had no connection with Master Ridley.'

'I see.' Scorby shrugged. 'Gilbert Ridley. Yes. We

will talk of him after I have read this letter. Please share some spiced wine with my men while I retire to read this. I would offer you more, but my wife grew too holy for this household and took herself off to a nunnery. Things are still confused beyond help.'

Martin did not wish to spend any more time with Scorby's men than he had to. 'It would take but a moment to discuss my business. Could we not talk now? I need not tax your household at all then.'

'No, no. There's plenty wine. You see, it is a letter from my fair cousin. A letter I have awaited for some time. I will attend you much better after I have satisfied my curiosity.'

Reluctantly, Martin and Ambrose accepted wine from Scorby's surly companions. Martin had a bad feeling about all this and silently contemplated the room. Ambrose tried to engage the men in conversation, but even his considerable charm failed to elicit a smile or a cordial word from the men. The four sat and waited, Martin and Ambrose exchanging worried glances, the retainers glaring alternately at the door through which Scorby had disappeared and at Martin, the three dogs breathing loudly and snorting in their unpleasant dreams.

At last, the two companions rose. Thank God, Martin thought, they're going to leave us alone. But to his dismay, the men yelled to the dogs and the monsters leapt upon Martin and Ambrose, knocking them back over the bench and trapping them under their huge paws. They stank of raw meat and urine. Scorby's men tied Martin's hands behind his back and tied his legs, then did the same to Ambrose.

'Please, please, my hands. Do not cut off the circulation to my hands,' Ambrose begged them.

323

The retainers laughed and called off the dogs.

'You might sit them back on the bench,' Scorby said from the doorway. He sounded delighted. As if this were sport. Tanner stood next to him.

Martin growled as he was unceremoniously heaved onto the bench. 'What is the meaning of this? We come here in good faith, delivering a letter that you might have received much later had we left it with the Dean of Ripon as we'd been asked, and you have your men attack us? And tie us up? Are you mad?' He winced as they heaved Ambrose up on the bench next to him. Blood dribbled from Ambrose's mouth. 'You're animals.'

'It is nothing. Just bit my tongue,' Ambrose whispered.

Martin kicked his bound feet up into the groin of the man in front of him. As the man howled and clutched himself, Martin noticed a signet ring on the man's dirty hand. Will Crounce's signet ring. 'Sweet Jesu,' Martin murmured, realising what that must mean. What all this must mean. 'The Archbishop delivered us into the hands of my nemesis.'

'The Archbishop did not,' Ambrose hissed. 'It was your idea to deliver the letter.'

'Indeed.' Scorby had resumed his seat. 'And how did you guess at your misfortune?' He chuckled. The hand that played with the fur trim on the collar sported a ruby ring.

How had Martin missed it before? 'You and your retainer wear the rings of dead men.'

'Clever, Wirthir. Do you know, my cousin is angry with me that I have not killed you yet.'

'Your cousin? You mean the letter?'

'Yes. Pity you did not recognise the seal of Mistress Perrers. Alice Perrers. The King's beloved.'

'Perrers?' Martin groaned. It could not be worse. 'When I knew her she had no seal.'

'When you took her money and then sold her name to that Chiriton swine, you mean. Well, yes, my dear cousin Alice has risen rather quickly. She gave birth this autumn to King Edward's bastard son. It has enhanced her position quite remarkably. Clever Alice.'

A bastard son for an ageing King. Alice Perrers would now wield great power at Court. As long as she silenced any accusations of treason. 'What has she promised you?' Martin had money hidden away. Perhaps he could bribe this madman.

Scorby nodded to Tanner, who moved to stand behind Ambrose. Scorby smiled. 'I am to be invited to Court as soon as— Well, she is angry with me, but when I deliver proof to her that I have completed my task, she will relent.' He stood up. 'Tanner, hold the musician.'

Tanner grabbed Ambrose. Martin lurched up, but he was grabbed by the other two men.

'Loosen Wirthir's bonds and bring him over by the fire,' Scorby said. 'You know what I must do.' He walked away as the two men hoisted Martin up and took him over to a table by the fire, then untied his hands and held him still.

Scorby approached with a sword in hand, a gleeful glint in his eye. 'Sweet Alice is angry about the hands, but it was my Kate's request. And in her memory, I must complete her father's curse.'

As Martin and Ambrose screamed their protests, the men forced Martin's right hand down on the table. Martin looked up in horror at the lust in Scorby's face as he lifted the sword with both hands.

Sweet Saviour, forgive me my sins. And give him strength to do it right the first time. In a moment of dreadful clarity Martin watched the sword descend. It took for ever to reach him. He howled at the sight of his blood rushing forth long before the searing pain hit him. And then Martin stumbled, almost fainting.

Ambrose broke out of Tanner's grasp, but the dogs were waiting. 'Martin! My God, Martin!' Ambrose was yelling.

Martin looked over at Ambrose and wondered woozily why his friend was on the floor, pinned down by the hounds of Hell.

'Pity that poor Kate could not witness the end,' Scorby said. 'She hated you the most, Wirthir. Said you'd killed her brother.'

'Cauterise his wrist, for pity's sake,' Ambrose pleaded. 'Martin, can you hear me?'

'I hear,' Martin whispered, steadying himself against the table. But it seemed that Ambrose spoke from a distance, and the room buckled and changed shape as he stood there. His right hand hurt unbearably. 'I do not think I can stand up much longer,' he whispered. Strong arms caught him up.

'Take them below,' Scorby ordered. 'I will visit them shortly.'

The dungeon with its seeping walls and fetid air was appropriate for a house with a moat and drawbridge. Ambrose wondered what the family protected itself against. But his thoughts were all for Martin as he was dumped, unconscious, on the filthy floor. They'd tied a rag on his mutilated wrist, but it was already soaked with blood. Ambrose dropped to his knees beside Martin and put his head on his friend's chest. His heart still beat. Praise be the Lord. Where there was life there was hope.

'Please untie my hands so I might assist him,' Ambrose begged the man who wore the signet.

'And what do you think you might do, eh?'

'I can at least try to stop the bleeding.'

The man brought his torch closer and examined the blood-soaked rag. 'I suppose, being in the dungeon and all.' He untied Ambrose.

'Could you bring some wine for the pain when he wakes?'

'He won't be living much longer. The Master has plans for him.'

'But you can die of pain.'

The man snorted. 'I'd be dead ten times over.' He spat in the corner. 'Die of pain!'

'There will be no more sport for Master Scorby if Martin dies of pain.'

The man looked uncertain. 'I'll see about it.' He closed the heavy door behind him.

Ambrose sat down and took off his jacket to untie the lace that attached one of the sleeves to the leather vest. It was a thin but strong leather lace. He dug in the filthy straw until he found a small, thick twig. Gently he slipped the lace under Martin's mutilated arm and tied the lace tight just above the elbow, then stuck in the twig to twist the lace as tight as possible. Martin whimpered. Ambrose lifted Martin's head onto his lap and smoothed his sweaty brow.

And then he began to sing. He sang anything and everything he could think of. His intention was that no matter when Martin waked, he would know instantly that Ambrose was there.

Ambrose's voice was hoarse by the time a timid servant came in, bearing a pitcher of wine and two cups. 'You've a voice like an angel,' the woman said.

327

'We heard you up above. Hide these under the straw after you have some. For later.'

Ambrose drank gladly, and when he lifted the cup to Martin's lips, his eyes fluttered open and he drank a little. Ambrose helped Martin sit up. Martin drank more.

'Praise God you have not given up, Martin.'

'I should. Perrers. Her uncles won't let me live.'

Ambrose helped Martin drink more of the wine. 'Now try to rest again.'

'The singing. Bless you.'

Ambrose folded his jacket and made a pillow for Martin. He finished the wine he'd poured, then hid the jug and cups. Getting up, he paced to keep warm while he sang. When he felt the stiffness go out of his legs, arms, and back, he sat down again and took Martin's head in his lap, singing all the while.

Ambrose had taken two breaks for wine and movement, and the light from the high, barred window had vanished long ago when Scorby came down with his two companions.

'Lift him up,' Scorby barked to his men. They lifted Martin and held him upright between them. 'It occurred to me that you might bleed to death. And since that is not the death I've planned for you, I'm going to cauterise that nasty wound. Now aren't you grateful?'

Martin slumped between the two men, his eyes fluttering as he tried to open them and keep them open. But he was terribly weak.

'You offer me no thanks, eh? Well, perhaps you do not believe I mean to be so kind.' Scorby clapped and a manservant came in with a jug and cup. 'Brandywine, Wirthir. From the cellars of my father-in-law, may he

328

rest in peace.' He filled the cup and handed it to Ambrose. 'Help him drink. It will go better for him with a good dose of brandywine in his belly.'

Ambrose helped Martin drink. 'They are going to burn the wound, Martin. It is a good thing. It will heal better afterwards. But it will be painful.'

Martin nodded, understanding. After a few gulps of the brandywine, he whispered, 'Enough, Ambrose, my friend.'

Ambrose stepped aside. He wished there were something he might do to lessen Martin's pain, but he could think of nothing.

The men dragged Martin out of the cell.

'I must go with him.'

Scorby smirked. 'It is a good show, 'tis true. And you have entertained the household so nicely today. *Certes*, I will allow it.' He grabbed Ambrose by the arm and they moved forward, the manservant hurrying after with a torch.

They took Martin down a passage to a room with a stone floor, a fire pit in the centre. A fire burned smokily in the pit. Tanner sat by it, heating an iron rod that was flattened on one end. Martin managed to move his feet enough not to stumble. They sat him down on a bench closer to the fire than Tanner's. As they pulled at the cloth binding Martin's stump he cried out.

Ambrose tried to break away from Scorby and go to Martin, but his captor held him firm. 'God's mercy, moisten the cloth before you pull it off,' Ambrose cried.

'You heard him, men, moisten the bandage,' Scorby said.

They did so, and it went better for it.

Scorby turned to Ambrose. 'How did you get the bleeding to stop?'

'I tied a lace up high on his arm.'

'Should we remove it now?'

'Dear God, I don't know.' Ambrose felt stupid. 'Perhaps after you've burned it and bandaged it again.'

Scorby nodded. 'You heard, men. Now be done with it.'

Tanner lifted the smoking rod from the fire and applied it to the stump the two men held out towards him. The stench was sickening. Martin's face was contorted with the pain, but he did not cry out. Tanner touched the rod to the wound several times, then thrust the rod back into the fire and reached for a grease pot.

'What is that?' Ambrose asked. The contents looked crusty and vile.

'Lard.'

'Up in my pack there is an unguent jar. Could you let me apply some of that instead?'

Tanner looked to Scorby.

'Forget the lard. Let them use their own supplies. That suits me.' Scorby turned to the manservant. 'Go up and get the gentleman's pack.' He turned to the two who still held Martin up. 'Let him sit while we wait. And his friend here can give him some more brandywine.'

Ambrose held the cup to Martin's lips. Martin helped himself with his left hand and took a long drink. With a shudder, he wiped his lips and looked over at Scorby. 'I don't understand.'

Scorby chuckled. 'You mean why I'm suddenly kind?'

Martin shook his head slowly. 'No. Why Matthew Ridley hasn't come back and ripped out your balls.'

'Matthew—?' Scorby looked confused for a moment, then shook his head, as if impressed. 'You have been thinking. I am amazed that you can still think so clearly. Matthew Ridley.' He smiled. 'He is a double-agent, you see, working both for John Goldbetter and our King – well, Alice Perrers and her uncles, who are the King's most loyal subjects at the moment. Matthew will agree to nothing that will hurt the King, or us, of course. His father had the wrong loyalties.'

Martin rubbed his forehead with a trembling hand. 'And you are a cousin to Perrers?'

'Indeed. We are a close-knit family.'

Ambrose frowned. 'How did you convince a son to turn on his father?'

'We convinced him that his father was a thief and a traitor. Which was true, but so are all the wool merchants. Or they would be if they had the right connections. King Edward has not endeared himself to them.'

Ambrose began to piece it together. 'They are the family you crossed, Martin?'

'Aye.'

'But the Perrers family – they sold to the Flemings against the King's orders,' Ambrose said.

Scorby grinned. 'And it is for that knowledge you shall die tomorrow. In daylight. Where I can watch you suffer. Ah!' The manservant entered with Ambrose's pack. 'Give it to the singer. He can find the medicine and apply it.'

Scorby paced around the room with his hands behind his back while Ambrose gently smoothed the unguent on a square of cloth, then pressed it to the wound. He removed the leather lace and used it to bind the cloth to the stump.

Scorby grabbed Ambrose again. 'Let's get you back into your nice chamber now.'

The men helped Martin back to the dark cell,

dumped him down in the foul-smelling straw, then shoved Ambrose in after him.

When the footsteps had died away, Ambrose crawled over to Martin. 'Can you hear me?'

Martin moaned.

Ambrose lifted him tenderly and carried him to the drier side of the little room near the door, again using his own jacket for his friend's pillow. He went back and found the wine and cups in the straw.

'Can you drink some wine?'

No answer. He leaned down and reassured himself that Martin still breathed, then poured himself a cup of wine and drank. Leaning against the wall, he chanted the mass for the dead until his voice gave way. Then he curled up beside Martin and slept.

Owen was puzzled as they rode into the yard of the inn at Alne. 'Why here?'

'It's the best inn between York and Ripon,' Thoresby said. 'Wirthir is a traveller. He'll know it.'

'Aye, Your Grace,' the innkeeper bowed, pleased to be of assistance to the great Lord Archbishop. 'They were here last night.' He cast an uneasy eye on Owen. 'Is there trouble?'

Thoresby did not answer, thinking of his own concerns. 'They?' He looked at Owen. Owen shrugged.

'The foreigner was with a town wait from your city, Your Grace. He wore the livery of York.'

'Astute man, to know the liveries of the great cities.'

'And it please Your Grace, 'tis my business to know such things.'

Owen nodded. 'That would be Ambrose Coats travelling with him.'

'They left this morning, not in a hurry. Still, they should be in Ripon by now.'

'Do you know the Scorby family?' Thoresby asked.

The innkeeper shrugged. 'You can't live hereabout and not know them.'

'An unpleasant family?'

The innkeeper shrugged again, uncomfortable under Owen's one-eyed stare. 'They're trouble. Paul Scorby, the young master, he's got his men with him all the time. And men like that, they're looking for a fight. My tavern clears out when they come. Bad for business.'

Thoresby threw his pack on a table by the fire. 'Do you have a room where we could eat in private? And a place for us to sleep?'

'Aye, that I do, Your Grace.'

When they were settled in a private room with table and fire, Owen asked, 'Why stay here? Surely any abbey or noble household would welcome you.'

Thoresby leaned back in his chair, massaging his neck with one hand, his eyes closed. 'They would be curious about my travelling this way, would want news of Court. I want peace and quiet.'

Owen fixed his good eye on the Archbishop, studying him while he was unaware. Thoresby's eyes, always deep-set, seemed sunken, as if the man slept little. And yet his face held the ruddy glow of the day's ride. So it was a spiritual not a physical malady that the Archbishop suffered since his Christmas visit.

'You returned early from the Christmas Court.'

Thoresby opened his eyes and sat up. 'I hire you to interrogate others, not myself, Archer.' He poured himself some ale.

'It might help me to know more about Alice Perrers.'

'And she is exactly the demon I wish to forget.'

Owen shrugged and sat back with his ale.

When Ambrose woke, he could not get his bearings

and wondered why his cat made such a strange, whimpering sound. Then, in the dim light from the window high above, he saw Martin. He had rolled away from Ambrose during the night and lay in the middle of the room moaning. It all came back to Ambrose in a rush of horror. He woke Martin and gave him some wine. Amazingly, Martin's forehead was cool.

'I dreamed my hand was crushed,' Martin said, his voice hoarse and weak. 'I could feel it. Such pain. Throbbing as it swelled. But when I reached for it— He will not let either of us out of here alive, Ambrose. I've damned you. *Mon Dieu*, I never meant to involve you. I tried to keep you out of all this.'

'I know, Martin, I know.' Ambrose smoothed back his friend's hair. They were sitting quietly when booted feet stomped down the stone stairs and a key rattled in the door. Tanner came in with a torch, followed by two of Scorby's men, one of them carrying a camp chair, then the manservant with a tray of bread, cheese, and a large jug. At the end of the procession strolled Paul Scorby, looking refreshed and elegant.

'Good morning, my guests. I trust you slept well?' He stood, awaiting an answer.

'Tolerably, under the circumstances,' Ambrose said.

Scorby's man set up the camp chair near the door. Scorby sat down. 'Then it is time to break your fast and heat your bellies with some good ale. And while you eat and drink I shall entertain you with the whys and wherefores of your fate.'

Scorby motioned to the manservant to put the tray down on the floor and leave.

Martin looked at the food, then back up at Scorby. 'If we are to die, why waste food on us?'

Scorby cocked his head to one side. 'Oh dear. Is pain making you cranky? Or is it too much brandywine last

334

night? Or a lovers' tiff? Have you two argued? You see, I'm quite observant. I've noticed the tender regard. It is much as I imagine the King regarding my cousin Alice. That was your mistake, you know, Wirthir. Underestimating the appeal of my cousin. But then you have no idea what a man finds appealing in a woman, do you?'

'I am hardly the only person astonished by your cousin's success with King Edward. Alice does not meet most men's criteria of beauty. Even her disposition is unlovely.'

Ambrose did not like the direction of this talk. 'Quiet, Martin. Eat something. Do not get yourself excited.'

Martin shrugged. 'You say your cousin is angry with you at the moment, Scorby. Why?'

'Ah. Because I have taken my time with your deaths. Being a woman, she does not understand that death is an art. Just like your music, dear Ambrose. I murdered Crounce first, the most innocent – to both you and my father-in-law the most painful loss. It was delightful how Gilbert Ridley wasted away with his guilty conscience. And then, when he was at his weakest, I finished him. But I confess I dallied also because Kate so hated you, Martin. She wanted you dead first. She was so passionate in her pleading.' Scorby closed his eyes and smiled, remembering. 'Dear, dear Kate,' he murmured, his eyes still closed, 'I was sorry to slit her throat.' He opened his eyes. 'That one I did myself. I did not want my men touching her. She would have been too much of a temptation for these pigs.'

'So the whole family but Mistress d'Aldbourg is gone now,' Martin said. 'Did you murder Alan in prison?'

335

Scorby nodded. 'That was the first step. And buying off Goldbetter, which was simple. But my cousin Alice is so angry with me because you were the most important to eliminate. You know so much about so many people. Do you remember, dear, scheming, double-crossing Martin, the information you sold my uncles about Enguerrand de Coucy's hidden money?'

Ambrose was amazed. 'Even Princess Isabella's husband was involved in this? You have been a busy man, Martin.'

Scorby laughed. 'Too busy and smart for his own good. That is the information that got Alice her position at Court. Had you been more cautious about your customers, you might not be about to meet your end.'

'With all this, I don't understand why I was not your first victim,' Martin said.

'As I said, there is an art to this. Besides, they were easier to find. I thought their deaths would flush you out. And they did.'

Ambrose felt a tightening in his stomach, realising how fate had tricked them. They had come here purely by chance. Scorby must be mad – but much good it did either Martin or him.

'So – at least have some ale, gentlemen. And then we will escort you out into the crisp January fields and let your blood melt the hoar-frost and fertilise the pasture for spring.'

Twenty-six

Revenge

Owen woke before Thoresby – he had given the better pallet to the Archbishop and the old wound in his left shoulder ached from the hard, lumpy bed. He got up, stretching and loosening his joints, then went outside to relieve himself. Returning, he found the innkeeper watching over the stoking of the fire and thought to ask him some questions about Scorby.

But the innkeeper was still put off by Owen's appearance. 'I don't know why the Archbishop of York be travelling with your ilk, but I don't trust it.'

'I'm his man. Do his spying for him.'

The innkeeper squinted at him. 'How'd you lose the eye?'

With a sigh, Owen told the tale, despite being thoroughly sick of it. As usual, the story won an admirer.

'Captain of Archers to the old Duke Henry? Well, now. Forgive the caution of an old man, but I'm all alone out here with the family and servants and no protection, see.'

'We'll begin afresh,' Owen said. 'Now tell me. How

337

much time would we waste going first to the Scorby manor before heading into Ripon?'

The innkeeper bowed his head and considered, which involved much muttering and tapping of fingers on the table. At last he looked up. 'With your steeds, a day if you just ride around, then go on to Ripon.'

'And what sort of welcome might we expect?'

'Welcome?' the innkeeper snorted. 'No welcome, but an arrow from the gatehouse and the drawbridge up against ye.'

'So there's a moat?'

'Aye. And there's talk of a serpent-like creature living down in the muck. You'd do better to follow His Grace's plan to head for Ripon.'

'How well were the travellers armed?'

'Swords. Knives. One of them had a whip. That's all I saw.'

'Neither had a bow?'

The innkeeper shook his head.

'So how do you think they would fare at Scorby's gatehouse?'

'Ah.' The innkeeper nodded. 'I see the problem.'

Owen clenched his fists in frustration and turned to look out at the frosty morning mist. The trees just across the courtyard were only discernible because he knew to look for them there.

He turned back to the innkeeper, who watched him intently. 'Do you know the layout of the Scorby lands? Could you show us a way to come in from behind?'

The innkeeper frowned and pulled on his ear. 'Why would I be knowing a thing like that?'

'Where I grew up, a lord's land was the place of choice to train bowmen. We started with small bows and small prey, and worked our way up. Nothing like poaching to teach one to be alert as well as go after a moving target.'

The innkeeper chuckled. 'So ye're a man o' the land, eh? Well, I could tell you how it used to be. But no one goes near it now.'

'I daresay His Grace would consider it worth double our bill for last night.'

The innkeeper's eyes opened wide. 'Ye'd pay double?' He bobbed his head then, accepting the terms. 'Come without. I'll draw it for ye.' They stepped outside into the glistening fog. The innkeeper found a twig, then squatted on the packed mud and drew a rough map of the Scorby land.

Owen guessed by the detail that the property was considerable but not immense, and that it would be difficult to patrol it all constantly. The defences were primarily at the front, where they would make the greatest impression.

'You've been most helpful.' Owen rose, his knees crackling from the long squat in the damp cold. 'Would you stoke the fire and put out some food in the room we ate in last night?'

His host nodded proudly. 'We've already lit the fire.'

'You're a good man.' Owen went up to see if Thoresby was awake.

The Archbishop was pulling on his boots. Owen noted with interest a jewel-handled dagger strapped to the Archbishop's right ankle.

'That's a work of art.'

Thoresby turned, startled.

'The handle of that dagger on your ankle.'

Thoresby looked down, then back up to Owen. 'You recognise the handiwork of your own people. It is Welsh made.'

'Taken as booty or received as a gift?'

339

Thoresby chuckled. 'You always think the worst of me. It was a gift, Archer.' He pulled on the boot and stood up. 'So. I take it that instead of riding straight to Ripon you think we should see if Wirthir walked into Scorby's web?'

'Were you listening to my conversation with the innkeeper?'

'I saw the two of you squatting in the mud when I went to the privy.'

'I think we should pay a visit to Scorby.'

'Was he able to suggest a discreet approach?'

'Aye. It's much closer than I'd thought. We'll be there before midday.'

The Scorby land was gently rolling on the far east, but buckled into hills with rocky outcrops and sparse top-soil to the west. The manor house had been built at the far west of the arable land. Owen headed for a spot just south-west of the house, where the innkeeper had assured him a track had been worn by poachers that would keep them hidden from any watchers near the house until they were directly behind it, in a blind spot, shielded from the house by stables.

The enveloping fog had given way to a winter sunlight, pale and low to the horizon. The frost had melted from the trees, but still crunched underfoot. As they turned onto the poachers' track that wound through a valley between two outcrops, they once again moved into crystalline trees that shimmered in a vaguely glowing mist that was the best the sunshine would do all day.

'A God-forsaken place,' Thoresby said as they moved into the shadowy valley.

'I'm glad the innkeeper did not mention any folk

tales about this place. I've enough imagination to make it uncomfortable.'

'I was a boy in the Dales,' Thoresby said. 'And I don't care for such valleys in winter, which is the season here for half the year.'

'No wonder you're not fond of it.' Owen checked that his bowstring was still dry and warm in the pouch at his waist, then wrapped his cloak closer about him. 'We'll come out behind the outer stables. From there we can perhaps detect if anything is up – if Scorby's busy slitting more throats.'

Thoresby crossed himself. 'This Paul Scorby sounds a cursèd soul.'

'You'd be the one to judge that, being a churchman.'

They rode on in silence, chilled by the vapour that the sun drew from the frosty earth and trees but could not dispel. The stony hills towered on either side. Their horses were skittish and took all their attention.

In time, they passed beyond the outcrops and rode out along a tree-lined stream where the sun again warmed them a little. They let the horses drink, though slowly at first for the water was icy. Then they proceeded with caution. The stables should be near. They walked their horses, listening, keeping the horses away from the rocky edges of the stream where their hoofs would clatter.

Roof-tops appeared beyond the trees, then the outline of long, low buildings. They tethered their horses. Owen strung his bow and crept forward to scout. Thoresby stayed behind until Owen could discover whether Scorby and his men were about and where they were. It would not do to have their horses taken from behind.

Owen stayed downwind of the stables so that the horses housed there would not scent an intruder and give him away. A whinny and the sound of a hoof against wood told him his precaution had been wise. He dropped down and studied the moated manor house beyond the stables. An old, venerable house. Moss crept up the walls surrounding it. A brackish stench came from the moat.

Owen crept closer. As he watched, a door opened in the wall and six men emerged. They climbed onto a rickety bridge that led across the moat to a point near the stables. It was not a drawbridge, but a makeshift affair that would be burned down at the first hint of trouble. One of the men stumbled and was roughly steadied. Owen squinted. The stumbler was Martin Wirthir. Something was wrong with his arm. Ambrose Coats walked behind Martin with his hands bound. Scorby made up the rear.

Careful to keep low and out of sight, Owen slipped back to Thoresby and told him what he'd seen.

'You think they're coming here for the execution?'

Owen nodded.

'What's our plan?'

'With four of them, I think you'd best surprise them on horseback, while I'm up on the roof of an outbuilding with my bow. When they see you, I'll stand and shoot before they can turn round.'

'I can wield this sword.'

'Good. I count on it.'

They mounted and rode up to the stables. Owen tethered his horse once more and climbed up on a roof with a slant to it, behind which he could crouch until Thoresby rode forward. Thoresby guided his horse around the building, bending low over the beast's neck. The procession of men had passed over the bridge and was moving through brush at the edge of the moat, towards the stable yard. Thoresby sat, waited until he could hear them, then burst into a gallop, yelling like a banshee. He shot past the six men, moving their attention away from the stables. Owen rose, taking aim.

With an angry yell, Scorby ordered his men to go after the intruder. Owen shot one in the shoulder, another in the back of the leg. They both stumbled, howling in pain. Thoresby heard them and turned.

Scorby spun round, spotted Owen, drew out a knife, aimed to throw. Owen put an arrow through Scorby's upraised wrist. Scorby dropped the knife and fell to his knees, clutching his arm.

The man with the arrow in his leg writhed on the ground in pain. The third, unwounded man went after Thoresby, who reared up and brought his sword down on his attacker, slicing through shoulder and neck. The man slumped to the ground, motionless. The man wounded in the arm took off for the bridge. Owen shot him again, this time in the leg, then jumped off the roof and cut Ambrose's bonds.

Wild-eyed, the musician grabbed a pitchfork and yelled, 'Scorby, you bastard. Look at me.'

Scorby turned, snarling like an animal, and lurched to his feet still clutching his arm, the arrow quivering.

Ambrose let out a war cry and threw the fork at Scorby with a precision and grace that amazed Owen. Scorby screamed as the tines pierced his torso. The impact threw him backwards to the ground.

'Ambrose!' Martin yelled.

But the musician was not finished. Ambrose ran to Scorby, grabbed up his knife, picked Scorby up by the hair. 'For Will, Gilbert, Jasper, John, Kate, Martin, and myself.

'"Therefore to Hell I shall you sink—
Well are ye worthy to go that gate."'

He slit Scorby's throat.

Martin sat down hard in the dirt. 'Sweet Heaven.'

Ambrose dropped Scorby, then the knife, and walked away towards the moat, slowly, like a sleep walker.

Owen went after him. He'd seen many a soldier walk into the line of fire, oblivious of the danger, or even mutilate himself in horror at what he'd done.

Ambrose stood at the edge of the moat, staring down at his bloody hands.

'That was quite a feat of arms,' Owen said quietly.

'I gave up hunting to protect my hands. But I was good as a boy.'

'Are you all right?'

Ambrose turned to Owen with a questioning frown. 'I remembered those lines of Will's from the *Judgement*. It was a gift – I could not repeat them now. I felt as if God was looking down on me and smiling. Blessing me. But that cannot be.'

'You looked like Christ harrowing Hell. Perhaps for a moment you were inspired.'

Ambrose closed his eyes. 'I cannot accept that. I am responsible for what I have done.'

'Then accept the thanks of all of us for doing what we all wished to do.' Owen put an arm around Ambrose and felt the man trembling. 'Part of your elation is shock, my friend. You did what you had to do. It is finished. Come. Let us get the others and go back to the house.'

Thoresby stood frowning over Scorby's bloody corpse. 'I wanted him alive.'

Ambrose joined the Archbishop. 'I will accept any punishment you deem fitting. But I am confused. You did not hesitate to kill Scorby's lackey.'

Thoresby shrugged. 'He was useless to us. Scorby might have given us information.'

Ambrose shook his head. 'He was the Devil, Your Grace. How could you trust anything he said?'

'You enjoyed killing him.'

Ambrose looked down at his blood-stained hands. 'I did. I was seeing the look in his eyes when he lifted the sword to hack off Martin's hand.'

Thoresby, surprised, looked at Martin. 'His hand? Sweet Jesu, I had not realised.'

Owen, too, had noticed only that Martin held the arm close to him, as if wounded. Now Owen squatted and unwrapped Martin's bandage. 'Cauterised. I'm surprised they took the care to do that.'

'He was the Devil, I tell you,' Ambrose said. 'He did not want Martin to fall into a faint – he wanted him to experience all the pain of his execution.'

Owen rewrapped Martin's arm and glanced towards the house. 'How many men did Scorby have here?'

'The gatekeeper was the only one other than the servants who stayed behind,' Ambrose said. 'We must get Martin back to the house. He is very weak.'

'Can you walk to the house?' Owen asked.

'With help.' Martin blinked as if his vision were blurring.

Owen helped him stand. 'We'll come back for the bodies. Let's get over there and see what's what.'

Ambrose supported Martin while Thoresby and Owen led their horses into the stables, hiding them.

'Help me,' the man with the wounded leg wailed as they began to leave him. Owen crouched down, broke the arrow and removed it. Then he tied the man's hands, hefted him up, and took him into a stable stall. 'You'll be warm enough here until we return.' He brought the other wounded man in and removed his arrows. 'Keep each other company,' Owen said, tossing them a flask of brandywine.

The four set off, Ambrose helping Martin walk. Owen held his bow ready, Thoresby had his sword drawn. No one challenged their approach, though they could see a few people huddled in a small doorway in the wall. The people scurried away as the small party approached, all but the woman who had brought Martin and Ambrose wine in the dungeon.

She came forward. 'The gatekeeper's ridden off. I doubt he'll stop till he reaches water.'

Thoresby nodded to her. 'The other servants. Will they trouble us if we look around?'

'No. They wish you no harm. They are but frightened, and worried what is to happen to them.'

'I will speak with them when we're ready.'

They passed through the wall and into the yard surrounding the house. Owen and Thoresby circled together, while Ambrose, helping Martin, followed the servant inside.

The yard was deserted but for a few chickens and a pig that wandered about looking for scraps. The drawbridge was down, the gatehouse empty. In the distance, several dogs barked.

Thoresby gestured round the cheerless yard. 'I should not be so surprised the gatekeeper fled. What was there to keep him?'

Owen walked over to a stable built against the wall. One horse remained within. 'I wager there were two horses before. If the gatekeeper has ridden away, we will not catch him.'

Thoresby shrugged. 'The men we left in the stables are as likely to be useful as he was. We must be satisfied with them.'

'Ambrose is right, you know. Scorby might have lied to the end.'

'You cannot understand, Archer. I needed him to take to Windsor and destroy Perrers.'

They entered the house.

Martin sat slumped in a chair by the fire. Ambrose sat near him, clenching a cup of wine in trembling hands. They spoke in angry whispers, not looking at each other.

Owen put a hand on Thoresby's forearm to stop him from going forward. 'They have been through much these past days. Let them talk.'

'What about Wirthir's condition?'

'He is weak, but there is no fever.'

'Let us be useful then. We'll search the house.'

'What are you looking for?'

'The letter from Alice Perrers to Scorby.'

'Why?'

'I can at least take that to the King as proof of her treachery.'

Owen turned his head so that his good eye looked right at Thoresby. 'Why do you care?'

'She is not worthy of him. Her presence at Court is an insult to Queen Phillippa. A gentler woman never lived.'

'If he is determined to have her by him, the King will not thank you for this.'

'Do you know what, Archer? I care not what the King thinks of this.'

Seeing that Thoresby was determined, Owen called to the servant who had met them at the wall. 'Where would Master Scorby have kept letters and important documents?'

She led them to a chamber off the main hall. A table, some chairs, a brazier in a corner, and several chests. 'Shall I light the brazier for you?' When Thoresby nodded, she headed for the door. 'I'll get some coals.'

Owen stopped her. 'We left two injured men in the stables across the moat. Someone should get them and bring them to the house.'

'But where should we put them?'

'Do you have dungeons?'

'Aye.'

He'd thought they might. 'Put them there.'

She nodded, frightened, and hurried away.

Owen poked through the ashes in the brazier. 'I fear he burned it, Your Grace.' He held out a few small pieces of scorched parchment.

'We will look anyway.'

Hours later, they'd come up with nothing.

'I could use some wine,' Owen said, pushing away the last of the documents in front of him.

Thoresby threw a handful of rolled up papers against the wall. 'Was there ever such a cautious monster?' He rubbed the bridge of his nose, sat back, drumming his fingers on the table. 'Perhaps there is another place where he kept more important documents?'

Owen stood up. 'We must get Martin back to St Mary's. Brother Wulfstan will ensure that the arm heals well.'

'We could send Wirthir up to Fountains Abbey. They have an excellent infirmary. Then we can complete our search.'

'Your Grace, where would we begin? If we return to York, we can ask Anna Scorby where her husband might have hidden incriminating documents.'

Thoresby considered that. 'Clever. That is exactly what we will do.' He stood up. 'Come. Let us have some food and get some sleep. We will start out at first light.'

Out in the great hall, Ambrose sat alone by the fire.

'Where is Martin?' Owen asked.

'I put him to bed in the chamber up above. He could barely support himself. And if we are to ride tomorrow, I thought he must rest.'

A servant poured wine for the Archbishop and Owen. Thoresby drank. 'Perhaps, Master Coats, you would tell us exactly what happened here? You decided to deliver the letter yourselves, is that what got you into this predicament?'

Ambrose nodded wearily. 'We thought to ask Scorby about his father-in-law, if he could remember Master Ridley speaking of enemies. We had no idea we were in the midst of Ridley's enemies – and Martin's – until we were well within, and they set the dogs on us.' He suddenly looked round. 'I have not seen the dogs today.'

Owen remembered the baying in the wood beyond the gatehouse. 'I think they're off hunting. If we raise the drawbridge, they will not return with their prey.' He called to the servant and asked her to get some men to see to it.

'We could also use some food,' Thoresby told her.

The woman curtsied. 'There are salted meats, cheese, winter apples and yesterday's bread, Your Grace. 'Tis not noble fare, but the master did not bother with anything fancy since Mistress Scorby went away.'

'Food is food. It sounds a goodly feast at this moment.'

The woman hurried away.

Thoresby turned back to Ambrose. 'Continue with your story, Coats.'

Ambrose recounted the ordeal, leaving out only his singing.

'How did Scorby treat his men?' Thoresby asked. 'Do you think it likely they would know anything?'

'I doubt it, but I cannot swear. I did not watch them much after Martin was injured.'

Thoresby pushed the key the servant had brought over to Owen. 'Go talk to them. See if they know anything of use.'

The men sat up as best they could when Owen entered the room. Their wounds had been bandaged. 'You realise that Master Scorby is dead?'

One nodded, the other just stared sullenly at Owen.

'The Archbishop will decide what is to be done with you.'

'We knew naught of what he meant to do,' said the one who had nodded. 'He was our master. We were bound to obey.'

'What is your name?'

'Jack, my lord. An' this here's Tanner.'

'Who gave your master his orders, Jack?'

The man snorted. 'Nobody gave him orders. He said he was above the law. He was soon to be knighted.'

'Who was going to make him a knight?'

Jack shrugged. 'The King, I suppose. Who else can make knights?'

'Which of you slit the throats?'

Jack flinched. 'We obeyed orders.'

'Which of you?'

'I slit one of 'em,' Tanner said, speaking at last, 'the first one. Our friend Roby, one the Archbishop cut down, he slit the other throat.'

'Who killed Kate Cooper?'

Tanner grinned. 'Master Scorby did that all by himself. Wanted no one sharing her. Said he was inside her when her heart stopped beating. Said it was the best he'd ever had.' He laughed.

Owen slapped him. 'You're scum, Tanner. I don't want to hear your voice again. Or see that smile.'

Owen turned to Jack. 'We need to find Master

Scorby's papers. Where else besides the little room off the main hall did he keep such things?'

'I don't know. Honest, I don't. He wasn't one to tell us much.'

Owen believed him.

At dawn, they departed the manor. Thoresby had gathered the servants the previous evening and ordered them to watch the house well, Anna Scorby would be returning soon. They were to feed the prisoners until the mistress arrived with men to take them away.

By midday, a light snow was falling. Ambrose rode close to Martin, watching that he stayed alert. He could see the pain on his friend's face, and the effort it took to keep upright. Thoresby had hoped to ride straight to York, but with Ambrose's coaxing he agreed to stop at the inn at Alne for the night.

Martin was much better for a good night's sleep. He rode better the second day, and when he entered York he asked if he might wait until the following day to go to St Mary's. 'Ambrose and I have things to discuss.'

Owen saw no harm in it.

Thoresby did not like it, but desisted. 'They'll be separated for a long while,' Thoresby told Owen as they parted at the minster gate. 'I'm going to take Wirthir to Windsor. He can tell the King about Alice Perrers and her family. Who better?'

Owen had begun to walk away, but that made him turn back to Thoresby. 'Martin won't like it. And what sort of reward can he expect?'

Thoresby shrugged. 'He is a pirate and a foreigner. I care not whether he likes it or not.'

Owen pulled up the hood of his cloak and walked away, disgusted.

Lucie listened solemnly to Owen's long tale, saying nothing until he recounted Thoresby's parting words about Martin. 'He learned nothing from his treatment of Jasper! How can he think to deliver Martin to the woman who had arranged his death? Is Thoresby human?'

'Human, yes. But arrogant. He hates Alice Perrers and nothing is more important than bringing her down. Yet what can we do? Perhaps Martin will find a way to get lost on the way.'

They sat up late, mulling over possible escapes. At last they went up to bed with nothing resolved.

Ambrose made up a pallet next to the brazier while Martin drank some of the brandywine the Archbishop had given him to get through the night.

'I don't know that we should spend the night here, Ambrose.'

'You want to go to the abbey now?'

'No. I'd like to get out of the city.'

'Too late for that tonight. The gates are closed.'

'Damn. Well, play something soothing and I'll try to rest. We must be up early. Before anyone else stirs.'

'What are you worried about?'

'They spent a long time searching for the letter we delivered.'

'What are you getting at?'

'They found nothing, right?'

Ambrose nodded. 'I heard some such pass between them.'

'So who could go with the Archbishop to Windsor and be his witness to the Perrers family's perfidy?'

Ambrose, the pallet ready, sat down next to Martin. 'You're thinking he means to feed you to the lions.'

Martin nodded. His forehead and upper lip were beaded with sweat.

Ambrose felt Martin's forehead. 'You are hot. You must lie down under the covers and sweat this out if you're to travel.'

Martin let himself be led to the pallet. Ambrose tucked him in. 'Do not worry, Martin. You are not destined to be a martyr.'

Ambrose took up his crowd and played softly until Martin snored. Then he tiptoed around, getting some rope and a good hunting knife. He had work to do before morning.

Twenty-seven

The Quick and the Dead

L ucie tickled Owen's nose with a feather until
  he sneezed and sat up, rubbing his eyes.
    'Good morning.'
He lunged for her with a growl.
She giggled and rolled away. 'Not yet.' She stood
up just out of reach, wrapped in a thick shawl and
nothing else. Which was obviously not enough, seeing
how she shivered.
  Owen, too, felt the cold outside the covers. 'Damn
you, come back to bed. I don't want to put my feet
down there yet.'
  'I know. And you need not if you stay quiet and
listen to what I've decided.'
  Owen retreated under the covers. 'What you've de-
cided about what?'
  'About Martin. Do you promise to lie still and
listen?' Her teeth had begun to chatter.
  Owen laughed. 'Cold out there, eh?'
  'My feet are going numb.'
  'Then why not come back to bed?'
  'You must promise to lie still and listen.'

'That seems reasonable. Why wouldn't I do that?'

'You have that look in your eyes.'

'What look?'

'Please, just promise. I shall be frost-bitten if you don't hurry.'

'How do you know you can trust my promise?'

'Damn you.' Lucie got back on the bed, but stayed atop the bedclothes, clutching the shawl about her.

'Come on, under the covers before your toes fall off. I'll behave for a few moments.'

Lucie wriggled under the covers. 'Holy Mary, Mother of God, it's cold this morning. I cannot feel my toes.'

Owen reached under the covers and grabbed her icy feet, holding them in his warm hands. 'Now tell me this decision.'

'You are going to Ambrose's house, as planned, but instead of escorting him to the abbey you will warn him and Martin to leave the city.'

'A good plan if Martin were in a condition to travel.'

'The Perrers family will destroy him, Owen. He cannot go to Windsor with Thoresby. And once at St Mary's, how can he escape?'

'I'll talk to Brother Wulfstan. Perhaps he can devise something.'

Lucie shook her head. 'Martin must not go.'

'I don't want him to go to Windsor either, Lucie. But he cannot escape the city right now. He is too weak.'

'Then we'll hide him.'

'Where?'

'I don't know yet, but we will.'

'Thoresby is no idiot.'

'I should have gone to warn them before you woke. But I thought you would be reasonable. That you had a heart and a conscience.'

355

'I do, damn it. I just cannot see how we can hide a wounded man from the Archbishop.'

Lucie bit her lower lip and thought. Suddenly she sat up, smiling. 'We'll take him to my Aunt Phillippa.'

'Lucie, what would she think?'

'She will agree when she hears what he faces.'

Owen thought about it. Freythorpe Hadden was a large manor. Surely they could keep Martin hidden there.

'All right. I will take him there today.'

Lucie threw her arms around him and hugged him tight, then pushed him away. 'Now hurry.'

He stared at her bare shoulders, bare breast where the shawl had slipped away. He moved her feet so that she could feel how she affected him. 'You mean for me to go at once?'

She let the shawl fall the rest of the way. 'Not quite yet.'

As Owen crossed St Helen's Square, he began to have doubts about the plan. How could they be certain that Lucie's father, Sir Robert, would agree to hide Martin? Freythorpe Hadden was his manor, not Phillippa's. And even if Sir Robert agreed, could they trust him not to give Martin up when the Archbishop's men appeared? Not so much perhaps the Archbishop's, but Thoresby was Lord Chancellor. Sir Robert had been long in the King's service. Would he be able to put aside that habit of loyalty?

By the time he reached Ambrose's door, Owen had decided to make the offer of Freythorpe, but to be honest with Martin about the flaw in the plan.

He knocked. Waited. Knocked again. Waited. Put his ear to the door, heard nothing. But then it was a thick door. He pushed with his shoulder. The door opened.

The house was dark, though a few glowing embers in the brazier assured him that someone had been there recently. And had covered the fire.

Owen felt around, found an oil lamp, lit it from the embers, climbed the ladder. A chest in the loft sat open, empty. He went back down the stairs, lit a few more tapers. It appeared that anything that might have been a personal possession had been removed from the room. On the floor was a bloody length of rope, and by the back door a bloody footprint. He opened the back door, stepped outside into a pearl-grey dawn. No one out here. A few steps from the door the ground was blood-soaked. Some bloody rags had been discarded nearby.

Owen did not know what to make of it. Could something have caused Martin's wound to bleed that much? Or could someone have broken in last night and attacked Martin and Ambrose? But who? Only the gatekeeper had fled the Scorby's – unless the servants had released Jack and Tanner. Owen could think of no reason the servants would trust that the men would not harm them if released.

Could Martin and Ambrose have staged the blood to confuse him? Had Lucie actually come here during the night and warned Martin? No. She would not have gone through the exercise this morning of coming up with a plan if she'd already set one in motion. That was not the way her mind worked.

With all their personal possessions gone, Owen had little hope of finding Martin and Ambrose at the abbey, but he closed up Ambrose's house and went on to St Mary's anyway.

He knew he was right about Martin not being there as soon as he saw the pleased surprise on Brother Wulfstan's face.

'Good morning, Owen. I was about to take Jasper to the refectory. Will you join us?'

Owen looked at the boy, standing straight and smiling shyly. 'You are so much improved you can eat in the refectory?'

Jasper nodded. 'I like eating there. Someone reads while we eat and everyone is quiet. I have never been in such a quiet place.'

Wulfstan put a fatherly hand on the boy's shoulder. 'So. Did you come to visit Jasper before the shop opened, or did you have another errand?'

'The Archbishop asked me to escort a man here this morning – Martin Wirthir. But Martin is not at his lodgings, and I see that he is not here. Have you heard anything of this?'

Wulfstan shook his head. 'Perhaps Abbot Campian knows of this man. If it will not upset Lucie to have you gone so long, come to the refectory and share our humble meal. You can ask Abbot Campian after we have broken our fast.'

Owen accepted the invitation. While he ate, he thought about what he had meant to do this morning – disobey his lord. Who was he to judge the Archbishop's motives? And yet to obey blindly was to join company with Jack, Tanner, and Roby, who had obeyed their master Paul Scorby without question.

So had he been wrong, all those years in Lancaster's army, to obey blindly and expect his men to do so? Now that he knew the personal, selfish reasons the King had for the war in which Owen had lost his eye, he knew he could never go back into service and not question his superiors.

Had he been a fool? Would he be damned at the Last Judgement for all the lives he'd taken?

The reading ended. Wulfstan tapped Owen on the

shoulder and nodded towards the abbot, who had risen and was turning to leave. Owen crossed over to him. Abbot Campian nodded, motioned to Owen to follow him.

They did not speak until they reached the abbot's chambers.

'What brings you here so early on a winter morning?'

'I was to escort an injured man to Brother Wulfstan this morning – Martin Wirthir, a Fleming. But when I went to his lodgings I found him gone. It occurred to me he might have come ahead, though I held little hope of that.'

'Why?'

'His lodgings had been packed up.'

Campian frowned. 'A disturbing development. I did receive a message from His Grace last night warning me of this man's arrival. But no one has come.'

'I thought not.'

'So you think he left the city?'

'It was not only Martin, but also the friend he lodged with. All of their belongings are gone. Surely they did not both move to another house.'

'But if one of them is injured, how can they travel? And why?'

'I don't know.'

The abbot fixed a keen eye on Owen. 'Forgive my contradicting you, Captain Archer, but you do know why.' Campian held up his spotless hands. 'Do not worry. As it is the Archbishop's business, I would not presume to insist that you explain.'

'Thank you, Father.'

Lucie had already opened the shop when Owen returned. 'You have been gone a good while. Have Martin and Ambrose come with you?'

'No. They are nowhere to be found. And there was something passing strange at Ambrose's house.' Owen told her about the blood.

She was as puzzled as Owen was. 'I wish they had told us their plans. Now we will wonder about them.'

'I stopped at St Mary's, though I knew it unlikely they had gone there. Not after packing up the household.'

'Did you see Jasper?'

'He is doing well. Limping, but going to the refectory and chapel.'

Lucie smoothed Owen's hair back from his face. 'You feel chilled. Go back to the kitchen and let Tildy give you something warm. Then I need you out here to see to customers while I sew up some bedstraw pillows for Alice Baker.'

Brother Michaelo arrived shortly after midday. 'Abbot Campian has informed His Grace that Martin Wirthir never arrived at the abbey.'

'No doubt. I went to escort him this morning and found the house deserted.'

'Might His Grace know why you did not inform him of the situation?'

'I meant to after closing the shop today.'

The nostrils flared. 'Indeed.'

Owen came around from behind the counter, squaring his shoulders. 'Do you think to question my honesty, Michaelo?'

Michaelo took two steps backwards. 'I will tell His Grace what you have told me. Go in peace.' He left quietly.

'Mistress Digby.' Tildy opened the door wide.

'Aye, 'tis Magda, child. Get thy master out here.

Magda needs a hand with sommat.'

Owen stepped outside. It had begun to blow and there was a dampness in the air. A storm approaching. Owen squinted in the dark. A handcart stood outside the gate. Magda motioned him over. Inside was a freshly slaughtered pig in a wooden tub.

'Be quick, then. Carry it in. 'Tis for thy family.'

Owen carried it into the kitchen.

Tildy's eyes lit up. 'What a great beast.'

Lucie invited Magda to sit down by the fire. 'It's a most generous gift, Mistress Digby.'

''Tis not from Magda. 'Tis from the musician and Pirate. This belongs with it.' She handed Lucie a piece of vellum.

Lucie frowned over it, then burst out laughing. She handed the note to Owen.

'Mistress Wilton, I have taken action at last. May this pig give you and Captain Archer much joy. Ambrose Coats.'

Owen looked up at Lucie, who was dabbing her eyes with a corner of her apron.

Magda's eyes twinkled too.

It irritated Owen that he could not see the humour they obviously saw. 'What is so funny? What does he mean, "taken action at last"?'

Lucie reached over and squeezed Owen's hand. 'Remember his neighbour's pig? I asked Ambrose why he did not report his neighbour if the pig bothered him so, and he said that he did not like to start trouble with his neighbours. I think it was because of Martin and the secrecy necessary. Ambrose did not want his neighbour to look for a reason to get even.'

'This is the neighbour's pig?'

Magda nodded. 'Killed it last night.'

'So you've seen Martin?' Owen said.

'Aye. Pirate suffers much. But Magda cleaned the arm, packed it with healing herbs, and tucked Pirate and Angel in a nice, safe place. They'll not feel homesick, they brought everything with them, even the cat.' She chuckled. ''Tis good sport, eh? The Crow will not find them.'

Owen smiled. 'Thoresby will be disappointed.'

'Good.' Magda stood up. 'Must leave thee. Magda has had a long day.'

Lucie stood up. 'Thank you for bringing the pig and the news.'

Magda nodded at her. 'And a good time for it, eh? Thou shalt need plenty meat this winter.'

'True enough. I will come see you soon.'

Magda nodded. 'Magda will see thee right. Dame Phillippa shalt have naught to complain of.' She hobbled out of the kitchen.

Owen turned to Lucie. 'What did she mean?'

Lucie took his arm. 'Tildy, will you lock up tonight?'

'Yes, Mistress.'

Lucie led Owen up the stairs and closed the door behind them.

'All right,' Owen said, 'what does Magda know that I don't know? Are you with child? And you've told her but not me?'

'I am, but I didn't. She just knows these things, Owen. So? What do you think?'

'I don't like these games.'

'It is no game, Owen.'

'Why didn't you tell me?'

'I'm only just now certain. Believe me.'

'You're not sorry?'

'Sorry? What a fool you are!' Lucie hugged him.

Owen reached his arms round her, but stopped,

uncertain.

Lucie laughed. 'You don't mean to deprive me of hugs till high summer?'

'High summer?'

Lucie pulled Owen's arms around her. 'For pity's sake, Owen, don't make me regret what our love has wrought.'

'The babe might grow up to be a soldier.'

'Better that than an archbishop.'

Now Owen hugged her, but not as hard as usual.

Twenty-eight

Blood Enemies

The King greeted his Chancellor warmly. 'So you have returned, John. Does this mean you found your murderer and have him safely locked up in your dungeons? Or perhaps you've executed him already.'

'The major accomplices are dead, my King, but not the one who conceived of the murders.'

'And is he locked up?'

'On the contrary. She is living the life of royalty.'

Edward raised an eyebrow. 'She? Your villain is a woman?'

'A most cunning woman.'

'Living the life of royalty? What do you mean by that, John?'

'She is here at Court, my lord.'

'At my Court?' Edward stood up abruptly, walked over to the fire, held out his hands to warm them. 'I hope you are not going to accuse Mistress Alice.'

Thoresby felt a chill run down his back. How had the King guessed? He had told no one here

364

at Court. 'Why do you say that, Your Grace? Why Alice?'

Edward turned a stern look on Thoresby. 'She told me that she imprudently let you know she was privy to information about you that you would prefer no one knew. She has worried that you would try to discredit her before she could convince you of her discretion. You had made her fear you distrusted her and disapproved of her presence at Court.'

All cleverly true – except the fear part. Alice Perrers feared nothing. What could Thoresby say? 'I was thinking of Queen Phillippa, how ill she is, how much love she needs. It seemed cruel to let her see you with the Perrers woman.'

'You would judge your King?'

'Forgive me. I saw it as a spiritual matter.'

'And so you were about to accuse Alice?'

'I did not say that. I confess that she is right in fearing that I distrust her and disapprove of her presence at Court. You have a wife, Your Grace. A most loving, beautiful, gracious—'

'Enough! You do not have to recite my Queen's virtues for me.' The blue eyes had turned cold. 'But I wonder what has changed in ten years, John. When I loved Marguerite you did not preach at me.'

Thoresby felt the courage draining from him. He gulped some wine while he thought what to say. Marguerite. Obviously the Perrers bitch had told Edward. Sweet Jesu. 'The circumstances were different ten years ago. Marguerite was at Court, but not acknowledged as your mistress. It was all discreetly done so that no one would guess your relationship, particularly the Queen.'

There was a nasty glow in the King's eyes. 'Discreetly. Yes. As I recall, you pretended to be smitten.

You escorted her here and there. And into my chamber. But perhaps you did not pretend, eh, John? Or did you act the part so well that you grew to believe it yourself?'

'Your Grace?'

'I have here a copy of a letter in which you swore your fealty to the fair Marguerite, described her body in intimate detail, and claimed the babe that she died trying to bear was yours.' With his ever present jewel-handled dagger, Edward poked through some papers on the table, squinted, selected one. He held it out to Thoresby.

'Your Grace.' Thoresby took the paper, but did not look at it at once. He remembered the letter. Why had Marguerite not burned it as she had all the rest? What could he do? He held it up to the light, skimmed it. Dear God, it was worse than he'd remembered. The moles between Marguerite's buttocks and beneath her left nipple, the seal-like bark she made as she rode him to ecstasy.

How ridiculously in love had Thoresby been to write such things? Completely, totally, overwhelmingly. And Marguerite had died so soon after he'd written the letter.

Thoresby knelt to his King, his head down, his right hand to his breast, his left hand crushing the letter.

'Useless to destroy the letter, John. 'Tis but a copy.'

'Forgive me, my lord. I was put in the way of temptation and could not resist.'

Edward touched Thoresby's head with the dagger, then lifted Thoresby's chin. The King smiled on his Chancellor. 'You are forgiven, John. And for that you must thank Alice. She has made me see that I never really loved Marguerite. She was a pretty thing, a toy.

I lusted for her body. But I did not love her. Not as I love Alice. Or my Queen. Stand up, John. Let us embrace and let the past rest.'

Thoresby stood and let himself be pulled into the King's crushing embrace. 'Your Grace has the noblest of hearts.'

Edward beamed down on Thoresby. 'So.' He slapped Thoresby on the back. 'Now. Do you still accuse Alice?'

Thoresby took a deep breath. 'Her cousin, Paul Scorby, had his men murder two members of York's Mercers' Guild. He would have murdered another man if I had not intervened. Scorby claimed that he had received his instructions from his cousin Alice.'

'Did he? And in what form? Letters?'

'Yes.'

The King held out his hand. 'Then give them to me.'

'I cannot.'

'Do you have them?'

'No, Your Grace. But his widow is searching the manor.'

The King threw his head back and laughed heartily. 'Oh, John. Your holiness of late has addled your wits. I hope that you did not let this man go on the strength of this claim, for I assure you that is why he told you such a thing – to be set free so he might escape the country.'

'He is dead, Your Grace.'

'Good. For you never will find any letters, I am certain. Alice was an innocent when she came to Court. And while here she has been treated so gently that she could have neither cause nor opportunity to get caught up in such a plot. And let that be an end to it.'

'Her uncles put her up to it, Your Grace. Scorby was to kill the people who knew how the Perrers bought their way to you.'

Edward reared up, threw his dagger at the table, where it stuck, vibrating. 'You say that people buy their way to me, John? Is that what you think of your King?'

'I – it is what he said, Your Grace.' Thoresby hated himself for snivelling.

'Get out of here before I change my mind, John.' The King's voice was quiet. Menacing.

This time it was Alice Perrers who discovered Thoresby waiting for her. He lifted his own jewelled goblet to her. 'I believe your cellar is even better than mine, Mistress Perrers. Or shall I call you Alice since we know such intimate details about each other?'

Alice hesitated, then dismissed her maid. 'To what do I owe the pleasure of your company, John?'

'I wanted to thank you.'

The cat eyes darted nervously around the room, the daringly low-cut bodice could not hide the frightened breathing.

'Do not worry, I've brought no one with me. Not on such an intimate errand.'

'Intimate?'

Thoresby stood and walked over to Alice. Insolently, he placed a hand on her chest.

'You are drunk, John.'

He shook his head, squeezed a breast.

Alice gasped, but did not move away from him. 'You wanted to thank me?'

'Yes, indeed. You have reminded me that I am but a man, Alice. A man with passions. Heat. I lie awake at night dreaming of the pleasure of ravishing you.

Isn't that a healthy sign?'

'I am not Marguerite.'

'No. No, you most assuredly are not Marguerite. My love for her was gentle. Not like the angry passion I feel for you.'

He put an arm around her waist, one hand still on her chest, and stared into the cat eyes.

They did not flinch. Alice did not move. Thoresby could hear her heart pounding. He felt his pounding. He reached down and sank his teeth into her right breast. She screamed and tried to pull away. He held her tight until he tasted the salt of her blood. Then he let her go.

She slumped against the wall, crying out when she looked down and saw the tooth marks. 'You're a monster.'

'No, just a man, seeking vengeance. My King loves breasts. And now you will have to cover one for a while. Or explain. Which might be amusing in itself.'

Alice stared at him, her hand on her wound. Suddenly, she burst out laughing. 'Pity we are sworn enemies, John. I would enjoy more rounds with you.'

'I am sure we shall meet again, Alice. You have not won. Not the whole battle.' Thoresby took up his jewelled goblet and left with the pleasant taste of her blood in his mouth.

The Archbishop returned to York in March and sent for Owen.

As Owen entered the Archbishop's chambers, he noticed that Thoresby looked pale.

'It did not go well, Your Grace?'

'It went well enough – though the King could not be bothered with my claims. Alice Perrers has bewitched him.'

'Anna found no hidden papers, so I could send you nothing to support your accusation.'

Thoresby nodded. 'I received your letter.'

'You stayed a good while.'

'I left Court last month. I have been visiting some of my deaneries. I think now I shall withdraw to Fountains Abbey to think on my future.'

Owen nodded to the chain of office that glinted in the firelight. 'For all that, you are still Chancellor.'

'For now. For perhaps only a little while longer.'

'What do you mean?'

'That is one of the things I must decide. Whether to step down.'

'And then she wins.'

Thoresby closed his eyes, sank back in his chair. 'She is the Devil's creature, Archer. Mark my words. When the King lies dying she will take what she can and desert him. She is cold and unnatural.' He opened his eyes. 'But no, she has not won.'

'With treason she bought her way to Court, with murder she covered her trail, but what is it that holds the King?'

Thoresby shook his head. 'The illegal wool sales were her uncles' doings, not hers. And it was they, too, who used information about Enguerrand de Coucy to buy Alice's introduction to the Queen. But the murders and the hold on the King, yes, that is all Alice Perrers, young as she is. She has eyes like a cat's, Archer, an intelligence that misses nothing, no nuance of speech, no gesture, and a body clothed to reveal its youthful bloom. But it is her spirit – the power that emanates from her – that arouses.' There was an odd flush to Thoresby's cheeks as he thought about her.

370

'She aroused you, Your Grace?' Owen tried to imagine the cold, bloodless man before him in a state of passion. He could not.

Thoresby opened his eyes and laughed. 'Another man might take offence at your shock, Archer, but I am pleased by it. My mask is back in place.'

'Are we finished with the deaths of Ridley and Crounce?'

'Yes. Pity we had to lose our best town wait in the reckoning. Did you warn him away, Archer?'

'No. Though Lucie and I had decided to. They had already gone.'

'And you've never heard another word from them?'

Owen shrugged.

'You know where they are.'

'No.'

Thoresby stared at Owen for a long moment, then shook his head. 'You have changed, Archer. You are growing into this life. You are learning to use the ambiguities to your own advantage.'

Owen shrugged. 'The money Ridley gave you for the Lady Chapel. Have you decided whether it is blood money?'

Thoresby smiled a little. 'I am certain it was, Archer. Yet I am but a man. Is it not fitting that I accept an imperfect tomb?'

Owen stopped at the York Tavern to improve his mood with a tankard of Tom Merchet's ale. Tom joined him.

'So 'twas our King's leman ordered the bloodshed.' Tom shook his head.

'Take care you forget that as fast as you've learned it, Tom. The King would call it treason to speak of it.'

'But sure she's too young to have plotted it all?'

'Her uncles put her on the path. It was they who traded the wool illegally and bought the information from Wirthir about the King's French son-in-law. Either de Coucy or the Princess Isabella then bought their silence by presenting Mistress Alice to the Queen.'

Tom frowned, thinking. 'It was Kate Cooper had Scorby chop off hands?'

Owen nodded.

'A woman with a black heart,' Tom muttered.

'She could not forgive her father's ruin, her brother's death.'

'Was it her poisoned Ridley?'

'No.'

'Bess had a mind to tell Mistress d'Aldbourg what her Kate did to our John.'

Owen drank down his ale. 'I'm sorry for that.'

'Bess didn't tell her after all. Said it might kill her, and she'd not have such a stain on her soul.'

'Bess is a good woman. And wise.' Owen stood up. 'I must get home to Lucie.'

'Aye. Tell Bess to come home. There's a lad come to see her about working in stable. I'd thought to offer work to Jasper, but Bess says he's learning to read and write.'

Owen nodded. 'He thinks he'd like to apprentice to Lucie.'

'Well, some good'll come out of much evil, then.'

'Precious little.'

Tom shrugged. 'We must be content with it.'

Author's Note

Many people think of history as mighty figures, epic events, and statistics. But at their best, historians bring the past to life by suggesting the motivations of the mighty, like a biographer with a clear thesis of the subject's inner life. Historical novelists or dramatists go further by reducing the mighty to human scale. Shakespeare put a human face on Richard III in his fatal battle by using the fact noted by one historian, that the turning point for Richard was when he was unhorsed. The Bard lets us witness Richard's tragic awareness as he cries, 'A horse! A horse! My kingdom for a horse!' Novelists and dramatists paint in the detail of the period, set the mighty in motion with imagined dialogue, and create the less than mighty characters missing in the historical records, those Owen Archers and Lucie Wiltons working secretly behind the scenes, those Bess and Tom Merchets providing the lodging and brewing the ale. Believable characters bring history to life.

A key element in any study in character is motive. Motive traces the trajectory of an action from stringing the bow through setting up, aiming and hitting (or missing) the target. What fascinates both historian and novelist is that any one event seen through the eyes of different participants suggests completely different motives, and it's the sum of the motives that culminates in the epic events. For a mystery writer, there is an additional fascination in how many people have motives for any crime, innocence being at times little more than a lack of opportunity.

The Lady Chapel's plot hinges on King Edward III's manipulation of the wool trade. Motive: to finance his repeated attempts to add the crown of France to his English crown. The wool trade was of vital importance to the economy of Flanders; Flanders was of strategic importance in Edward's war with France. Edward's scheme was to influence supply and demand to such an extent that the Flemings would support Edward rather than the French King in order to protect their economy. But Edward did not inspire confidence and trust in his own merchants – he gave them rights and revoked them ruthlessly, and promised monies that his scheme failed to raise; nor did he learn from the failures of the first year – he bullheadedly went on with the scheme. In effect, he pushed the merchants on both sides of the English Channel to devise means to continue their trade illicitly. In general, their motivation was to make a living, but in some, opportunity for unrestricted trade inspired greed. Merchant companies such as Chiriton & Company and Goldbetter & Company steered a daring course, sometimes winning, sometimes losing.

But in the fourteenth century, even in the heat of business, people were keenly aware of their mortality and tried to secure a comfortable after-life. Gilbert Ridley was tending to his soul when he offered a generous sum to Archbishop Thoresby for York Minster's Lady Chapel. Lady Chapels were common additions to churches and cathedrals in the fourteenth century, when the cult of the Blessed Virgin Mary was strong. Mary was seen as the gentle intercessor between God and man. In a time that suffered plague, war, famine, deluges and drought, the Virgin was embraced by the people as the Mother who would beg God the Father to forgive His

374

erring children and spare His hand. The placement of the Lady Chapel was usually on the east end of the church, behind the high altar. The chantry priest appointed to the chapel would say daily masses there dedicated to the Virgin. John Thoresby, Archbishop of York from 1352 to 1373, built York Minster's Lady Chapel to house his own tomb and those of six of his predecessors. He also provided for the chantry priest. Motive: the obvious one was that he saw the chapel as a lasting monument to his power and holiness. But I put forth another. At this point in his life Thoresby was an ageing man, increasingly disillusioned by the King, and his thoughts often turned to his own passing. Like Ridley, he wished to secure his place in Heaven, and in building the Lady Chapel he expressed his hope that the Blessed Virgin Mary would intercede on his behalf.

As I present it, part of Thoresby's rift with the King was Alice Perrers. He saw her as a meddling commoner, an insult to the ailing Queen Phillippa. Alice's influence over the ageing King Edward III, particularly after the death of Queen Phillippa, was the great scandal of the time. And yet this powerful, enigmatic, controversial woman left little record of herself, and as surviving descriptions of Alice Perrers were written by her enemies, even those are suspect. There is no record of her relationship with John Thoresby. I based my portrait of Alice on F. George Kay's *Lady of the Sun: the Life and Times of Alice Perrers* (Barnes and Noble, New York, 1966), and then seasoned to taste. Alice Perrers' motives were complex – love and devotion to the King mixed with ambition and the need to secure her future; being mistress to a King, especially one who was quite old by medieval standards, was to walk on quicksand because the King could die at any moment and leave her defenceless in the midst of her enemies. Being a commoner, she lacked the family connections that might have protected her. It is interesting that what her high-born enemies appear to have disliked most about her was her business savvy.

The Mercers' Guild was a trading company, later known as the Merchant Adventurers. Representatives chiefly of the wool industry – mercers, drapers, hosiers, dyers – the guild members were the wealthiest citizens of York, especially the mercers, or wool merchants. In this period, the term 'merchant' was applied to the large traders, the petty retailers and also the artisans who bought their own raw materials, produced their own wares in their own workshops, and sold the wares direct to their own customers. The mercers of York dominated the city council. Of the 88 mayors of York between 1399 and 1509, 68 were mercers. Archbishop Thoresby would have taken great pains to solve the murders of two members of this guild in his jurisdiction. And, of course, the Archbishop would wish to clear Gilbert Ridley's name so that he could make use of the merchant's generous donation to the Lady Chapel with a clear conscience.

It is not surprising that this influential guild was responsible for the elaborate play *The Last Judgement* that formed the finale of the York mystery plays on the feast of Corpus Christi. The guild had the money to invest in a pageant wagon with various levels and a platform that lowered Jesus Christ from heaven to earth. *The Lady Chapel* opens on the feast of Corpus Christi, as the pageant wagons of the guilds of York wind through the narrow streets of the city, stopping at stations set up along the way for the players to present the set of roughly fifty plays (the number varied over time) depicting the history of mankind from the Creation to the Last Judgement. These were elaborate undertakings; preparations began in early Lent. (An abbreviated, four-hour production is now performed in York in the ruins of St Mary's Abbey every fourth summer.)

Town waits participated in the Corpus Christi celebrations. They were musicians who received an annual stipend from the city treasury as well as livery and, sometimes, free accommodation. They performed on specified occasions for the mayor and the corporation of the city and provided special music for ceremonial occasions and royal entries. In York they held a special position in relation to the minster, regularly performing at Pentecost and on the two feasts of St William. In *The Lady Chapel*, Ambrose Coats is therefore a civil servant and hence his concern about keeping out of trouble.

Ambrose plays two medieval bowed instruments, the rebec and the crowd. The rebec belonged to the generic family of fiddles. It was a pear-shaped instrument, typically with three to four strings, held either in the armpit or across the chest. The bow was held as fiddlers hold theirs today. Its pitch was described as high, its quality shrill. It was used often as a drone instrument.

The crowd was the ancestor of the Welsh 'crwth'. It was an adaptation of the newly imported bow to the long established lyre (or Anglo-Saxon 'hearpe'). It typically had parallel sides, and most English examples had some form of neck. The number of strings varied from four to six. It was most commonly held at the shoulder, pointing downwards. Typically sounding at least two notes at once, the crowd was described as melodious and harmonious.

For further reading about King Edward III's financing of the war, I recommend Scott L. Waugh's *England in the Reign of Edward III* (Cambridge University Press, Cambridge, 1991) and E. B. Fryde's *Some Business Transactions of York Merchants* (St Anthony's Press, York, 1966). For further detail on the musical instruments, see *English Bowed Instruments from Anglo-Saxon to Tudor Times* by Mary Remnant (Clarendon Press, Oxford, 1986).

*   *   *

Also available from Candace Robb

The Apothecary Rose
An Owen Archer Mystery

**Read on for an extract from the first
Owen Archer Medieval Murder Mystery . . .**

Master Roglio took great pains folding his astro-
logical charts and tucking away the tools he had
used to examine the eye. Owen noted a tremor
in the physician's hands, the tensed shoulders of a
man holding his breath, eyes that would not meet
his. Master Roglio stank of fear. Owen glanced at
the Duke of Lancaster, who glowered in the corner.
An old man, but Lancaster's power was second only
to King Edward's. Displeasing him was a dangerous
business.

It would be Christian to wait with his question,
but Owen had waited three months for this moment,
and he could wait no longer. 'The flesh heals, but the
eye remains dark. You see no change, eh, Physician?'

Roglio's eyes slid to the old Duke, who sat forward,
interested. Roglio raised both shoulders in an eloquent
shrug. 'God may yet work a miracle.'

'But you cannot,' the old Duke said with a snarl.

Roglio met the Duke's steely gaze. 'No, my lord.'
He managed not to flinch.

The flesh healed, but the eye remained dark. One
eye. God had created man with two for a purpose, no

doubt. And blinded Owen in one. A purpose to that as well, no doubt.

Owen had made good use of two. Lancaster's prize archer, he had trained the others, drilled them, risen to captain. An achievement for a Welshman. No animal escaped his arrows. Nor man. He'd taken care to kill only for food or in obedience to his liege lord. And all for the honour and glory of God.

Christian charity had robbed him of all that. A jongleur and his leman. Bretons. More independent than the Welsh, Owen had thought. They had no reason to spy for the French. The leman helped herself, flirting with the men. The soldiers would make good use of her. But the jongleur was doomed. The men did not find him entertaining. Only Owen understood the Breton songs, and only with effort. The language was a bastard mix of Cornish and French. The men grew restive. Killing the jongleur, now that would be better sport. Owen argued to release him. And won.

Two nights later, the jongleur slipped into camp and slit the throats of the best prisoners, those who would cost the French nobility most in ransoms. Owen caught him. *Ungrateful bastard. You were shown mercy.* The leman crept up from behind. Owen spun round. A thrust meant for his neck opened the left eye instead. Roaring, he plunged the sword into her gut, retrieved it, and, turning round, did not see the jongleur on his left until he'd sliced into Owen's shoulder. Calling on the bowman's muscles that gave him enough strength to wield a broadsword with one hand, Owen sliced through the jongleur's shoulder and down beneath the neck. Once the Bretons lay in pools of their own blood, Owen slipped to the ground in a hellfire of pain. His last soldierly deed.

Now what?

Everything must be learned over again. He'd not bothered till now, thinking the half-blind state temporary. A passing discomfort, like all his wounds. When an unseen obstacle tripped him up, he shrugged it off, a small penance for his many sins, a lesson in humility. Not an easy lesson. Familiar objects looked foreign. The world appeared lopsided. When he blinked, it winked out.

Owen learned the value of two eyes. With two, a mote in one had not blinded him. It was a mere discomfort. Now it rendered him as helpless as a babe in arms.

Complete darkness. He knew it possible. Death, too, was possible.

It changed everything.

The old Duke argued that Owen's loss of sight did not render him useless – an archer aimed with one eye shut. And the strength would return to his shoulder with work. But Owen saw his blinding as the result of his own faulty judgement and the shoulder wound as the inevitable result of his blinding. A one-eyed man was vulnerable. He would endanger those with whom he fought.

Lancaster let him be for a time, then surprised him. 'You are a natural mimic, Owen Archer. In my service you have mannered yourself a knight. Your accent is rough, but the marcher lords carry the accents of their borders. And better than a lordling, you are a free man. No one owns you, you have no family honour to defend, you do not seek power through secret alliances. I can trust you. With a little education I might use you well as my eyes and my ears. What say you?'

Owen turned his head like a bird to study his lord with his good eye. Lancaster possessed a strange humour and was adept at maintaining a level voice, devoid of emotion. But at this moment the old Duke's gaze was level, lacking amusement.

'I would be your spy?'

The old Duke grinned. 'Yet another virtue. A blunt thrust to the heart of things.'

'A spy with one eye would seem almost as useless as a one-eyed archer, my lord.' Best that he say it. Someone would.

'Not to mention how conspicuous you are with your leather patch and angry scar.' The old Duke chuckled, enjoying the moment. 'Your unlikeliness becomes a disguise.'

'An interesting line of reasoning,' Owen said.

The old Duke threw back his head and roared with laughter. 'Spoken with a lordling's delicacy. Excellent.' A sudden sobering. Lancaster leaned forward. 'My son-in-law called me a master tactician. And that I am, Owen Archer. Power is not held by attending the King and fighting battles. I need trustworthy spies. You were of great value as Captain of Archers. You can be of greater value as my eyes and ears. But you must know the players and the plots. You must read well both men and their letters. Will you apply yourself to the learning of this?'

A spy worked alone. Owen's incompleteness would endanger no one but himself. It appealed to him. 'Aye, my lord. Gladly.'

God was merciful in His designs. Owen spent the night in chapel giving thanks. He might yet prove useful.

Two years later Owen stood in the back of Westminster Abbey church, part of the old Duke's funeral retinue. God had lifted him up to strike him down once more.

He could not expect that the old Duke had arranged for his future. If the dukedom had passed on to Lancaster's own son, perhaps that might have been. But the old Duke had only daughters. The new Duke of Lancaster, John of Gaunt, was a son-in-law, husband to the old Duke's daughter Blanche, and he was the son of King Edward, which made him a powerful lord in his own right. He could hardly be expected to employ a one-eyed Welsh spy. Owen had thought much on his future the last few days. He had some money earned in the Duke's service. His best plan so far was to arrange passage to the continent and on to Italy. Many princes, much intrigue. Someone would find him useful.

He worked on his aim until his good eye blurred with fatigue and his arms and shoulders twitched. Still a sure shot, almost as strong as before. But vulnerable on the left. He worked on spinning from a crouch, and strengthened his neck so he could turn sharp.

And then John Thoresby, Lord Chancellor of England and Archbishop of York, sent to Kenilworth for him. Thoresby was in London seeing to the King's business. Owen was to join him there.

Owen accepted the proffered cup and tasted the wine. He had not tasted better, even at the old Duke's table. The Lord Chancellor and Archbishop of York treated him nobly. Owen could not think what he might want.

John Thoresby leaned back in his chair. He sipped his wine with quiet pleasure. A fire crackled beside them in the hearth that warmed the private anteroom. Tapestries caught the firelight and lent the warmth of their vivid colours to the room.

With his one eye, Owen could not look at the tapestries without being obvious. It required turning the head this way and that, especially for those on the left. There was only one solution. Be obvious. Praise the man by praising his possessions. He turned his head, letting his one eye span the room. A boar hunt began to the left of the door and continued around the room, finishing with a feast in the great hall, where the beast's head was presented to the victor. The separate tapestries formed a complete set, designed for this room, for the fit was perfect. 'The tapestries are exquisite. Norman work, I think. The close weave, the deep green. Norman for certain.'

John Thoresby smiled. 'Not all your time in Normandy was spent on the battlefield, I see.'

'Nor yours in negotiations.' Owen grinned. He must not seem cowed by the honour of sharing wine in the Lord Chancellor's chambers.

'You are a bold Welshman, Owen Archer. And adaptable. When the old Duke asked that I take you into my service, I thought his mind muddled with pain. He did not die with ease, as you may know.'

Owen nodded. Lancaster had died in agony. Master Roglio said the old Duke's own flesh devoured itself from within so that he could at the end consume nothing but water, which exited his body as a bloody flux. Owen was moved that in the midst of his agony his lord had remembered him.

'He trained you to listen, observe, and retain.' Thoresby watched Owen over the rim of his cup. 'Is that correct?'

'Yes, my lord.'

'So much trust might have overwhelmed an ordinary archer.' Thoresby kept his eyes steady on Owen.

The Archbishop was easy in himself. Honesty would be Owen's best ploy. 'I lost the sight in one eye, which I thought was death to me. My lord's trust lifted me up from despair. He gave me purpose when I thought I had none. I owed him my life.'

'Owed him.' Thoresby nodded. 'And you owe me nothing. I merely consider honouring an old comrade's request.'

'You might have ignored it, and only God would be the wiser.'

Thoresby cocked an eyebrow. A grin danced on his lips. 'The Archbishop of York would deceive a man on his deathbed?'

'If he judged that it were better for the soul in his care.'

Thoresby put down his cup and leaned forward, hands on knees. The Archbishop's ring shone on his finger. The chain of Chancellor glittered in the firelight. 'You make me smile, Owen Archer. You make me think I can trust you.'

'As Archbishop or Lord Chancellor?'

'Both. The matter concerns York. And two knights of the realm, dead before their times, in St. Mary's Abbey. Do you know the abbey?'

Owen shook his head.

'Good. I want someone who can be objective. Make inquiries, note the facts, report them to me.' The Archbishop poured himself more wine and gestured for Owen to do the same. 'We serve ourselves. I wished to have no ears but ours this evening.'

Owen poured himself more wine and sat back to hear the story.

'I must tell you that the new Duke of Lancaster is interested in you. You might do well with Gaunt. It would be a secure future – more so than with me. Mine are elected positions; he is the son of the King, and Duke of Lancaster for life. I tell you this because you might have cause to speak with him. The second knight in this matter was one of Gaunt's men.'

Owen considered this wrinkle. Gaunt was dangerous, noted for his treachery. Owen could well imagine the sort of work Gaunt would give him. To serve him would be an honour, but it would not be honourable. Not to Owen. Surely God had not raised him up from the ashes for such work.

'I am flattered that two such powerful men offer me employment, and I thank you for giving me the opportunity to choose. But I prefer to serve the Archbishop and Lord Chancellor. I am better suited to your service.'

Thoresby cocked his head to one side. 'Not ambitious, I see. You are a freak in the circles in which you dance at present. Beware.' His look was serious, almost concerned.

A shower of pain rushed across Owen's blind eye, hundreds of needle pricks, hot and sharp. He'd taken to accepting these attacks as warnings, someone walking on his grave. 'I am a cautious man who knows his place, my lord.'

'I think you are, Owen Archer. Indeed.' Thoresby rose, poked the fire for a moment, returned to his seat.

Owen put down the wine. He wanted a clear head.

Thoresby, too, set aside his cup. 'The puzzle begins thus. Sir Geoffrey Montaigne, late of the Black Prince's retinue, makes a pilgrimage to York to atone for some past sin. We do not know what sin, for while in the service of the Prince, Montaigne's behaviour was beyond reproach. Something in his past, perhaps. Before joining the Prince's army he fought under Sir Robert D'Arby of Freythorpe Hadden, a short ride from York. Montaigne's choice of St. Mary's at York for his pilgrimage suggests that his sin was linked to his time in D'Arby's service. So. He arrives in York shortly before Christmas and within a few weeks falls ill of camp fever – the ride north jarred open an old wound, which weakened him, causing a recurrence of the fever he'd suffered in France – all this according to the abbey Infirmarian, Brother Wulfstan – and within three days Montaigne is dead.'

Thoresby paused.

Owen saw nothing odd in the story. 'Camp fever is often fatal.'

'Indeed. I understand that after you were wounded you assisted the camp doctor. You treated many cases of fever?'

'Many cases.'

'Master Worthington praised your compassion.'

'I'd had the fever myself but a year before. I knew what they suffered.'

The Archbishop nodded. 'Montaigne's death would have gone unremarked but for another death at the abbey within a month. Sir Oswald Fitzwilliam of Lincoln, a familiar face at the abbey, making retreats for sins that were only too easily guessed at by all who knew him. Shortly after Twelfthnight he falls ill with a winter fever. It worsens. He sweats profusely, complains of pain in his limbs, has fainting spells, fever visions, and within a few days he is dead. A similar death to Montaigne's.'

'A similar death? But it does not sound like camp fever.'

'Towards the end, Montaigne was much the same.'

'The Infirmarian poisoned these men?'

'I think not. Too obvious.' Thoresby took up his cup and drank.

'Forgive me, Your Grace, but how do you come into this?'

The Archbishop sighed. 'Fitzwilliam was my ward until he came of age. An embarrassing failure for me. He grew to be a greedy, sly creature. I used all the weight of my offices to get him into Gaunt's service. I did not make friends in doing so. I assume my ward was poisoned. And though I do not pretend to mourn him, I should know his murderer.'

'And Montaigne?'

'Ah. As far as I can determine, a God-fearing man with no enemies. Perhaps his death is unrelated.' The Archbishop leaned back and closed his eyes. 'But I think not. The deaths were too similar.' He looked up at Owen. 'Poisoned by mistake?' He shrugged. 'Or was he merely better at burying his business than Fitzwilliam?' He smiled. 'And here's an interesting item. Montaigne did not give his name at St. Mary's. He called himself a pilgrim. Humble and plain. Or sly?'

An interesting puzzle. Owen liked the prospect. 'What inquiries have you made so far?'

'A few questions, enough to discover that Abbot Campian thinks they both died of natural causes. Hopes they did, is more like it. He fears we'll wrongly accuse his Infirmarian, Brother Wulfstan. And the Archdeacon of York assures me that if there had been a hint of trouble his Summoner would know of it. I hand it to you, Owen Archer. Disregard them. Begin at the beginning.'

'In what guise shall I present myself in York?'

'I think that something as close to the truth as possible will suit the situation. Present yourself as a soldier who has lost his taste for killing and wishes to begin afresh. You are looking for honest work in the city, with a small behest from your late lord to support you in the meantime. My secretary, Jehannes, will doubtless come up with something before you arrive in York. You will of course have all the funds you need. You will go to Jehannes when you arrive, and whenever you have need of anything. The Archdeacon of York would normally arrange all this, but I would rather he not know about your purpose.'

'You suspect him?'

Thoresby smiled. 'I suspect everyone at this point.'

'Everyone but Jehannes.'

Thoresby nodded.

'And after I complete this task, what then?'

'We will see.'

Owen left with mixed feelings. No need to take ship to Italy. He had an interesting puzzle to solve. But it was a mental challenge, not at all a physical one. Fishing for clues, catching people in lies. Not his best talents. It bothered him a little. What bothered him more was presenting himself as one who had lost his taste for killing. Did the Archbishop think that true? It was not. Given a just cause, he would kill again. He had not lost his nerve. Did the Archbishop think him a coward? His face grew hot.

But no. The Archbishop would not hire a coward. He must push that thought from his mind. Doubts would keep him from doing his best. And he must succeed. Success would secure his future in England. God still watched over him.